Praise for the novels of E. E. K

Dragon Avenger

BOOK TWO OF THE AGE OF FI

"Knight breathes new life into old conventions.... Here is no warmed-over Tolkien playground, but a new world breathed to life and populated with fascinating characters we long to hear more from.... Knight, a master plotter and world builder, alternately surprises and delights, keeping us on the edge of our seats.... Knight has written a classic here, a kind of *Watership Down* with dragons—a book that will be cherished for generations to come. It is, simply, a grand tale, full of the mystery and wonder fantasy readers long to discover and too often find absent in modern fiction."

—*Black Gate*

"[A] gritty coming-of-age story.... Knight makes the story complex enough to entertain readers of all ages." ・ —*Publishers Weekly*

"Knight offers a thoroughly crafted fantasy world.... For a lushly unique fantasy read, look into *Dragon Avenger*, as well as its predecessor, *Dragon Champion*. You'll never look at dragons the same way again."

—Wantz Upon a Time Book Reviews

Praise for Dragon Champion

BOOK ONE OF THE AGE OF FIRE

"Smoothly written ... a bloody, unsentimental fairy tale."

—*Publishers Weekly*

"*Dragon Champion* is an enchanting story of a young dragon's search for answers to help him understand what it is to be a dragon. This is a heartwarming story full of adventure, where good deeds and friendship always succeed. The characters are wonderfully endearing, and the adventures that Auron experiences as he grows into an adult dragon are exciting and entertaining. A superb introduction to what I hope will be a wonderful series." —The Eternal Night

continued ...

"The author of the Vampire Earth series has crafted a series opener with a refreshingly new protagonist who views the world from a draconic, rather than a human, perspective. A fine addition to most fantasy collections."

—*Library Journal* (starred review)

"Knight did a great job of hooking me into the story. . . . This concern and attention to the details illustrate how strong the overall feel of the book is—Knight clearly is building something more in this world, and the amount of back story to the characters and creatures is very impressive. . . . Very entertaining—the characters were genuine and the world full of depth. With the ending Knight gave us, I am very interested to see where he takes these characters next."

—SFF World

"E. E. Knight makes the transition from the science fiction of his Vampire Earth series to a fantasy saga with an ease that is amazing but not surprising with someone with his enormous amount of writing talent."

—Paranormal Romance Reviews

Praise for The Vampire Earth novels
VALENTINE'S RESOLVE

"Knight flavors action with humor in [*Valentine's Resolve*]. . . . Classic apocalyptic SF on a grand scale is always scary, but Knight makes it terrifically entertaining as well."

—*Publishers Weekly*

"Knight has managed to write a book six that keeps fans thirsting for more in the series. . . . [He] maintains a tight point of view, controls scene transitions beautifully, and never wavers in tone. His main character, David Valentine, keeps readers coming back for more."

—Science Fiction Weekly

"E. E. Knight brings excitement and interest to his Vampire Earth series. . . . [David] is an extraordinary character who turns the Vampire Earth war into a compelling tale."

—Alternative Worlds

"Knight mixes bits of military SF, survivalist fiction, the alien invasion story, and other elements including more than a mild dose of horror. . . . I'm entertained following [Valentine's] adventures, and it's nice to have some evil vampires, even if they do come from another planet."

—Don D'Ammassa

"Knight manages something that is not always a given in an extended series: he's kept it fresh and engaging, not only by providing a new story line for each episode, but by changing locales and supporting cast. . . . Knight maintains a high level of interest. He's a good, strong writer with a definite gift for building character and milieu without beating you over the head with it, and he never lets it get in the way of the story. Yes, this one is certainly worth the time—and it looks like all the preceding books are as well."   —The Green Man Review

VALENTINE'S EXILE

"Compelling pulp adventure. . . . The sympathetic hero, fast-paced action, and an intricately detailed milieu set in various well-imagined regions of twenty-first-century North America make for an entertaining read."
                                            —*Publishers Weekly* (starred review)

"*Valentine's Exile* isn't an average vampire novel. . . . The vampires and their soul-sucking Lovecraftian masters are like Dr. Moreau on steroids. This is nicely drawn horror: not gross, not psychologically terrifying, but very creepy. . . . E. E. Knight is a master of his craft. His prose is controlled but interesting, and his characters are fully formed and come to life. The point of view is tight and rigidly maintained, and the transitions are beautifully handled from scene to scene. The novel maintains a sense of place, with touches of sound and taste keeping each setting vivid and acute. Consistent tone and voice and excellent pacing keep the reader glued to the action and adventure. Even the futuristic touches are drawn with just the right tweaks of reality: never overdone, no R2-D2 types, no *Trek* guys. E. E. Knight's work is creative and the voice is his own."   —Science Fiction Weekly

"Knight gives us a thrill ride through a world ruled by the vampiric Kurians and filled with engaging characters and grand schemes, and promises more to come."   —*Booklist*

"The Valentine series is still going strong. Each book reveals new secrets concerning the world, which expose new levels of complexity . . . I'm looking forward to more."   —SFRevu

"The latest addition to Knight's popular alternate-Earth series maintains the high quality of its predecessors, combining fast-paced action/adventure with the ever-popular vampiric threat."   —*Library Journal*

BOOKS BY E. E. KNIGHT

THE AGE OF FIRE SERIES

DRAGON CHAMPION

DRAGON AVENGER

DRAGON OUTCAST

THE VAMPIRE EARTH SERIES

WAY OF THE WOLF

CHOICE OF THE CAT

TALE OF THE THUNDERBOLT

VALENTINE'S RISING

VALENTINE'S EXILE

VALENTINE'S RESOLVE

FALL WITH HONOR

Dragon Strike

BOOK FOUR OF THE AGE OF FIRE

E. E. KNIGHT

A ROC BOOK

ROC
Published by New American Library, a division of
Penguin Group (USA) Inc., 375 Hudson Street,
New York, New York 10014, USA
Penguin Group (Canada), 90 Eglinton Avenue East, Suite 700, Toronto,
Ontario M4P 2Y3, Canada (a division of Pearson Penguin Canada Inc.)
Penguin Books Ltd., 80 Strand, London WC2R 0RL, England
Penguin Ireland, 25 St. Stephen's Green, Dublin 2,
Ireland (a division of Penguin Books Ltd.)
Penguin Group (Australia), 250 Camberwell Road, Camberwell, Victoria 3124,
Australia (a division of Pearson Australia Group Pty. Ltd.)
Penguin Books India Pvt. Ltd., 11 Community Centre, Panchsheel Park,
New Delhi - 110 017, India
Penguin Group (NZ), 67 Apollo Drive, Rosedale, North Shore 0745,
Auckland, New Zealand (a division of Pearson New Zealand Ltd.)
Penguin Books (South Africa) (Pty.) Ltd., 24 Sturdee Avenue,
Rosebank, Johannesburg 2196, South Africa

Penguin Books Ltd., Registered Offices:
80 Strand, London WC2R 0RL, England

First published by Roc, an imprint of New American Library,
a division of Penguin Group (USA) Inc.

First Printing, December 2008
10 9 8 7 6 5 4 3 2 1

Copyright © Eric Frisch, 2008
All rights reserved

Map by Chuck Lukacs and Eric Frisch.

 REGISTERED TRADEMARK — MARCA REGISTRADA

LIBRARY OF CONGRESS CATALOGING-IN-PUBLICATION DATA:
Knight, E. E.
Dragon strike E. E. Knight.
p. cm.—(The age of fire ; bk. 4)
ISBN 978-0-451-46235-0
1. Dragons—Fiction. I. Title.
PS3611.N564D738 2008
813'.6—dc22   2008022286

Set in Granjon
Designed by Alissa Amell

Printed in the United States of America

TO HOWARD ANDREW JONES
A THANE OF STICKY-HILTED SWORD AND SORCEROUS FLAME

AGE of FIRE THE DRAGONS STRIKE!

BARBARIAN LANDS

THE INLAND OCEAN

HYPATIA

THE RED MOUNTAINS

IRONRIDER SWEEP

OLD ULDAM

FALNGES R.

EMPIRE OF THE GHIOZ

THE KU-ZUHU

HORSE-DOWNS

ANAEA

BANT

SUNSTRUCK SEA

YELLOW SAND

TUVALEA

CHUSH-MEREAMAE

THE BLACK TIP

KOMOD

WINDBREAK ISLES

Dragon Strike

BOOK ONE

Adapt

GRANT A FAVOR TO ONE GENERATION OF HOMINIDS, AND YOU'LL FIND
THEIR SONS TWICE AS DEMANDING — AND THRICE AS FORGETFUL.
— *AuRel the Bronze*

Chapter 1

AuRon son of AuRel, the scaleless dragon who lived upon the Isle of Ice, watched his sons blink in the brassy sun of the dazzling northern spring.

In the winter, AuRon had learned, the island saw constant snow, coming in waves from low iron clouds. Summers were alternately foggy and rainy, save for a brief, enchanted dry spell after midsummer. But the turning seasons, spring and fall, slow getting started but always lingering thanks to the warm ocean currents, made up for the rest.

As though in apology, spring had brought wildflowers to the thin patches of soil clinging between granite spurs where the wind died. Their yellow and blue and white heads looked up, as bright as sun, sea, and sky. Incredibly, insects already danced and buzzed between the blooms, keeping low, out of the wind, where the sky heated black earth and turned melt into mire.

AuRon looked at his sons, pride making the armored fans covering his neck hearts twitch. In a few months they would breathe their first fire and become drakes. Ausurath, a little heavier than his brother, had big back haunches on his red-scaled body and was a fine jumper, forever pouncing on his brother. Aumoahk had an odd, overlarge slit of a right nostril that showed dark against his golden scale, a reminder of a bloody brawl with his brother.

On their first trip into the Upper World he taught them about wind and shadow and the course of the sun. The second time his mate, Natasatch, accompanied them with the two sisters. Both glittered as green as their mother—of their five eggs AuRon and Natasatch had four hatchlings; one, sadly, never emitted so much as a flutter of a heartbeat and became unwholesome. Natasatch solemnly burned it as the others began to tap.

The excitement of the trips aboveground cut down on the fighting between the males. Traditionally males fought to the death upon emerging from the eggs, driven by mad instinct, but the two adults together managed to keep throats and limbs intact.

Once they could be made to understand that the survival of all might depend on an extra set of ears and nostrils, they settled into almost playful enmity. Underground the two males wrestled and bit and yeeked little battle roars at each other, stealing each other's fish and mutton through diversions worthy of their army-smashing great-grandsire, scattering their sisters to corners of the cave, then collapsing into sleep with tiny teeth locked on each other's limbs. More than once the family gathered for a meal with the smell of the bleeding brothers in the air; then it was time for wound licking and lectures.

Exhausting business.

Aboveground, in the overwhelming space of the Upper World, AuRon was relieved to see that they shrank against each other, tail to tail and staring from heads frozen in fear.

The awe soon faded. The male hatchlings, with the energy and curiosity of their age, lost their fear of the open sky and distant horizions. But for AuRon the trouble had only begun. Their sire had to do a good deal of wrangling to keep them close as he tried to teach them of game trails, grazing, water, and spoor. But their attention was difficult to hold with big snowfoot hares bounding away at their approach, all bouncing hindquarters and flapping ears.

Gently grabbing one scrambling set of shoulder blades with his teeth-covered lips, then prodding the other back in line with his stiff, regrown tail, AuRon envied his mate. The females kept tight to their mother's belly and listened attentively. When they acted, they cooperated. His sons dragon-dashed after every bee and showed all the sense of a field mouse.

On the third trip, AuRon decided it was time for them to learn a real lesson.

This time he went up first to check Zan the tradesdwarf's work before loosing the hatchlings on the world. The Chartered Company line-trader, a grizzled old northerner who might be mistaken for a hairy stump, was on his way north for a season's trapping and skinning. He had chuckled when AuRon described what he wanted to fashion, and he'd done a typically thorough dwarf's job in exchange for a bag full of dragonscales sloughed off Natasatch over the winter.

"Rafer be hunting beasts with mother and sisters," Ausurath complained.

"Watch your brother's approach. See, he's keeping downwind from the camp." AuRon had to stifle a *prrum* as he watched.

Aumoahk tested the air around the "camp." His slit nostril seemed to wink at AuRon as he breathed.

AuRon watched his son sniff and listen before exposing himself and then zigzagging up to the camp. Aumoahk's scale would gleam better if he'd eat the bits of scrap brought by the tradesdwarf with the same enthusiasm that he swallowed the few coins of AuRon's bare hoard, but he was cannier than his more enthusiastic brother.

Aumoahk found the three dummies lying in their circle around the stones of a nonexistent campfire, oars serving as spears resting over "shoulders" of burned man-furniture and rotting fishnet. Aumoahk became overexcited and squeaked out his little roar and charged the nearest.

A thunderous barking broke out from the rocks above the "camp."

AuRon spread his wings and glided down to the camp, where Aumoahk was play-fighting with the wolf. The wolf, a grandson of his old friend Blackhard named Birchfang, and his sleek mate dashed in and danced out, nipping at the new drake's flanks, first one dealing with the more dangerous front end, then the other.

Aumoahk made a gurgling noise and the wolves yelped and dashed to avoid the coming sputum.

The drake vented his frustration and his fireless bladder on some innocent bracken. The air turned sour and sulfurous.

"You missed the sentry," AuRon said, landing and pointing clumsily with his tail. Its small size and the off-putting step down in flesh from old stump to new tail struck him as ugly, but Natasatch didn't seem to mind.

Wolf eyes and ears poked around a sharp piece of blue shale.

"What did I tell you about your flame? You'll be hungry tonight with an empty firebladder, and all the hungrier when you get none of whatever your sisters bring back."

"You thsaid they'd be wulnerable when on the ground asleep," the drake said, glaring at the wolves.

"I told you they might have dogs," AuRon said. "Men, well, they might as well be those bundles for all they use their noses and ears. That's why they travel with dogs. Dogs that come out of the soundest sleep at the whiff of a dragon."

"Wolves aren't dogs," Aumoahk complained. "No fairz using wolves."

"No, wolves are smarter, as they don't have men to do all their thinking for them. If you can creep up on a wolf, no dog will ever give you trouble."

A cry carried across the valley. Strange to hear a wolf-howl in the bright morning sunshine. Ausurath took the cry as his cue to jump on one of the scarecrows. He kicked a bottomless bucket serving for a head down the hillside.

AuRon cocked an ear, reminding himself to send Ausurath off to retrieve the bucket.

"News, news, hear me, O Good Wooooooooolves!" he heard.

"The blighters are probably fighting again," AuRon said. "Every cairn-building starts a feud."

He'd invited a few families of blighters from the rugged North-west Coast of the Inland Ocean to settle on the isle, where they could mine and herd in safety, trading the rather poor ores to be found on the island for the protection of the dragons. While not as intelligent as elves or as industrious as dwarves, they were easier to deal with than other hominid races.

He glanced up the hillside, where Natasatch was watching Istach and Varatheela stalk some goats. Varatheela's tail quivered just like his sister Wistala's on the hunt. Istach tended to be quiet and reserved, perhaps because of the odd dark stripes on her green scale. The males were forever quoting some bit of hatchling rhyme they overheard their mother say when the parents thought their hatchlings asleep.

She born with stripes looks to a bitter fate,
As many suitors as stripes, but never to mate.

Istach gave as good as she got. She liked to weave the scales on her brothers' tails as they slept, so when they twitched to wakefulness each yelped as the scales pinched or tore free.

He sighed. Of the six dragons of his family, he was the only survivor. Unless his brother, maimed in the hatching duel, still lived. Not that he deserved his heartsbeat. He'd betrayed the rest of them to the dwarves.

Oh, Tala. It's a hard world—for both dragons and goats.

Natasatch raised her head as well. She'd picked up enough wolf-speech to understand an alarm.

"O good woooooooolves! Strangers on the island, trail and spoor on morning-side downwind, to the burned clear and fjord-caves. Pass this news to Firelong, O Good Wooooooooooolves!"

Birchfang hopped up on a smooth-topped rock that reminded AuRon of a sea turtle he'd once met and began to pass the news.

"Don't bother with that," AuRon said. "I heard. Thank your pack, friend. I'll fly north to Grass Point and bring back a moose for you first chance I get."

Birchfang's mate looked at her husband, pride shining in her eyes. Though they were both young, they'd already founded their own pack. The freshly named Mist Hunters had a range nearly as great as the whole woodlands of their birth. Here there were no men to catch wolves in cruel traps and nail their pelts to barn doors and fenceposts.

Natasatch and her hatchlings joined them. While the hatchlings swapped stories and the males set to wrestling again, AuRon relayed the details Natasatch had missed. At her request the wolves repeated the warning so she could learn.

"See, the wolves are worth a few sheep and goats. More than," AuRon said.

"I never disagreed, my love. Remember, the words were Ouistrela's. She hates fish and shell-crawlers and blubber and begrudges every mouthful of red meat. She resents the wolves, and you for bringing them."

Ouistrela was a brave dragon-dame. Her fury had helped free the glacier-hung Isle of Ice from the dragon-breeding wizard. But without an enemy to fight, she quarreled at any opportunity, and AuRon had long ago learned that something about his leathery skin put her off.

"I'll see what this is about," AuRon said.

"We'll help you fight the invaders, fazer!" Ausurath yapped and Istach rattled her *griff* in agreement.

"A fight is the last thing I want," AuRon said.

"Stalk in caution, AuRon," Natasatch said. She used his name only when she grew serious. Otherwise it was "my love" when she felt playful and "my lord" with a good deal of nostril-twitching when he waxed pompous and imperious over family policies.

"A scaleless dragon learns early to do nothing but," AuRon said, nuzzling the closed *griff* at the back of her cheek and tapping his hatchlings each on the snout with a *sii*. They shared a brief, affectionate *prrum*.

He launched himself into the air and first found Zan the trades-dwarf. Zan wandered the coasts in an open oarship with a blighter crew. In return for exclusive rights to take beaver and ermine from the patches of woods in the soggy central valley, he did odd jobs and carried a few messages. AuRon suspected that some of the other dragons on the island traded loose scale for a few coins or bars of working iron, but that was their business.

Zan denied any knowledge of strangers and warned AuRon not to burn his boat and oarblighters by mistake.

Then he turned east and found the yearling wolf who'd passed the warning, and from him met up with the sister of Birchfang's mate, who'd discovered the stranger's trail.

The she-wolf was only too happy to leave off digging for chipmunks and trot over to guide him, ears and tail up at the prospect of a good hunt.

He found them in the old dragon-rider caves. First he tracked by scent, then the echo of stone being moved and orders issued.

They were seeking treasure, not revenge, then. There'd been one or two unfortunate encounters with men of the barbarian coast, come through dangerous seas to avenge brothers or fathers. Better still, there was no smell of dogs. Hominids were hard enough to deal with without their snarling hounds hanging off your throat and loins.

Good. Treasure-hunters would have more regard for their skins.

They'd set a few warning-traps in the outer passages, strings of scrap metal hung from wires designed to spin and clang like wind chimes at the low bits of the tunnel ceilings where a dragon's back might strike them.

But AuRon wasn't in a hurry; he was more curious than outraged at the trespass. He crept through the caves as wary as though the Dragonblade might be lurking around the next bend.

Hearing faint tapping and scraping, he stepped forward into the old baths. The water no longer ran, though a few pools of brackish water were refreshed at every rain and bore a thick film of glowing moss and lichen.

They'd left footprints. A small party, fewer than ten.

At the other end of the baths he discovered a sort of wood contraption full of springs and wires with an ugly barbed javelin set in it, triggered by an old shutter set on a peg. Interesting. If he stepped on the shutter, it would flatten a peg, which would release a line, which he guessed would fire the awful thing.

The hatchlings would have to see this. It looked clever enough to be produced by the dwarves of the Chartered Company.

They were at work in the old dragon-rider dining hall, which could perhaps be mistaken for a throne room, for it had elaborate stonework and there was a raised area at one end where musicians had once played.

To enter, he first had to unhook another pair of chains designed to loose some dozens of thin metal disks. None of it smelled as though it had been dipped in poison. He tucked them behind his ear. The hatchlings would have their fill of metal tonight!

Moving a scale's breadth at a time, he put his head into the room, making use of shadow.

Two candles and a lantern lit the scene.

The strangers were prying open rusted doors at the old lifting chutes that carried food up from the galleys. A rather filthy dwarf looked like he'd just crawled down the old toilet-dump.

He made a quick count: three humans, two elves, and the dwarf scraping himself with an old chair-leg. They were well arrayed for battle or for climbing, with gear and assorted deadly-looking weapons. One of the elves was an attractive female, insofar as he could judge, and had long black vines of hair that matched the feathers of a raven perched on her shoulder in shine.

"There's some kind of blockage. A vault door." A voice echoed up from the galley chute. "Greasy as sausage-gut in here. Can't get a grip."

They'd found the old lift-platform at the kitchens. Surprising that some metal-hungry hatchling hadn't crawled down and devoured it the way all the knives and skewers had disappeared. Of course, it was big, so it would have had to be broken into bite-sized pieces. Not worth the effort.

"At last! I told you!" the raven-toting she-elf said. The other elf ignored her, lost in a stained book. "That burned lodge was a waste of effort. The vault is down there."

So they spoke Parl. Good. He'd forgotten what little Hypatian he'd learned, and dragon-throats weren't designed for the grunts of the barbarous northern tongues.

"The wizard's vault!" the dwarf said. "But why so small and frail a lift? Gold is heavy."

"All the slower to sack it, then," a man put in. He had a close-shorn beard and black teeth. AuRon thought a few good rinses with fine sand after mealtimes would benefit him in breath and health.

He fought down a snort. The only thing they'd find in the kitchens would be piles of charcoal and skeletons of rats. Why couldn't they chase fables somewhere other than his island? He'd better warn them off before Ouistrela sniffed wind of their presence.

"May I help you?" he asked in Parl.

"Yi! Yi!" the male elf shrieked, loose pages flying as he vanished behind a shelf that had once held casks of ale. "Dragon!"

" 'Tis Shadowcatch the Black, returned," the elf's raven squawked in birdspeech. " 'Ware, for he's fierce."

"No, 'tis AuRon the Gray, standing in a bit of cave-dark," AuRon said back in the bird tongue.

The vine-haired elf froze, head cocked.

"Get me out of here," a voice echoed up from the lift-shaft.

The dwarf swung a vast shield, fitted at the front with a spear-head and ugly spikes all around the sides, big enough to cover him entirely save for another spike at the peak of his helm. The men, led by the big brave fellow with trimmed facial hair and black teeth, upped their swords and spears. One held a round shield covered in green dragonscale. AuRon felt his firebladder pulse.

"Spread out! The creature can't burn us all," the trim-faced man said. He raised a coal black sword with gleaming silver edges.

The explorers spread out.

"I've no need to kill anyone," AuRon said.

"Dragons deceive with their tongues!" the dwarf shouted, creeping forward behind his shield. AuRon heard clicking noises echoing from behind the shield and wondered what sort of contraption the dwarf was readying. He thought it best to get down behind a broken pillar.

"Am I to die in this dark hole? Help!" the voice from the shaft called. "Pull, for the love of Stormbeard!"

"A coward at heart, like all its kind," the man with the black teeth said. "Lurking in the shadows."

AuRon raised his head. "Let's have some light and—"

He ducked again and an elvish arrow clattered off his crest. An instant sooner and it would have been in his eye.

"—warmth, I was going to say," AuRon finished, risking a peep around the fallen pillar. The men and the dwarf were still stepping forward, moving from pillar to overturned table to heap of old pottery, wary and ready for flame.

"Fyerbin, check that passage," the voice from the shaft echoed as they did so. "Fyerbin, scale that wall. Fyerbin, crawl down that hole. I'm always going first and I'm always getting the shaft. Did you hear that, Halfmoon? *Getting the shaft—*"

"Shhh," the elf with the raven said. "Ghastmath, hold there. Let's hear what the dragon has to say."

"Never!" The dwarf stamped an iron-shod foot. His beard held only the dimmest kind of red vestigial glow—either he was a very poor dwarf or he'd washed away much of the glowing moss that most dwarves cultivated in their beards.

"Fyerbin seven-toes, thanks to that blighter at the Ghioz borderpost. Fyerbin, bones forgotten in this cold hole. What goes on up there?" The voice echoed up from the hole.

The men looked as though they were nerving themselves for a charge, and the dwarf sidestepped down the side of the dining hall, keeping stone to back and pointed shield to dragon.

"Perhaps if you told me what you seek?" AuRon asked.

AuRon dashed across the back of the dining hall, spreading a curtain of fire. It pooled and burned, even on the floor slippery with muck.

"The wyrm's emptied his fire," the dwarf called. "We've got it!"

"Now we've the advantage," the man with the black teeth said, leaping between two puddles of flame with silvered sword whirling elegantly.

"Would somebody restrain him before he hurts himself?" AuRon said, backing toward the entrance arch.

"Ghastmath!" the elf called. "Let's hear the dragon out."

Ghastmath, the black-toothed man, ignored her, but the dwarf had more to say: "Tell that to my dead uncles, after our good king Fangbreaker listened to Wistala the Oracle—"

AuRon froze in shock.

"She mazed him into folly," the dwarf continued. "Don't listen!"

"Repeat what you said, dwarf," AuRon said, rounding on the little carbuncle of shield and helm.

The warrior Ghastmath, fire reflecting on his blade and cutting red shadows into his face, lunged forward with a cry. The point of his blade pierced AuRon's breast—

AuRon whipped his head down in riposte, hooking the human under his shoulder plate with the tiny spur on his nose—an egg-breaker that most dragons lose within a week of hatching—and hurling him across the room. The blade clattered to the floor, smelling of dragonblood.

Kung!

A projectile like a small boat-anchor shot out of the dwarf's shield, trailing a line. AuRon hugged the floor.

"Beast moves like old Gan himself." The dwarf added a few curses that AuRon remembered from the push-pull dwarves in the traveling towers.

The line fell across his back. He reached up with a *saa* and grabbed it. The dwarf fumbled with gear behind his shield.

AuRon yanked the line hard and the dwarf flew across the dining hall and landed at his feet. AuRon had not yet grown to a size where he could easily carry a metal-clad dwarf in a single *sii,* especially if the dwarf decided to struggle, so he settled for perching both *sii* on his back.

AuRon heard joints popping.

The dwarf grunted and almost succeeded in rising. Dwarves were counted the strongest of the hominids, but this one must have the thews of an ox.

"Can we stop this nonsense?" AuRon asked, ducking under another arrow coming for his eye.

"*Ssssst!*" the elf-archer cursed.

The man Ghastmath rolled over, cradling his side. "What's holding you back?" Whether he spoke to AuRon or to his wary men, sheltering behind pillars, AuRon couldn't decide.

The dwarf produced a short blade. AuRon bore down until he dropped it with a gasp.

" 'Tis AuRon the Gray at that, he that killed the Wyrmmaster, the Wizard of the Isle of Ice," the raven chattered in the elf's ear. "He'll keep a bargain. The Iwensi Gap dwarves once trusted him to guard their caravan-coin."

"Yes, dragon, let's talk," the elf with the raven said. "Sheathe weapons! Put down that bow, Cattail."

"And get Fyerbin out of this reeking hole!" called the voice from the shaft.

The elf stepped forward, and her raven fluttered warily to the ceiling. "My name is Halfmoon. I've no tokens of parley, but I'm willing to share anything we find with you."

"Uninvited guests to our island could set things right with an apology."

The elf went down on one knee and spread her arms, bowing. "The birds told us no dragons inhabited these caves," she said, as the others helped Ghastmath to his feet. "We hoped our presence on the island would pass unnoticed."

"What are you after?" AuRon asked, letting the dwarf rise. "Gold? The produce of the old Thortian mines? The jewels of Krakenoor, taken in the great sack?"

The men stirred and glanced at the elf. The dwarf, whose left arm hung funny, struck it hard against a pillar and sent it home with an audible click.

"Pogt," the dwarf grunted. "The creature's fouling the very air. I want out of this dragon-reek."

"Little of the gold came here," AuRon continued, licking the wound in his breast clean. "The old Wizard Wyrmmaster wasn't after fortune or glory. He spent much of what he stole buying allies or building those dragontowers. Dragons have nosed all through these caves, despite the evil memories of our bondage. Nothing like a mouthful of gold to keep the scale healthy, you know."

"I told you it went to Juutfod and Gettel in her damn tower. She's as rich as the ten kings, I'll swear," Ghastmath said, picking up his sword with a wary glance at AuRon.

"The sooner we're back there safe, the better," the dwarf grumbled. "This is a run-out mine."

"Ghastmath, make yourself useful and put some of your wound-salve in the dragon's injury."

"Waste it on a dragon?" Ghastmath said, drawing himself up with a hint of a wince.

"Thank you, I'll attend to my own," AuRon said.

"If it's poisoning you fear, Ghastmath will pour some on his tongue."

Bother the wound.

"Now, if you want my permission to explore these caves and discover lost toilet sinks and old rag-weaving rooms and sidemeat closets and then leave the island in an unburned boat, you'll have to pay a . . ." What would the Chartered Company dwarves call it again? ". . . A usage fee."

"May we hear the fee before we accept?"

"Only a piece of information. I would hear a story from the dwarf, regarding a name he used."

"Done," Halfmoon said.

The dwarf crossed his arms and broke wind; the echo of it startled the raven off its perch. "That's the only story a dragon will get from me. Short and nasty."

AuRon yawned. "Which might describe the rest of your

scrounging little lives, should some of the dragonelles learn of your presence. They still bear a grudge for scores of stolen eggs. And they like to hunt in packs. What sort of sport would you make, I wonder?"

Ghastmath shifted as though nerving himself for another strike.

"Raise that sword and I'll take the arm that wields it," AuRon warned.

The elf spun, seeming to work her body in two directions at once. Her leg moved up behind Ghastmath's ankles as a stiff arm flashing the other way caught him across the chest.

Ghastmath struck the dirty floor with a sound like a dropped platter.

"This is a parley, fool," she said.

"You're quick," AuRon said. "Happily, your wits match your reflexes."

She ignored the compliment. "Ask the dwarf for the story, AuRon son of AuRel."

AuRon made an effort to look unaffected. "I'd like to hear about this Oracle dragon. I haven't heard a story of a dragon from anywhere but here in years."

The elf laughed. "Oh, that's an easy one. It's to do with the humbling of the Wheel of Fire dwarves and the barbarian wars. I heard bits of it myself at the Green Dragon Inn at Rainfall's bridge from the innkeeper himself. He knew Wistala, still does."

After hearing the tale, bits and bobs that made so little sense that AuRon wondered if the humans had invented a tale to suit themselves, he was so excited that he bade the party a farewell forgotten as soon as the words were voiced and almost walked into the javelin-trap on his way out.

Wistala. His sister.

Alive after all these years. At least he hoped. She'd made powerful enemies, it seemed.

The Isle of Ice could support another dragon. As long as she liked fish and shellflesh. How had she survived so long out among men and dwarves? To hear the tale, she'd humbled both the Wheel of Fire dwarves and the Dragonblade.

Which reminded him. He took up the trap to play with and secured the metal chimes for Natasatch and the hatchlings. They would make a fine treat for dessert after celebrating his daughters' first hunt.

It would be hard to leave them, even for a little while. He'd have to ask Ouistrela to keep an eye on the cave.

He conditioned himself for another distance flight with a short trip north to Grass Point. He didn't find a moose for the wolves, but he did manage to snatch up an elk floundering in a spring mire.

Natasatch accepted his decision to leave the island in search of his sister. The first time she'd heard his voice as a full-grown dragon, he'd been calling Wistala's name in that horrible chicken coop of a prison she'd been chained in.

"A dragonsire always feels the urge to roam far as his hatchlings come aboveground," she said. "Even if I find your devotion to a memory strange."

"Perhaps it is because we were separated so young. Had we both matured properly, I may have gone off and left her to her home hunting range. But if she still lives, I must tell her that there is a place where dragons live in safety."

"And beastly weather," Natasatch said. "I will welcome her to this little cave, my love. I'm sure she has much she could teach our hatchlings, if she's survived in the Upper World all these years."

"Thank you, my love."

"Since you are wingbent on a-dragoning, may I make one request of you?"

"Of course."

"Some gold. Our hatchlings need it for their scales to grow properly. These ores we're clawing up out of the mountain seams, all they do is stave off desire for metals without supplying much scale-weight. Aumoahk's are coming in crooked about the nose—that's a bad sign.

I could break one of Varatheela's scales with my claw. There must be places where you could find coin."

"I would hate to fight or rob for it. Perhaps I can earn some as I did with the dwarves."

"I hope you will consider your hatchlings as you consult your conscience."

"Let us not argue on our parting. I promise, I'll return with gold whether or not I find Wistala."

"Some of the dragonelles will be glad to hear you have gone. More sheep for them."

Chapter 2

Cold trail, Wistala thought. *Pogt.*

Auron—or rather AuRon, for he was a fledged dragon now—kept vanishing like a desert mirage just when she approached.

Despite the blighter guide's assurance, it didn't look like the sort of chamber a living legend would inhabit. Her tread's echoes chased each other in and out of corners—nothing but empty dark.

At first check, she thought the cavern had a rather cramped ceiling for a dragon, especially one as old and great as NooMoahk. AuRon had always been a bit on the smallish side, so maybe he found it comfortable.

The empty, old air made her hearts hurt. For so many weary journeys to end in the same way . . .

Was this the end of the long hunt?

Her pursuit had wasted years—well, not wasted, the exploration of other civilizations and cultures having rewards that rivaled a mouthful of gold in flavor and benefited one far longer—chasing down tales of AuRon across the kingdoms of the east.

It seemed every waterfall and cavern had rumors of a color-changing dragon living as a guardian spirit or soul herder or guide into the afterlife.

She disliked the East. For all the prosaic beliefs about a dragon's role in the order, there was an ugliness to the relationship between the hominid rulers and the ruled that was appalling to one used to the courts of Hypatia. The continual decapitations ordered by the powerful there appalled her—she once saw a man killed in a matter of seconds for accidentally tripping a warrior's horse. Cross-legged priests, speaking in metaphor while surrounded by burning incense that smelled like roasting rat turds, described life as an illusion and death as a blessed gateway to a higher reality, or a new life as a dragon, even.

Easy for the priests to say. No one dared execute one of them.

Though the peoples of the vast East threw her coins and said prayers in strange tongues to her—she had to retreat to the most challenging of mountainsides to sleep in peace—she learned why so few dragons could be found there. The lesson came in the form of ropes and chains when hunters snared her at a warm spring where she paused for a few days of bathing and fire-nit removal.

Luckily for her the hunters had never met a dragon who knew the trick of hooking a chain around a rock so that no matter how many men they put on the dragline, all they'd do would be to part the chain.

She allowed one of the hunters to live, though she bit off his two bowstring fingers to encourage a change of profession. In exchange for mercy he told her rich lords believed that ground dragon-bone turned into a soup of dragonblood stock gave them renewed youth and vigor. Every old warlord with a garden full of concubines sought it.

She still had three arrowheads buried deep in her shoulder as memorials of the trap and a divot in the scale at her collarbone where they'd plunged the iron hook in. The divot she didn't mind—she'd never be counted a beautiful dragonelle, as her neck and tail were both too thick—but when she reached above the shoulder joint with her right *sii* the arrowheads pained her.

While searching the desert wastes to the south she met a trading caravan of white-turbaned merchants traveling under the protective banner of the Ghioz, a mask of gold with snakes for hair. In exchange for a few loose scales, she heard a tale of a dragon warrior-king, leathery-skinned and silent, invisible as a mist, terror of the southern jungles—and leader of fierce blighter hordes.

Wistala lied and said she sought vengeance against the leather-skin, switching AuRon's place with her copper brother so that she wouldn't be trapped by making up details as she told her tale.

They offered help in finding him.

Consulting their maps and following their directions, she found the mountains at the northern borders of the jungle easily enough.

She didn't see fierce hordes of torch-bearing blighters. Instead there were woven huts giving way to more-substantial wood-and-brick constructs with green gardens and planters, and lodgepoles decorated and dyed into fascinating shapes. Tempting herds of shaggy-backed cattle and sheep thick-wooled after a mountain winter stood about pens and improvised shelters of trees bent together with branches tied, piles of hay and fodder high and dry on wooden platforms. She saw stacks of wool.

She'd arrived during shearing season, it seemed.

It was hard to find a spot outside the principal blighter settlement's gates where she could land that wouldn't result in melons being crushed. She settled for the edge of an orchard, scattering the water bearers down the slope toward their town.

The blighters assisted her, eventually. Their headmen argued and fought through two risings of the moon that night, screaming, baring fangs, one slamming down his staff in disgust, but there were no knifings or head-bashings that tales of blighters' savagery would lead one to expect.

Best of all, no decapitations.

She resolved to put a paragraph about this land in her journal, if she ever returned to Thallia and told her story to a quick-writing scribe.

From what she could tell of their shouting they didn't want to be *ruled* by a dragon again—though all acknowledged the advantages of one being present in the area. The last one had turned back an invasion from the south and scared the waste-elves out of the dry foothills in the north, fearing some horrid beast called a "revengerog." She spoke to several who'd served their "dragon-lord"—gray, scaleless skin with faint black stripes, when he wasn't the color of whatever vegetation he rested against. He'd given up his throne and gone off with some pretty little bronze—odd how hominids called such variations of dun colors of dragonscale—human wench, though reports on her homeland conflicted. Some said east, others west, others north. He'd come back once six seasons ago, scarred and bearing an undersized, pinkish tail, to pick up some personal treasures he'd left behind. His stay had been brief: only one night's feasting, one day's admiration of a military display. He'd promised to return, so if she wished to enjoy their hospitality until that happy day . . .

Finally they led her up an old pylon-strewn road to a massive scar in the mountainside, a great cave like some yawning mouth filled with snaggletoothed ruins. Runnels of mountain rock stretched from cavern floor to ceiling, all thickly bricked with old dwellings, holed and tumbledown as broken crockery. There were no bears but many bats. The guide told her stories of Old Uldam in its glory, when the blighter charioteers used the crowns of human kings to decorate their wheel hubs.

The blighters had kept one wide lane clear running back to where the cave narrowed, and then down, somewhat in the manner of a dragon throat. It was easy to imagine the dwellings as teeth.

"The greatest of cities—once," said her guide, who proudly named himself the sixteenth son of Unrush Uthvhe-Rinsrick. He spoke Parl tolerably well. "When commerce was to be had between the worlds of sun and dark. Before the demen. Before the promises of Anklamere that turned to death."

Wistala, who sought secrets and histories the way some dragons chased the purest refined gold or hominid females or rare wines, listened to the mishmash of legend and folklore as they passed through the tumbledown piles of mud-brick. Anklamere was a sort of devil to several cultures; once he'd ruled the world from the kingdoms of the east to the city of Hypat at the mouth of the Falnges River on the Inland Ocean. They said his rule had once stretched just as far in the Lower World, too. She'd much rather hear of NooMoahk, but the blighter said that he'd died when he was still upon mother's teat, and the name had an evil reputation, for he'd often forgotten old promises and stolen cattle or taken lives in his dotage.

Scores of warrior blighters now guarded the tunnel entrances, the mouth of the cavern, and a great yawning sink they had to traverse under hanging pots of bubbling, torch-heated fat. They greeted the sight of a dragon with a mix of babbling consternation and kneeling reverence.

The guide told her these were the sacred Fireblades. They'd won victories under AuRon and replenished their aged and injured from the tallest and strongest of the clans. Now they dwelled near the holy dragon cave.

The warriors slaughtered bullocks right and left, and their leaders told stories of the splendid hunting in the jungles to the south. Their enemies to the south and west, the Ghioz, feared dragons—all she would have to do would be to appear in the sky and they'd turn back. In return the blighters would hammer heavy cups and urns and fill them with the blood and sweetbreads of game—or their enemies.

A number of the Fireblades bore recent scars, closed up with pins of bird-bone. Helms and shields glinted with fresh strikes and digs, still gleaming bright against the more weathered metal, but whatever had happened they did not boast of it.

She probed the pit with ear and eye. "Do enemies come up that hole?"

"It was once a great well-pool, but the demen diverted the flow and NooMoahk did not put it back in order."

Demen? She knew something of them through the dwarves. Odd, carapaced hominids who scuttled around in the dark places of the world and prayed to mysterious shining gods. Gods who demanded sacrifices.

"The Fireblades had a hard battle with Ghioz men, the Stonebuilders," her guide said. "They sought the sun-shard."

"What's that?" The name tugged at Wistala's memory, but she couldn't quite place it.

"You see in a moment. It is the living heart of our old empire. Stolen long ago. NooMoahk restored it to us after Anklamere's fall."

More tough-looking blighters idled here, eating and dueling. Heavy axes propping up mountains of muscle and studded hide of those on watch.

"The Fireblades," her guide said. "Guardians of the sun-shard."

They stirred and gaped at her as she passed. "The witch doctors were right! A new guardian comes!"

"The ancient dragon-cave," the well-spoken blighter said. "Here NooMoahk placed the sun-shard, taken from the tower of Anklamere. Here AuRon advised our king to build rather than fight. Here in its light my tutor taught me the tongues of the subject races. It is a wonder of the two worlds. You could be its keeper, mayhap."

An arch of clear light shone at the center of a circular, fanged dais. This was no prism reflecting torchlight. The reflections shifted and danced, as though it lived.

She would have to give an account of this to the librarians at Thallia. A relic of Anklamere might be of enough interest for them to send scholars to study it, if the blighters could be persuaded to have "subject races" tread on holy ground.

Perhaps she could come to terms with them.

"I will refresh myself. I can repay your hospitality with more than just words of gratitude."

The peoples in the east had given her coins just for breathing in their presence while they made prayers. She had quite a collection sewn into the trim harness that carried her notes and maps and records of her travels that she would bequeath to the Great Library at Thallia.

Wistala sniffed around—dragon odor lingered long, and a scent remained, the tang and taste of male dragon, but whether it was Au—

Her head locked and her eyes widened. Off in a corner, bathed in the glow of crystals like the ones she'd seen in Yari-Tab's tumble-down, only much brighter, stood stone-and-wood shelves lined with books, and scroll cases, and boxes.

She left the sun-shard and made straight for the shelves.

Heaps of paper lay rotting on the floor, or scattered around in wads. She opened a crumpled page.

"Strange lost tongues, but the pictures interest, mayhap," her guide said.

The paper bore a smear, obscuring faint ink. The blighters had been wiping themselves with pages torn out from ancient texts.

She took down a leather-bound volume, not even feeling the twinge in her shoulder as she reached, opened a book, and looked at the first leaf. A strange design of three equilateral triangles overlaid on a thicker fourth—her savior and mentor Rainfall had taught her some geometry—the memory of him dried her throat. She unrolled a scroll. Someone had added the same icon to the top of the scroll in ink of a more recent vintage than the faded writing.

Someone had gone to great trouble to collect and mark these volumes.

Tomes and tombs! And the blighters were cleaning their tailvents with it. Funny and sad at the same time.

Her studies in the archives of Hypatia concerning the history of the librarians supplied the name. The signet of Anklamere.

She may not have found her brother, but she'd discovered the half-legendary library of Anklamere.

AuRon's cold trail couldn't get much colder. Perhaps he would return for more books.

"I think I shall stay for a while, if you have no objection. Perhaps a season? Pray tell, what are the winters like here?"

Her guide slapped himself about the belly and chest. She'd not mixed much with blighters until now, but she guessed he was pleased. She just hoped they wouldn't ask her to go hunt the revengerog, whatever that was. Food, rest, and some quiet to study the library would be most welcome.

"I have a few requests, in the interests of making our association a happier one," she added. "First, no one touches the library. Second, your warriors wash away their filth somewhere other than that trickle in the corner, as I'm not fond of drinking sewage. And last," she said, trying to keep her mouth from watering so much it spoiled her Parl, "tell me more about the game found in the jungle."

So subtle was the sun-shard's effect, Wistala at first attributed it to her imagination. Or its light, allowing her to read more quickly.

She'd brought a few volumes onto the formidable-looking dais to read in better light—and hold up the pages to a bright enough source to allow her to see the icons written in subtle inks at the edges of the triangles, some form of categorization—and she found the words came easier, tongues she'd last read years ago in Rainfall's library came fluidly, she even fancied a deeper understanding of the scribes' words.

Awa, the dwarf philosopher whom she'd never been overly fond of thanks to his elaborate metaphors and disjointed manner of writing, rose in her esteem when she read him by the light of the sunshard. But then when she returned to a passage that had echoed in her mind by the ordinary lights of the library he seemed leaden and obtuse again.

Though she had to be careful about falling asleep in its presence. She had dark and disturbing dreams when this happened, awaking as though from a nightmare, hearts pounding. Yet for the rest of the day after one of these nightmares she was oddly vital, with a hatchling's curious energy.

She tried to get more about its history out of the blighters, but to them it was only "bigger-than-big magic."

"The old tower star fell to earth. From it came taming of fire to make wheel and blade and bowstring, which raised the *Umazeh* to glory," Vank, her blighter interlocutor, said. He'd found a bit of old cloth, a weave of red and gold, and tied it about his head and neck to show his status. "Then Anklamere stole it from us and used it to enslave the charioteers. He placed it high in his tower and let it glow until it rivaled the green wanderer in the heavens."

His conversation left her bored and impatient, missing Rainfall's nimble discourse or Ragwrist's jokes and laments about his state of poverty.

Vank tried to give her a servant to clean her scale and teeth, a bow-legged old blighter named Harf, an escaped Ghioz slave. He claimed he'd been a body-servant to dragons in the mountains off beyond the plains of Bant. Hundreds of dragons, a powerful empire—he was quite the most extraordinary liar Wistala had ever met. She'd flown all down the spine of mountains running west of the Inland Ocean chasing rumors that turned out to be founded on some bird-creatures.

Of course, to a blighter any big flying creature might seem a dragon. Still, all the detail he'd worked out, with tunnels and a whole hidden society of dragons dug in like rabbits in a warren inside a mountain. Perhaps he'd found that his stories enhanced his prestige among the others.

Wistala had learned long ago to clean her own scale and suck up and spit out river-sand to scrub her teeth. But she did let Harf set up bed and tenting on her doorstep, with orders to keep blighters from defiling any more texts.

An entourage of tribal elders visited her, paying obeisance to the crystal and asking what she'd seen on her hunting flights. They seemed most worried about the river to the west, their informal border with a province of the Ghioz. The Ghioz had crossed the river and were "digging holes" in some of the Pine Hills, a green serration on the horizon visible from the mouth of the great cave-ruin.

Ghioz riders had even explored some of the foothills of the blighter mountain range. They'd been chased off with a hail of flung spears and arrows and slingstones, but the Fireblades who'd seen action in the old Southling war under AuRon feared they'd be back.

A chastened enemy might return. A one-eyed Fireblade insisted that not even the ghosts of destroyed enemies ever troubled him again.

Wistala could understand their worry. She'd grown up in the human lands of the old Hypatian Empire. The Ghioz on the other side of the mountains had grown from minor trading partner on the Sunstruck Sea to rival. Geography, a few good thanes in the mountain passes, and the traditional friendship of elves and dwarves in their own lands who'd shared in Hypatia's ancient glories kept their terrible queen on her side of the mountains.

But, still, her wondering turned to worry. Wistala supposed that the choice cuts of meat and tasty organmeat sausages were inducements to stay. They even presented her with bits of old chain and nail and cooking iron along with raw gold and silver ores, gritty but satisfying in the slime that came to her mouth to aid it in its downward slide. *NooMoahk's tribute,* the blighters styled it.

She'd seen one war; one war was enough for her temperament. But the idea of all these irreplaceable old books being torn up and used to start campfires or finish a bowel evacuation pained her. She could almost hear Rainfall weeping when she thought of its destruction by ignorant blighters or a heedless invading army.

That night, she fell asleep among them, counting old scrolls the way some dragons counted tasty, jumping sheep.

A deputation of the Fireblades with Vank at its head roused her the next morning with a snarling drum that made her think of desert snakes and their rattle-tails. Irritated, she was tempted to knock the whole lot of them down with her tail.

"Greenscale goddess," Vank said, as she smacked her lips to bring moisture to her dry mouth. "The Ghioz have crossed the river. They cut down trees for a stockade in our western woods, rich with wild boar and redmonkey."

She wasn't surprised that he named her two favorite blighter preparations. Vank was full of himself, not stupid. He'd acquired a new belt of gold and silver rings.

"I hope you don't want me to fight them."

"No, keeper, no. Horblikklak, the Fireblades' Marchchief, intends only to make a show of force and ask them to talk."

Wistala dredged her memory. The Fireblades had a three-headed leadership. Their Marchchief saw to the day-to-day organization and training of the warriors. The Battlechief, a bent oldster who used a captured battle-standard for a staff, would direct them in fighting.

The Youngchief picked likely male blighters, saw to their supply, and learned from the other two. It was an old system from the ancient blighter glory, when a Battlechief might command tens of thousands represented as bits of skulls on three-dimensional maps in boxes of dried sugared sand instead of the few hundreds squatting in their storied ruins.

Horblikklak, whose name meant "Mountain Lightning" in the blighter tongue, stepped forward, quick and flashy as a warty mountain toad—which is to say not at all.

"Tell the dragon—" he began.

"I've improved my understanding of your tongue," Wistala said. The language had come fast, as though she'd learned it in the egg. "You may speak to me directly."

Some of the blighters made coughing sounds at her pronunciation, but she'd made herself understood.

"We talk to Stone-men, to Ghioz," Horblikklak said. "You fly in distance, watching. When we signal with banner, you fly to us and circle, so they see we speak truth about presence of dragon."

"Will you speak truth about willingness of the dragon to go into battle?"

"Some truths best left unsaid, mayhap," Vank said, digging in his oily ear as he examined her cavern's ceiling.

"Just don't start a fight and expect me to rescue you. I've no quarrel with these men."

Vank made a digging motion with one long arm, but the gesture was lost on Wistala. "The sight of a dragon will make them wary. The runaway, Harf, said the Ghioz fear dragons. Dragons knock down stone cities."

Scales and tales! Evidently the blighters here liked a good liar. Well, she could do with a little exercise. For eye as well as wing, she'd been reading too much.

"I agree. Show me the signal and so on."

It took a few days to set up the meeting with the Ghioz, then a spring storm delayed it still further. The two sides arranged for it to be held at an old rockpile that the blighters claimed was a quarry from Krag's old glory. The Ghioz insisted it was an old stoneworks of theirs, and even dug up old tools bearing Ghioz marks that old Horblikklak thought suspiciously free of rust and rot.

Vank told her the history of meetings with the Ghioz. Their first meeting generations ago had been deep in the woods beyond the great river that, if her maps were correct, flowed all the way to Hypatia and the Inland Ocean. In those days the woods were the halfway point between the blighters and the Ghioz. At that time they arranged to take lumber from the forests across the river. After a bloody incident between human woodsmen and blighter hunters, they held a second peace council on the "Ghioz" riverbank, the new border, two generations ago. The next one after that was on the blighter side, once the Ghioz claimed rights to use the river to float their lumber down to their province on the east side of the Red Mountains. When that had happened, most of the Fireblades were running naked chasing beetles. Now it seemed the Ghioz claimed a vast swath of territory on this side of the river, and the new "halfway" point was practically on the doorstep of Great Krag.

She saw the Fireblades' banner, a tall wooden construct that reminded her of a small boatmast. It took four blighters to carry it from base point to base point, plus two more to roll the heavy wheel base it rested in when traveling. Assorted skulls, broken shields and sword hilts, black dragonscale etched with chalky pictographs, and long strings of vertebrae like Rainfall's old Winter Solstice decorations of whitebell blossoms rattled against each other or chimed in the wind. It had lines to the top where the blighters could run up signal flags for those too far away to hear orders. Vank pointed out a bronzed bit of dragonclaw, some sheath AuRon must have shed and given to them, when they told the story (again!) of their great victory when they burned the war machines in the southern jungles.

Wistala's throat tightened as she touched the bronzed memento of her brother.

Horblikklak showed her how they would rock the banner back

and forth like a tree in a heavy wind when they wanted her to fly up and circle.

Wistala couldn't resist a predawn flight over the Ghioz encampment the day of the meeting. She knew enough Ghioz history to wonder if the Fireblades weren't walking into some kind of trap. The Ghioz stockade was impressive, sensibly sited against a looping, swampy stream on a low rise. She drifted on the fresh spring breeze as she passed over the camp, not daring to flap, and smelled coalsmoke. Even at night there was the sound of wood being chopped and hammers at work. The Ghioz had cut down trees and fitted the trunks with sharpened stakes and set up war machines—nothing like the juggernauts of the dwarves, of course, but she suspected they were lethal enough. And there was fresh earth everywhere; they'd dug pits or trenches to confound a blighter charge.

The Ghioz fought like dwarves, it seemed.

She returned to the Fireblade camp and fortified herself with a blood pudding the blighters made for her and some crisped bits of hide from the evening's feast. They had a pile of bones and joints, but if she had to spend much time aloft a bellyful of rattling offal wouldn't be a welcome companion.

"If you have to vent something on an enemy, better fire than what comes out the other end," Mother used to say.

She climbed a pile of rocks with a good view of the land between the Fireblade camp and the meeting site half a horizon away. Treetops bubbled across the valley leading to the distant ridge of the Ghioz camp. The old quarry made a chalky scar in the greenery.

She settled down for a one-eye-open nap. She'd perfected the art in her travels across the endless expanses of the east. Hunting horns, faint in the distance as the birdcalls from the adjoining woods, indicated that the two sides were approaching each other. Then relay signalmen took up the call, long sonorous swan-honks relaying the news of a peaceful meeting.

With that, she launched herself aloft.

Good thing she hadn't eaten all those joints. Her stomach writhed in anxiety. She hoped the blighters wouldn't get riled up and start a battle in the expectation that she would come to their aid. Or suppose the Ghioz decided to launch a quick strike—according to the Fireblades they had some tough riders called the Red Guard who patrolled their eastern borders.

What kind of dragon was she, to dread battle so? She'd once been fierce enough in avenging her family's destruction, dared the dwarves to fire their weighted harpoons at her. Now her *griff* twitched at the thought of a few arrows flying in a far-off forest.

Well, the appearance of bravery and bravery itself were identical to all but one, and she'd never had difficulty keeping secrets.

She didn't mind surveying the forest. The trees looked tall, straight, and sturdy on this well-watered ground west of the mountains. She dipped and looked down tumbling streambeds choked into pools like blue jewels on a string by beaver dams. The blighters, or lightning in a dry season, had burned open meadows in between stands of older timber, and these were thick with ground birds and game on hoof. Herds of deer hurried, a brown-backed flood, for tight-laced branches as she passed over. She smelled sweet berries and saw the muddy smears of wild pigs tossing ground cover for nuts and sweet roots.

No wonder the blighters wanted the forest.

She promised herself a pig hunt in these woods before too many days passed. She'd probably have to examine the game-trails closely and then find a place to lie in wait, making use of wind and dew to hide her scent. Pigs weren't easy to catch, but their ample, tasty flesh more than made up for the effort.

More blighter horns!

She flapped higher, alarmed that they'd joined battle, but the encounter seemed to be ending peacefully. The Fireblades sang as they marched away from the meeting place, shaking their standards until the battle-banners seemed like dancing giants accompanying them on the march.

The Fireblade mass exploded into various shades of green.

"As best as best can be," Vank said, when she alighted to hear the news. "We told them to get back on their side of the river, or there would be bloodshed and unceasing war so long as man dared walk in our woods."

"That's the way to treat men," a warrior interrupted, thumping fist against his small round shield, edged with swordcatchers. "Like dogs! Fierce enough until they meet a fight. Then they tuck tail and scuttle. Scuttle!"

"Aye!" another barked.

"And?" Wistala asked, ignoring the byplay.

Vank managed to dance without moving his feet, waving his arms first one way, then the other. "They agreed to withdraw. True! Their prospectors, who thought they found gold, were mistaken in any case. 'Profitless mine,' they said." Vank had to use Parl to quote them accurately. "No profit! No profit! Ghioz never move but for profit. The men will be gone. They promised to withdraw their huntsmen and break camp. Tonight!"

Only Horblikklak seemed downcast.

"Too easy!" he grunted, as he sent out more flank-guards, pointing and swatting his warriors into position. "Too many smiles. Too much promised."

"I see," Wistala said, opening her wings. Maybe she should take one more flight around the Fireblades as they entered the thickest part of the forest.

"One more!" Horblikklak interrupted. "Too big a pile of rock in thick-axled wagon, covered by tarp and guarded, in the center of camp. 'Profitless mine,' my dung!"

Chapter 3

"Tyr, you have won another victory," the messenger from the Drakwatch reported, puffing the whole length of his sides. The stretched skin against his sides where his wings would soon emerge was swollen and cracked.

The Copper dragon, Tyr of the Lavadome RuGaard, Imperator of the Dragonfumes of the Lower World, Courses Wet and Dry, Sunned and Cavenighted, the Three Lines, Seven Hills, Grand Guardian of Egg and Hatchling, Scale and Song, Fiery Heritage and Winged Future, as that gassy firebladder NoSohoth liked to style him, reclined on a small projection overlooking the old sand-floored dueling arena. He dismissed two blighter thralls who'd been polishing his teeth.

The projection, once used to attach the ropes and pulleys thralls needed to extract a deceased loser from a duel—a duel in theory could be stopped at any time, but some dragons made it a point of honor to die rather than cry vanquished—was still being rendered fit for a Tyr. Thrall artisans, under direction from NoSohoth, had smoothed and saddled the stone and were slowly filling in etchwork of the pleasing *laudi*-like designs commemorating his victories in Bant and Anaea, and against the Dragonblade.

The Copper preferred to hold court in the old dueling pit. He'd killed the Dragonblade here, but happier was the memory of the dragons roaring in triumph as his hag-riders fell. The chamber yawned big enough to admit many dozens of dragons, and it meant less of a climb to the gardens at the top of Imperial Rock for dragons, and yes, even the occasional free thrall, who wished an audience.

He'd outlawed dueling to settle differences, which was just a way for dragons to determine which one was rich enough to hire the best thicsy

Skotl duelist. Poor dragons had to do their own fighting, and more often than not they died.

At his hatching the Copper had come off worse in duel. His maimed left *sii* still gave him an awkward gait and an uneven frame owing to the overdeveloped shoulder of his right.

Now dragons were supposed to take their differences to the leading dragons of the Seven Hills. And if they couldn't work it out between each other, they came to him and pleaded. It made for many a wearying day hearing them out and deciding which to favor or how to divide guilt.

Dueling still took place on the quiet, of course, beyond the river ring around the Lavadome, but he made sure his mate didn't invite reputed duelists to any of the feasts atop Imperial Rock.

In compromise to the dignity of his rank, he had two golden perches added, flanking his saddle-shaped rock. Brightly colored *griffaran* with well-preened feathers and sharpened talon-extenders stared owlishly down on the sandpit. Though smaller than the dragons, they were quicker, with beaks strong enough to break a dragon's neck and talons that ripped through scale. *Griffaran* could fly in spaces where heavy, big-winged dragons couldn't hope to launch, like the river tunnels that allowed quick travel in the Lower World, and up through the mountainside cracks near the Lavadome.

The Copper gave a pleasant nod to the Drakwatch courier.

"I won?" the Copper asked. "I've conquered precious little this morning beyond from my tortoiseshell of hot kern."

That brought a few polite chuckles from senior members of the three lines who idled about the sandpit. Some, like the rather dull red CuBellereth, were simply busyhaunches who liked to drop anecdotes about the Imperial Court at their home hills. Others, the blue CoTathanagar, for instance, engaged in office seeking, constantly putting forward relations for assignment.

Luckily dragons he respected and trusted also lounged nearby. Word had spread that good news was on its way. NoSohoth saw to it that messengers bearing good news trumpeted it to an audience. Bad news crept up the thrall passages to the anteroom off his sleeping-chamber.

The Copper burped as he listened to the messenger's report. His kern wasn't sitting right. He'd had nothing since last night but a little kern in blood pudding. The Copper wasn't fond of the taste of the stuff, but dragons who lived long underground benefited from the grain. Usually it aided the digestion—there wasn't a bullock so tough and stringy that it didn't settle better when followed by a nice hot gruel of kern. Odd.

Poison? His cooks, dragon and thrall, had tasted of it right in front of him, and assisted him all through the meals to prevent them from running off and bringing it back up in some waste-chute.

The messenger was running on about another victory over the demen. Paskinix, the Deman-King, had requested an "accommodation in recognition of the change in circumstance."

The Copper clacked his teeth good-humoredly. NoSohoth had probably coached the courier on his wordplay. Irascible old Paskinix, tough as a dug-in scale-tick, would have used blunter phrases. A canny warrior and formidable opponent, even in defeat he made a plea for peace sound like a demand.

"The old northeast passage lies open," the courier continued. "The Star Tunnel echoed with the sound of your Aerial Host as they flew and broke the enemy. Now the Firemaids explore regions long-lost to dragonkind."

At a mutter and a nod from NoSohoth, the messenger repeated his words, roaring out the news. The fierce noise elicited growls and stamps of approval that seemed to require a nod of acknowledgment from their Tyr.

Just so, the Copper thought. When he heard word of the size of the Star Tunnel, he asked HeBellereth if he thought the Aerial Host could be brought into action. Dragons could ferry elite human thralls about easily, or men could fight from dragonback.

"Captives?" the Copper asked.

"Ten claw-score or more and two of their generals. One general is wounded and seems likely to die."

"Have them brought to the Lavadome. Paskinix will have to come to Imperial Rock if he wants them back."

"HeBellereth sent them along behind me in those cockleshell boats of theirs, under beak and claw of the *griffaran*. They should be arriving at the river ring even now."

"Thank you for such a complete account," the Copper said, and the courier swelled.

"So large and dangerous a group of captives should be supervised," NoFhyriticus, a scaleless gray Anklene who served as the court physician, said. "Demen have surrendered before, just to get spies or assassins inside the Lavadome." The Copper liked having him around because he rarely spoke, but when he did it was something sensible.

"Perhaps my nephew SuLam—" CoTathanagar began.

"I'll go meet them myself," the Copper said, stretching. Maybe exercise would settle his stomach. It had been a hearty feast last night, three bullocks to commemorate Tyr FeHazathant's ending of the civil wars and peace in the Lavadome. Perhaps the kern was an irresistible force meeting an immovable mass of roast hides. His mate, Nilrasha, Queen of Imperial Rock, called his selection of fried hides crass when he should be claiming the tyrloin.

"Offal fit for kitchen thralls and cave-mouth beggars," she'd said, even after he told her that the taste brought back memories of his days in the Drakwatch caves. In some ways Nilrasha struck him as a regrettable queen, but she always spoke her mind. Few other dragons on the Imperial Rock could make that claim. The Copper thought Tyr FeHazathant's Queen Tighlia, dead but no more forgotten than her besung mate, a model, at least in her public behavior. Nilrasha relished the glitter of her position more than its duties.

Though the thralls loved her. They called her Queen Ora, after an old nickname the blighters had given her during the fighting in Bant. It meant "lucky." She liked to award thirty days' rest from duties or relocation to the sunny Upholds to thralls who showed good judgment or skill or even a pleasing song, and she left punishment of lawbreakers to her mate.

He was skeptical at first, but her system did get more work out of the thralls, if they had a chance at reward, though there were others who maintained you'd get twice the sweat with a simple threat of being turned into a feast. Problem was, she also bestowed her blessings on thralls belonging to others, which caused grumbling in court.

But at the end of the wing, he admired her. She was the one dragon in all the Lavadome who never brought him a complaint.

Being Tyr reminded him of the snake-cave where he'd met his bats, three claw-score years ago and three. Every time you broke the back of one, another slithered silently up behind you and struck.

He knew he was a young Tyr, a compromise from different factions because he'd arrived at the Lavadome a hero of the *griffaran* and a stranger to each line and faction. His role in the rising against the dragon-riders four years ago settled him into Lavadome legend. The dragon-lords of the Lavadome's cave-stitched hills thought he'd be pliable with bits of egg practically still sticking to his scale. His bad eye and withered forelimb brought pity, contempt—some even called him cripple or used his old Drakwatch nickname "Batty"—in private.

But the old Tyr FeHazathant believed in him enough to issue his blessing before he died. Or so he'd been told.

That was the worst part of being Tyr. Not being able to trust the words others spoke.

Which is why he set off to see the demen prisoners himself.

He set out with a few of the court and his *griffaran* guard. They made an impressive procession, with their Tyr at the head of the file. One of the advantages of copper scales was their versatility. They looked blood-colored in the low light of tallow dips, and in the brighter light of the vast underground of the Lavadome, lit by rivers of liquid rock flowing down the mysterious walls of its horizon-wide crystalline bubble, they positively burned like embers. When polished to a fine smoothness by soft wire brush and scouring-rag by his body-thralls, of course.

"Are you leaving Imperial Rock, my love?" Nilrasha, his mate, asked, alighting. If anything, she was sleeker and more beautiful than when she'd first sprouted wings, every scale trimmed and polished, scale around her eyes subtly painted and etched. She'd been drawn down from the gardens atop the Rock by the circling *griffaran*.

"Just to the river ring. I haven't been out enough lately. I need exercise. My digestion . . ."

"I'm feeling it too," she said. "We are in sympathy. I was just thinking a swim would clear it. But must half the court follow us?"

"There are prisoners to see. A curiosity."

If he'd been feeling well that rising the trip would have been a pleasant walk, especially with his beautiful mate drawing attention away from his limp with her playful chatter and shifts of wing and tail.

The Lavadome burned gloriously today as the northern lines of glowing liquid earth ran down the transparent crystal, a vast bubble that had created the Lavadome in old years beyond count. At the top it peeked from the volcano's caldera so that frosted sunlight was admitted. More marvelous still was the way it dispersed and conducted the heat of the lines of lava so the entire dome simply became pleasantly warm. Normally the south had the better view, but the flow sometimes rerouted itself.

But instead of enjoying mate and view, he dragged a sour stomach as he had to pass the jagged barbs of Skotl hill, so naturally dragons great and small crept out of their holes, drawn by the bright wing-feathers of the *griffaran* bodyguard advertising his trip as they traced endless double-loops above him.

He limped along, three-legged. His left front leg wasn't quite as useless as it once was. Nilrasha, falling back on lore she'd learned as a hatchling attending to old, battle-scarred Firemaids so that as succor flowed one way wisdom might trickle another, worked it and massaged it and worried it with tooth and tongue until he felt—well, not so much a tactile sensation as a sort of warmth. Now he could extend it and lock it in such a way that he could rest on it, rather like a tired thrall's leaning on a rake or bearing-pole.

It was nice to halt here and there and take the view, giving his good *sii* a chance to rest as he leaned on his not-quite-useless forelimb.

"Mighty Tyr RuGaard," a rather plump blue bellowed at one halt, bowling over a couple of drakka who'd climbed a rocky perch to watch him pass. "My thralls are stealing from me. None will confess the crime. I'd like an Imperative to eat a few as an example to the rest."

RuGaard didn't give a waggly tail-tip scale for the gizzards of unknown thralls, but the Lavadome had few enough. Most dwarves starved themselves rather than work for dragons, blighters fought among themselves so you had to limit the number in a household or appoint a strongman to keep the others in line—who would then cripple or kill a third of your servants every year through beatings—and as for elves, you might as well try to capture and keep a cloud for a pet. Demen hardly bred in captivity. That left men. With men you had to be careful in feeding and watering and housing or they died like flies.

"What are they stealing?"

"Food, of course."

"Men will steal. Be thankful yours are such poor thieves."

"Tyr, my brover sits on my neck," said one little green hatchling, rather undersized for a Skotl. A bigger, bristling silver hatchling rolled an eye to watch the *griffaran* above, as though thinking about timing a jump. "Tell him to stop."

"Bite or claw whatever you can reach and don't stop until he gets off," the Copper said. "Leave enough marks and you'll get invited to join the Firemaids as soon as you light your first flame."

"Truly?" the hatchling asked.

"Of course," Nilrasha said. "I've placed my eye on you ... er ... young prospect."

"S'ank you, shining Queen," the hatchling said, swelling and raising her neck.

Speaking of which, the Copper thought to her as they moved on, *did you review this year's first-oaths yet?*

By tradition the Tyr's mate led the Firemaidens, young dragonelles learning to guard shaft and mouth and passage of the myriad tunnels around the Lavadome. Those who didn't mate often continued in their duties and became Firemaids, warriors oathed for life and the most respected band in the Lavadome, feted in every hill. Though she'd never breathed word, some of the senior Firemaids turned tail to Nilrasha, as she'd broken her Firemaid vow to mate, but the Copper didn't want to stick his snout into female squabbling and get it singed.

Don't bring that up now, she thought back at him.

Some dragons bowed deeply, others just bobbed their nose-tips, and a few put heads together—mind-speech didn't come easily to Skotls—to discuss their Tyr as he walked by, his withered left forelimb giving him an odd gait.

A bit of green flashed across the fields, parting a rather sickly flock of sheep grazing on hairy lichens. The procession halted again.

"Tyr," a young dragonelle said, throwing herself down before him with neck turned full round to expose the lesser hearts beating behind her chin. "My name is Yefkoa. My parents wish me to mate against my will . . . to . . . to SoRolatan."

The Copper knew him. SoRolatan was another Copper, though brighter and with less of a blood-tinge to his scales. A former Upholder at the tip of the Empire's southern wing, he'd grown rich mining for the ores dragons needed—indeed craved—for a healthy growth of scale. Rumor had it he had a jade or two. Now he wanted multiple mates?

"SoRolatan has a mate, does he not, dear?" the Copper asked.

"But barren, poor creature," Nilrasha said, glaring at the frightened, skinny little thing, her wings hardly dry from emerging. "The old Upholder's daughter in the Six Ridges, you'll remember."

The Copper had come to the Lavadome practically as a hatchling but had never quite developed the ear for politics, intrigue, and out-and-out gossip that most dragons born there seemed to possess. He tasted the air next to his mate's cheek in gratitude for her smooth supply of detail.

"I suppose you have someone else in mind?" the Copper asked. Yefkoa seemed a sleek young dragonelle with an attractive set of wings, even folded and decorously tucked. He understood SoRolatan's interest. The Copper was mated, not dead.

"No, Tyr. I . . ."

She kept looking at Nilrasha as though fearing a bite.

"Spit it out," the Copper said.

"I want to fly. Out in real air under real sun."

The Copper wondered if she wasn't one of those back-to-nature dragons. She'd clearly never tangled with crossbows or war machines.

She looked healthy enough, and had nice lines for air, as far as he could judge such matters. "Flying, eh? How fast are you?"

"Fast!" she said. "Just watch."

She hopped nimbly onto a rock and opened her wings—every set of male eyes upon her—and launched herself into the open air of the Lavadome. She gained altitude fast, then dropped into a gliding, tail-balanced swoop. Reflected burning earth turned her glittering young scales to meteors as she rounded the Imperial Rock and returned.

The Copper would have liked to fly like that. His artificial wing joint allowed him to stay aloft and maneuver, but he was no aerialist.

Fortunately the wind of her landing dried his eyes.

Skotl. All brawn and no brains, Nilrasha thought to him. *Don't let a nice pair of wings make you do anything rash. SoRolatan is an important and influential dragon.*

Mind-speech is a strange thing. The closer two dragons are, the better their communication link. Sometimes Nilrasha preempted his thoughts, but she was better at guarding hers. Whenever he probed to find out about his first mate, Halaflora, for example—

Ahh, the past is set. You're Tyr, you need to be thinking about the future, as yet unformed.

"Name the Upholds, the dominant hominid race in each, its principal product for the Empire. You can really impress me by naming the Upholder as well," the Copper said.

"Ha-errr," she began, settling her wings in a way that made his hearts beat faster. "Bant, mostly blighters, produces fleshstock— sheep, I mean—and grain, the Upholder is... NiThonius. Far Anaea, humans, produces kern, the Upholder is... is... Ru—no, CuPinnatax..."

If you're really planning to sit through this, I'm going to go on to the river and have a bath, Nilrasha thought. But she made no move to abandon him in so public a manner.

"The Aerial Host could use you," the Copper said, cutting her off as she mentioned that Yellowsand, to the southwest, offered only rare spices and herbs and a few jewels grudgingly extracted from the waste-elves there in return for horseflesh. "But remember, fly only at night, unless it's an emergency or over the home mountains controlled by the *griffaran*. We aren't ready for the surface yet."

"And SoRolatan? His hoard-offering to my family?"

"I'll see to it that it is replaced—within reason."

You've made an enemy today, Nilrasha thought to him.

And also a friend. She's young—she'll be around longer.

Young dragonelles forget favors like clouds lose water, she thought back. Old dragons like SoRolatan hold grudges like dwarves keeping beard-light.

There were several castrated dragons in the Aerial Host, survivors from the brief but brutal reign of SiMevolant and his human supporters led by the Dragonblade. Though unable to produce heirs, they would still like having her around. And if she found some *laudi*-painted young flier with seed intact who sang his lifesong to her and managed to catch up on a courting flight... well, a few generations of eggs inheriting their flying skill would do the Empire equal good.

If SoRolatan made too much of a stink, he'd ask HeBellereth to send the dome-guard Aerial Host for endurance training over SoRolatan's hilltop. Airborne dragons had to evacuate their bowels sometime.

He sent a message to HeBellereth, and the dragonelle practically licked his good *sii* clean with her tongue, bubbling gratitude like the old hot pool that had belonged to one of his predecessors.

If mutters arose from the spectators they took care that their Tyr did not hear them.

Nilrasha moved off toward the river ring.

A second messenger spotted his *griffaran* guard and corrected their course to the landing where the demen were held prisoner.

Of all the hominids, demen struck the Copper as the oddest. They looked like bits and pieces of other creatures fixed together with that liquid stone the dwarves used and men imitated. Bits of them about the shoulders and spine reminded him of scuttling pinchg-prawn with their carapaces enclosing tasty flesh. They had long, strong fingers, and toes for probing and gripping, and big eyes oddly set slowly blinking on either side of their pointed scabby heads. They had long, knobby-kneed legs that reminded him of frogs or toads, folding themselves neat as dragonwings against their sides when they sat. If a squatting demen closed his eyes you'd almost think him a stalagmite.

Which, he supposed, was the point.

They could squeeze into crevices one would think a snake couldn't wriggle through too.

They were fast on their feet, though when panicked they shot in different directions, which, according to the reports he'd been hearing and sending on to the Anklenes to be recorded, was their one weakness in battle. He'd seen them working in the Lavadome often enough to know they could be cruel, especially to other races put under their supervision.

This assortment, bereft of their nets and crystal-tipped spears and slingstones that broke into ugly fragments in a wound, looked much the worse for their experiences. A deman was an emaciated-looking thing compared even to an elf, and these were thin as kern-stalks in a drought.

They squatted, mud-splattered and smelling of the river, chained or roped or weighted fixed to boat-bottom, half in the boats and half out and with that nasty thrall-dealer Sreeksrack—or so everyone called him. He had lost his honorable dragon name long ago—something having to do with a duel, Nilrasha said. He was a Copper as well, but of a bronzeish hue that reminded the Tyr of his father.

No one minded owning thralls, but the business of gathering and evaluating and culling them was best left to others.

Sreeksrack bobbed his head, trying to get his Tyr's attention.

Captives taken in war belonged to the Tyr—though by tradition they were quickly sold, adding to the hoard of the Imperial Line. Vast sums moved in and out of the hoard overseen by NoSohoth. There were always coins rattling in NoSohoth's gold-gizzard as they digested and turned to scale, but if a mouthful here and there kept so efficient a servant to the family line loyal, the Copper was willing to part with it.

Poor thralls. What must it be like to be rowed across the river ring in chains, nothing but toil to look forward to, even if it was under the splendid burning streaks above?

The waters of the river ring sagged, bordered by muck and sand. Must be the end of the dry season in the Upper World. He remembered it as a chaotic time during his service in Anaea. Men always went a little crazy then, perhaps from heat and thirst.

The Firemaid in charge of the captives bowed. "The prisoners from the deepest Star Tunnel holes. We finally found their lair. 'Twas in a grotto too tight for dragons. Your sister countermined, hiring dwarves."

The dwarves must have thought it a fine deal, getting paid to help destroy their bitterest enemies.

What the Lavadome was to dragons, the Star Tunnel was to the demen in this part of the Lower World, or so he'd been told. It had been the work of years clearing it, and they'd lost dozens of dragons and even more dragonelles. Every time they thought they had won it, the demen opened some new portal and attacked from an unexpected quarter.

"This is but a token of the tally," the Firemaid said. "Their leaders. The others follow, perhaps a thousand."

A thousand! He heard Sreeksrack choke back a hungry yelp. A vast number in the Lower World, which was often as inhospitable as bare desert or cold mountaintop. Of course, the Star Tunnel had many exits to the surface. A few in his retinue licked their chops. There would probably be wounded and sick to eat. Every hill had a few clan recipes for deman. Their thin leg-flesh practically melted in butter.

Paskinix, no wonder you are willing to deal at last. It seems I have much of your army. In the darkest days of his youth in the snake-haunted bat caves he'd learned that the best way to kill a snake was to crush its head. No matter how powerful the coils of the body, without the head it was nothing but a meal.

The Empire had taken the demen body—and the head was no doubt wondering what to do with itself. At dreadful cost, but dragonkind now held as much of the Lower World as the great wizard Anklamere ever had. They wouldn't have to worry about raids on the trade lines, and drakka and drakes would be freed up from the watch-posts.

The Upper World, soft and ripe in the sun as the sweet fruits brought down for the thralls and livestock, beckoned to his imagination.

He walked along the line of prisoners. Disarmed, sullen in defeat, they were marked as a fierce warrior race only by their carapace decor. They had bits of bone, dragonteeth, what looked like dwarf-skull and blighter-fang dug into or piercing the organic platework about their shoulders. Some had painted their battlescars, others filled an empty ocular cavity or torn-out ear with a baby *griffaran* beak. But appearances could be deceiving. These were war-chieftains who'd fought fire-breathing dragons a hundred times their weight to a standstill for *years*.

Seemed a shame to put such specimens to work herding cattle or shoveling dragon-waste.

Now would be the time to announce a grand victory feast. NoSohoth eyed him, subtly smacking his lips. Deman organmeat— especially the liver and kidneys—sharpened the eyesight and kept one clearheaded.

The Copper turned to face his procession and cleared his throat, feeling sluggish. They wouldn't like the speech, but the sooner it was done with, the better. Then he could find a comfortable spot on the riverbank to sleep.

His first word turned into a shocked breath. Pairs of eyes widened and he heard a few gasps. Before he knew what had happened, he felt a flutter of feathers across his back and a deman-scream cut the riverbank.

Two *griffaran* rose into the air, one with the head and arm of a deman in its claws, the other gripping a leg. A jagged shard of crystal, long and slightly curved, spun as it fell. It broke into ugly barbs as it struck the ground just behind his bad *sii*.

Above, the deman parted, messily.

Other *griffaran* of the bodyguard swooped down, batting at the demen with their wings, knocking them back into the mud and among the boats.

It occurred to him that from behind, his withered leg left a rather attractive target just under the shoulder joint. A clear path to his heart for just such a blade.

He'd have to see that what was left of the weapon was given to Rayg for study. Rayg, a scientific-minded thrall of rare gifts, and dwarf-trained besides, might find it interesting, especially since it had somehow survived a prisoner search.

Cosseted in the Imperial Rock, he'd forgotten lessons learned as a hatchling and drake. Poor old NeStirrath would have had a few choice words about *that*. Anger, mostly at himself, brought him round to face his enemies, and he felt the *foua* in his firebladder pulse, wanting out in the rush of nervous energy.

He spat, and an oily film splattered into the mud. Old injury in a fight with egg-raiding demen had left his firebladder missing some element or other that caused his *foua* to ignite. He could spit up a tiny flaming gob easily enough, but regular dragonflame was as beyond him as aerial acrobatics were.

This one had come within a few steps of breaking a crystal point into his chest-heart. Fate, it seemed, didn't want him fighting demen.

Embarrassment at his misfire calmed his anger better than any soothsaying.

"Not quite defeated yet, I see," he said to the demen in their darktongue. "I'm sure Paskinix will strike a fine bargain to get you back." He turned his head—held high and out of leaping reach—back toward his assembly.

"Odd, though," he said, keeping to the darktongue, "that Paskinix should not be taken along with his chieftains. I would hope that if the Firemaids were giving their lives in defense of the final refuge in the Lavadome I would be with them at the last."

"If I might offer—" Sreeksrack began.

"No, you may not," the Copper said, preventing him from naming a sum that might impress even NoSohoth. "These aren't some scale-seeking thieves sneaking down the Wind Tunnel. They're the toughest warriors the Empire has ever been matched against."

He felt woozy and thick-tongued. Better get the words out while he still could.

"I speak now as Tyr. The demen are to be conveyed to Imperial Rock and placed next to it in the west hollow. Just shift the horseflesh elsewhere. I want them to march, not drag chains, mind you, with the youngest hatchlings lining the way so that they may see examples of bravery and valor, paying their respects as dragons of the Empire should. Whether they become thralls or not—well, let's see what Paskinix says about getting them back. Now, you must excuse me."

He dashed off toward a riverbank rockpile quickly enough that the bodyguard circling above had to swoop to catch up. There he brought up the remains of his breakfast before collapsing.

"Tell Rayg—poisoned," he managed, as the alarmed *griffaran* fluttered above, before blackness swallowed him.

Chapter 4

The Copper woke, looked around at the rich tapestries and mats covering the cavern walls. Gold and silver thread multiplied the lamplight. The soothing aroma of *oliban* made itself at home in his nostrils. He welcomed its aromatic visit.

In the shadows of the ceiling, two pairs of red eyes glinted and blinked.

"Nilrasha?" he rasped, feeling for her mind.

"She's holding court in the gardens," a human voice said. "Would you like some water?"

The Copper blinked the mist out of his eyes and saw Rayg Sable-cloak. Despite his hominid birth, Rayg had as fine a mind as any of the Anklenes. Six years ago Rayg had married his body-servant, a lively but almost silent girl named Rhea. The Sablecloak family lived in the sunlight near the Southexit, and the Copper gave him leave to be with them whenever Rayg could be spared from his projects—a rare occurrence.

The Copper kept meaning to free him entirely, but it seemed there was always one more task that only Rayg could accomplish.

Rayg desired seeing his family settled out of the Lavadome in wealth and comfort. Now that his children were old enough to be helpful, one of them usually attended him in his workshop beneath the *griffaran* nesting areas, which employed a few skilled blighters and a strange dwarf who kept his beard and skull shaved. When the Copper had inquired, Rayg explained that the dwarf had suffered some irredeemable disgrace and labored so that he might still send a decent income home in the form of dragonscale.

"How did I get back here?"

"You were in a delirium. You don't remember, then?"

The Copper searched his memory. He remembered viewing the demen, then bringing his breakfast up. Then there was some dream about a trek across Bant with lions watching him the whole way, and swimming, swimming in water that alternated hot and cold.

He heard dragon-voices out beyond the beading that separated his sleeping-chamber from the rest of his chambers—the hygiene annex with its trickle and paired pools and his private gallery looking out on the Lavadome and the little trophy alley that led up to the formal court hall. They were cramped quarters, probably not even filling the egg shelf in the cave he'd been born into, but it was easier to relax with comforting stone close around and tight corners where enemies could not mass and might be surprised.

"How long have I been with fever?"

"Three lightings," Rayg said, referring to the glow of refracted sunlight or moonlight through the apex of the Lavadome. Probably about a day and a night in the Upper World. While dragons in the Upper World adapted to a sun-based schedule easily enough, in the Lavadome they alternated long-sleep, long-active, short-sleep, short-active, mixing according to humor and necessity. The Anklenes kept to a system based on the changing of the *griffaran* guard every twelve dwarf-hours.

"Send NoSohoth in," the Copper said, lifting his head. He felt tired, but remarkably clearheaded. "I believe I hear him in the trophy-hall."

NoSohoth, on entering, sprinkled another *sii* of quartz-like *oliban* on the brazier and tested the aroma with his nose. With a satisfied snort he bowed his way into the sleeping chamber.

"My Tyr—"

"Is awake," the Copper said, forestalling expressions of joy at his recovery. He sensed a tension in NoSohoth, even with the relaxing aroma so thick in the air you could almost see it. "What's the matter? Is Nilrasha ill?"

"No, my Tyr. But many are."

"A plague?"

"Food poisoning," Rayg said. "It's this year's new kern."

Kern was the most beneficial when it was freshest, so most dragon larders and storehouses sent the older stuff off to be cattle-feed or thrall-gruel when a new batch came in. Mothers of hatchlings mixed it up with blood, or rolled organmeats in ground kern and flamed the mash so that their progeny might grow long and strong.

"Bad kern?" Careless of that CuPinnatax. He'd appointed him Upholder of Anaea because he seemed an intelligent—though idle—dragon. CuPinnatax's grandsire FeLissarath had been the Upholder there for many years under the old Tyr. The Copper had served there before events in the Lavadome changed the entire course of his life.

"Not to smell or taste or sight, my Tyr," NoSohoth said, but then he'd put CuPinnatax forward for the Upholdership.

"I put it under a dwarf-lens," Rayg said. For a human who could speak Drakine credibly, he cared little for courtly niceties. "There's some kind of blight on it, a brownish spore-like organism. It doesn't appear to make the kern itself less wholesome, or interfere with it in any way I could detect, but once introduced into the digestion, it thrives and putrates. Cattle and sheep and pigs it affects hardly at all; they grow gassy and distended, but that seems to pass in a day. It sickens and slays chickens, and with dragons it appears to be taking the young and infirm."

"Take?" the Copper said. "How many?"

NoSohoth seemed unaccountably impressed with a new tapestry in the sleeping chamber. The Copper saw him deftly add more *oliban* to the brazier with his far *saa*.

"It is bad, Tyr," Rayg said. Even a dragon could read his expression.

The Copper's brain felt divided, flying in two directions. One part of him rushed backwards, trying to remember absolutely everything FeLissarath had taught him about kern. It was a crop dependent only on ample sunshine and rain as it ripened. Anaea, with its rich soil and high-altitude climate, was ideal in both, though once in a while a bad year or too much rain left the kern either undersized or rotting. FeLissarath had never mentioned any kind of blight that sickened dragons.

"Prepare yourself, my Tyr," NoSohoth said. "Most of the hatchlings are seriously sick. Some *sii*-score have already died—that we know of. Smaller drakes and drakka are also dying, but in lesser numbers. Of the aged dragons, it appears to depend on their appetite. Unhappily, the healthiest and heartiest eaters are falling victim."

"Where is my mate?"

"She just returned from visiting hills that have lost hatchlings. She goes out again directly."

Nilrasha might have her faults and enjoy the privileges of being Queen more than its duties, but she could be relied on in a crisis. Still, the sooner he appeared the better.

"With most of the dragons, it seems to have affected them to some extent as it did you. They bring their dinner up, or sluice it out the other end, and suffer from a fever."

The Copper's head cleared. "No one's to eat another mouthful of kern. NoSohoth, I want every healthy dragon in the Rock out in the hills helping the parents of hatchlings. Sick parents can't nurse their young. Rayg, what might help?"

"I'm no physiker, especially of dragons," Rayg said. "Fluids usually help, whatever the malady or injury."

"That will just speed their passing. Unconscious dragons will choke," the Copper rasped. Rayg loved to build tunnels out of air.

"Of course, if you apply by the mouth."

"How else are they supposed to get liquids?" NoSohoth asked, rolling his eyes.

"I saw one of my masters keep a cow with a broken jaw alive with injections through the . . . tailvent, you'd say."

"Can you manage this, and teach NoFhyriticus the Gray and a few body-thralls?"

"I can make nozzles easily enough. Hollow bones will do. Cow or sheep bladders would work for the liquid—for adult dragons you'd need whole ox or pig skins. The liquid—hmmm." Rayg muttered a few words in a language the Copper suspected was Dwarvish. Then he returned to Drakine. "Nothing fancy there. Water with the smallest portion of salt would do. Join them with gut. I can do all the work in your kitchens."

"Make at least eight. One for the Rock, seven for the other hills."

Rayg gave a curt bow. Was he losing a little of his hair? The Copper hated to think of such a valuable thrall aging. He'd have to make sure Rayg spent his declining years in some congenial Uphold with his family.

Assuming he could be spared.

"Am I excused, then?" Rayg asked.

"Of course. NoSohoth, aid him. If Mother Kyrithia herself is needed to wash out bladders, see that she does it."

Mother Kyrithia ran the Imperial Line's kitchens. She predated old Tyr FeHazathant and was indulged and bowed to more than the Copper. But she could make the stringiest old rock-lizard taste like the tenderest cut of veal.

There his mind went again, flying in two directions.

NoSohoth lingered. "And the old?"

"We'll do what we can for them, but it's the hatchlings we must see to."

"One thing, my Tyr," NoSohoth said, glancing at the ceiling where the bats hung.

"Yes?"

NoSohoth put his head close alongside the Copper's and dropped his voice to a whisper. "As it stands now, this is a tragedy. Grieve with the families over their dead, and you will have their love and respect; the love between you and the hills of the Lavadome will be refreshed and renewed as it was in the days of your victory over the Dragonblade and the hag-riddens. Send this human in with his contraptions and his potions, and no doubt some hatchlings will die in any case. Suddenly you are responsible for their deaths. The physician's dilemma."

NoSohoth was always counseling the safety of inaction.

The Copper had received only one piece of wisdom from his parents once pushed off the shelf by the Gray Rat, a suggestion that he try to overcome. Somehow that had stuck with him more than all the lessons he'd learned in the Drakwatch caves, or the deep knowledge of the Anklenes. He would rather try to overcome this wretched blight than be a dignified picture of grief.

"Let them hate. Even a handful of hatchlings saved will count for more in the long flight. Our numbers are few enough."

"My Tyr—"

"Do your best, NoSohoth. Perhaps I'll put you in charge of the kern trade from now on, if you don't mind one more burden."

NoSohoth's *griff* fluttered in excitement. "Speak not of burdens. The Empire and my Tyr have all I have to give. Virtue in the performance of one's duties—"

"Find some reliable, scientifically minded Anklene to examine the kern-trains on arrival. Oh, and have Rayg show this blight to the physician." The Copper had to cut NoSohoth off, or he'd be talking until a new coat of scales came in.

The thought of some gold quietly changing *sii* as a dragon was selected for the position might run NoSohoth's mind down happier paths.

"A wise decision, my Tyr," NoSohoth said.

"Now go help Rayg in the kitchens, would you? He'll need some intelligent thralls who are used to working close to dragons. Start with the body-thralls."

"Yes, my Tyr."

"Tell my mate I'll be with her shortly."

"Yes, my Tyr."

After NoSohoth left, the Copper looked up at the red eyes in the shadows above.

"Wail. Gnash. You've a long flight ahead of you."

The bats dropped and glided down, landing on each wing close to the shoulder. They patted and nuzzled his ridge of collar muscle in a manner some might find affectionate, if the observer didn't know they were searching for a vein.

The Copper had met a family of overlarge cave-bats as a hatchling. They had a taste for blood, and loved dragonblood above all things. Though it made them a little tipsy and insensible, it also had caused them to grow into bats of enormous proportions.

He'd adopted a line of bats, or perhaps they'd adopted him, much in the way a toothy lamprey adopts a whitefish, and they had become his most trusted—albeit dirtiest and laziest—servants. He'd cured them of fouling his sleeping chamber out of necessity. Nilrasha wouldn't stand for bat-droppings.

"A sup, pleassse?" Wail keened.

"Not yet," he warned. "I want you clearheaded."

They hardly resembled bats anymore. The Copper wasn't sure he understood what had happened, but everyone from Rayg to the Anklenes had their theories. The first generation of young bats raised on dragonblood grew uncommonly large and strong, flowers of batdom, long-lived and healthy. The second and third generations showed some odd . . . changes. Mutations, in Rayg's strange word. Wail and Gnash, sister and brother, the first of the fourth-generation bats, fed almost exclusively on dragonblood as they grew into massive, thick-snouted, big-toothed, ridge-browed brutes with scaly skin and almost dragonlike claws. One of the Anklenes went so far as to call them gargoyles, a race that was thought to have died out over a thousand years earlier, along with their creator, Anklamere the Sorcerer. They hardly hung upside down save to sleep deeply, preferring to perch in the manner of *griffaran* when awake.

Wail was rather brighter than Gnash, so he turned his snout to her.

"You know the way to Anaea, right? You came along with me when CuPinnatax was installed as Upholder."

"The west road, the lake, the bridge, yes—yess," Wail said. She ran her red tongue across her fangs. "A hungry journey."

"And you can help yourselves in a moment. In Anaea watch the kern. Examine the fields, especially the crop just coming up now. You know kern, right?"

"Tall green stalks, yes—yess," Wail replied.

Gnash nodded. "Birds and mice and bugs among the stalks, good crunching."

"Crunch away," the Copper said. "But observe the crops. See if anything is being done to the kern, especially as it ripens. Look and see if anything is being put on it, either before or after it is harvested. I'll send more of your kind to act as messengers. Or Wail, send Gnash if it's important enough. He's a fast flier."

"Yes, yess," Gnash said. "Fly the faster, I."

"Now you may take some blood."

He wouldn't call either of them particularly intelligent, but they were wily enough and followed clear instructions.

Sadly, the bats had lost much of their numbing saliva that had made feeding earlier generations almost pleasant thanks to the light-headedness, but the wounds they made still healed clean and quick. The Copper winced as they opened his skin. But it was worth it to have eyes and ears loyal to him, though the rest of the dragons in the Lavadome thought of bats as vermin and found his "gargoyles" positively creepy.

Even those who secretly burned out their nests admitted the over-sized bats had helped free the Lavadome of the hag-riders.

The bats burped and belched as they suckled, then rested briefly before taking off. The Copper poked his head out of his gallery and watched them disappear in the direction of the western tunnel, then headed up to the garden.

He felt exhausted and he'd hardly moved a dragonlength.

A little extra pallor wouldn't be noticed. He'd been ill, after all.

After a long, slow climb—the best pace he could manage—he found Nilrasha holding informal court around the feeding pit. The pit, scene of innumerable feats, was a low, bow-shaped trench-walkway with stairs going down to the kitchens where bearer-thralls could bring up platters. At formal feasts a continuous snake of joints and ragouts and racks and quarters, punctuated by the occasional squab on a skewer, passed under the dragons of the Imperial Line.

Now only two thralls with platters of cold cut meat and toasted munchrooms passed, probably because Nilrasha felt it was impolite to have company without offering at least a gesture.

At the center of the walkway was a sandy pit, usually reserved for hatchlings of the Imperial Line. There'd been some fine tussles and games among the hatchlings, always the best part of any dinner, to the Copper's mind. Now the pit held only a single green corpse, resting on its side.

All the assembled dragons quieted at his approach and regarded the dead hatchling silently.

The Copper took a breath. He didn't care for any of her company.

There was LaDibar, one of the senior Anklenes, at the honored position to her left where the freshest dishes arose. In his youth the gold had been proclaimed a genius, a prodigy, a dragon of rare mind and discernment. The Copper didn't dispute any of it, but for having such a rare mind he never did much of anything useful with it.

A handsome young couple of almost perfectly matched Skotl dragons sat across from Nilrasha. He was red and she, of course, was green, but their snouts were much alike. SiHazathant and Regalia were high in the Imperial Line; the mystical said they were SiDrakkon and Tighlia reincarnated. No one disputed that they were related to SiDrakkon through a cousin; their father had died bravely in battle against the hag-riders when first they arrived. Their hatching was still talked of, for they came from a strange double-egg, sharing a single egg-sack, though both had been rather small in consequence. When SiHazathant was losing to his brother in the hatchling contest, Regalia fought at his side and together they triumphed.

They'd been inseparable ever since. Regalia served with her brother in the Drakwatch by a special dispensation during SiDrakkon's rule—it was either that or SiHazathant would have had to go into the Firemaidens. It hadn't been as awkward as some predicted. She'd proved herself equal to the drakes, and she had a dragonelle's ability to hold her temper. They were both unusually grave for dragons of their age, as though in private mourning of some unspoken grief.

The third dragonelle was an unmated female Wyrr named Essea. She didn't have any particular talent or skill that the Copper could discern; if anything, she was a silly gossip, but she was of the Imperial Line and a friend and confidante of Nilrasha. The rest of the Imperial Line looked rather down on his mate because of her humble birth—Nilrasha had come out of the hovels at milkdrinker's hill—and slighted her whenever possible. The Copper was grateful to Essea for her unstinting kindnesses. She'd helped Nilrasha acquire a modicum of courtly manners and speech.

In a sense he and his mate were both outsiders to a line that they ostensibly led. He'd been adopted high into the Imperial Line by Tyr FeHazathant after rescuing a batch of *griffaran* eggs; she'd mated him after the overthrow of the hag-riders and the Dragonblade and taken the title of Queen. They were more popular in any other hill than they were in their own home caves.

Thus the emptiness of the gardens as Nilrasha mourned.

"It is good to see you well, my Tyr," Regalia said, and all but Nilrasha gave a *prrum* of agreement.

The Copper looked at the dead little hatchling at the center of the sandpit. A Skotl, but small, even for a hatchling. Her jawline, the lift of her protective *griff*—

"This was Tilfia," Nilrasha said, speaking low, as she did when unhappy. The Copper felt a little stab behind his breastbone. For all the bluff and strength that he admired, she sometimes sounded like the tired, defeated drakka who'd dragged herself out of that Bant waterway after the lost battle with the Ghioz. "I didn't know her name."

"The hatchling who complained about her brother sitting on her," the Copper said.

"I should have known her name," Nilrasha said.

"You can't expect to know every hatchling," Essea said, pressing tail to tail with her friend.

"Tighlia did," Nilrasha said. Regalia's eyes lit up at the name. FeHazathant and Tighlia, of Wyrr lines and Skotl, had mated and put an end to the civil wars that had almost emptied the Lavadome, and the Anklenes had suggested that FeHazathant take on the ancient title of Tyr, a kingly name out of dragon legend dating back to Silverhigh, if not before.

"We'd rather have you as Queen," Essea said. "Tighlia was a scold. And a traditionalist."

Nilrasha yanked her tail out from under Essea's. "Tighlia watched me win a whole sheep in the single leap and triple leap as a hatchling, and invited me into the Firemaids herself. She never forgot a name. I can't even be bothered to learn them in the first place."

"How many have we lost to this plague?" the Copper asked.

"Eight dragons. It seems to be hitting the Wyrr hardest," LaDibar said. "Fourteen hatchlings and a drakka. We also lost Gubiez in the Anklene hill."

"Rayg says the cause is a brown growth on the latest train of kern."

"Oh, scut," LaDibar said. "Bad meat, perhaps. But a disease that attacks kern wouldn't bother a dragon. Completely different entities, sun-eating and meat-eating. To think—za! Now, perhaps a poison— but no one's mentioned a smell or taste."

"Grieving over her is just making everyone miserable," Si-Hazathant said. "Enough mourning. We're not her parents. Let's be done with this." He opened his mouth and reached for the little body.

"Don't touch her!" Nilrasha roared. Regalia hooked her neck neatly under her brother. "I said she'd go into the Firemaidens, and go into the Firemaidens she will. Her bones will rest in the cairn, and in a generation or two some other young hatchling might make a talisman out of a piece of her scale. As far as I'm concerned, she died in battle."

"Battle?" LaDibar said. "What battle? There's been no battle. To think!"

"Don't be so sharp that you're brittle," Nilrasha said. "Someone's been at work at the kern, to poison us."

"Dragons?" Regalia said. "Treated like parasites? Like bat—or scale-nits, I mean?" Her eyes flamed even brighter than they had at the mention of Tighlia.

The Copper would have chuckled if he hadn't trained himself not to betray his emotions in public. Regalia had a good head on her neck. Nilrasha had better instincts, or perhaps she was just reading half-formed suspicions drifting through his own mind.

"To think! Is it so strange for natural food poisoning to take the weak?" LaDibar said. "That human is just puffing himself up again. He strings a few words of Dwarvish together and everyone calls him a savant. Za!"

"LaDibar, if you're so sure Rayg's wrong, feel free to eat the hatchling," the Copper said. "We've mourned. Let's finish it."

Nilrasha took a breath and glanced at Essea. Essea tightened her lips and drew in her head a little, a signal for dignified silence and attention.

"Barbaric custom," LaDibar said, after just long enough of a pause to make the Copper suspect he'd been searching for a way to refuse and keep his dignity. "We don't eat drakes or dragons, so why eat hatchlings?"

"Very well," the Copper said. "SiHazathant is hungry and already offered to perform the service. With the word of one of our most respected young Anklenes to guide him, I'm sure he'll have no qualms, and if something should happen, well, Regalia's legendary for her forgiving nature."

Regalia settled her *griff*. Not quite a warning rattle, but her brother shut his nostrils and raised his head away from the hatchling.

"Yes," LaDibar said. "Well, in circumstances like these, I think it meet to test your caution, and take caution in your tests, as we say in the temple when probing the unknown. Our Queen's wishes should be respected, in any case." He tilted his head complyingly at Nilrasha.

Nilrasha scooped up the hatchling, and for a dreadful *griff-tchk* the Copper feared she would swallow the corpse herself in her misery. But she merely made for the grand stair.

"I'll be at the Firemaiden cairn in mourning for some time," she said, forming the words out the side of her snout with difficulty.

Her coterie bowed deeply as she left. Essea raised herself up for a moment as if to follow, then thought better of it. Or maybe she just wanted to discuss the Queen's strange behavior with the others.

Nilrasha mourned through several lightings. Two more old dragons died. Rayg's strange, inverted manner of obtaining fluids allowed the remaining sick hatchlings to recover with the resiliency of young blood, with the exception of one poor little soul who hardly breathed as Rayg attended her.

Privately, the Copper credited Rayg with more than a score of lives saved against that one which would have been lost anyway. He must think of a suitable reward—one that didn't deprive the Lavadome of Rayg's services, of course. The offer of having his own (golden!) chair installed in the throne room didn't impress the quirky human. Much of the rest of the Copper's thinking as to rewards was met with a shrug.

The Copper suspected that Rayg chose the gesture just to revolt him. The humans' tendency to apparently dislocate their shoulders at will turned the stomach.

Rayg, when the crisis was past and after a good deal of work and experimentation, discovered that washing and boiling wouldn't remove the strange blight, but long roasting in a dry pan rendered it harmless—and made the kern almost indigestible.

Nilrasha struck the Copper as less eager for bows and baubles afterwards and more attentive to the hatchlings of the Lavadome.

Whether this was a passing resolution or a real change he couldn't say.

He liked seeing her so concerned with the hatchlings. It was part of her duty as Queen. He would like to see it become more than duty—he would be gladdened by some hatchlings of their own.

They hadn't had any luck with eggs so far, but between the two of them they had battle injuries that might make a clutch an impossibility.

If they did have a clutch, he would try something new with the males, separate them somehow until they could be made to understand. He and Nilrasha could set the style. Perhaps others would follow. Females in the Lavadome outnumbered males on the order of two to one or more. They always had, but did that have to mean they always would? With another hundred males, the other dragons wouldn't be so puffed up with their own importance. He could establish real dragon settlements in other places in the Lower World—the Star Tunnel, for instance. And perhaps dragonkind could look once more to the surface and put an end to lurking in the Lower World in fear.

He spoke about it once to Rethothanna. She was his favorite Anklene. She'd completed the first, and so far the only, history of the Lavadome. It was like a lifesong, only horribly long and complicated. You couldn't even listen to the whole thing in one sitting, and he had patience for stories.

"Yes, others before you have had the same thought. In the days of Anklamere it was enforced, of course, but dragons weren't much better than thralls back then.

"Tyr FeHazathant, glory to his name, had the same thought very early in his time. It fractured the Lavadome again. EmLar and his back-to-nature group quit the Lower World entirely and took off for the surface."

He sounded NoSohoth out on the matter, and the old courtier's head dipped as though his hearts had stopped. The Copper decided that he would cross that chasm when he was more secure. As it was, he waited for word from Anaea. He sent a message to his fool of an Upholder with a report of the bad kern and a request to look to the next crop with extra care. He also asked for full details about the last batch—had it been planted in an unusual place or had some trick of weather or infestation given the Anaeans difficulty?

He doubted both—Anaea's high-altitude plateau enjoyed mild, sunny weather the year round, cave-like in the cool of the night and pleasantly cleansing brightness in the day.

What he really waited for was news from Wail and Gnash. Three more fourth-generation bats were coming along nicely—Nilrasha offered up her blood regularly, saying it helped her sleep—but they were still learning the hills of the Lavadome and the holes of the principal dragons.

One worry dominated all the others. What would happen when the supply of even the old kern ran out? It would mean long, slow debilitating illness and eventual madness.

Oddly, none in the Lavadome talked of it. At least not that he heard.

Chapter 5

Years later, when Wistala thought back on it, that last summer of peace and quiet isolation that stretched into fall remembered better than it had lived.

At the time she was surfeited by the blighters and their endless celebrations. They celebrated that year's calves maturing, the winter's births who had survived to take their first steps and yap their first words, the fruit and crop harvests, the extraction of the fall's honey from the hives, the young females becoming maidens, and the young males taking their first real warrior-spear. The festivals blazed loud and vigorous and colorful and musical and all that, but one was very much like the other to her senses, and she preferred the peace of Noo-Moahk's library to massed dancing.

In time, even the library galled her. She couldn't read quickly enough to get through, and each scroll parsed out increased her sense of frustration.

Her mood was the crystal's doing, she finally decided.

Wistala distrusted the crystal. Delightful as it was for casting light on her reading, fascinating as it was to stare into, since the slightest shift of one's head brought different images—at times she thought she saw dragons, at other times a great tower, not quite circular and flat-headed as an anvil—it sometimes made her doubt her own mind and will.

She'd heard and read stories, of course, of travelers too long on their own who became crazed. At first she wondered if her own mind was the one at fault. The crystal, though smaller than a troll, reminded her of the one she'd fought on Rainfall's bridge. The way it leaned forward, as if inspecting her, watching what she was doing over her shoulder, the way Auron used to try and sniff out whether she was concealing a juicy tidbit or just a dried-out old slug under her *sii*.

She rapped it once—accidentally, she told herself—as she turned, but it did not shatter or fall. Instead light played head-quick-tailchase around the inside, up and down, back and forth, in and out, until the center of the crystal seemed farther off than the distant horizons of the eternal plain she'd crossed while traveling east.

That night dreams of Father's death, bloody-mouthed dogs hanging at his sides, brought her out of her slumbers more nervous and exhausted than she'd been when she settled down.

She decided to leave. While hunting was good and the blighters had been making necklaces of brass rings for her to eat—new, hardier scales were coming in to replace the travel-thinned coat— eating water buffalo and forest deer wasn't going to help her find her brother.

The library needed sorting. A few of the oldest and most interesting volumes could be brought to the great Hypatian library at Thallia, proof of the odd heritage of the blighters of these mountains. Then others could travel with trade goods for the rest. She suspected the blighters would part with their paper and skins and tablets easily enough. And those strange gems, so like the ones that Yari-Tab had showed her in the ruins of Tumbledown what felt like an age ago—they kept the collection dry and free of dust. She would try to sneak off with just one and see if it still worked after being removed from its post in the living rock.

I will leave! she silently told the crystal, as she counted the books she'd selected.

Her imagination said it answered back.

She yawned, and when she turned again to the samples she'd selected from the library, the volumes had vanished!

Sniffing for enemies and searching with her ears, she probed the darkness. Had she been robbed while her back was turned?

She hurried over to the shelves. The volumes she'd selected rested in their usual places on the shelf. Whoever had put them back had even arranged them so the container-titling could be more easily read. And one scroll case, which had been resting on the shelf below where it belonged when she found it, was back in its rightful place among its supporting scrolls.

Strange thieves, who would return property better organized than they found it.

Hearts pounding—she couldn't say why—she removed the scroll case again. With some diligent labor, she reassembled the collection she intended to take along on her departure.

She ate a haunch of leftover ox she'd kept hanging in the cool, dry air at the top of the chamber and settled down for a nap, instinctively circling her selection the way a dragon often slept around its hoard, resting her jaw upon the uttermost end of her tail-fringe.

"You won't get them this time," she said to the crystal, keeping an open eye on it as she nodded off. One-eye-open sleep wasn't nearly as refreshing—you didn't dream, though your thoughts sometimes sang to you.

And if you do, I'll just leave without them. You'll see.

When she woke, she was a good deal less surprised to find the books removed. As she stalked over to the collection to see if they'd been put back in their proper places, she had the strangest feeling before she even knew why. Then it came—she saw a bit of loose ox-flesh on the floor. It must have dropped from her mouth at some point—but she hadn't visited the collection in between eating and settling down for her nap. Could she have been—

A harsh clatter of gongs sounded, echoing down to her cave. Alarm! Alarm! ALARM! came the shouts, distant and echoing, from the entrance to her cave. "A dragon comes!"

A dragon? Could it be AuRon? Why would they be giving the alarm?

She swarmed up the old well, past the guards who were unaccountably throwing extra logs on the fires that heated their oils to pour down the sides of the pit should the demen come again, and to the old city at the throat of the massive cave-mouth.

The dim purple light, just framing the hanging towers at the cave-mouth, told her it was the early dawn. The cave-mouth faced southerly and it looked a clear morning. At this time of year the sun would shine full into the cave as it came up.

A perfect time to attack. The blighters would be fighting both sun and enemies.

Flame blossomed at the cave-mouth at one of the hanging, fang-like towers—the long, unbroken one where the blighters kept a small watch of archers, for they could see well down the long switchback road on the mountainside. Wistala caught a flash of white scale reflecting in the fiery bloom.

White? She'd met a white dragon once, in her almost fruitless search for others of her kind. A great, elderly queen of dragons. She saw the dragon swoop down, strike something with its tail, and rise vigorously as a second dragon, a green, dove, dropping a curtain of fire at the cave-mouth.

Two! One she could handle. She knew Uldam's ruins, where she could spread her wings and where she had to tuck, where there were deep shadows and where the sun would fall. She would have the advantage. But two!

First one, then three, then a little less than a score of Fireblades rushed forward to the aid of their comrades.

Now more battle-horns echoed through the cave. She saw the mates and their hatchlings—or spawn, children, was that the word?—of the Fireblades fleeing from the more intact of the homes to take refuge in caves and wells. Older Fireblades lurched out of their dwellings, supporting themselves on the shoulders of youths still with downy tufts about the head and shoulders rather than a true blighter's mane, carrying bows and crude imitations of dwarven crossbows and spear-throwers.

"Why you wait?" a warrior called to her as he hurried forward, a spear in each hand and the unlatched buckles on his helmet jingling.

"To see," she said.

Liar. Because I hate fighting. Only the crows benefit.

"The rest of you, stay here," she told the gathering Fireblades in their own language. "Block up the tunnel here as best as you can. Your friends may need somewhere to retreat. I want to be able to just squeeze over the top."

One of the grizzle-hairs nodded and barked at the others. There were big casks handy, full of fat for the boiling cauldrons and mead for the warriors—they could make a start by rolling those forward.

Maybe she could drive them off somehow by just showing herself. It would be a bold pair who would dare attack a female in her cave. What if she had hatchlings to defend, and a mate lying in wait to attack from behind as soon as they flew against her?

She launched herself into the air, cold-hearted and wingtips a-shiver. Where was that dragonelle who faced giant trolls on Rainfall's bridge or challenged war machines of the Wheel of Fire dwarves?

A yellow halo grew over the horizon to the south. Soon the sun would be shining down the cave-mouth.

She rolled and alighted, gripping the cave-ceiling and bracing herself with her tail at the upper root of one of the pillars of mountain-muscle. Hard rock full of natural ridges and crevices offered her claws purchase. She must be hard today.

The green vomited a long stream of flame, scattering it here and there among the mostly empty outer ruins. The Fireblades kept some sheep and goats and sickly cattle near at those roofless hovels. She must have seen motion and spewed.

She wasn't much of a fighter, Wistala decided, or at least inexperienced. She'd loosed her flame too high, scattering it into droplets and losing much of the effect. You might do that if you were trying to burn a field of crops and teach some encroaching settlers a lesson, but fighting blighters with plenty of time to see the firefall and doorways and alcoves to shelter in wouldn't be bothered by such a display. And a dragon had only so much flame. If her firebladder wasn't empty now, with that first gout still in burning puddles along the entry-road, it must be very nearly so.

The white dragon was a good deal more effective than his mate or sister or ally or whoever she was. Wistala guessed he was a male; she was pretty sure she saw horns rising from his crest. He dove, tilting his body to keep scale to enemy, terrorizing with beats of his wingtips and strikes of his tail, screaming as he descended. He drove the blighters back from their battlements flanking the great road.

White knew hominid fighting.

He'd taken out the most dangerous threat with his first flame, the watchtower at the cavern roof. Now he could terrorize the Fireblades without having to worry about stones or javelins being flung down upon him.

Silly Green and Canny White. If she could surprise Canny White, down him before he knew she'd joined battle, she'd be able to handle Silly Green.

A coiling serpent, dark as a pit viper and mindlessly purposeful as a stream of ants, could be seen on the road outside the cave-mouth. Men on horseback, with banners at intervals, red leading silver followed by a purple, the third higher than the rest, with a rather dispirited green bringing up the rear. It must be a vast number, at least in the thousands, to fill such a length of road. She could hear the steady thunder of their hoofbeats on the old grass-stitched stones.

The sun climbed as though eager for a better view of the contest.

It would take too long to crawl. She went forward, glide-rest, glide-rest, in a series of barrel rolls, keeping to the darkness in the shade of Krag's great roof. The attacking dragons harried the disorganized blighters, their quarry rallying only to be dispersed by one of White's dives and then running again.

They must have known a dragon lurked in the area, but neither seemed very watchful. Perhaps they were carried away by the excitement of alternately smashing and driving the blighters, or assumed that since she hadn't yet shown herself, she never would. Did they think she was some roaring male, who would announce his presence half a horizon from the fight?

Canny White saw some blighter archers falling back toward the rear of his cave. He must have decided that he'd rather fight them from the air, despite the arrows sticking out of neck and arms. Blighter bows were better for bringing down deer than dragons; while they made decent enough bows and stout strings out of mountain-lion sinew, their heads and shafts weren't as sharp and true as elvish arrows or dwarvish bolts, and they lost velocity quickly when fired upward. Despite the arrows, Canny White swept behind them, and flapped briefly atop a broken old three-level home to push roof and chimney down on the blighters in the lane below.

Wistala saw her chance. She dove, wings folded like a hawk, gaining deadly velocity with every length in the vast cave.

She struck Canny White square at the base of his neck with a body blow. Being thick and muscular had its advantages—he bent like one of the blighters' recurved bows and crashed into a house on the other side of the road, sending white scales flying off and falling like snowflakes.

Ha!

Wistala opened her wings and turned toward the other, resisting the urge to admire her handiwork beyond seeing Horblikklak, who'd kept his archers and a few other blighters fighting as a disciplined unit, send spearmen toward the white twitching under the fallen walls.

Arrows sang up and struck. Luckily they didn't penetrate much farther than a full-grown scale-nit. Stupid fools, shooting at their ally!

Wistala rose toward Silly Green, who hung in the air at the entrance as if puppeted by strings. Wistala flapped hard and shot toward her like a dwarvish javelin.

Silly Green didn't care to meet her. She turned tail and fled, with Wistala fast behind.

Probably by accident, Silly Green did the one thing that could have saved her—she headed almost straight up once out of the cave. She was more lightly built than Wistala, and the heavier green couldn't quite match her angle of ascent. Wistala just bit off a mouthful of tail and banked to see the riders below.

They were almost to the old pylons covered with etchings of

proud blighter faces and sealed casings of war-trophies. Wistala wondered how best to loose her flame.

A third dragon's silhouette swooped out of the sun. Three! They'd kept a reserve outside in case she appeared. The sun was too bright for her to make out much, save that he was big and heavy about the forequarters and therefore most likely a male.

She turned back for the cave. An open-air fight would be difficult, especially if Silly Green joined the stranger.

As she passed over the head of the column she loosed her flame and the riders scattered—well, most of them. The scream of horses followed the twin whorls of smoke in her wake. Poor horses! They hadn't chosen this battle.

She felt arrows pluck at her wings and break off in her side, and she chanced a glance back. The column of riders had divided into a fork, circumnavigating the pool of dragonflame. Archers had dismounted and were firing from the—what was that military term again? *Flanks,* that was it. Some dwarf who'd started off in life as a butcher and become a general had codified war in his volume describing the long, grinding war against the Charioteers.

Strange how the mind raced in battle. An arrow stuck through her tail like a crossbar. She didn't even feel it.

She flapped up to the cavern roof and alighted on one of the great pillars, built up with clay cisterns and lead pipes of an old gravity-well that had fed the king's citadel, a sort of triangular fortification anchored by rocks carved into shapes like mammoth-tusks. The Fireblades under their war-chief manned what was left of the battlements there, with long slides greased on both of the remaining towers. Strong young blighters stood ready to send stones down the slides, which could be turned and tilted to better aim the dropped projectiles at those beneath the walls.

The riders streamed in, and the two columns turned into three, the thickest heading straight down the wide road for the citadel. Their hoofbeats echoed in the cavern like the roar of a waterfall, and the sun glinted off of polished helm, shield, and spear-tip.

Too few blighters. Too few. Perhaps they would content themselves with plundering the ruin. Except there was no plunder, just old broken brick and bat-haunted roof.

The third dragon appeared again, bearing a cylinder that looked like a sawed-off tree trunk. She couldn't quite make him out, silhouetted against the sun. He flapped hard, gained a little height, and at last she could see him.

A reddish copper color that might be called orange, broken by dark stripes, six good-sized horns—

DharSii!

She knew him. They'd met, briefly, years ago in Sadda-Vale, where she'd searched for others of her kind. She'd found only a handful of indolent dragons, comfortable and uninterested in the world outside their steaming valley.

Her thoughts, racing a moment ago on two wings and all four legs, stilled, fading like the ink on one of those ancient scrolls in Noo-Moahk's cave.

DharSii carried a heavy column of stonework, one of the columns that flanked the road near the entrance to the old city. He flapped one more time, strain on his face, and dove for the citadel.

She dove as well, leaping from her perch, wings open only enough to allow her to guide her fall. If he saw her he gave no sign of it. Instead he released his load, which fell like a huge arrow toward one of the old towers. She just managed to strike the stone as she crossed under him.

Arrows flew up, peppering both dragons, with no more effect than the flowers tossed at young blighters passing through the end of their final mating ceremony.

The stone tumbled, missing the top of the tower, where it would have smashed the blighters and their rock-slide into gory streaks. It struck the wall below, sending rubble falling into the city and out into the gate-lane in front. Dust clouded the air.

Each dragon completed half of a double-loop.

DharSii gaped at her, hardly moving his wings. He alighted on an old terrace, rows of garden-troughs thick with shadeweed. His ribs heaved as he caught his breath.

Wistala returned to the cavern roof.

Some of the riders chased their quarry like rabbits through the old streets and alleys, vaulting obstructions with wild cries.

Blighters streamed down from their battlements. With the wall in the old citadel broken, they hurried for some old hole, she guessed. The city had any number of ancient undercourses for the disposal of waste or retention of water. Perhaps they made for some secret bolt-hole.

Canny White had retreated to a corner near the entrance, blood making dark stripes on his sides even more vivid than DharSii's natural ones. He did not seem eager to rejoin the fight. As for Silly Green, she was nowhere to be seen. Perhaps she was soaking her tail-tip in the chill of a mountain stream.

She had to delay the riders. Wistala mastered herself. One more effort, and then she would return to the back of the cave.

DharSii cried out as she flew, but whether he was calling to her or summoning the white she couldn't know.

The front of the column fell into confusion as she came at it, wings beating hard. Carts and horses wheeled—

A presence behind, coming fast—must be DharSii.

She banked a little to stay out of striking distance, took a breath so she might better press her firebladder—

Whoosh! Whoosh! Whoosh!

Sparks and smoke and rattling—what evil was this?

Three projectiles like the oversized javelins dwarves fired from their war machines flew toward her, not arcing like arrows but spinning like a playful squirrel running along a straight branch. They trailed smoke and flapping lengths of line with ugly barbed hooks.

"Down!" she heard DharSii shout. He struck her on the haunch.

Why he warned her, she couldn't say. She struck some old roofs, scattering rotted thatch like dandelion tufts.

The missiles passed howling and sparking just above her, their ugly flail-tails thick with barbs and hooks dancing a mad jig in their wake.

She banked to the rear of the cave and made for her old hole lest some other aerial monstrosity be launched at her.

DharSii thrashed, entangled in one of the things, raising dust and debris in an old plaza.

Wistala saw ugly sights in the streets below as the human warriors discovered a little hovel of Fireblade females and their babes. Hominids must love death for death's sake—there was no other way to explain the bloody scene there.

She returned to the rear of the cave and the tunnel to the old downshaft and library. Only a few elderly warriors remained, calming frightened mates and wailing spawn.

"The city is lost," she told them. "If there's some secret tunnel where you can flee, you may wish to take it. I can delay them here for a few moments. Then they will come."

A grizzled one-handed blighter began to give orders. Most obeyed, but one or two of the females ran into the ruins, whether in search of their mates or because they thought they could escape through rubble and rooftop, Wistala didn't know.

She settled herself at that last, half-built wall, tried not to listen to the screams and clatters echoing from farther out in the vast cavern. And always, always was that waterfall echo of hooves.

A dragonback moved among the ruins, wing-spurs high and proud. DharSii surmounted a fallen building and rested between two vast chimneys. His snout and neck and shoulder bled, but not profusely, and one sail of wing hung, cut into ugly tatters. He'd taken worse from those terrible contraptions than she had.

He came within a dragon cry.

"Wistala, I remember," he said.

"DharSii of the Sadda-Vale. How is your aunt and the rest?"

His nostrils pulsed. Perhaps he found the exchange of pleasantries amusing. "The same. As always." He stalked a few more paces forward.

He'd added another ear-ring, well, not quite a ring, more of a smooth squiggle, of what looked (and smelled!) like the rarest of white gold.

He marked her gaze and lowered his *griff* enough to hide the decoration. Or was it just decoration? Did it hold some significance to those slaughtering men?

"You'd better move along," he said. "The battle is lost. The Ghioz have some business in these caves and then they will depart. You could return in a day or two."

"Behind is my cave. If any of them wish to contest my claim, I look forward to the contest."

DharSii took a reluctant breath. In a flash he shot forward and fell upon her, not biting but trying to pin her to the mound of rubble half blocking the passage. Or perhaps trying to pull her out.

He was frightfully strong, but she had plenty of grips for limbs and tail, and though her thick body would never be called elegant, anyone who tried to overcome it would admit it was powerful. She rolled him off hard enough to feel the impact through the rock and retreated a little farther behind the mound.

The smell of blood and dragon—male! *Male!* MALE!—both frightened and excited her.

"Did you think I spoke idly?" she asked.

"Of course not," he said.

"Perhaps you could convince your host to leave."

"They're blighters. Hardly hominids, even. What could you possibly care about them?"

She panted, but even more than the air in her lungs, his hateful tone invigorated her spirit. He was the sort of dragon she could hate as fiercely as admire.

"Even blighters have their charms if you get to know them."

"I rather doubt that. How did they buy such loyalty? All I've seen in these mountains is bits of copper and brass."

"I'm not loyal to them. I'm loyal to my sense of right and wrong."

"If there's a wrong here, it's that dragons are fighting among themselves in some hominid squabble. You've injured my companions, and taken very little harm in return. You could fly out of this cave knowing you'd given better than you received in defense of this rubble."

"I could say the same to you. You three tried, and lost two dragons. Only a fool would press the contest after that. You could retreat with honor intact."

"I told the Red Queen I would clear these caves when they met my price," DharSii said. "Clear them I will."

"You just said they're nothing but a rubble. What do you suppose your Red Queen wants with rubble?"

"For all I care she just likes holding parades and parties when they've won a victory. You know humans. They like to cheer and celebrate deeds others have done, whether it's their armies beyond the domes or some slathering hound in a fighting pit right beneath them."

"Interesting choice of imagery. You're no better than a trained dog, to my mind."

"I'll leave that to opinion. I'm certainly richer, and I have my independence."

"For now. Until the Red Queen decides she needs to chain you up at her door."

DharSii snorted. "Let her try. I'm more careful than that, and she needs me and my dragons too much to chance it."

"Then you may die when she meets an opponent greater than herself."

"I'd simply switch allegiances. The strongest faction is always willing to buy more strength. They pay a little less than the desperate, but it's more enjoyable to win." He looked at his tattered wing. "Less hazardous too, but that doesn't seem to enter your reckoning. I shall have a long job with hemp and dart here tonight."

"Some victory. Leaving those awful horsemen to skewer screaming children."

"You've not seen much of the world if you're surprised by such behavior. You can't expect better from blighters or men." He lowered himself, set his wings at an angle to deflect blows, wing-spurs up and ready to close on neck or tail, and advanced, bent a little to his right side so his tail could be brought into action as well. "I give you one more chance to show the sense I credited you with those years ago when you quit the Sadda-Vale."

Wistala felt her fringe rise. "Don't speak of last chances to a dragonelle with jaw and limbs intact."

He dragon-dashed forward.

She washed the wall in flame as she retreated. He broke through the wall of fire as though it were nothing but a winter mist.

"You think pain will deter me?" he asked. "I am a dragon. Pain only makes me more resolved."

"I never doubted your dragonhood. But it's well-singed."

She edged back. She could make one last stand at the mouth of the tunnel to the library-cave. She would have good tunnel to defend and he would be contending with verticals. He'd be fighting her and his own weight.

Wistala wondered why he didn't roar. Male dragons, in her limited experience, made a good deal of noise when they fought, especially when in pain. DharSii conserved his breath, struck, struck again. She'd never felt such power in a blow before. It reminded her of a mountain-troll, toughened by climbing. He struck, not biting, but stabbing forward with nose-tip and tail-point, and with each strike she heard her own scale breaking.

He battered her. He never closed, never came to grips in a manner that might allow her to claw or bite. She managed to latch on to his crest, but came away with a bloody *sii* and a torn-out claw when he recoiled.

"Yield!" he said, his voice oddly calm. "Cry settled! Cry, curse it all, cry!"

"Never!" she managed, wondering what in the six skies "cry settled" was supposed to mean.

His nose guard was cracked and sat askew, giving his snout the appearance of being bent a little. If she weren't so battered and bruised, she might have laughed.

Her tail felt emptiness behind. She'd been driven right to the brink of the pit—

She batted one of the cauldrons filled with hot oil with her tail. It broke loose from its chains and sent a shower of oil toward him. The oil hissed as it struck on his flank and he scrambled to get out of the way.

Seeing a chance, she rushed forward, slipping as she passed over the spilled oil, hardly hot anymore after expending its burn in the first instant of striking the cool stone.

They reared up, grappling, biting and snapping. Wistala had always counted herself strong, and for a moment she bent him back—

But then her *saa* slid.

The oil might have cooled, but the footing was treacherous. DharSii lunged. She heard his hot panting in her ear, felt his breath beating at her neck as they strained, his *griff* locked in hers. Her tail sought purchase but found only empty air—

Then she was over.

She fell with a shriek. Just as she heard DharSii gasp something—it may have been "no"—her own frightened wail overwhelmed his word.

She tried to open her wings, a natural instinct, but while the chasm was wide it was not wide enough for that. She heard something snap, felt a shock, heard a flapping and realized one wing was broken, whipping wildly as she spun down—but the other was open, turning her fall into a crazy spin, like those spinning one-winged seeds those tall trees dropped in Hypatia's northern forests.

She bounced off the wall, or a projection, and continued her fall, some instinct keeping that one wing open.

It was the most terrifying moment of her life.

Later she wondered how long she fell. It felt like an eternity, a day, but it couldn't have been more than a few moments, for when she finally struck she could still see a circle of light above, not quite a star but far smaller than the moon.

Her eyes perceived a bump in the circle. Natural irregularity, one of the oil-pots, or DharSii?

She'd landed on something spongy. The soggy slap shocked her; she felt wet, clinging wet, all around.

Stunned for a moment, she could only lie there, looking up at that far-off circle of light, a wet, rotting smell like a barrel-full of last year's swampwater, alternately revolting and comforting—the latter because a dying dragon would have more important things on her mind, one would think, than mouldering water.

Of all the dragons in the world to appear here—she couldn't have been more distressed if she'd just fought AuRon. Of course, there weren't many dragons left; she'd looked hard enough when she first uncased her wings. Would the hot oil scar him?

Then it struck her that her first thought upon landing, before judging her injuries to determine if they might be her last thoughts, was of the dragon she'd just fought.

She chuckled like Rainfall amused by one of old Stog's mulish tantrums, a very undragonlike noise, but the laughter of elves infected all who heard it into imitation.

She cleared her mind with a determined effort and shifted her weight, testing limb and tail. Pain in her injured right wing stabbed, a fast, deep, twisting spear that bored right up through her shoulder muscle and shut her eyes. Her wing was more than half closed and hung at a strange angle. It also hurt when she breathed on her left side, though whether that was related to her wing or not she couldn't say. Rainfall had done some sketches of her muscles once, just for his own satisfaction, and commented that a dragon's entire body pivoted on the wing nubs.

Strangely, the most painful wound was that arrow in her tail. Of course the punctured flesh had a chance to grow tender. Luckily both sides of the arrow were still visible. She broke off the feathered end, then extracted the head by pulling it forward.

Fierce new pain made her eyes water. She spat out the arrowhead. Good workmanship, and the metal was well shaped and wholesome-smelling. She swallowed it.

Tangles and angles, she had more important matters at snout. She blinked and tried to clear her head.

The blighters had said something or other about this being an old well. She wondered. Down here there were ancient stairs, not masonry but steps cut into the rock itself, wide steps, even so that a full-grown dragon might use them, spiraling up. They must end somewhere above, for she was sure they did not go all the way up to the blighter defenses at the top.

Rainfall's laboriously taught logic told her that the stairs must have been built, then, by someone who didn't particularly desire access to the surface.

The cave she'd fallen down widened at the bottom like a bell, and it was filled with mushroom-like growths. Water soaked the muck here. She sensed that it moved, so it must be coming from some-where and going to somewhere. She stood up, rather shakily, and surveyed her surroundings. It seemed there was some sort of lip or ledge above.

She could reach it by rearing up on her hindquarters. She shifted her *saa* and heard an alarming snap, but on inspection she discovered she'd just broken a moldy rib cage with muck and growth clinging to it. She dredged up a skull with tail-point and perched it upon tail-tip and brought it up to her eye.

Blighter, it seemed, and judging from the heavy brow, jutting jaw, and oversized incisors it had probably been a big male. Fallen from above or killed somewhere else, dumped here where the odors would only bother dark and feed the mushrooms.

She sniffed the big mushrooms, especially the smashed caps that had cushioned her fall. A second leafy undergrowth covered the well-floor, oblong pads, big and spongy enough for a blighter to sleep upon. Both smelled wholesome enough to eat, if she was in the mood for vegetation. She also smelled slug-trails, and for a moment stood again in the egg-cave with Auron and Jizara, with Mother watching from the shelf. The memory relaxed her. She could do with a nap.

Mustn't!

The moldiness of the mushroom patch overwhelmed her nose, but another faint scent drifted down from above, one she couldn't quite identify further than determining it was animal. First she raised her neck, testing limbs and tail, then reared up and explored the lip above.

The stairs broke at the ledge, and she sensed a tunnel of some kind—there was airflow. After their brief interruption, the stairs continued up again.

If she was to regain the surface she would need her strength.

She found the origins of the water, a mostly blocked-up crack in the wall. She lapped and lapped again, her head clearing with every swallow. The water was pure and clean and cold, thankfully, and even had a faint soda-mineral taste that pleased her exceedingly. Real dragon-water, this. No wonder the mushrooms thrived on it.

She cautiously ascended the stairs to the ledge, poked her head in the tunnel. Still that faint odd animal smell.

"Gaaaa!"

She recognized the bray of a goat. What in the worlds was a goat doing down here? She stuck her head farther into the tunnel. It seemed a natural one, curving up and rising a little, thinning as it did so like a dragon-neck. The goat looked lame, dragging a broken rear leg. Had it tumbled down the shaft and survived a miraculous landing on one of the spongy pads?

Poor thing. She could make a quick end to its suffering, and get a meal besides. Just what she would need to get herself back up that shaft.

The goat fled as best it could, and she took two quick steps after it, opening—

Kzzzzzt!

Odd. Stunning sensation. Her senses fled for a moment. She felt suspended, nowhere in time and space, cognizant only of what felt like a strong blow somewhere on her back.

The ground struck her under the chin, hard. She sensed motion all around. She smelled ozone, as though fresh from a thunderstorm, and suddenly she was with Auron, who was comforting her against the terrifying flashes and noise by tempting her with the taste of raindrops on her tongue.

Cries and shrieking voices like birdspeech broke out all around. The sounds were kind of a pidgin Drakine mixed with clucks and hoots and croaks, a jamboree of mismatched winged creatures.

She recognized the dragon-name NooMoahk.

"*Mizz!* Anklamere's *grook* cracker works *bakka* still, *ptuck*! Dragon-dropper, *yak*?"

"*Yak! Cluck-glug!* We *braaak* NooMoahk! *Chukku-na*."

"*Nip! Nip! Dulg mak* NooMoahk, got us dragon-she!"

"*Nie-hruss,* ventwipe."

The motion resolved into dancing forms seen through eyes incapable of focus, but she felt rather easy about it. Something fixed about her snout. She smelled a hot melted-metal scent. She recalled stories of killing dragons by pouring hot lead in their nostrils and other horrible hominid tricks, but she felt oddly complacent about the idea of it happening to her.

One eye focused and she saw a heavy leather band, studded and reinforced with hot rivets, stuck about her nose.

A bent-over shape, almost folded over on itself with an assortment of strange plates and spines and bits of creepily soft-looking flesh showing beneath and violet eyes brighter than any wildflower she'd ever seen stepped forward. It supported itself on a curved stick studded with what looked like hatchling teeth.

She heard a clattering above and rolled one eye up. Some cave above, with false cave-wall broken away . . .

A trap. She'd stuck her head right in.

Other hominids, vague in the dark, not quite so curled up but still bent, with legs that stuck out sideways and up more like spiders than men, rushed here and there with lines and chains.

"Ye speak to Paskinix, dragon," the creature said. For a moment she couldn't say which language it spoke.

"I've lived four generations, dragon, four!" it continued to her in competent but unaccented Drakine, tearing off a piece of raw and bloody goat-haunch with teeth like broken rocks, "waiting for another crack at NooMoahk. Didn't expect that greased projection and the undermined crack when ye climbed down the shaft, did ye? Well, thy recklessness cost ye a wing. Thy Tyr thought he'd sneak in the back door after bashing in the front, eh?"

Wistala couldn't have responded if she'd wanted, since the band was fixed too firmly about her snout. She wondered which one of DharSii's dragons called themselves *Tyr*—an old title from the tales of Silverhigh, wasn't it? His Drakine was odd. Either he didn't know proper word order and emphasis or he'd picked up some dialect or archaic form.

The thing, which Wistala decided must be a deman—it was definitely a hominid, if a bizarre-looking one, and certainly no dwarf—straightened, supported by its toothy prop.

"Aye, ye've driven me out of my gardens and streams to this forgotten corner of the higher darks." It grew animated and splattered her with goat-blood as it gestured. "Trading bits of glass for a goat-meal when once I dined on tender young *griffaran*. Ney more sulfur-soaks for Paskinix, thanks on thy cursed sisterhood. And yon Tyr, acting all lofty and demanding I come call him and negotiate," Paskinix said. "Well, I'll let him know I've my own token in play this game, ye can be sure."

He looked up and down her uninjured wing as other demen fixed lines to it. Another did something abominable about her hindquarters and hiccupped out a few words.

"Ney eggs coming, eh? Well, bad for us," Paskinix said.

Wistala found the strength to swallow the drool accumulating in her mouth and began to feel a little better in body—but much, much worse in spirit. Taken by some deman with a grudge against dragons that she knew nothing of—

She heard a grating sound and a sort of sculpture of metal and wheels like a cart—but all backwards, for the wheels were at the top, spinning as uselessly as an overturned turtle's legs—was dragged up next to her by the demen. A deman clad in greasy-smelling leather and thick gloves thrust a sort of bright two-headed spear at her and . . .

Kzzzzzt!

Her whole body jumped within the restraints even now being secured without her willing it, and consciousness faded—rather pleasantly—to the sound of the old deman cackling.

Chapter 6

If it weren't for the bridge, AuRon would have never found the place.

He traveled at night, resting at rocky, inaccessible coves on the Inland Ocean. He hoped he'd find that inn before too long. The fall winds were kicking up and storms would soon come out of the northwest, cold furies of wind and sleet, coming ashore as though angry for having to pass over all that water.

At first he flew up the wrong river. When he reached a fork in the river without the bridge appearing and explored both branches just to come upon an old ruin he'd once camped under with a now-dead dwarf friend, he knew he'd gone wrong.

He explored farther south, flying up a vast river-mouth that for a while was indistinguishable from the Inland Ocean itself. Then it narrowed into true river, though a wide one. Just before dawn he came upon the bridge, a massive construct with a patched span in the middle. He vaguely remembered this bridge from his travels in Djer's cart.

It seemed the sort of place humans frequented, so he flew a little farther upriver and found a forbidding cliff with a nice stretch of sand under it. The river had retreated somewhat because of the season, but there was good fishing in the pools and the tangles of waterweed were thick with pinchy-crawlies. He hadn't had the freshwater variety in years, and he enjoyed himself before settling down for a brief nap.

He woke in the afternoon. It was a pleasant fall day and the air beckoned. He took off and rose high in the sky and flew back toward the bridge. Once there, he followed the road north and came to what might charitably be called a town on the edge of some vast collection of fields and pastures, with forest to the west and what looked like some mining cuts to the north near another tangle of roads.

He checked the smaller of the enclaves first, circling slowly lower and lower so as not to alarm the population with too quick a descent.

Nevertheless, he saw cattle and pigs driven into the woods and sheep scattered in the hedges under the frantic efforts of boys. Fools. If this was a livestock raid he wouldn't dawdle so.

Dragon-eyes had their uses, and he spotted a sign out in front of the inn, just as that strange collection of hominids had promised. A green dragon, sure enough, though they'd rather stylized the icon.

He found an obliging field, grazed short within sight of the inn's roof-peak, and settled down to wait. The woods were kept far enough back that he would have plenty of warning of arrows if they shot, if they had bows strong enough to cross the field, that is. An open hill behind guarded his rear.

Boys, probably shepherds' sons, crept from tree to tree with what they thought cunning stealth and woodcraftiness. A summer running with the wolves to the north would do them an improvement. He watched a fistfight break out among four or so and the loser went running home—or perhaps was dispatched with a message.

Downwind, dogs barked endlessly. He couldn't help his odor. If the dogs didn't like it that was just too bad.

The field smelled mouthwateringly of horses and cattle, but there was no helping that. He'd wait.

When the locals finally showed up he understood the delay. They came in some numbers, in fits and starts and with much discussion at each advance. The collection dribbled away as it crossed the field. A tall female, with comely hair by human standards and evidently well able to feed her young, judging by the fit of the long robe, stood next to a figure swathed in blankets and a heavy, droopy velvet hat, carried on a litter by two stout-looking men.

"My name is Lada, dragon. May we approach in safety?" she said, enunciating carefully in Parl. The figure swathed in blankets seemed to find her pronunciation funny, as she heard a rather raspy chuckle.

"I came for converse," AuRon said. "Parley. Please."

The one who called herself Lada made a gesture in the air with her right hand and they stepped forward. The two litter-bearers kept glancing back at the others hovering nearer to the inn or in the middle of the field. A local dog dashed halfway out into the field, let loose with a terrific bark, and ran back to his humans with tail tucked.

How Blackhard's pack would have snickered at such behavior.

They came a little closer into an easy distance for humans to speak.

The one swaddled in blankets tipped her head up. "Here I was waiting on the wrong dragon. I waited for the green and the gray shows up."

AuRon recognized the face beneath the droopy hat, mostly because it wore an eyepatch. Hair like winter birchtwigs supported the brim of the hat. It was the elf, Hazeleye, both his capturer and his rescuer. Happily, she'd collected the debt for freeing him long ago, which had resulted in the overthrow of the dragon-riders of the Isle of Ice and his mating with Natasatch. The wizard who'd organized and purposed their race war against the other hominids had once told him that elves were like tree bark on poplars—peel back one layer of plotting and a new one appeared underneath.

"Wistala. Her name's Wistala."

"I know that. She's a good friend to this place and we all long for her return."

"Why is that?" AuRon asked.

"Her counsel would be most valuable," Hazeleye said.

"Then you don't know where she is."

"I'm afraid she went off east hunting you, AuRon," the one called Lada said. "She has been gone for years. But then she was a rover."

"I'm sorry to hear that," AuRon said. "Couldn't you have told her you dispatched me to—"

Another yap broke in on his thoughts and the dog dashed away then. He'd come a few paces closer before barking, but shortened his warning.

"I haven't seen her since before the dark days of the dragon-riders," Hazeleye said. "Thank you for finishing them and freeing the dragons from their thrall."

She'd spent her many years in the study of dragons. AuRon believed she was one of the few hominids with any true understanding. And better, sympathy.

"Are you unwell?" he asked.

"I feel the fall wind more than I once did. Do you think we might continue this conversation indoors?"

"You have a barn nearby?" AuRon asked.

"Better than that. An inn. The owner was a good friend to Wistala too. He's hanging back there in the crowd with his wife. You could get your head through the door in back with ease."

If this had come from any other hominid but the Dwarves of the Diadem AuRon would have expected a trap, but trusting Hazeleye had always been to his benefit. Hers as well, seemingly. He would trust her one more time.

The dog barked again from just behind the foremost party of humans.

"I've no objection. Could we get that idiot dog tied down?"

The tall woman, Lada, signaled to the people behind and a boy retrieved the dog.

The party decamped and headed for the inn. AuRon finally grew disgusted with the litter-bearers and had them seat Hazeleye on his shoulder, gripping the simple strap-harness he wore when traveling. The dwarf trader had made it, inlaying rings of steel held by iron bands for securing packs or bags such as a mule might carry. Hazeleye seemed to have some difficulty with her legs, and kept them well swaddled in their wrap of blankets.

"This brings back happy memories," she said in her learned but unaccented Drakine. "It has been long and long since I rode dragonback."

"I would fly, but I fear you'd fall off," AuRon returned in kind.

"Yes, I would need a saddle."

"No more saddles for me."

"That's certainly your choice," she said. "But a shared journey is a happier one."

AuRon was tempted to reply that it depended on who was wearing the saddle, but he held his tongue.

They walked up a path through the pines—AuRon curled his neck high and back so that Hazeleye wouldn't be smacked by branches—and so crossed a dry streambed and came upon the back of the inn. AuRon smelled tempting livestock. Better still, roasting meat. Also woodsmoke, pitch, horses, bodywaste, straw, and all the other smells that went with hominid habitation.

He picked pine needles out of his crest and horns while the others went inside. A broad man in a leather apron opened the top half of the back door. He had flecks of gray in his thick hair and a drooping mustache.

"Welcome to the Green Dragon Inn, firebreather," the man said, not at all in awe of a dragon sticking his head through the back door and surveying the great room like a living trophy. If anything, he seemed pleased. "She's mine, and proudly bears Wistala's mark on the sign at the front. Any friend to the original Green Dragon, as my Elvish lodger says you are, is a friend to me and my family."

AuRon warmed to the innkeeper's manner. He was rather like his old barbarian friend Varl, with the same hearty confidence and eager eye. Were that all men spoke so to dragons!

The innkeeper was saying something about quantities of food that would be ready by sunset, but AuRon didn't need words. His nose said there was beef stewing, sheep roasting, and best of all . . . sausages. He hadn't tasted a good greasy sausage in years. His eyes almost rolled up into the backs of their sockets at the thought as the man asked what he might bring hot from the kitchen.

"Sausages, yes," AuRon said. "As many as you can manage."

"Ah, you're a dragon after my own heart. Have you ever had a

Thickwurst? Stuffed with garlic and ground liver and onion? And for those with a taste for it, ginger."

The common room itself seemed comfortably stuffy after the manner humans liked. Everything, from shutters to furniture, was stoutly hewn, planed smooth, and a bit smoky. Faces of—oh, what were they called—cats, that's it, stared at him from the warm corner between hearth and dried woodpile and atop the chimney mantel. Between the chairs around the fire and the bar, a big round platter that looked like it had been made out of a barbarian shield held broken nutshells. Another cat scratched at the shells, sniffing suspiciously at a mound.

Hazeleye settled herself in a chair by the fire and took up a long white pipe of the kind AuRon had seen sailors smoke when at their ease.

She cocked her bright eye at AuRon. "Never used to smoke. Filthy habit. But it's soothing, now that my last seasons are in sight. Herself over in the great house is a fair herbalist and her mix doesn't half take my aches and pains away."

Hazeleye drew deep on her pipe and sighed out a thick cloud of rather sickly-sweet-smelling smoke.

Lada, standing quietly at the door, smiled. AuRon didn't know hominid expressions well enough to distinguish pleased from wistful.

"What can you tell me of my sister? How did she come to this place? When did you last see her?"

"That's some tale, dragon," the innkeeper said.

"She went off years ago, before the Dragon-rider Wars," Lada said.

"For all we know she's returned," Hazeleye said. "Perhaps to those librarians in Thallia."

"Not without calling back here," the innkeeper said.

"Her old cave is unoccupied, save for a few kestrels and such," Lada said. "Perhaps she left some sign or instructions there we wouldn't decipher, or even recognize."

"She went in search of her brother. I know that," the innkeeper said.

"I am her brother," AuRon said. "I'm AuRon. Auron, as was. Known briefly as NooShoahk on the Isle of Ice."

"So it is true then," the innkeeper said.

"Strange fates have befallen all your family," Hazeleye said.

AuRon wondered about the use of the word "all." She'd been partly responsible for the destruction of much of his mother and sister, in an ancient pact between mercenary egg-hunters and wicked dwarves.

But she'd freed him from bondage and a probable death on the Isle of Ice.

Wrimere Wyrmmaster, the Wizard of the Isle of Ice, once told him that elves wove truth and lie into invisible strings through which they manipulated the other races. AuRon didn't believe him—elves spread out across the world spending all their time manipulating others would have difficulty knowing who lied about what to whom. But Hazeleye's motives for anything, from freeing him to asking him to find the Isle of Ice and kill the wizard, were her own.

"Why are you waiting for Wistala?" AuRon asked.

"You may not believe this, but it was to pass news of you. It's come to my ears what happened on the Isle of Ice, that you've mated and so on."

"How did you hear that?"

"Shadowcatch. He's become quite the sea dragon these past two years."

AuRon wasn't sure he wanted events on the Isle of Ice generally known. He switched over to Drakine.

"You wanted to give her news of me?"

"Yes," Hazeleye said. "At one time or another I've thought each of you dead. I'm happy to be proven wrong. I'd like to know more about both of you. I'm at work on my last book, and I doubt I shall write the last word before this form dies."

"So you're still interested in dragons."

"Few can claim to know more about them than I."

AuRon decided to ask what was on his mind. "What happened to your legs?"

"I've lost most of the use of them. I can stand, just. I need assistance to walk."

"I am sorry for that," AuRon said. "An accident?"

"No." She drew deep on her pipe. "I was tortured. Those fools in Ghioz thought you could break an elf's spirit by breaking her body. That Queen of theirs. You'd think one of her kind would know better."

The Copper remembered his friends there. "Naf allowed such a thing?"

"It was Naf's fault I was brought before the Queen. I was living quietly in the mountains and she had need of an expert on dragons. I was fooled once. Never again."

"Naf—Naf didn't . . ."

"Of course not. He helped me escape. He's an outlaw now. If he still lives."

"Outlaws! He's one of their great commanders."

"He disobeyed the Queen. That put an end to his rise among the ranks of the Ghioz."

"What about Hieba?" He'd watched her grow into a woman, saw her look at Naf with the same love she'd once shown him.

Hazeleye shrugged. "With Naf, I hope. The Red Queen is no kinder to her own sex than to men."

"Where is he now?" AuRon wondered if he should offer them refuge in the north. Not on his island, of course—men came with trouble the same way dogs carried fleas—but he could settle them on one of the more hospitable coasts nearby. He could use some intelligent humans in the nearest port. If nothing else, just to keep strange parties like the treasure hunters from getting themselves eaten.

"On the Hypatian border somewhere. I haven't seen him since he sent me north in the company of a traveling circus, some time ago. But I suspect they won't be safe for long."

Something poked at his tail. AuRon removed his head from the inn and saw a small boy fleeing toward some chicken huts, where others, equally scruffy, were beating him to the tree line. A dropped stick lay next to his tail.

Insolent little pup. Well, it would be a story for his family over the dinner-meal.

He returned—well, his head returned, anyway—to the common room. "Why? Is Hypatia sending him back?"

"War is coming between Hypatia and the Ghioz. You can feel it building all along the border."

AuRon didn't give a loose tooth for humans and their battles.

"The Queen of the Ghioz wanted to know about dragons to use them in this war?"

"I expect. She probably took the idea from the wizard. He laid many strong places low with his riders, and the tales are told everywhere."

AuRon's indifference began to melt. These people seemed reasonable, even kindly, and they'd been good to his sister. Hazeleye had been treated cruelly, but she herself had been responsible for cruelty in the past, and the world had a way of putting itself back in balance just as a hot, dry summer was often followed by an extra-cold, extra-wet winter.

As for a war between Ghioz and Hypatia, the more damage their armies did to each other, the less likely either would be to molest the dragons on the Isle of Ice. Let them kill each other off, the more the better, and good riddance to them.

His harsh thoughts, as they so often did, softened the more his mind worked on them, like a wolf gnawing at a tough bone. These humans seemed content to be friends with dragons and let Wistala come and go as she would. Indeed, they seemed to honor Wistala's memory. Dragons could do with more of these sorts of friends among the hominids. Did this Ghioz Queen allow the same freedom?

"I suppose you will tell me that the Ghioz have Wistala beholden to them and are using her in this war."

"I know they have at least three dragons. One is a female. I did not get a close enough look to say whether it was your sister."

"With riders and so on?"

"No. The dragons flew as dragons should. Still, I wonder what hold the Red Queen has over them."

"Probably a weak one if she sought your knowledge of dragons in order to tame them," AuRon said.

The arrival of dinner prevented further discourse. The innkeeper had both hot and cold meats, bread, cheeses, and different forms of vegetable matter, mostly mashed and baked or peeled and jelled.

The innkeeper brought out a platter of sausages especially selected for AuRon, some hot and some cold. He talked about the mixes of meats and herbs in each, and spoke of eggs as the perfect companion to sausage in the morning, breads at midday and through the afternoon, and cheeses their favored partner in the evening.

AuRon tasted a few and asked him to continue the discourse.

He then begged AuRon to sample a suite prepared just so, calling for two dozen eggs to be specially cooked so the dragon might eat his sausages in proper order. If all humans were as hospitable to dragon-kind, the world's history might be happier.

"Oh, yes, many's the sausage I prepared for your sister," he said, as he filled mugs for his guests from a barrel. "A good friend she was—if she'd not been with us the night the barbarians attacked, I don't know what would have become of us. Slaves or worse. Luckily we were too small to be of any notice in the Dragon-rider Wars, which I hear you put a stop to. Traffic's good on the road again, with people fleeing the troubles to the south. Only those with coin to spend make it this far."

AuRon ate heartily, politely leaving the best bits of roast and stew to the others and devouring the bony leftovers. *Giving your stomach something to keep it busy*, as Mother used to say.

Some of the younger humans held their nostrils pinched shut as they ate—AuRon knew that dragon odor was reckoned unpleasant to those not used to it, though Varl claimed it drove away bedbugs.

The tall robed female corrected them before he could compose a joke. The room needed a joke, with this talk of war and those fleeing it, and he never was good at them. Only the innkeeper seemed to be enjoying himself; Lada was grave, Hazeleye thoughtful, the members of the innkeeper's family harried.

"Did my sister give any indication of when she might return?"

Lada sighed. "She said she would probably be gone for a year or more. It's been six. I hope nothing has befallen her."

"She's a mature dragonelle. Perhaps she found a mate," Hazeleye said. "The lead male the Ghioz had, he seemed a fine specimen."

"I'd like to visit this cave of hers," AuRon said.

"She left her books at Mossbell, where they'd be looked after," Lada said.

"She reads?" AuRon asked. Strange how they'd both picked up the habit.

"Wistala holds the title of librarian," the innkeeper said. "There's another story there, getting that title."

"Title?"

"It's a Hypatian rank," Hazeleye said. "The Hypatians are fond of their various ranks. Military, priestly, judicial, scholastic, and of course governing. You can get honorary titles for sport or artistry."

AuRon itched himself under the chin with the bottom of the doorframe. Some greasy, sausage-scented saliva had found its way down there. "How interesting."

"It was a trick of my father's, for the preservation of his estate," Lada said. "Wistala owns most of this land, in a manner of speaking."

"There was talk of making her thane," the innkeeper said. "That's an ideal thane, to my mind, one who's never around to collect his taxes."

The room chuckled at that.

"My full belly asks for sleep," AuRon said. "Thank you for the sausages, innkeeper."

"Jessup does for friends," he said.

"Would someone aid me in finding that cave you spoke of?"

"I know the way," Lada said.

"Can you ride a dragon bareback?"

"I'll have to shut my eyes the whole way," she said. "I'm not one for flying."

"That wouldn't be much help in finding the cave."

"It is not a long trip on foot. I'm used to walking, and these woods are no longer dangerous."

They said their good-byes. Hazeleye seemed lost in her pipe, shifting her blanket-covered legs this way and that before the fire.

Lada led him out across grassy hills. AuRon smelled horses and cattle, but saw only a few of the latter, who shied and milled nervously when they smelled him. Now and then he heard hoofbeats as groups of horses fled his approach.

AuRon liked the smell of Lada. It had been long since he had had a human female tickling his nostrils, so to speak. The scent excited him; though he was hundreds of years from being counted an old dragon, her scent made him feel young, as though he'd just uncased his wings.

"So, by those robes you are a person of importance," AuRon said, passing the time. To talk he'd have to keep close to her. "Do you have a title too?"

"I wonder if she will return," Lada said, as though she hadn't even heard his question. "It seems I always lose my loved ones a year or two before I learn to value them. I'm a foolish, foolish woman."

"That cannot be true," AuRon said. "These people look up to you."

"They look up to me because they looked up to my grandfather, an elf of great mind and experience, yet who looked beyond even his own faculties and experiences for greater wisdom still."

She'd pushed Parl to the limit with that last speech. She knew how to wring every drop of meaning from a trade tongue, whatever her imagined failings. "Elf. So you're partly elf?"

"Yes."

"Then tell me. What is Hazeleye hiding under that drooping hat?"

"She loves dragons, you know."

Could this human never answer a simple question?

"She's found different ways of expressing that love."

They walked in silence past some sweet, almost rotten-smelling vines, which she told him were "hops." Her grandfather, and some elf relative named Ragwrist who now lived on his old estate of Mossbell, had advised the innkeeper that along with the sweet honey-mead he offered he should give his patrons a choice of bitter beer. AuRon listened attentively and remembered none of it except her smell. And so they came to a cliff-top with a good view of the moonlit bay. Only the faint susurration of moving water and a gentle fall wind broke in on his thoughts.

Wistala had chosen her cave well. Ample food to be had, defensible, and water wasn't a problem. Of course it was near hominids, but they seemed to get along just fine. Though according to his father, favors granted to one generation were oft forgotten by the next.

"What will you do?" she asked.

AuRon wondered about this woman. She was so different from the spirited Hieba he'd watched grow from a girl. Her slightly sad manner reminded him of Mother, when too long parted from Father.

He wondered if comparing a human to a dragon somehow dishonored their memories.

"Have you not decided?" she said after a moment.

Lost in his thoughts again. Well, he could give as obscure an answer as she. "I'm going to have a good nap in this cave. Then in the morning I think I'll dive and see if I can't find some big crabs deep out in the river there. It seems to have a rocky, sandy bed and that's just what they like. Then in the morning I'll trade the crabs to that innkeeper for some more eggs and sausage."

"I mean about your sister," she said.

"I haven't made up my mind."

"If you do see her, tell her we miss her here. We're a little worried about that pass the Wheel of Fire used to guard. We've heard that Ironrider scouts and traders have ridden through, armed, with no more than a wave from what's left of the dwarves there. It will take a strong heart to rally Hypatia's north, if they should ever send more than scouts and horse-traders through, for we'll get no help from the south."

Why couldn't humans ever solve their own problems? No wonder the dragons of Silverhigh grew weary of fighting.

"This is good-bye, unless you remain among us many days," she said. "I may be called away. We've a mother-to-be in the shepherd hills and the cold is bringing illness."

"Thank you for guiding me. The walk did me good. I've flown too much of late."

She half smiled. "May I touch your nose? Your skin is so different from your sister's."

He dipped his head and felt her hand pass down his snout. She giggled.

"Your skin ripples."

"Little buds rather than scales," he said. "They change color."

"I noticed earlier. Remarkable. Farewell, AuRon. Return for more sausages. You'll be as welcome as your sister. Will you?"

He decided to answer her question. "You can tell Hazeleye that I believe I'll have a word with those dragons allied with the Ghioz. They might have knowledge of my sister. Their Queen owes me an old debt, which I shall collect."

"I would have wished you a good journey before. Now I'll light candles to guide you past doubt and ignorance and into knowledge."

AuRon cleared his throat. "Candles. Does that work?"

"I doubt it. But it's nice to think it does. Horrible thing for a priestess to say."

"I'll remember you to my sister," AuRon said, taking one final deep draught of her air. "Assuming I find anything more than a memory."

Chapter 7

Wistala couldn't make sense out of Paskinix's orders to his dreadful, taunting demen.

They put her in a filthy, cramped widening of a tunnel that they couldn't be bothered to clean. She had to have water brought to her, one precious bucket at a time, and she begrudged every splash and lost drop, as they never gave her quite enough to slake her thirst.

The demen were unhappy to have her alive, grudging her every mouthful of the wretched, rotten food they ate, but unwilling to kill her.

They bothered her in every way possible, kicking and prodding her as they passed, throwing their filthy, ropy waste at marks on her side and flank as though engaging in target practice, and not letting her sleep with their continual noise on the part of her guards, but they did not cause her any real agonies.

They smeared a piece of hollow wood, like bamboo only knobbier, with her blood, yanked out a few scales, then clipped off the tip of her *sii* inclaw. She guessed them to be trophies or mementos of some kind. A grim sort of humor came over her at the thought. The last trace of her existence might decorate some deman's hole.

They taunted and teased her over her injuries and situation, but hinted that she would soon be released to return to her kind.

The demen were clever enough in their brutal way. They inspected her bonds each time the guard changed, striking her on the joints with stout metal rods that they carried constantly. With little to do but observe, Wistala decided they used the rods to send signals. She saw them *rap-tap-tapping* the sides or floor of the tunnel, or listening to faint banging sounds and grumbling among themselves.

She suspected half of their ill temper was from short commons.

There were constant squabbles over food as it was shared out, and a thicker slice of mushroom could be cause for much head-butting and spine-yanking.

One night—morning—*who could say when it was?*—shortly after her capture, a good deal of tapping woke her. Her agitated guards jumped up and shouted. Two of them picked up a stout spear with evil-looking, twisting fluting to the edges and put the tip against her side.

"No! Please," she managed out the side of her mouth—awful last words for a dragon. *Oh Father*—

But they didn't ram it home—instead they listened while her mind raced. She was chained such that she couldn't strike the point away with tail or neck or limb, and even her wings were secured by a pair of chains running beneath her belly to the injured wing.

Her injured wing—it would hurt. . . .

A faint roaring—undoubtedly a male dragon—echoed in her prison.

Awful moments passed, trying to judge the roars—drawing closer or no? Then more tapping and the demen with the spear relaxed.

More tapping still and they hooked claws and snorted and honked into each other's faces. She wouldn't care to have another dragon clearing its nostrils right into her face, it was almost as bad as men picking and digging at their dirty corners.

She was gaining enough of their language to guess they were enormously pleased with something. Paskinix made an entrance with a few warriors, one much singed about face and fingers. Paskinix's spines alternately drooped and waved like sea fronds as he spoke.

"Ye own comrade came down the shaft. Turned him back easy enough and would have taken his head, but he's a cursedly good nose for traps."

He? She wondered if it was DharSii.

"The orange one with black stripes?"

"I didn't see much of yon roaring cockspur. He's been pricked good, cowering in the muck bottom anow. Too many shafts in him to think about climbing out. We'll let him bleed out and then hit him again."

More warriors arrived, displaying gory weapons under her nose. She shut her nostrils to the smell of dragonblood.

"Now he'll be of a mind to bend, that he will," she thought she heard Paskinix tell his warriors as they hurled themselves about in celebration. They jumped around, overleaping each other like startled frogs.

Never dance out your victory over a living dragon, she thought. But hope was hard to come by.

Why would he come after her? To finish her off, or to rescue her? To tempt her to join his flying circus and kill not for food or for honor but at the orders of some greedy hominid queen?

She hated him anew at the thought. Then there was another thought, and a third, equally hateful.

Because they were all about him.

She turned her back to the revels and pretended to go to sleep, moving her good wing within its limits as though to block the light.

Working at her bonds as she never had before, Wistala pulled and twisted, not minding the ripped-out scales or the blood smearing the metal. Her blood might lubricate the shackles and let her get a *saa* free. If she could just—

Kzzzzt!

That lightning-smell again and her mind emptied. Her thoughts were concise and clear but oddly unmoored.

It seemed easier to just drift off to sleep . . .

Paskinix stood by her nose when she woke, waggling one of those rubbery digits at her. A moment later? An hour? A day? His spines made stabbing gestures toward her, threatening like scorpion tails. That odd machine huffed behind him.

"Ye'll be free in yon Tyr's own good time, once his neck unbends at last."

They zapped her again so the lesson might sink in.

She was beginning to welcome the surcease of hunger the sparks brought. But no point telling them that.

"Tomorrow we all dine on dragon meat!" Paskinix promised, and his throng beat their rods on stone in clattering celebration.

Wistala wondered, rather dully, whether they meant hers or DharSii's.

The demen learned a lesson about counting breathing dragons dead the next day. Just after a meager breakfast Paskinix stormed back into her little run and struck the inoffending guards keeping watch over her, knocking them this way and that with sideswiping kicks.

"Climbed out! Three spears in him and yon scaly devil climbed out! No sign of the watch I left. Down three, and naught but bloody footprints showing for it!"

He raised his club and gave her a couple of bashes about the neck. Then he threw down his club and squatted with his face to the wall, his spines rising and falling in a confused manner.

The guards tried to ply him with one of those hollow tubes, opening it so a sweet-tart smell, like molasses and juniper, wafted into the tunnel. He put his mouth to it and worked the other end, and Wistala heard a sucking sound. Then he threw down the tube.

" 'Twas my plan to lead my people to greatness," he said in his strange Drakine, his back still to her. "It all went wrong in the war with the dwarves. I thought myself mighty clever, sneaking down the river. We'd raided up the Ghioz palace itself and came away with riches. Why not do the same to the dwarves? They and their cursed battle boats."

"The Wheel of Fire?" she asked.

"Ye know them?"

"I've fought them too."

Wistala told her tale, briefly, of how she had brought down King Fangbreaker and of the gruesome battles she'd seen, showed the long-healed scars in her wing-leather. Paskinix made excited wheezing sounds as she told of the slaughter of the dwarf-column sent into barbarian lands.

He folded his hand under a bit of carapace and worked a crack in the cave wall, widening it and sending bits of stones flying as he twisted his armored limb-shell this way and that. "I should have taken that offer yon old Tyr gave me. Not that new whelp with his damn trained monkeys riding dragonback, I mean the old Tyr. His Cussedness. An alliance."

"You didn't?"

"Nay. I thought I'd just gamble, try and master the wizard's crystal, what with NooMoahk's yon cave empty and echoing. Thought it'd show me a path to victory, ye see. But someone'd put heart in the blighters and they fought like mad. We were long licking our wounds from that beating. I even thought for a while that some blighter genius had been born and unlocked the crystal's secrets. But they never followed us down. Next thing I knew the Star Tunnel was full of mad dragons under that green demon. Oh, she's taken the better bits of the Tyr and his mate."

It was like trying to piece together an entire song from a line or two at the end. In any case, he seemed in no mood to hit her again.

"May I offer something?"

"Words of comfort from a dragon? Nay."

She took a careful breath. "You could release me. I'd serve as an ambassador to this Tyr. Perhaps he'd renew the offer that other fellow made."

"Oh, aye. One of the Tyr's own Firemaids. Ye'd keep my interests close to heart, I'm sure."

"You're clever, but you don't know everything, Paskinix. I know nothing of this Tyr or his dragons. I fell into the Lower World thanks to a quick slip and a long fall."

His spines stiffened, then relaxed again.

"A good try, Firemaid. Well done. Ye almost had me with that lying tongue."

With that he rose and shuffled off.

*   *   *

Wistala felt herself growing thinner on slight rations and lack of exercise. Secretly, she rejoiced at it. Much longer and she would be able to slip out of her bonds.

To pass the time she improved herself in the demen tongue so she could chafe her guards for more water or a chance to clear out the filth coating one end of her alcove. They gave her some bits of dried mat-leaf and she scrubbed and sponged vigorously. The harder she worked the thinner she would get.

But the demen knew their business. There was only so much one could do to swell a joint when they stuck a finger in to test the bonds. They tightened her shackles.

That night she wept, truly wept, for herself. A very undragon-like response to difficulty. Mother would tell her to hide her tears and think of a way to improvise a solution.

She fell into an exhausted sleep, but felt better and more clear-headed for the crying jag. Now that the frustration was out she could think again.

Later, she had the most extraordinary dreams. DharSii figured in them, and her blood ran hot and quick at the events. Except his *griff* kept poking her just beneath her right neck heart.

Waking, she came eye-to-face with a snaggletoothed horror. It was like a bat, but vastly overgrown and with a faintly scaly snout.

It licked bloody lips with a long tongue.

Impossibly, the nightmare spoke. "I'll let 'em know," it whispered in good Drakine. "Thanks for the sup, gentledragon. I was perishing for a taste. Good thing you reek of blood 'n dung; never would have found you otherways."

The horror of this thing!—wretched claw-winged thing!—clinging to her neck overcame her. She let out a startled gasp and it sailed off into the tunnel dark, silent as a passing cloud.

"Now what?" one of the demen asked.

"I—I had a bad dream," she said, more than half wondering if it was true. No, she smelled her own blood.

"Quit worrying at the bands," the deman said. "I'm sick of wasting good whiz and ferment washing out your wounds. Serves you right if you get a hot throb and croak off."

She passed through two feeding cycles of next to no rations. The demen fought when one tried to cut off some of her tail to eat.

The wound in her neck healed so quickly and so clean she wondered if she'd dreamed the whole conversation with the bat-creature. Perhaps it was a craze brought on by thirst. She'd never been so thirsty in her life—thoughts of water tormented every waking moment.

By obeying every order in an instant and affecting a servile wheedle, "learned my lesson and learned it well, sirs," she received an extra bucket of water. She'd just drained the second bucket when an ominous clatter broke out. First one, then another, then another rod echoed, a quick, steady tap.

"It's dragons come!" one guard said to another.

"Get the skewer," the one in charge said.

Wistala's hearts raced. She resolved, if she saw the other end of this, to die before anyone chained her like some wretched dog again.

They ran toward her with that great twist-headed spear.

She didn't let them plant it. In agonizing pain, she swatted the point down with her wing as they approached. Her injured wing gave way afresh, the pain of the old injury back and redoubled.

But the force of the blow knocked it out of their hands. She managed to roll over part of it, a sloppy move more than half accidental.

The demen dragged and dragged, trying to extract it.

"Get the cursed machine!" one yelped. "Spark her off it, for dark's sake."

More delay. She felt blows of signal rods but didn't care. Delay! Delay! Delay!

One of them took to rapping and she felt the zap of the magical lightning before she heard it. She jumped.

They dragged their spear free.

She heard a faint *whoosh* of flame being loosed and thought she saw shadows dance far off down the tunnel.

The blade poked into her side, just above her mainheart.

"Hold! My fellow shes are coming," Wistala said in their tongue, wishing she knew the deman word for *surrender*. "A fresh-killed dragon, and I expect I'll spurt a bit as you ram that thing home. Shouldn't be too hard to find a couple of demen reeking of dragon-blood. I wonder what they'll do?"

Their big frog eyes widened still further. "Oh, bury it," the biggest of the guards said. "We kill a prisoner and they'll hunt us to the bottom hole."

"Aye—Firemaids avenge their own," his friend agreed.

This time Wistala was happy to be taken as a Firemaid and she made no effort to dissuade them.

"No, kill her," one of the demen at the contraption said. "One less dragon, and we can hide and then come back and eat up for once on her body."

"Liver as big as a boat," one said, saliva dripping.

She saw Paskinix himself leaping up the tunnel, rapping the wall each time he landed.

"Rally, rally, all rally," he called. "Don't kill the prisoner. We need her to negotiate. But for your mother teat's sake, rally!"

"Rally? With what?" a guard asked.

"Our bluff's been called," the one at the lightning-fork agreed. "Escape!"

Paskinix began to stagger, exhausted. Fire behind silhouetted his spines.

"Save the machine!" the one at the sparking two-tipped spear called.

"Save your lives, you breedslime," the big guard said. "Find a hole tight and dark!"

They rushed off, pushing and pulling their wheeled contraption, dragging the great spear.

"Cowards," Paskinix called.

Wistala knocked him off his feet with a painful sweep of her wing.

He folded himself into a squat, facing the wall as before.

"Always figured I'd be finished in my sleep from one of my sons, not some stinking dragon."

Wistala saw green scale reflecting firelight. Two wingless drakka raced forward and began sniffing around at trails, and a third leaped on Paskinix, who made no move to resist. His spines hardly twitched as she settled her *saa*-claws against his gut.

A fledged female, not much older than Wistala but with a much smaller fringe, surveyed the scene. She saw other heads behind and heard faint, frantic taps here and there in the distance.

"Flame and fame, you're in wretched shape," the dragonelle said in oddly accented Drakine. The grotesque bat rode her head, hanging about her *griff* like some kind of leathery, hairy collar. Wistala noticed her wings were striped with purple, yellow, and white. "Half starved and broke-winged. Best have a meal right away, so you've the strength to get out of these damp holes."

"He did not kill me when he had the chance," Wistala said. "I will not kill him."

Paskinix turned wide eyes at her.

"I'm hungry," the one on him said.

"No," Wistala said. "Please, let him live."

"Good work, Takea," the painted stranger said. "That's the way to hold down a prisoner."

In fairness, he hadn't resisted, Wistala thought, but the drakka seemed pleased. Her undersized fringe rose.

"Thank you, from nose-tip to tail," Wistala said. "My name is Wistala Irelianova."

"And I am Ayafeeia, ranking Firemaid," the painted rescuer said.

"Thank you, Ayafeeia."

"She's of the Imperial Line, matekin to the Tyr himself, or have you forgotten?" the drakka atop Paskinix added.

"I never knew to begin with," Wistala said. "Must I bow?"

The youngster half dropped her *griff*. "It would—"

"Not be necessary. In fact, I will bow to you, as you're a visitor, and I'm grateful for your help in capturing this villain." She looked at the youngster. "Takea, since he's your prisoner, take charge of him."

The young dragonelle narrowed her eyes in thought. "Deman, put that bucket on your head and take hold of my tail. If the bucket comes off or you let go of my tail, I'll gut you."

Paskinix's spines rippled but fell again.

"I wish you'd let him go," Wistala said. "He spared me once."

"He didn't spare you any food, by the look of your ribs."

"His warriors starved too," Wistala said, not quite believing she was defending her tormentor.

"Have you ever seen quicksilver poured out on glass?" Ayafeeia said as the youngster led her captive off, the bucket rattling against his neck plates. "I did as a youngster in the Anklene hill. This one's just as quiet and twice as slippery." A dragonelle followed the pair at a nod from Ayafeeia.

"Don't worry about him; whatever he gets it's less than he deserves, the old egg-thief. Let's get you out of those chains, stranger, cleaned up, and see about that wing. Would you care for some toasted deman leg? There's a lot of it about this morning. Stringy, but that's war."

They walked what felt like a terribly long distance, though the more rational part of Wistala's brain knew it to be but a short journey. It just felt doubly far because they climbed two steep rises and her wing pained her with every step, despite the soft hominid-made hemp-lines the drakka had fixed to it to support it. That horrible bat creature or one like it flapped back and forth, scouting ahead and checking behind.

"It's that exhausted I am," it complained.

"You'll get your sup," Ayafeeia said. "Just get us back to the Star Tunnel."

Wistala shuddered. It was one thing for a beast like that to creep up on you and bite, quite another to offer your own neck. Ayafeeia was made of stern scale inside as well as out.

She did seem a dragonelle to be admired. The four female dragons she led, and perhaps twelve drakka—they moved about so much and smelled so similar, thanks, she guessed, to identical diets, that she wasn't sure she wasn't counting the same ones twice—deferred to her orders instantly. Odd to see dragons, evidently not related in any way, acting as obediently as hatchlings under the watchful eye of their mother. Perhaps more so—hatchlings liked to test their mother's limits and act up as soon as that great watchful eye closed.

Could the discipline be this Tyr's doing, or was it just that they loved Ayafeeia as some sort of surrogate mother?

They drove Paskinix mercilessly. He couldn't walk long without his support, and when he flagged they spat a *torf* of flame onto his back. He bore the pain with grunts and gasps, but no cries, and reeked of burned flesh.

Wistala wished she'd had more experience with dragons. The only ones she knew at all were those of the Sadda-Vale, and—

DharSii again. Put him out of your mind.

Oh, if only she'd made more of an effort to find out about those Ghioz dragons. Perhaps if she'd gone to them, talked, the whole fight could have been avoided.

Of course there was the disturbing possibility that these "Firemaids" were allied with the Ghioz through their Tyr. What if she had dropped off the spit only to land in the fire?

They came to a chute requiring a short climb and Ayafeeia, listening to Wistala's breathing and pulse, called a rest.

"But we're practically under the Star Tunnel," a dragonelle demurred. It was the first resistance to Ayafeeia that Wistala had seen.

Ayafeeia listened to Wistala's breathing. "The stranger needs a rest before we climb. Besides, I smell water, and it seems to me there was a trickle here."

"It's that thirsty am I, too!" the bat creature croaked.

One of the energetic young drakka found the trickle and Ayafeeia let Wistala drink first. Wistala noted that all around the trickle there were cracks and holes where the water drained off—above, in the walls, below. Cave moss, an odd pinkish kind, gave it an eerie glow. Wistala felt doubly bad, considering what she was contemplating.

Ayafeeia kept Paskinix away from the cracks, and had water brought to him, using the bucket he wore.

They started up the chute. Wistala positioned herself so she climbed just behind the straining Takea, who was dragging Paskinix up like a fisherman with a catch on the line.

"Remember what I said about being your ambassador," she murmured to Paskinix in his own tongue.

"I do," the deman-king whispered back. "Ye shall always have my gratitude and friendship, and that of my people, if ye get me out from under yon little witch's burns and claws."

"Slipping!" Wistala screamed, giving Takea's tail a good bash with her head. Paskinix leaped on her neck and wrapped those long, thin legs about her, and they dropped together. They bounced off the dragonelle behind them.

Wistala was careful to let her tail absorb most of the impact of the short drop. But there was no need to let everyone know that.

"Wing! Auuuuu!" she shrieked, loudly enough to deafen a dragon.

Paskinix scrabbled off in the direction of the trickle's faint glow.

Two of the drakka slipped down to aid her, but she rolled and thrashed about so they looked at her rather than seeking Paskinix. By the time a dragonelle climbed down, he was gone.

"After him!" Takea cried.

"He's slipped," Ayafeeia said. "He's worse than an eel."

Takea glared at Wistala. "You helped him. You let him go."

"None of that until we're back in the Star Tunnel," Ayafeeia said.

Wistala, with many a moan of pain that needed little acting of the kind she'd seen displayed in Ragwrist's circus, made the climb once more.

At the end of the climb she had to pant long and hard before she could take in the wonder surrounding her.

She could see why it was called the Star Tunnel. It was a vast, vaguely triangular passage, wide at the bottom and narrow at the top. Little serrations of light, like long stars, dotted its peak.

Lower down, the stone was smoothed, cut in a fashion that reminded Wistala of a tree chipped and shaved by an ax, only in segments the size of a dinner platter. She wondered what sort of tool had the power to do that to stone. And what sort of arm had driven the tool.

"That's the surface, a good hundred dragonlengths above," Ayafeeia said. She stuck close to Wistala on the climb and offered kind words the whole way.

"Maybe it is for the best that Paskinix got away," she said. "If we'd torn him to the bits he deserves, it would just make what's left of the demen resentful. As it is, they're beaten and they know it. The last thing they need is a martyred king to put a spark back into them. They're an awful hominid, the worst in a way. Either groveling at your feet or clawing at your throat."

"So what is intended for me?" Wistala asked.

"It's my duty to take you to the Tyr. We lost two drakka fighting our way to you—we thought you were a captured Firemaid, and we've lost a few down these dark holes—and the Tyr will want a report."

"His mate will hear how the stranger helped Paskinix escape," Takea said.

"I can find a watch-perch for you," Ayafeeia said, rounding her head on the youngster. "You can use that voice calling out to let us know you still breathe."

Wistala learned she liked the smell of other dragons around her. It was comforting, almost like being against Mother's belly again. She wanted to stretch, really stretch out in some dry cave and have a sleep.

"Don't worry about the Tyr. He's a good sort," Ayafeeia said. "Not much to look at—I shouldn't say it but I will. A little stupid-looking, with that bad eye of his, but sound instincts when he speaks that make you forget how he looks. Oh, and be sure to bow to his mate and compliment her. She's the watchdog of his reign."

Another of the dragonelles cocked her head at Ayafeeia. Ayafeeia snapped her *griff,* not so much a warning for a coming fight as an expression of confidence in speaking as she chose. "Now, let's get back to our thralls and see about properly bracing that wing. I've set three claw-score broken wings and I know: you'll get air under you again. It looks much worse than it really is. I'd take a break over a cut ligament anytime."

Chapter 8

AuRon knew the way to the northern territories of Ghioz, as he'd crossed it once before. He'd last seen his former human ward, Hieba, and her mate, the laughing warrior Naf, there some three years ago, plus a season.

He made a brief visit to the dwarves of the Chartered Company. They fed him in one of their high halls, its opulence much reduced and obviously rebuilt after damage in dragon-attack during the wizard's wars. The dwarves told stale stories and grumbled much about a Ghioz "embargo"—whatever that was—and gave him one piece of interesting news: they had acquired a messenger-dragon. Scarfang was a former fighter for the Wizard of the Isle of Ice who'd come to the dwarves' doorstep to visit where a dragon-friend of his had fallen in the battle. Finding the residents willing to let enmity be carried off down the river, the dragon inquired if the dwarves had knowledge of his comrade's fate. The dwarves had no good news—they'd finished the wounded dragon—but since all seemed amenable despite the effusion of blood on both sides, the dwarves hired him as a flying courier.

AuRon had never met Scarfang, but he congratulated the dwarves on their new line of business. Which just gave them an excuse to talk about the collapse of their trade routes east. The Ghioz had formed some kind of alliance with the Ironriders and only Ghioz caravans now traded between the rich kingdoms of the Great East and Hypatia and the Dry South.

"More wealth buys them more allies which buys them still more wealth," one of the partners grumbled.

AuRon left the dwarves to their complaining and flew south.

First he went to the pass where he'd last met Naf and Hieba.

The pass had changed a little. What had once been a precarious trail hugging the side of the mountain was now a road, more or less, allowing wagons to use the pass rather than the foot traffic it had seen before. He wondered if the iron road of the dwarves had quit bringing cargo from one side of the Red Mountains to the other.

The lonely tower at the top of the pass, with its ready signal pyre dry under stout canvas, looked much the same.

He remembered some effort at a flower bed, probably a touch of Hieba's. A new stable covered the ground where the flowers had been, and much more besides—what looked like a storeroom set into the side of the mountain and a war machine ready to hurl missiles down the road toward Hypatia.

The tower was now flanked by a wall blocking the new road, and it looked as though lumber and iron had been gathered in preparation for installing a gate. Small subsidiary watch-posts, one higher on the slope and one lower, looked like stony shepherds' huts in positions chosen more for the view than comfort.

He circled the tower for some time, using the same long, slow, descending loops as he had over that little village with Wistala's Inn, as he liked to characterize it.

No sign of Naf, but much heraldry in the form of banners of various colors and designs and many more horses than the stables could hold.

They neither took alarm—even the reasonable precaution of hiding their horses—or attempted to signal him. He had no desire for converse. They might order him out of Ghioz or try to put a poisoned arrow in his eye as they talked.

Naf had spoken, more than once, of his dreams of freeing his people from the Ghioz. AuRon had hoped against hope that he held his pass still, so he could at least look at his homeland, but saw no sign of him. He certainly would have come out and signaled if he'd been there.

AuRon descended the eastern side of the mountains into Naf's homeland, the province of Dairuss, and circled over the City of the

Golden Dome, his joints aching at the long day flying at high altitude, and looked down on the seat of the Ghioz government in the north. The city had swelled, it seemed, absorbing the population that had fled the wars on the other side of the mountains. He had just reconciled himself to an end of flying for the day when he caught a flash of scale off to the east.

That dot against a cloud was a dragon, no doubt. Too much neck and tail for anything else.

AuRon, thanks to his scaleless skin, could fly like an arrow when he chose, and he chose to intercept the unknown dragon, who seemed to be following the river bordering Dairuss north.

The dragon moved slowly, either exhausted or burdened. At first he turned a little toward AuRon as though interested in speeding the encounter.

With the day ending, AuRon had the slight advantage over the stranger of having the sun at his back. He could see that the unknown dragon was a red, with dark stripes descending his scales. Odd color scheme. His own skin had dark stripes too.

Suddenly the dragon dove. As he turned, AuRon saw he bore some sort of harness, a smaller, simpler version of his own. If he had a rider it was a fat, well-wrapped one hugging saddle and scale with all four limbs.

The stranger turned belly-up and his harness fell away, twisting as it dropped to the trees below. It was no rider after all, but some sort of cargo-saddle such as mules and packhorses wore. For a moment AuRon dipped and turned to follow the faster-moving object—a natural instinct but one Red Stripe used to advantage. Released of his burden, he fought for altitude, and AuRon found that Red Stripe had the sun painfully behind him and advantage of wind and altitude.

"I've no wish to fight," AuRon bellowed.

". . . stay . . . or . . . below me," the stranger called back, keeping his advantage as AuRon rose.

AuRon almost tried outclimbing the strange dragon to regain dominance in the encounter, but the cautious half of his brain took over and had him glide inoffensively back toward the dropped pack. Why reveal to the stranger just how fast he could climb?

"Might we land and talk?" AuRon called, and flew closer, repeating the offer.

"You first," Red Stripe called back.

AuRon swooped down, tilting his body first right and then left, a quick way to drop but still have plenty of momentum in case you needed to fly off to avoid an attack. Plus it allowed him to keep an eye on the stranger.

Red Stripe imitated him and they found a wild brambly patch in the woods. There were thick thorns here and AuRon guessed it flooded in the spring, judging from the grasses and reeds. But now it was dry.

The stranger neatly retrieved his pack from where close-packed trees had caught it, with some loss of branches. It must be a heavy burden. Nevertheless Red Stripe extracted it with a mad flap of a hover and a dip of his tail.

A neat trick. AuRon didn't want to be impressed. Every instinct told him to bristle and assert himself in the presence of a strange male, but he couldn't help the impulse to admire such a deft move.

AuRon flattened some of the thorn bushes about. There were game trails crisscrossing this clearing. Whatever lived here must have a thick hide.

Red Stripe dropped his pack near them in the tangle of brambles and set down. He dug about behind his *griff* and then approached with whatever it was held in his right mouth. The gesture drew attention to the fact that he wore a gold earring. The decoration unsettled AuRon. It reminded him too much of the fixtures for lines on the wizard's trained dragons.

"I am AuRon of the Isle of Ice," AuRon said, taking the stranger's part in greeting, since he'd moved to intercept Red Stripe. His store of dragon etiquette was about as deep as a puddle. He dipped his head.

"I am DharSii of Sadda-Vale," the stranger said. If his nose dipped, it only just moved.

AuRon wondered at the name. It was "Quick-claw" in Drakine, but he'd never heard of dragons named for objects or their alleged attributes. It struck him as odd.

This DharSii stared at the old hatchling egg horn still perched between his nostrils for a moment, as if making sure of his eyes. Dragons usually lost their egg horn soon after hatching, but AuRon had fought the itch to rub it off and kept his, and it had saved his life in the hatching combat with his brothers.

Too small to be a weapon anymore, its only use of late was for aiming small, precise globs of fire for the amusement of his hatchlings.

"I am sorry if I alarmed you with my approach," AuRon ventured. DharSii had impressive size, rugged scale, a keen, watchful eye, and healthy horns projecting from his crest, rather more outward and up than most dragons, almost in the manner of an ox. AuRon wouldn't care to fight him.

"Care for some oliban to ease the words?" DharSii asked, extracting the tube from his mouth. He reared up and fiddled with a cylinder, put some quartz-like granules in his *sii,* and held them out to AuRon.

"What's that?"

"It's a distillate of rare woods to the south with a most relaxing aroma. The smell is more intense in liquid form, but it stores better as a crystal, even if the effect is diminished. The aroma is exceedingly pleasing, if you've never experienced it."

The stranger had a fanciful way of speaking. AuRon wondered what hid behind the camouflage of words.

The stranger pinched some of his aromatic treasure into a nostril, grinding it between his claws. He gave a soft, satisfied snort.

"That rather washes the fatigues of the day away," DharSii said. "Are you sure you won't have some? Don't worry, it's merely a pleasant sensation. It doesn't intoxicate like a shaggy mushroom or wishweed."

AuRon wondered if it was some trick.

"No, thank you."

DharSii put his cylinder away. "I've heard of you. A dragon named Shadowcatch told me about the rising against the men who were hatching dragons. It's an honor to meet you."

"He should have dragonelles do most of the fighting," AuRon said, uncomfortable as always at the thought of people discussing him. "What is the Sadda-Vale?"

"The home of some distant cousins of mine. A remote spot in the north, east of the Red Mountains—you do know the Red Mountains?"

"You'll fight a cold wind," AuRon said.

"I've fought worse. I have just completed a war for the Ghioz."

"The Ghioz pay well? My island is poor in metal, you see."

"I thought so, once. But the problem with selling out tooth, wing, and scale is that they temporarily belong to another. I'm determined that from now on if I must fight, I shall have the choosing of my opponent."

"You wouldn't know if a dragon named Wistala was also hired at some time?"

His counterpart stiffened as though AuRon had snapped at him. "Wistala?"

His usual loquacity seemed to have fled.

"She sometimes goes by Tala," AuRon said. Something about the red's manner drove AuRon to caution; he decided the less he revealed, the better for all. This DharSii must not know they were brother and sister or he would have said so. "She's an old ally of mine, from before the freeing of the dragon-isle. . . . I believe she long thought I was dead."

"I have very bad news for you. She fell in battle. But a moon cycle ago."

AuRon's heart felt as though it had dropped out of his chest and lay pulsing on the thorns below.

"I fear . . ." DharSii began. "I fear the demen killed her. She fell down a chasm. I went down after her." He raised his wing, and AuRon saw torn scale, fresh-healed wounds still weeping, and blackened marks that might have been burns.

AuRon tried to find words.

Red Stripe read his mood. "I can't offer you any hope beyond saying I saw no body. I do not know absolutely that she is dead. I left her a message saying that she is to come to the Sadda-Vale at once if she ever gets out of that hole. Circumstances in the form of a counterattack by blighters forced me to quit the location."

AuRon tried to imagine what another dragon might say. "I am sad to hear that. Our hunts together are one of my happiest memories. She was a clever dragonelle," AuRon said.

"You admired that too, did you? Did she consider you for—"

"Oh, there wasn't a thought of mating," AuRon said.

"Why? The lack of scale? She was of generous mind. I doubt she would have refused you on that account. She would adapt."

The use of Father's maxim—that he must adapt to new circumstances—rather shocked him. Had this DharSii been close to Wistala? Why wouldn't he say if they were mated? He had worn the expression of one who had lost a mate ever since her name had arisen.

"I—I'm mated already," AuRon said. This DharSii had a quick mind, and it would occur to him that just because he was mated now, it didn't mean that he had always been besung. But he showed no sign of it.

"I am happy to hear it. Is there a clutch?"

"Our first, just over their first year."

He tore up ground with one *sii* as he spoke. "My compliments. Were it not such a long flight to the Sadda-Vale, I would offer you hospitality with my relations. They dote on stories of hatchlings."

"I could use an introduction in Ghioz. I'd like a chance at earning a harness of coin myself. As I said, our island is poor in metals, and we have hatchlings."

For the first time since Wistala's name had come up, DharSii looked at him, close and thoughtful.

"This isn't—this isn't another infiltration."

"What can you mean?"

DharSii's *griff* didn't exactly rattle, but they lowered visibly. "As I told you, I heard your story from Shadowcatch. The Red Queen makes war when she must, but she's no mad-dog. Ghioz is the coming hominid power—anyone can see that—and I enjoy its favor. I wouldn't want anything to upset my position."

"I can leave you out of it. Just tell me where I may find her, and I'll thank you for news of my . . . my friend."

"It will cost me but half a moon. I feel as though I owe you something for the sad news I bear. The winds to the north will be that much fiercer, but I've come through worse storms."

"Thank you."

"I warn you, she can smell out deception."

"I thank you for the warning, but it's not necessary."

"You'll lay your throat on that?"

AuRon wondered at the grim-sounding phrase. Well, he certainly intended no harm to the Queen of the Ghioz. "If that will set your mind at ease, yes, I lay my throat on it."

"Let us rest before turning back south," DharSii said. "I've been sleeping on sandbars, but this tangle would serve to guard us. Shall we take turns keeping an eye open?"

AuRon turned a circle, like a wolf, and settled down. "I will stay up first, while I consider how best to mourn my friend."

"Know that she was resolute to the end." Then more quietly: *"Were that she hadn't been!"*

DharSii woke him before dawn and they hunted the game-trails. They found some scab-hided boar, and by each taking an end of a game-trail through the thickets, managed to burn one of the fattest, though their trap didn't work as well as they would have liked, for the others shot off grunting through the roots. But dragon-roast pork made a fine breakfast, seasoned by a rosy smoke from the thorns.

The successful hunt mated his admiration of the dragon with enjoyment of the time spent in his company. He could be talkative when asked but preferred silent contemplation, division, and digestion of their meal. A word or two on the merits of game roasted in skin against gutting and tenderizing in a tree for a day or two satisfied both.

They halted once on the flight south, and AuRon prodded DharSii for details of the battle that cost him Wistala. As he relayed details, an awful suspicion grew—mountains to the southeast, a great cave, an old ruin, blighters . . .

It sounded as though the Queen of the Ghioz had made war on the blighters he'd once more or less presided over as an ally. But why had the Queen attacked the old ruins? Unless broken pottery and dust had suddenly become valuable, he couldn't see the reason. A murder-raid would be better directed at the blighter villages on the southern slopes of the mountains there. For NooMoahk's library? For that queer crystal the blighters worshiped?

He wondered how Wistala had fallen in with mercenary dragons, murdering blighters he knew to be about as peaceable as any hominids he'd met in all his travels. Wistala, seeking death and pillage? Of course, he'd changed much in coming to maturity. Perhaps she had also, and not for the better.

AuRon saw ships scattered along the river, and camps full of soldiers.

"Is there a war?" he asked, flying over men marching back and forth in an empty paddock and archers practicing on scarecrows.

"Soon," DharSii said.

"She doesn't need dragons for war?"

"Oh, she does. It's the dragon who is tired of war in this case."

They came to fertile lands and fields full of livestock. DharSii pointed out brickworks kilns and limestone quarries, docks and warehouses, roads, bridges, and neat little towns with wide streets. Each had a temple with a golden dome somewhere near the center; some domes were great, some, at quiet little crossroads, no bigger than a dragon egg.

AuRon asked about the domes.

"That's the seat of power for the local titleor."

"Titleor?" AuRon shouted back over the wind, not sure he had heard what was obviously a hominid term correctly.

"That's the Ghioz word. It translates into Parl as *overking*, but that's a little clumsy for me. I find it easier to pronounce Ghioz."

"So they're a kind of miniature king?"

"Oh, it confuses even me. Here, drift close for a moment. The Queen grants or sells titles, say to run a warehouse or unload ships or even govern a province, and in return the hominids pay a title-tithe. Those that run their affairs profitably get the chance to buy more titles. Titles are ranked by the coin used to pay—brass, silver, and gold. If you're the owner of one or more golden titles you're a very important Ghi man indeed. Those titleor that lose money so as not to pay the title-tithe, get their titles revoked. It's possible for one successful dwarf, let's say, to have a score or more titles. It gets horribly complex, especially since provincial governors get a chance to grant titles in their own province in the name of the Queen, sharing the proceeds with her. That's why the Ghioz grow so. They're always looking to start up a new province."

How did hominids find time to make so many squalling whelps when they had to cope with such complexity every day? Strange schemes of the two-legged!

They turned off the river and followed a smaller branch into the mountains. AuRon guessed their destination from far off. He could see the cuts and shapes to one spur of mountain, flung far out and divided into claws, like a two-digit *saa*.

On the way there they encountered giant winged avians. AuRon recognized them. He'd seen a few, far off and high up, in his explorations of the southern jungles during his years as dragon-friend to the blighters of the Bissonian Scarps.

"Roc-riders," DharSii said. "The Queen's latest obsession. She's breeding them as fast as she can. She learned some trick of taming them just out of the egg."

AuRon suspected he knew the trick, but he said nothing.

Three avians, with unnatural bumps of fur-swaddled men on

their backs, flew close. Their saddles and reins seemed light compared to those AuRon was all too well acquainted with from the wizard's riders. As to weapons, they looked like dwarvish crossbows.

"The threat's not the man," DharSii said. "It's those beaks and talons. They can outclimb and outturn a dragon."

"And a dive?" AuRon called.

DharSii winked. "Shhhh."

The riders were satisfied with a brief look at DharSii. They took their mounts higher, content to observe.

They approached the ending of a long-running stretch of the Red Mountains. The ridge was rather odd, rocky and sheer-sided, with grass at the top like a green rug running down from the tree line. Woods of trees that looked amazingly tall stood in a misty valley, with foggy clouds in two layers rendering the landscape gray and soft.

"That's the Queen's Wood, all around that spur," DharSii said. "The mightiest trees you've ever seen, tall cylinders of pine longer than dragons. I daresay older, too."

AuRon marked a prominence at the end of the mountain, before it divided into three steep fells.

"That's a mountain centuries in the making. It's an old place, terribly old. Supposedly there was a war fought between elves and dwarves over it long ago. It was supposed to depict that dwarf-legend Dwar with his face coming out of a tree, some legend of theirs. Or maybe the tree is the elves' doing, to make it look like his head is hanging from the branches—though I don't quite believe it because the head looks out of proportion. Then Anklamere took possession and decided it should be him, and off comes much of the beard—you can see they've made sort of a labyrinth below with bits of it—and the brow was reshaped to his noble form. Now, with the Red Queen's rule, they're reshaping it again to make it more feminine."

"Where does the Queen live?"

"That terrace built into the back of the sculpted knob. It doesn't look that impressive, but it's rich inside. There's a long path up the green spine of the ridge to her personal temple, and you can see her sacred flocks in their pens. We'll make for the path. There's a sort of amphitheater where she holds audiences. I watched one and she said very little, just swapped her masks around as she made judgments."

AuRon saw what he guessed was the amphitheater. The palace itself, set at the back of the under-construction face, didn't look nearly as impressive as the delvings of the Dwarves of the Diadem. A few little holes, some barred windows, a balcony and walkway here and there. It seemed a cold, lonely place, up there looking down on treetops with only the wind and a few soaring birds to keep you company.

AuRon spilled wind and drew close to DharSii again.

"She seems a long way from the city. What was it called again?"

"Ghihar."

"Ghihar."

"She doesn't go among her people much. She's supposed to be able to strike a man blind with her beauty—or her ugliness. It depends if you talk to a friend or enemy of Ghioz which version of that you'll hear. One of those roc-riders said an expectant mother can't so much as look at her shadow without miscarrying."

They landed on the greensward. AuRon smelled sheep and his mouth grew wet. Flying always gave him an outsized appetite.

DharSii stretched, a strange gesture, so different from the way his other dragons did—like a cat from the inn named after Wistala, first the back end, then the front.

"What now?"

"Oh, some watchman is sending a report to his captain, who will tell one of the Queen's servants, who will inform the Queen. She should be here. She has a winter palace near the coast and a summer palace up in old Dairuss, but she hardly uses them when she's busy."

"She's been so occupied lately?"

"Ever since we recovered that crystal she wanted."

AuRon shuddered, but couldn't have said why he did so.

"I think I picked up some scale-nits between my wings," DharSii said. "Do you mind?"

"Go ahead."

"They're vicious. Do you suffer much? I've never known a gray."

"They wash off easily with no scale to hide behind," AuRon said.

"Fortunate."

"Sometimes."

DharSii groomed, and then they settled into silence.

They only waited less than a dwarf-hour.

The Red Queen appeared to the sound of trumpets, riding out of her palace behind two white horses pulling a white chariot. A stunted human rode one of the horses, and another the back of her chariot, throwing his weight this way and that in the turns.

AuRon had plenty of time to watch as she approached. He understood the red part immediately—she wore garments of the richest red with a silvery metal accenting it. Her dressing reminded him a little of the battle flags he'd seen in the east, pinned to the back of horsemen, though these seemed more like streamers, projecting out and up like a peacock displaying his feathering.

He supposed it made an impression. But no bodyguard, no retainers, not so much as a courtier or a herald?

"Why doesn't she send one of her titleors to do her bidding?"

"She doesn't trust others to shade her judgments. Besides, she's fascinated with dragons. I expect she wants to meet you. She's been full of energy since our battle in the heart of Old Uldam. She's pleased that we retrieved that crystal. I'm sure it lights up her collection of treasures."

"Ah."

"Do not stare directly into her face. She wears layers of masks, a silk one with a porcelain one atop that, then there's the gold one she holds in her hands. On one side the face frowns, on the other it smiles. You'll do well to see that she keeps the smiling one toward you."

Watching her approach, AuRon decided the flight was worth it. He'd like a chance to meet so extraordinary . . .

Extraordinary what?

"Is she human?"

"She's the correct size for one, though she has some of the willowy grace of the elves. She's no dwarf or blighter, that's certain."

The chariot ascended the path at a trot. She entered their field and approached them like a serpent, bending first one way and then the other. The horses refused to settle in the presence of the dragon, and the other miniature human assisted his twin in holding them.

She gave a sweeping move of her hand and loose sleeve-fabric followed as though trying to catch up. She detached herself from the plumed carapace and came off the wheeled platform.

AuRon noted the decorative spikes at the center of the wheels.

He would have thought her a slim young man or an elf rather than a woman. She seemed scant for a female. The ones he'd known were full and curved as foxtails. DharSii hadn't been exaggerating about the masks. Her head was swathed in silk and she wore a mask on her face of the brightest white, shimmering like an unblemished moon.

Her garb still stuck out and up from the shoulders and hung about her as though she were traveling with her own tent in place. The coloring reminded him of a well-boiled lobster. She carried a large mask on a polished ivory stick, holding it in front of her face with the smiling golden face turned out. The face was masculine and reminded him of a beardless dwarf more than anything.

Odd. But then he'd always been told that powerful humans had strange fancies.

The horse-holders took the chariot up the path and away from the dragons.

AuRon couldn't help but be impressed. Most hominids were terribly timid around dragons, or overcame their instincts and started touching in a stockyard fashion. The Red Queen kept a full necklength of distance and looked up.

"DharSii, we knew that talk of never returning was a hothead letting off steam. It pleases us to see you back."

DharSii lowered his head. "Great Queen."

AuRon thought it best to imitate him.

The mask spun, flashing a brief frown before the smiling face turned to the dragons again. "Ever measured in your words in our presence. We thank you for relieving us from courtly duties and getting us out in the air. You have brought us another skyking?"

"A famous dragon out of the north, traveling in search of a comrade. His name is AuRon."

"Great Queen. Yes, I do seek another dragon. But we have other matters between us. Years ago a counselor of yours promised me lands in your Dairuss province if I performed a war-service against the Wizard of the Isle of Ice, the Wyrmmaster. This I have done. I come to claim Hischhein's bounty."

DharSii looked a little startled at this speech.

"Well done, dragon," the Queen said. "We are pleased. You come right to business."

"On which point I will receive satisfaction first."

"As to your comrade, you've met two-thirds of our Drakine retainers. Imfamnia still sulks in the hot springs on the western slopes, nursing her bruises."

She put a curved speaking trumpet to her lips and pointed the bell behind her.

"Pish, a reign cup, to wash out our mouth of the dust."

The servant hurried forward with a clay vessel over his shoulder and a thick carved horn cup in his hand. AuRon smelled hot copper and blood.

Which was what the reservoir within the clay and padding contained. It steamed in the cold air as he poured it.

"Hot calf-blood," she said. "Will you have some, AuRon? An arrival tonguefull is all I could carry, I'm afraid."

"I prefer mine still inside the meat," AuRon said.

"Ah, well, yes. We suppose a full stomach in back balances all that wing weight to the front."

She drank from the fragrant cup. AuRon noticed that it had a little channel in the lip shaped like a bird-neck that allowed her to insert it in the hole in her mask. The blood smelled warm.

"Ourselves, we hate the feeling of a gorged stomach. It makes us entirely too sleepy. Most of the digestive system is devoted to turning ordinary food into blood. We save ourselves the trouble so that we may think more clearly."

"The Great Queen is scientifically minded," DharSii observed.

"I'm afraid we have bad news, dragon. The lands Hischhein promised you were put under the supervision of your old friend, whose name has since been stricken from the rolls of Ghioz and become outlaw. They reverted to the Empire. Though as this had nothing to do with you, we will see to it that you are given their value in coin, though timberless grazing-slopes may not bring as much as you would like."

"That does not sound like justice to what was promised me."

"I'm afraid our counselor who made that promise has fallen into disfavor. I asked him to make an alliance with the Wyrmmaster, and the fool sent a dwarf to negotiate and instead made an enemy. I asked him to keep the peace on my borders and offer succor to ancient Hypatia, which sadly no longer seems able to control her destiny, to the misery of all, and instead we had war and throngs of impoverished refugees, elf, dwarf, and man. Finally he promised lands of Imperial Title in exchange for your services, dragon."

"None of this is through fault of mine," AuRon said.

"We will satisfy your claim. But first, satisfy our curiosity. What does a gray need with coin?"

AuRon bowed, trying to remember how the dwarves used to speak to the Ironrider princes on the plains. "Your majesty is a scholar of dragons?"

"More of an enthusiastic admirer. Are you a good flier?"

"I've won time trials, and the longer the distance, the faster I do."

"Great Queen," DharSii whispered.

"Great Queen," AuRon added.

"No scale to weigh you down."

"You are perceptive, Great Queen."

"Perhaps it's the lack of scale, but you look starved. We can see your ribs. We shall have food sent to you."

"Thank you, Great Queen," the dragons said, together.

The Red Queen laughed. "We should like to hear you sing, like two birds. We shall do you justice, AuRon from the north. Ghioz is always ready for a new friend. Let us forget Hischhein and that rebel Naf the Dome-burner."

"Perhaps. As long as the debts of Ghioz are not forgotten along with the names."

The Queen's mask at the end of the handle spun and spun again, as though she were deciding whether to show the smiling or frowning face. It ended up smiling.

"Look for us on the morrow. Perhaps we can fulfill more than our counselors promised. DharSii, are you back for the season?"

"No, Great Queen. I came only to accompany AuRon."

"Then we wish you a good journey again."

DharSii thanked her and bowed again.

The Red Queen, business done, turned and ascended to her chariot.

Food arrived, though the Queen gave no sign of having called for it. Blighters brought them each a skinned sheep in a barrow.

"What do you think?" DharSii asked, after they'd eaten.

"Different," AuRon said, wondering how much honesty he could afford.

"Do not cross her, if you know what's good for you. She doesn't forget her friends or her enemies."

"I am allowed to say no to serving her, I hope."

"I did," DharSii said. He looked to the east and took a deep breath. Then he opened his wings.

The expected jump-beat didn't come. DharSii turned back to AuRon.

"If I have kept things from you, it's because I heard your name and respect your deeds. I did not want us to be enemies. I hope you understand that once I have given my word, I could no more break it than I could divide myself to fly both north and south."

"If you've brought me here on false—"

"Oh, you'll have your gold. Fairwinds, AuRon. I hope we meet again."

With that, he flew away.

Chapter 9

The Copper watched the demen move almost as one from point to point beneath the west tumble—a sort of pile of rocks at the base of the Imperial Rock.

Gigrix, the general of the demen, had "exercised" his troops to keep them from fighting amongst themselves in their idleness. The Copper had taken to watching the exercises with Gigrix when he saw them moving around within their allotted space beneath the loom of the Imperial Rock and took to asking questions—for example, why so many of the evolutions required the soldiers leaping over each other's backs, the lower helping the upper to vault higher and farther.

Gigrix, clumsy in his Drakine, explained that in tunnel fighting, possession of a cave-ceiling often meant possession of the tunnel.

"An uphole was the only way for escape ye dragons," Gigrix said. "No dragon spit flame straight up."

"You're right there. Nothing burns hotter than your own flame, my old master in the Drakwatch used to say."

"Demans—he (sic-eek) natural instinct to flee down, into crevice."

"I would like to see those dragon-snares and arresting ropes you're so famous for using on dragons in action sometime. We've lost too many dragons to such devices."

"Ye—ye wish to see us—snare dragon? In true—In truth?"

"I've seen warfare on the surface, but have only heard reports of tunnel fighting. An exhibition of your prowess would be fascinating. Of course neither side must be hurt in the exercise."

"Of course!"

"Gigrix, I have a proposition for you. We're having trouble getting Paskinix to meet so that your release might be negotiated."

"If ye intend is . . . , demen have honor, sir, as dragons."

"No, nothing of the sort. I was thinking that perhaps you could choose one or two of your soldiers to send looking for him with a message that I wish to meet, Tyr to King, and settle this conflict. Demen and dragons have enemies enough on the surface without fighting each other down here."

Gigrix was as difficult to read as a *griffaran,* between the frog eyes and the sliding headplates and grinding mandibles with probing lips, especially when all chose to work at once. But his spines stiffened at last.

"Done, if ye wish to give the orders. I shall send two."

Two would be better, the Copper thought. They'll spend their time talking to each other.

"There's one other arrangement I'd be happy to offer for the comfort of your warriors," the Copper said.

"What would that be?"

"Dragons, I know, hate being long away from mates and hatchlings. I suspect it is the same with demen."

"What is propose?"

"That such of your people"—the Copper was careful to observe Gigrix's reaction to the phrase *your people*—"as wish to visit and cheer your warriors may come and live at some intermediate distance where they might make the trip in a day. I'm afraid I can't allow any of your warriors to leave their area to go visit them, but I will allow free traffic by whatever mates and spawn wish to visit. They could settle at the river ring, as long as they take care not to try to steal any *griffaran* eggs. What say you to that?"

"I—I give that think."

"You do that. Evidently there is no hurry. At least Paskinix is of that opinion. Perhaps I'm not offering the right guarantees of his safety. Would you advise me on that?"

"Yes. Yes," Gigrix said.

"He knows that we meet as equals, he King of the Demen, myself Tyr of the Dragon Empire. No humiliation, no victor and vanquished."

"The Tyr is generous. I, as general, admit that we beaten, beaten very. He cannot object."

"He may choose the location of the meeting. All I ask is the companionship of my guard and his word that we meet in fair parley, no tricks or ambushes. Is that an immoderate demand?"

"No. The Tyr shows courage. That last parley with fighting—it was quaking trick. I take no part in that."

"Of course. You are a warrior, with a warrior's honor. Your followers surrendered, and I'll die before I see them ill-treated or have the terms of the surrender broken. That is my promise to you, Gigrix."

"Your word is prove by better treatment than I ever expect, Tyr."

"I just hope it is soon. So you see no fault in my offer?"

"No—none!"

"Hmmm. Well, perhaps something is being lost in the messaging. This has dragged on far too long. I've nothing but admiration for the discipline and spirits of your warriors, but I hate to see them confined to a few dragonlengths of shabby holes."

"Shabby! Tyr, the Lavadome is a wonder. Holes are clean with sound water than accustomary, purify in from steam. See the living hot rock flow against the . . . the—"

"Crystal," the Copper supplied.

"Ah, *crystal*! Great magic. Very dangers. Yes, it is like a magma pilgrimage that never ends behind crystal."

"Ah, yes. Well, as I was saying, such fine warriors, kept waiting, though I commend you for keeping their minds occupied with exercise and training. How did we ever beat you? We could have used such skill in the skirmish with the dwarves at the hotflow."

"A sharp fight, eh?" Gigrix asked, his spines rising and falling.

"Yes, the dwarves had taken refuge on a rising slope up from the steaming river. They'd banked stone against flame, so our own fire ran down on the Firemaids, and they had a stout shield wall behind."

"Ha! The Tyr is wise, but I know how to fight dwarves in such a situations. You had water near. A good triple pump."

"Triple pump?"

"Easy to build, just copper tubing of different sizes, and some stout backs to work the handles. It throw stream of water farther than any dragonflame. I see a triple pump knock down a wall, dwarves behind shields? Spill 'em and send 'em rolling like toadstools. Oh, a sight, that to see." Gigrix seemed lost in his imagination.

"Well, if the occasion calls for it, when a peace of friendship instead of enmity is made, perhaps I'll ask for your assistance in a future fight. Reward the victory with herds of cattle and drink a toast of dragonblood over a pile of dwarf-heads."

"Dragonblood, my Tyr?"

"You've never had it?"

"Well, yes, in war . . . well, bodies and such."

"And how do you like it?"

"Made me a new-shucked deman. Could that I took six matings instead of the usual three."

"Ah. Well, the dragon-riders in the Aerial Host swear by it. Both they and their mates enjoy it regularly. A well-fed dragon's all the better for a little bleeding now and then, I always say. Their children raised with a sip on the seven-day grow up uncommonly handsome and strong."

"Amazing."

"How so? I've heard that in Anklamere's time dragonblood was used as a tonic."

"No, that ye share. My apologies."

"Well, there was some resistance to it at first, but they're used to the idea now. It's something of an honor, to play 'host' at a party for the riders and their mates. No dragon is ever forced, and there are enough volunteers willing to bleed a little."

Gigrix smacked his mandibles. That divided jaw of the demen— most unsettling. It looked too much like an injury.

"Would you care for some?"

"I . . . I would never ask."

"Oh, come, you've been most helpful to me today. You allowed me to watch your exercises, advised me on the offer to Paskinix—perhaps he's died and your warriors can name you the new king. That would simplify things. Look, your eating knife looks clean enough, and one of those water buckets would do."

"Not from you, Tyr!" But he did retrieve the bucket.

"Oh, come, a little blood spilled makes lasting friendship, I've found, and I'm heartily sick of counting demen as enemies instead of praising them as allies. Give me that."

He pinched the short, sharp knife between his *sii* and cut himself just inside the turn of his forelimb.

If anything, it didn't go deep enough. He had to continually squeeze his *sii* to keep the blood flowing into the bucket.

A small crowd of tired, dirty demen gathered to watch the strange ceremony.

Gigrix called to the others, and one brought a ladle with a bowl at the end.

"Fresh firewater!" a deman marveled. At least that's what the Copper thought he said.

Gigrix filled the ladle, and like a good leader, offered the first sip to his "voice"—the deman who bellowed orders and corrected the warriors in their practice evolutions.

Then Gigrix himself took a swig. He stood still, drinking, breathing deeply, spines rippling up and down on his back.

"Yes, my Tyr," he said, passing the ladle to the tallest and widest of his soldiers. His greenish tongue dabbed at the sides of his mandibles, and he muttered a few words the Copper did not recognize. "Just to think, some argued for a glory-charge instead of surrender! Here I am, enjoy a drink fit for a king."

"It is fit for a king," the Copper said. "What do you say, warriors? Wouldn't Gigrix make a fine king?"

Eager for their turn at the ladle, the demen whistled through their mandibles and gave off piping hoots.

The Copper worried the wound to increase the flow. He used to believe himself awful at politics. But one could learn—yes, one could learn.

Pleasantly light-headed, the Copper returned to the top of Imperial Rock at a slow climb, with many pauses to talk to both dragons and thralls, hearing small news of kitchen and nursing-room. He congratulated thralls on the birth of babies or the marriage of children and made a quick visit to a distant relative's cave to listen to the quiet taps inside three promising-looking dragon-eggs. He assured the mother-to-be he'd never seen such perfectly formed eggs. It portended great things for the brood, most certainly.

Then it was up to the gardens and down the shaft to the old cistern with his bats.

In the days of the civil wars, he'd been told, it held a reserve of water. During FeHazathant's day, the water was mixed with a paste of ash, strange rare salts, and other nutrients and used to feed the Imperial gardens.

He'd ordered the cistern emptied and new masonry pools built to feed the gardens. Now it housed his bats.

It was a slow climb through the narrow well hole with his bad *sii*, but fortunately a short one. He found himself among his bats.

These were the trusted elite, descendants of the bats that had guided him as a hatchling. Each wore a tiny foot-band of metal, identifying it as a Tyr-bat. It was a crime to kill a Tyr-bat, at least on purpose.

They were of all different sizes, from small and quick, who lived mostly by eating parasites clinging beneath dragonscale—many a dragon would be revolted at the thought of some filthy, greasy mammal doing him a service as he slept—to medium-sized, who ate flies in the livestock and thrall pens to the big, blood-drinking brutes. Then there were the monster-bats, those who for generations had been raised on dragonblood. Some of them didn't even sleep upside down anymore, but slept in cracks above the noisome floor.

The Copper was relieved to see that the floor had been freshly scraped. The bat offal was greatly prized by the Anklene herbologists for their gardens.

"Ahh! 'Tis himself," a bat called as he clambered in.

"Ooo, is there a sup? Perishing hungry I am," one squeaked.

"No. No blood this time," the Copper said, climbing carefully to the cave floor so he didn't slip in filth. His body-thralls would be burning their cleaning rags later.

"I need three quiet, very healthy bats, small and smart. The duty will require a good deal of flying and cave-sense. But on completion I'll give you a permanent place in the Aerial Host caves."

He had scores of squeaking, clamoring volunteers. Two brawls broke out. It was difficult to pick three, but he found two brothers who claimed to be descended from Enjor and one female who seemed better-spoken than the rest.

"You're Ging," he said to the female. He looked at one of the males. "You're Gang. You're Ghoul," he said to the bigger male, for his fur was a ghostly gray. "Come with me, you three."

He walked and they flew to the edge of the gardens and he looked down at the assembled demen. "Those are demen. Get to know their sounds, their smells, their voices. In another day or two, a pair of demen will leave that group. I want you to follow them. It will probably be a trip of some days. When they find another group of demen and meet with a big, sort of bluish one who walks with the aid of a big stick, you return and let me know where he is."

They had the usual questions about dying of hunger on the way— he told them that they would just have to sneak a sup from sleeping Firemaids, there should still be some left in the Star Tunnel—and of course, there were the demen themselves.

"Now, you can help yourself to a little of my blood. Just a little. I'm weak enough from feeding demen. You can clean out this cut, while you're at it."

Nothing like bat saliva for speeding healing, he'd found. Even Nilrasha thought it was disgusting, but she couldn't argue the result— the wounds healed thrice as fast with only the faintest of scars.

Thinking he'd done a good day's work, he told the thralls he would have an extra haunch of roast pork for supper. And perhaps a second or even third helping of that wine his adoptive grandmother used to be so fond of. He had blood to make up.

All the while he met that afternoon with NoSohoth, the smells coming up from the kitchens made it very hard to keep his mind on affairs in the hills. NoSohoth's droning lulled him, and he had to resort to his old training cave-watch trick of digging *sii* into *saa* to stay awake.

Unfortunately, dinner was spoiled by one of his thralls, the female in charge of the cleaning staff. She was a massive creature, as wide as she was tall, almost white hair bound up in a Tyr's household kerchief.

"Oh, sir. One of my scrubs, she found some strange odds and ends in your wizard's sleeping chamber. We're used to his strange devices, but we wondered about this."

A similarly wide young man, probably one of her family, moved forward with a bundle wrapped in a blanket. He unrolled it before his Tyr.

There was rope, a mallet on a lanyard, spikes, food, waterskins, hooks, spiked shoes with soft fronts for gripping.

"I know a runaway being planned when I sees it," the old woman said.

"This was in . . . Rayg's quarters?"

"Aye, sir. All between two boards in his bed under the matting. Clever, but she heard it sliding around when she moved the bed. No one can say my girls don't do a thorough job cleaning."

The Copper thanked her and told her to help herself to whatever she might find hanging in the Tyr's larder.

He didn't finish the meal with the same appetite as he'd started it.

Later, the Copper invited Rayg out into the gardens, so they might have a private talk under the red light of the flow. Other dragons and drakes and drakka enjoying the gardens and the fading light at the crystal circle in the top made room for him.

The Copper brought Rayg to the banquet pit and showed him the assortment of gear.

"Rayg, these were found in your quarters. Tell me what they mean."

"It's not obvious?" Rayg said in his good Drakine.

"False claws, lines—this is climbing gear."

"You've noted how old some of it is," Rayg said.

"Well."

Rayg lifted one of the spike-studded shoes. "See the rust. Years old."

"You were planning an escape."

"I had my reasons."

"Numerate them for me. Have I been ungenerous?"

Rayg wasn't behaving like a thief caught by his owner dragon. They might have been discussing the bulbs in the gardens. "Oh, I'll take you over the barbarians, of course. You are fair. You've been very generous to my family. They're prosperous and happy. The time I spend with them is wonderful. If another dragon became Tyr, however . . . Must I say it?"

"I intend to be Tyr for a good many years yet." It didn't do to mention the relative life spans of humans and dragons.

"It seems a Tyr doesn't always have a choice. You're the third Tyr since I've been here, I believe."

"Rayg, you're a great help to me. Indeed, invaluable. If you were to run away and be killed in the Wind Tunnel, as I'll hazard this gear is meant to ascend—"

"Oh, no. I won't run away on *you*, RuGaard."

For a thrall to use a dragon's name, let alone the Tyr—The Copper glanced around, but if anyone was trying to listen to the conversation they were as stealthy as his bats. The banquet area was empty.

"Hmmm. I'll give orders that you're allowed to have whatever sort of equipment you need for climbing. I'll say it's for your experiments. No sense having your life depend on this rusting old junk."

"Thank you, my Tyr."

"Will you tell me something, though? Why *do* you stay?"

"I like dragons."

The Copper thought that over. Strange thing for a slave, even a pampered and privileged slave, to say.

"You don't mind the smell, being underground?"

"Oh, the years have accustomed me to that. You're not cruel. I lived among barbarians when I was very young. Dragons aren't cruel to those in their power. They don't go out of their way to make captives miserable to amuse themselves."

"You're never afraid I'll lose my temper and eat you? I thought that all thralls, free or no, lived with that fear."

"Not particularly. It would be an easy death."

"What do you mean?"

"Have you ever seen a really old dwarf?"

"What does that have to do with anything?" the Copper asked, puzzled.

"I am getting to that. They get so they just sit. Can hardly lift a finger anymore, but too stubborn to die. Some get wheeled about in tiny pushcarts, for a time, while they still talk and give instructions. Eventually, when truly ancient, they lapse into silence. They get fed and washed off once a day, from the same contraption, a sort of portable pump you wear on your back. They might as well be a potato plant. Rows of statues in the hall of ancients." Rayg shuddered. "Just eyes, glaring out of this bird's nest of hair. I think death's better."

"You're not a dwarf," the Copper said.

"No one can accuse you of being of philosophical mind," Rayg said. "I only mean I'm troubled by the frailties of inevitable age."

"I'll see to it that a few of your children are around to help as you get older."

The Copper looked at Rayg. He knew him to be at least a score of years into adulthood, yet he still looked hale and hearty. He wondered if he didn't have a secret source of dragonblood or something to keep himself so youthful looking.

A pair of young drakes, glaring at each other, approached, but the Copper waved them off.

"More grievances to be settled," the Copper said, trying to put a briskness in his voice that he didn't feel. Rayg's talk of decline depressed him. "It is enough to make one wish for a return of dueling."

"But you hate duels."

"Oh, I'm just tired and I didn't enjoy my wine. Just last night I had my meal interrupted by two dragons—never mind their names; they were sort of a charcoal and a dull bronze. Charcoal sold a herd of cattle, an even score, to Bronze in exchange for three young thralls. By the time Bronze delivered the thralls and picked up the cattle, two of the beasts had sickened and died. Charcoal insisted that Bronze take the carcasses, as they could still be eaten.

"Neither could resolve anything between themselves, so they brought it to me. Bronze wanted to keep the ten kine but give only two slaves, but Charcoal demanded that the original deal for the herd be kept."

"What did you do?"

"I told Charcoal that if dead cattle were so valuable he should keep them and replace them with live beasts. Bronze claimed that he would be given two more sickly beasts and insisted on the return of one thrall and that anything else would be a cheat. Now both are more angry with me than with each other. United in their disgust at my decision, they had a fine session of tail-bowling after, it seemed."

"Dwarves had disputation hearings," Rayg said when he'd finished chuckling. "I saw one once. Part of one—I'm told it went on for much of the day. Each side brought several others to give their version of events."

The Copper couldn't dig teeth into it, but something about speaking to Rayg always settled his mind. Or the purge settled his mind and he was simply used to venting his firebladder—figuratively—in Rayg's presence. It often gave him ideas. Maybe Rayg's manner of settling disputes could be put into practice here.

"Speaking of disputes, may I ask you for a favor?"

"Of course."

"Those twins, SiHazathant and Regalia. They've been giving dragonblood to the expectant mothers among their thralls, trying to breed extra-strong humans or something. A little dragonblood is a fine thing, but a diet of it exclusively—the babies are born dead, or don't live long. Which is probably just as well. The mothers are deeply grieved by the . . . the mutations. One killed herself. Would you tell them to stop experimenting?"

Idle fools. Of course, it wasn't all that different from what he'd done with his bats, but the bats weren't dangerous to begin with and had been much improved by doses of dragonblood. Humans, on the other hand, were and always would be a threat.

All those old rumors about the Dragonblade drinking the blood of dragons he'd slain. If those two were to inadvertently breed a generation of dragonblades . . .

An ugly doubt crept in on claw-sheathed *saa*. What if it wasn't inadvertent? What if they were trying to breed another dragonblade, or two, or six, or a score? He would have to keep an eye on those two, and his eyes already had too many other dangers to be watching.

"I'll put a stop to that."

He sent Rayg and his collection of climbing gear away. Even if Rayg had dazzled him with lies, suppose he did escape? He owed such debts to Rayg—he should really grant him his freedom and let him enjoy the sunshine in the Upper World.

But it wasn't up to one sentimental, indulgent young Tyr. The Lavadome needed Rayg's skills.

NoSohoth spoiled his digestion with a new round of complaints from Upholds to the south and northeast. The Ghioz were stealing cattle, brigands were raiding their blighter allies on the world's end.

Nilrasha returned late, ill-tempered, tired, and footsore. She'd been accompanying some drakka in the Firemaidens on a fast training march to the river ring.

"On the return trip I brought a gift of fowl to SoRolatan at the Six Ridges. He's still smarting over that dragonelle you took out from under his nose."

"In a fair flight he'd never catch up to her. Fat old thing."

"Still," she said, "I had to listen to his fool of a mate babble while I tried to come up with new features to praise on a dragon remarkable only for how little there is to praise. I kept the compliments flowing through an entire meal to get a promise that his latest hatchlings would go into the Firemaidens."

"You play this game like you've been doing it since you were in the egg."

She looked off, beyond their little outer chamber. "You forget, my love, that I grew up on milkdrinker's hill. Only one rich dragon there—that bug Sreeksrack—and the rest of us were fighting over his scraps. It's the same game. They want what you have, only the stakes have changed. Under milkdrinker's hill it might have been a rusty shovel scoop or a scrawny old chicken. Now it's rooms looking out on the dome and or a share of oliban trade."

The Copper touched tail-tip to tail-tip. "You're the rock my rule rests upon."

"Quit cracking it and I wouldn't have to spend all my time filling cracks." She stared at him as though she were looking at him for the first time tonight. "My Tyr, you look positively bled! You weren't feeding those bats again."

"No. Demen."

"Oh, whatever—"

"That general of theirs, Gigrix, he'd had dragonblood before. I saw an opportunity."

"You'll lose his respect. A Tyr doing such a thing."

He told her about the twins' experiments with humans and Rayg's opinion.

"I'll have a word with their thralls," she said.

"You have influence even with theirs?"

"I've worked hard to have all the thralls come to me with their problems. Thralls know their owners better than their families, you know."

"I thought you rewarded them out of a kind heart," the Copper said. It would be hard to say whether he was disappointed, impressed, or some mix of both.

She snorted. "They're a tool, like claws, like tongue, like feasts."

"Like mating?" He half hoped she would lie to him.

She cocked her head. "Not ours, my love."

As the thralls cleared away the meal he put his neck across hers. Nilrasha tickled him with her *griff* and began to sing.

These were his favorite moments. He felt like a hatchling again, warm against his mother—or at least that's how he imagined a hatchling felt. He'd had only one brief moment with his own . . .

Chapter 10

They gave him a comfortable nook out of the wind that couldn't quite be called a cave, but it had a fine view of the mountains to the south, soft bracken to rest upon, and a windbreak. It smelled faintly of dragon, but not DharSii. AuRon found an old white scale, lost under the bracken and tinged with yellow and red fissures.

He idled for a night and a day. A pair of blighters wearing leather reinforced with dragonscale at the knees, shoulders, and elbows, well groomed save that they were barefoot, brought him a cartload of hams and sausages of assorted shapes and flavorings.

"More?" one asked in intelligible, if not intelligent, Drakine.

AuRon broke one open, sniffed carefully, tested it with his tongue, then took a taste. It seemed wholesome.

"This will do for now."

He ate lightly, just in case.

It was pleasant to be at this altitude. Back in the north, ice and snow would be thick in this fissure. He had just enough energy to find a cool stream for drinking and bathing.

When he returned from his bath he heard the blighters calling, blowing a horn and rattling a ring of metal against a rod.

He snuck up from downwind and startled them. It was good to keep in practice, but with the noise they made, he had little difficulty.

"Come, come. Eat! Soon she see you."

They had an offering in the form of some cooked organmeats, swimming in butter. He hadn't had butter in years, but once again forced himself to politely nibble.

A third hominid, this one a human, watched from a distance. He looked too stout to be much used to hiking up and down mountains, but ambled off as soon as they began their journey down the ridge.

The blighters led him down toward the scaffold-shrouded hill-side. There was an arched door at the end of the path, up a short rocky zigzag of stairs through a sort of wild garden, but it was too small for a dragon to squeeze through, though AuRon thought he might just make it if supplied with a little more butter to grease the passage.

Instead the blighters led him off down a gravel road and he smelled horses. A small field beneath the ear and cheekbone on the great face held bright green grass and a few horses, either the ones who'd pulled the Queen's chariot or cousins of theirs.

The blighters led him inside a sort of stone barn. He found the Red Queen in the stables, examining one of her horses' feet with a dwarf wider than he was tall, clad in a heavy leather apron and belt sagging under the weight of tools. The dwarf's sideburns were thick with glowing moss, brighter than any species AuRon had yet seen, and the rest of it showed no evidence of gold dust or other decor. The dwarf must have cared only about proper illumination for his work.

The Red Queen wore a sort of thick red canvas cloak that re-minded AuRon of those little cups at the end of handles that homi-nids used to snuff candles. She simply wore a light scarf about her face this time. AuRon found himself frozen in his tracks by a pair of startling blue eyes, heavily blackened about the rims with stenciling, which only drew attention to their size and clarity.

She said something quietly to the dwarf, who nodded.

The Red Queen looked at him and the corners of her eyes crinkled. He guessed she smiled. "It never hurts to pay attention to details."

"At your service, Great Queen," AuRon said, remembering DharSii's phrasing.

She took him farther into the mountain. The passages were wide, high, and airy—AuRon recognized dwarf workmanship when he saw it, though there was none of the impressive decor of the Char-tered Company.

"Details, AuRon, details. Of course there are always more than can be seen to. The trouble is, we can't be easily in six places at once."

She led him to a sort of domed chamber at the bottom of a divided staircase with a wall-fountain bubbling between the balustrades and more stairs descending back into the mountain from the chamber. Light came in, soft and diffuse, from twin slits in narrowing shafts, which AuRon suspected were nostrils. "Won't you excuse me for a moment? You may wish to admire the fountain, or refresh yourself at it."

AuRon contented himself with looking at the stonecraft. The back of the fountain was a mosaic of precisely measured square shapes, tipped sideways to be diamonds. They were arranged in an intricate design, rather thicker at the bottom and narrowing at the top. All he could think was that it was some highly stylized depiction of a mountain.

"Can you believe the blighters made that? It's a relic of Old Uldam. Yes, even the blighters once claimed this mountain as their own. But they didn't keep it long enough to make many exterior alterations, or we might have fangs to remove from the mountain-face."

She'd changed her wardrobe into a simple long dress, as spare as her previous outfit had been elaborate. Three silver brooches, elongated triangles, held it about her. He'd been right. Her figure was spare, but it just drew attention to her head. A translucent mask of swirling crystal cut to resemble—oh, he couldn't say—smoothed ice hid her face now. A light silk wrap of black with a hint of glittering gold covered her hair and neck.

She carried a lighter version of her previous mask. This one was ivory colored and had the appearance of stiffened, intricately sewn lace, with the same smile on one side and frown on the other.

"Red outdoors, black indoors, as simple as that."

AuRon regretted losing the magic of those brilliant eyes and wondered why the game to hide her features? Of course, if no one ever had a good look at you, they wouldn't know if you were aging or not, sick or not, or if perhaps you'd been replaced by another. He'd been told in his visit to the East that some monarchs had three or four identical wagon-chambers, to make assassination more difficult or so that none of their underlings might know whether their actual ruler or some underling was on his way.

"You believe in simplicity, Great Queen?"

"Life for us is complex. The calculations we commit before making a move sometimes take days or weeks, so we must keep the rest of our life as spare as possible. But we still must make an appearance.

"We are glad you could see that fountain, AuRon. We often pause by it and remind ourselves of the rises and falls of nations before Ghioz. Civilization building is long, weary work. I've raised a city of polished marble where once there were mud-and-straw huts."

"Are you a sorcerer who can turn air into stone?"

"Not that kind of sorcerer. Anklamere's way was a cheat. But we do know the secret of creation. The creation of anything is an act of will and mind."

She led him down the stairs and to another gallery in the mountain-face, much better lit than the one above. Her footfalls on the stairs were so light he wondered if he imagined them. This one he guessed was the statue's mouth. He couldn't see much, because of scaffolding and canvas in the way, but without the working equipment he guessed it would be a commanding view.

"Those trees down there, obviously they exist in the physical world. But isn't our concept of those trees flexible? The architecture of the imagination, as that dwarf put it. It's called the Queen's Wood, so the trees are ours. We can imagine the trees as sheltering game birds, or being cut down and made into scaffolding for another statue. There is enormous power in audacity. Your little 'Isle of Ice'—as we believe it's called on the Hypatian maps. We could just as easily name it Aurontos and appoint you our governor. The world entire belongs to us in our imagination. Life is slowly filling in the details."

AuRon wondered if she'd already sold the island to a would-be titleor.

"There are those who would dispute my claim," AuRon said. "And yours, Great Queen."

Apparently, it never hurt to imitate DharSii's manner. She tipped her head to him in acknowledgment of the compliment.

"Oh, we can outwait them. We can afford to be patient. If no other solution presents itself, we simply wait a generation or two. How soon they forget."

"Dragons live a long time," AuRon said.

"Not even those trees will outlast us, dragon. The Red Queen is eternal."

"You pass the title down to your daughter along with your beliefs?"

"Nothing so mundane. We simply can't be bothered to die. Too much undone in this world. Your wizard and men like him, they drop off and leave their work hardly begun."

"He was hardly my wizard. I regretted his life, not his death."

She spun the mask around to the frowning face. "Be careful, AuRon son of AuRel. Make an enemy of us and you make an enemy forever."

"Was he some titleor of yours, Great Queen?"

"No. The circle of men is folly. We are not so stupid as to not recognize the value of elves, dwarves—even blighters. We are happy to stamp out such nonsense. When some of his riders sought refuge here after his fall we took them in, but as soon as they started proselytizing that Man's First Destiny nonsense, we had their heads struck off. Little loss.

"We find our greatest challenge is in finding worthy intelligences to be our titleors. Oh, plenty want the title, but few the labor that goes with it. Then there are those who are diligent but require constant instruction or who are too hidebound by the teachings of their temples to do what is necessary to be effective."

"How do you measure 'effective'?"

"There is only one sure measure, dragon. Coin and goods of value. I learned long ago that men will try to substitute almost anything for coin: fair words, professions of love, promises of loyalty, sad stories, flattery, tears—yes, they will offer up all that, rivers of it, raging torrents, and all of it gathered together weighs as much as mist on a cattle-scale. It is the one who brings a chest of coin who has the ability to rise."

"You must have much coin."

"I'm not a dragon who piles it in a hoard. Let me give you some advice, AuRon. Put your gold to work. It is like seed. Pour it into the right ground and it will sprout tenfold. No, I do not have the great treasure-chambers that some believe reside under this mountain. What comes in goes out again, in the form of small presents to those who apply. A man comes to me and says he wishes to establish himself as a horse-breeder, I give him coin to buy his broodmares and land. True, there are those I never see again. But there are others who return in a few years with what I gave them raised tenfold. I offer a title. Then I see them again when they would have their son set up as a captain of one of my cavalry squadrons, or a daughter who could be most advantageously married with a larger dowry. Over his lifetime of labor, I see my gold grown a hundred times or more."

"I'm afraid dragons aren't much for such diligent labor, Great Queen."

"But they can talk to other dragons. We do have some dragons you might help us with," she mused. "We believe your face would be unknown to them."

"Who would that be?"

"Do you know the Lower World well? I wish for an emissary to the Lavadome."

"Lavadome? I've heard the word. A dwarven interpretation of a blighter myth, I thought."

"Oh, it's real enough. We don't know much of the Lower World, as you call it, but then we don't determine it would profit Ghioz to go to the effort to control it. In our calculation, there's little enough reward down there. Tunnels filled with nothing but dark."

"Is there coin in bearing your messages?"

"Yes. We wish to show you some of our chief titleors. If you could be obliged to accompany us to conference.

"You picked a fortunate time to arrive. Some of my northerly allies have come south to spend the season with me and miss the worst of the ice and snow, and Ghioz is soon celebrating the sun's death and rebirth, a most worthy of occasions, we think."

He followed her into some rougher tunnels. He smelled animal coops, cooking, spices, and ranker odors.

She led him down a passage that sloped rather precipitously, but the floor-stones were set in such a way that claws, or feet, had sound purchase. Out through a wide arcing set of doors, AuRon realized they'd come straight through the mountain and now stood beneath the great face with all the scaffolding. He had to duck his head to pass under some of it.

The trees and stones here had been arranged, and assisted by waxed canvas, in such a way that he could hardly tell whether he was inside or out. The pocket of mountain and the vast chunks of what had once been the dwarf's beard gave the appearance of walls, the great boles pillars, and the interlaced trees above a roof. Yet there were pools and streams, flower beds and fern-patches, and even sweet-smelling fruit trees scattered about the vast arena. Someone had cut the fallen rocks to provide rude seats and stairs to have access.

He suspected the area could have held many hundreds or a thousand, but at the moment there were some score, in little groups of threes and fives.

"Thank you for holding your business until a new day. We appreciate your patience," the Red Queen announced in Parl.

AuRon surveyed the faces. Mostly human, though he saw a few elves, their tresses resembling dried seaweed, fall leaves, and in one case a cascade of pumpkin seeds. Dwarves, also with faces veiled and beards alight with glowing moss reflecting gold dust and gemstones— very rich dwarves, it seemed. Five blighters squatted together on a single stone, devouring a basket of apples as they waited.

The largest contingent seemed to be men with dark hair and thin mustaches and beards carefully trimmed and shaped and beaded. AuRon recognized their garb. They were Ironriders of various tribes.

He remembered them as being described as very dangerous to those unfortunate enough to live within raiding distance during those rare intervals when they weren't warring with each other over pasturage and nomadic pathways.

One of the dwarves, particularly rotund, leaned on a thick, gnarled stick. Something about the pose tugged at old memories. What was the name of that thieving dwarf who'd tried to blame him? Sekyw.

Interesting that he'd found his way into the Red Queen's court.

"Stay near the entrance for the moment, AuRon. There are ceremonies and pleasantries we must endure. Such rituals have their purpose, but they weary after a twelvescore or two."

AuRon watched her mount a low platform and stand. Each of those at the conference lined up to greet and speak to her. Part of their tradition involved dipping hands in a cistern of water and drying them on a white cloth before meeting at the hands. With little to do but observe, he noticed that some she gripped by both hands, some only one, sometimes they crossed arms so right hand met right hand and left hand met left.

The Ironriders simply touched their foreheads to the hem of her dress.

Then they spoke. The Red Queen seemed conversant in many tongues. She rarely spoke at any length. When quarrels broke out she silenced them immediately.

Servants, human and blighter, brought food and drink around.

Finally she waved him over.

"This is AuRon, a prince of dragons out of the north," she said. "We think he may serve as a suitable emissary to the dragons of the Lavadome."

"I knew this dragon when he was but a wingless drake, I believe, my queen," Sekyw said. "We crossed the plains together in the traveling towers. I know him to be trustworthy." Sekyw shot a guilty glance at AuRon. "He did the dwarves great service in battle. He is loyal to his friends, very loyal."

"Ghioz looks everywhere for friendship," the Red Queen said.

The Ironriders said something in a tongue AuRon did not know, but he recognized the Parl word for *dragons*.

"Yes, yes, everyone must have dragons to accomplish their goal. That is the difficulty. There are so few, at least who will act with intelligence. Remember the stupidity of the ones used to human direction, how easily they died when left to their own devices in conquering the Chushmereamae Archipelago. I have sent you roc-riders for scouting, and that will have to do.

"So, what will it be, AuRon? I offer you a title, if you will take it. You'll find the duties light and our friendship worth thrice the pittance we ask in return."

"It is a poor island, Great Queen. It offers little except fish and seal-meat."

"But it does have dragons. Dragons, being intelligent, powerful, and winged, are the most useful of allies."

"Join? I cannot make up my mind about so important a decision without consulting others. My hatchlings, however, need coin, and need it soon if they are to grow up strong."

"Then you will find us a generous commissioner. We need a messenger to go to your kind in the Lavadome and offer them friendship. Through blunder and misunderstanding, we have fought at the Sloai horsedowns and in Bant. We were considering sending another as emissary, but his past in the Lavadome might carry along prejudice against our intent. You, as a fresh face, could be fairly heard."

"What would your message be, Great Queen?"

"The friendliest of messages. Only that there be a dialogue between worlds, upper and lower, so that we might settle disputes without bloodshed."

"Your terms?"

"Upon a dragon from the Lavadome attending as an ambassador to my court, and the appointment of an ambassador from Ghioz to the Lavadome, and the establishment of communications each way, we will present to you a ransom in pure gold coin."

"A ransom?"

"Do you know our weights and measures?"

"I'm afraid not."

"It is about the weight of a full-grown male bull."

"That is a substantial sum indeed."

"Then the terms are satisfactory?"

"The mission may fail. I would like to be compensated in that eventuality."

"One-quarter shall be yours, then."

"I do not know your customs, Great Queen. How do we call it a bargain?"

"There are seals and such that can be set upon paper, but they are only as good as one's word, and you already have ours."

AuRon decided that if nothing else, contact with other dragons would be beneficial. He hoped there weren't remnants of the wizard's old armada lurking in this Lavadome, nursing a grudge against the one who brought about their master's fall. "Then you have mine as well."

"We are always happy to come to agreement."

"Will you satisfy me on something?" AuRon asked.

The mask spun around, and briefly frowned, then the smiling side turned back again. AuRon judged it a warning to get to the point. "We have other business this day, but you have our attention."

"The friend I lost—DharSii spoke of her. How long had she been in the service of Ghioz? What were her aims and goals and so on?"

"Friend? Another dragon?"

"Yes."

"There is some misunderstanding. We never had her in our service. We are afraid she was friend to the blighters and guarding a very great prize. As an obstacle to our will, she had to be removed. DharSii was fond of her, and gave her every opportunity to escape destruction."

"She fought against DharSii, not with him?"

"That is our understanding. We regret that the encounter could not have ended more happily. According to DharSii, she was a worthy dragon."

After all these years. If he'd come east just a few months earlier. . . . why couldn't those cursed treasure-hunters have taken advantage of the first warm spring winds?

The last of his old family, gone. Why couldn't dragons stay out of hominid quarrels? But hominids acquired gold like ants seeking fallen fruit, and dragons needed that gold. So here he was, mixing in hominid affairs again.

Maybe DharSii was right about the Ghioz. They are strong, and a tree does better to bend with a strong wind if it wishes to keep limbs intact.

He still had his new family to think about. They must come first.

"Does this change matter?" the Red Queen asked. "You may alter your decision. We have no desire to place such a mission on unwilling wings."

"I am sorry that events went the way they did," AuRon said. "But I still need that gold. The sooner I may claim it, the better."

"Very well. Return to the fountain inside and we will have further instruction, and a small gift."

AuRon idled by the fountain, thinking. The Red Queen's evident desire for good relations with his island might be to his advantage after all. She seemed a wise ruler, and anyone who could bring different tribes of Ironriders together must be a diplomat to be reckoned with.

It grew dark outside and servants lit a few lamps. The staircases turned into pathways to shadow and doubt, but the flow of water remained constant. Eventually, even the faint sounds of stonecutting ceased.

The Red Queen reappeared, moving slowly but surely.

"A long day. We have ordered food to be brought to the stable door for you, so that you may eat before setting off, or sleep and then leave in the morning, if you prefer."

"Thank you, Great Queen."

"I have a simple message in Parl. Do you read it?"

"Yes."

She gave him a scroll-tube on an oversized chain. The clasp was big enough for dragonclaws to easily work it. He extracted the message and read it, a simple, friendly offer to establish ambassadors between Ghioz and the Lavadome so that future conflicts between the Upper and Lower Worlds might be avoided. There were three seals, of gold, silver, and red wax at the bottom.

"You need a badge of rank as well," she said, after he replaced the message in the scroll-tube. "Wear this to show you have our confidence."

The leather blighters appeared at a wave. One carried a long, thin chain with a crystal pendant dangling at the end. AuRon examined both it and the chain closely. They seemed harmless. The crystal was of unusual clarity, with just a hint of milkiness to one side. The stone didn't look like a diamond.

"Would you like it around your neck? DharSii wore his in his ear, back when he was an emissary."

"The neck would suit me."

The blighters fixed it around him as she showed him a map. He asked a few questions about the landmarks mentioned.

"So this bridge deep in a canyon cavern will lead me there, Great Queen?" he asked.

"There are other ways, we believe, but it would be better for you to take that one. It is the surest path, and well guarded so that your coming will not be a surprise. There is another entrance we know of in Bant, but there has been much blood spilled there. A message brought through Bant would just remind everyone of this."

The Red Queen walked around in front of him to admire the necklace.

"That does look well. We guessed the length just right." She raised the smiling mask to his face. "You are a brave dragon, AuRon."

"I might say the same about you. A Queen who converses with a dragon without fear or bodyguards all around."

"Oh, yes, I suppose you could envelop me in flame, if you were mad enough to do such a thing. But remember, I've far too much to do to do something as wasteful as dying."

BOOK TWO

Improvise

FATE FIGHTS ON THE SIDE OF THE PREPARED.
— *Irelia Antialovna*

Chapter 11

W istala, with food in her stomach giving her energy and a mind wishing diversion from the aches of healing, learned much about these "Firemaids" and the dragons they protected as they traveled from post to post.

It seemed there were three strains of dragonkind, according to her rescuers. The Skotl were reckoned the best fighters, as they tended to be the biggest and thickest of scale. They were also the most numerous, by a thin margin, though they were flexible enough to count any largish dragon as an honorary Skotl regardless of bloodline, so their counts couldn't be trusted. The Anklenes were the cleverest, as they'd once been close servants of the ancient Anklamere, who'd once kept and bred dragons much as dragons now kept other races as thralls. The Anklenes were the fewest and the most clannish. The Wyrr considered themselves the mortar that held the others together, noted for their cool heads and sound judgment and skill at song, story, and sooth.

All the Firemaids apparently thought well of their Tyr, and while there was some doubt as to his parentage, as he'd been orphaned young, each line seemed assured that he was, deep down, of theirs. The Anklenes argued his distinctive eye-ridge and classical crest as proof of their line's intelligence, the Skotl bragged that such hardihood in the face of battle injuries could only result from Skotl parentage, and the Wyrr praised the friendship he seemed to inspire in not only dragons but bats and thralls and such as well.

"It's more that what went before him was so bad, he seems thrice as great as he really is," Ayafeeia said when they chanced to be alone after one dinner when the Tyr's latest order that Paskinix should be told that a substantial chunk of his army was waiting for him to come and claim it in the Lavadome came down via a Drak-watch messenger. "He gets what he wants. He's just cleverer about it than most."

The irony of her situation appealed to her. She wished nothing more than that Rainfall was still alive so she could get back to his estate and tell him. She'd exhausted herself flying from the frozen north down the spine of the world to the south, searched the borders of Hypatia, across the endless plains, and even into the East seeking first other dragons, then AuRon.

All those horizons under her wings, exhausting days and sore nights. Wasted. Well, not wasted. A broader knowledge of the world could hardly be called a wasteful activity. But what she really needed was one slippery step and a fall into the Lower World to bring her into more contact with her own kind than she'd ever imagined.

The one filcher in her hoard was that drakka Takea.

"The Tyr must know about you helping Paskinix escape," she said. At every opportunity.

"And he shall," Ayafeeia said. "But from me, not you. All I know for certain is that an exhausted, starved, injured dragon fell during a difficult climb."

Wistala's exhaustion was cured by rest, her starvation was remedied by two-a-day meals—one could tell day from night in the Star Tunnel by taking a trip to one of the openings—and her injuries were set by blighter-thralls, who put a brace on the break and used a charcoal forge to seal it closed.

"It feels awful at first, like something's clutching at your wing. Quite unnerving," Ayafeeia said. "The itch feels like it will drive you mad if you don't keep yourself occupied."

Wistala took her up on it and tried to keep her mind occupied. "Who built the Star Tunnel?" she asked during one of the restorative meals. "Dwarves?"

"It doesn't look like dwarf-work," one of the Anklenes in the Firemaids said. "It's too dry for demen and as for blighters—why? They're comfortable underground, but they prefer the surface. The triangular shape, while structurally sound, wastes a good deal of space for anything but dragon-sized creatures."

"But we've no legends of dragons making it," Ayafeeia put in.

"The proportions are right for trolls. They're rather triangular. And they're so odd, it's easy to believe they're out of the Lower World."

"Trolls!" Ayafeeia said. "Where are there trolls? I thought they'd vanished."

"There are still some in the north, regrettably."

"Trolls! They are supposed to be strong," a Firemaid said.

"Fast, which is worse. And they can climb like giant monkeys."

"Best just to fly away and burn them."

"Well, they squeeze into cracks like spiders. They don't know fear. But if you burn them good at the tailvent—their lungs are to the rear—you'll drop them."

"How do you know all that?" Takea asked.

"I helped kill one, and just survived another. He jumped on me while I was flying through some mountains."

Takea shut her nostrils, and a few others whispered among themselves. The Anklene stared at her closely.

"You have a great deal of experience in the Upper World," Ayafeeia said.

"I've traveled it my whole life. I know Hypatia better than most areas, but I've been up to the icy wastes, I've seen the Sadda-Vale, the eastern kingdoms, and some of the Inland Ocean."

"No one could survive so many journeys," the Anklene said. "How were you not hunted?"

"By not giving them a reason to hunt me. I don't raid pasturage or pens, and if I must go hungry for a week to do so, I go hungry. One can always get by on badgers and skunks and so on. They're disgusting but easy to smell out."

The Star Tunnel went on for days. At one point it seemed to end in a sheer rock face, with a new tunnel, smaller and rougher, bored so that it joined up with the old, and a second break in it soon after, this one requiring a brief climb.

"Some change in the Lower World itself since the tunnel was made," the Anklene Firemaid asserted. "You can see the demen dug connecting shafts."

"This was where the hardest fighting took place. Every hill lost a dragonelle or a drakka here," Ayafeeia said, showing hidden pits full of broken spear points and holes that had fired javelins or whirling blades. "One day we'll build a shrine at the Bloody Cut."

There was a shrine, of sorts, in the form of a stack of demen heads. Wistala lost her count as she realized it was in the thousands.

The demen had done construction of things other than walls and traps throughout the Star Tunnel. There were small ponds where they stocked fish and shell-creatures, pens where they had kept livestock beneath platforms that brought fodder down from the holes, even smoking rooms for the preservation of foodstuffs.

"This one was filled with men. All withered, as though they'd been long dead. The demen like their smoked meat very dry," a Firemaid told her.

"We drove the demen away from their underground rivers. Many of these improvements are recent, to try and feed themselves. What's left must be mightily hungry by now."

"I think they eat each other," Takea said. "Drakka exploring fissures have found some dead demen. Always small and weak-looking, always with flesh and guts and brains removed."

"A shame," another Firemaid said. "Demen liver sewed up in their own skin and boiled with the brain is an old Wyrr favorite."

The others smacked snouts and licked lips in agreement. Wistala didn't care for the idea of dragons behaving like battlefield crows and tunnel rats. But after her enforced short rations, her mouth watered nevertheless, and she was forced to gather the saliva back in with her tongue just like the others.

While all but a watch slept, nose to flank or curled belly to back, Ayafeeia sought her out.

"Come. I want to see how that wing is progressing," she said quietly.

Wistala followed her to a wider section of the Star Tunnel, where bits of dead leaf and other fallen dirt from above had accumulated, making a soft bed for cave moss and mushrooms.

Ayafeeia plucked up a pair of mushrooms and ate them. "Dwarf food, I know, but they clean the bowel. Let's extend that wing, if you can."

Wistala found that she could, at the cost of some pain. Ayafeeia had her raise the wing, lower it, sweep it about.

"You'll fly again. Even if it doesn't heal entirely, we can have a lighter brace made for you," Ayafeeia said. "Our own Tyr uses a contraption that keeps the proper tension at the joint. But be sure you extend your wings now whenever you get the chance, several times a day. A little—a very little—strain on the wing will encourage it to heal more firmly."

"I feared—"

"Well, don't. I know it's instinct, one-winged birds make easy prey, and you're keeping it tucked tight, hiding the injury."

"Thank you."

"There's more. I've wanted to have a talk with you."

"Yes?"

"Now that you've regained some of your strength, I was wondering what you planned for the future."

"To continue searching for my brother. I don't know where he's gone, but if I return to the librarians in Hypatia perhaps they will have some news. I've asked my friends there to collect any news of dragons they hear."

"Ah," she said.

"You are disappointed?"

"I'm an honest dragonelle, Wistala. It's why I never rose far or won favor in the Imperial Line. Politics is not in me. I had hoped you'd use your skills and knowledge here, for the Lavadome and the Empire. For your kind. We're the last hope of dragons. One as well traveled as you must know that."

"Go on. I'll try and hear your words fairly."

"I'm no expert on the Upper World, Wistala, but it seems to me that dragons are just about done there. We've had several groups of back-to-surfacers leave, to live natural as dragons ought and all that rot, but we never hear from them or their hatchlings again.

"The one set of dragons we did meet were—well, the only word I can think of is *thralls*. They were thralls to men, dragon-riders who briefly arrived and made us part of their dominion. It's a story with much wickedness and a bloody finish, if you'd like to hear it."

"Maybe someday, when I'm a bit stronger of hearts, but I'll take your word for it. Where is this discourse leading?"

"I believe our kind is vanishing from the world."

Wistala couldn't argue with that. She'd seen few enough dragons in her life. These Firemaids were more than all she'd ever met put together.

"Perhaps. Your opinion of the surface is true enough. There aren't many dragons about."

"Dragonkind needs you. Your aid would be invaluable, if the Lavadome is to survive."

"What is the Lavadome to me?"

"Your original home, I expect."

"Whaaat?"

"It must have occurred to you that our dragonspeech is very similar."

"Perhaps, but I've not spoken with many dragons."

"I've talked with some of the dragons who formerly were under the thrall of riders. They're a slow and stupid bunch, and their speech is most odd. Half the time I must ask them to repeat what they say. I have no trouble understanding *you*. In fact, you're easier on my ears than some of the Anklenes, and I've been among them my whole life. I can't help but think we're related."

"How can that be?"

"How much do you know of your parents, your grandsires?"

"Very little. AuRon knows more, as he talked with Father about his song now and then, and Mother supplied a few details. I know my mother's mother was named Irelia."

"An Anklene name if I ever heard one. Was your mother clever?"

"Yes. I would call her clever. Father was always praising her ability with tongues."

"I suspect, Wistala, that you're from a line of one of those renegades. Some hated living much of their lives underground. Others objected to keeping thralls—they even compared it to Anklamere's enslavement of dragons, if you would believe such sophistry—and they left. There were those happy to see them go—more food for the rest of us and the voracious *griffaran*. But what I'm getting at, Wistala, is that you've come home. What are you going to do about it?"

Wistala felt as disoriented as after her crash down the well. "I—I need time to think. I've lived among hominids, so I'm used to new ideas, but this requires getting used to a new . . . a new *me*."

Ayafeeia crossed necks with her, and they stood so, feeling each other's blood pulse.

"Take your time," Ayafeeia said quietly.

Once past that break in the tunnel the Firemaids relaxed considerably. The party met with a magnificent blue with red stripes on his wings whom Ayafeeia called one of the "Aerial Host."

He bore a rider, but it was easy to see who was in charge. While Ayafeeia spoke to the dragon, the man fetched water and food for the dragon. The rider had no reins, but he did have a thick strap tethering him to the saddle. Ayafeeia later told her it was so he could turn around in the saddle to shoot his crossbow behind in flight. The riders did communicate with their dragons, through either words or leg taps, to let them know what they were doing, so a sudden turn or dive didn't "spill" their burden.

Wistala noted that the rider wore a sort of armor under his fur-trimmed cloak of blue dragonscale, the same shade as his dragon.

He flew off down the passage, evidently with a message. Imagine, flying underground! This Star Tunnel was a wonder of the world.

"What sort of men ride with the Aerial Host?" Wistala asked.

"Free thralls," Ayafeeia said. "There's talk of establishing an Uphold just for the Aerial Host so the men can raise their families among proper gardens in the sun. Though if I were the Tyr I might fear such a move."

"Why is that?" Wistala asked.

"I suspect the Uphold would prosper, and a rival might rise."

It seemed all the dragons in this empire lived in fear of another civil war. The previous one had lasted for generations, off and on, and ended only with the establishment of the First Tyr, FeHazathant. There were two short-lived ones after him, a brief domination by dragon-riders, and now Tyr RuGaard, who had inaugurated what he called the "Age of Fire."

"Our Tyr would not have us hiding in the dark. He promises a return to the surface," one of the drakka said. "When we are strong enough."

Wistala wondered. The world was an awfully big place, and it sounded as though even this empire had few dragons.

They marched on through the Star Tunnel, drakka out scouting ahead and behind. They came to another break, but this time the floor had fallen away, spanned by a single bridge.

"It's heavy enough to bear a dragon," Ayafeeia said, trotting across with wings out for balance.

The others followed in line.

"Maidmother, demen!" shouted one of the drakka who stood on watch, sniffing down into the chasm.

"Quick, across, on wing," Ayafeeia called. "Drakka who haven't crossed yet, ride! Wistala, hurry."

Hearts pounding, there was nothing to do but cross. She fixed her eyes on Ayafeeia and dragon-dashed across. She felt a thump on her left *saa* and slipped for one awful second. An iron hook rose, dragged across her fringe, but luckily didn't catch and fell off into darkness.

Wistala wondered what she would have fallen into if that hook had pulled her down.

But she finished crossing.

She hurried to the others, grouping so as to fill the Star Tunnel wall-to-wall.

"You're hurt," Ayafeeia said.

Wistala saw a gash in her *saa,* and wondered what had made it. It looked like an ax blade that left a ragged end to the wound. She was bleeding, badly. Blood coated her *saa* and was already pooling, though she'd just planted her foot.

"Tuck it tight, tight as you can. That will slow the flow," Ayafeeia advised.

The last of the drakka dashed back from the edge of the chasm. "Many hundreds, Maidmother! Coming up each side."

"We should run," a dragonelle said. "This is not good ground, too wide."

"Wistala can't run."

"Too bad for her," Takea said.

"How do we live, Firemaids?" Ayafeeia asked loudly.

"Together!" they responded.

"How do we fight?"

"Together!"

"Then how should we die?"

"Together!"

Now they could hear breathing from the darkness around the break in the tunnel. A shadowy mass of movement, like some mass of seaweed thrown up by a nighttime surf, resolved into individual shapes.

They came, limping, pairs of demen supporting each other, a larger deman dragging a smaller evidently unable to walk.

They all shared one attribute: bright, dry eyes. Wistala would never forget them, bobbing in their reflected light, hundreds of pairs of fireflies, each in its own dance.

"Drakka! Skirmish line, single length!" Ayafeeia called.

A dragonelle on the other side of the column tossed demen this way and that, stomping and swinging her tail. She saw one knocked off into darkness by a tail swipe. A wet splat sounded out of the shadow.

The drakka dashed ahead and fell into line with admirable speed, as though the only thing that mattered in their young lives was getting noses into line, the space of a fully extended tail between them.

She could hear the steps of the demen horde now, a sound walking through spur-deep leaves to faint claw-taps.

"Drakka! Loose flame!" Ayafeeia bellowed.

Orange gouts of flame struck the foremost.

"Drakka! Protect the rear. Firemaids, scale wall, three across!"

As the drakka dragon-dashed to the rear, the remaining six dragonelles dropped into a strange back-to-front set of interlocking pairs. The three biggest dragonelles plopped their backsides down, hugging ground, tails pointed toward the enemy. They swung their tails back and forth, not in unison, but at random. The backward-facing dragons watched flanks and rear, the forward-facing dragonelles held their breath as the demen surged through their burning, fallen comrades. The flames showed the approaching forms admirably.

The other three dragonelles filled the spaces, *sii* just behind the backwards-facing *saa*.

Wistala stuck close to Ayafeeia, who kept one eye on the approaching demen and the other on the dragonelle who'd reduced the flanking attack into smears of blood and twitching bodies. She breathed fire into a hole.

The demen charge broke against those swinging tails. Demen were crushed between two meeting tailswipes, or batted against the Star Tunnel's walls, or knocked head over heels before being crushed like an insect under a branch. Those few who dodged through the maze of movement, brandishing frightful-looking barbed swords and spears, met lashing *saa*-strikes that separated torso from legs or sent entire bodies flying, leaving only the spinning head to bounce off the tunnel floor like a dropped melon.

The mass piled up, just out of reach of the waving tails.

"Firemaids, loose flame!" Ayafeeia bellowed.

The tails flattened against the mass of haunches as the three dragonelles emptied their firebladders. Wistala smelled the hot, oily smell of dragonflame and the flames burst among the demen as though howling, dancing, blue-orange-yellow beasts rampaged in their ranks.

Keee, keeee came the screams from the demen, hissing like Widow Lessup's old kettle before making the morning infusion.

"What's left is running," one of the Firemaids called, spitting to cool her mouth.

"Drakka, finish them," Ayafeeia said. "Run and pounce, before they get back to their holes."

It wasn't a battle anymore, if it ever was. It was an extermination.

Wistala couldn't watch the rest.

They had to relocate, to remove themselves from the reek of blood and waste.

"It doesn't usually go that well," Ayafeeia said, as the Firemaids settled down to a meal of the vanquished. "If they'd been quicker and quieter, as demen usually are, it might have gone ill. I've been engulfed before. It seems they suddenly flood up from the floor and walls and you're in a sea of them. You're lucky to form fighting pairs."

She and a pair of drakka, returning from the fight with gore-smeared mouths and *saa*, attended to Wistala's wound. They dusted it with some kind of ground lichen and wetted the root that Wistala knew as dwarfsbeard to revive the sticky strands before laying it on and binding it with sponges.

"It's a shallow cut. They always look worse than they really are," one of the drakka said, checking the bindings. "You'll be limping for a while."

"Well, Wistala. I'd say you arrived just in time to see the last of the Demen War," Ayafeeia said. "I envy you. You can tell your hatchlings a fine story someday."

"I should think you'd have a better one," Wistala said. "You led the fight."

"She—" a Firemaid began.

"Wistala," Ayafeeia said, "the Firemaids take a most solemn oath of celibacy, so that we may be more devoted in defense to the Empire. Hatchling survivals are two to one favoring the female, so we must do much of the work of defense of those who do take mates."

One of the dragonelles licked at her torn and riven scale. "Oath or no, some recant at the first opportunity, like—"

"Enough of that," Ayafeeia said.

Wistala couldn't help but be moved at such an attitude. This green bodyguard had saved her life twice now. She'd often despaired of finding a mate—she'd once promised her father that she would avenge their family's destruction by having many hatchlings—but if she couldn't have her own, she could certainly protect those of others.

But she was also a Hypatian librarian. The title meant much to her. Would she have to renounce her Hypatian rank if she joined these sisters from the Lavadome?

"Tell me more about how one becomes a Firemaid," Wistala said.

Chapter 12

T he chief dragons of the Lavadome met in the map room.

The map room was a minor wonder. It was the design and labor of one of the Copper's predecessors as Tyr, the thrall-sniffing sybarite SiDrakkon, begun in the days when he assisted Tyr FeHazathant.

SiDrakkon took the idea from a map the Anklenes made of the Lavadome, formed in three dimensions out of the poured stone the dwarves made. He turned one of the Tyr's old hoard-rooms into a map room and had the Anklenes re-create the Upholds as though viewed from high above, mountains and rivers and forests in miniature.

The only shortcoming was that one had to be careful where one stepped, for some of the peaks proved fragile.

The Copper thought the map rather shortsighted. It encompassed only the Upholds of the Dragon Empire of long standing, from Anaea to Bant. The rest of the world did not exist unless it bordered their Empire. But then, SiDrakkon always had lacked imagination to match his ambition.

Already, thralls with artistic talent had started painting the walls with the representations of the rest of the Upper World. It didn't look quite right, but SiDrakkon's artisans had done such a lovely job with the mountains and rivers that he couldn't bear the thought of tearing them down and starting afresh.

The Copper listened to HeBellereth's chief of thralls report of matters in the southern and northwestern Upholds. The human captain could more easily step through the sculptures without obstructing the others' view.

NoSohoth had to be present to keep track of decisions and opinions and supervise decorum. HeBellereth had to be there to give his opinion; he'd just returned from a tour of the Upholds with a few snout-picked fast-winged scouts of the Aerial Host. HeBellereth wasn't the quickest of the dragons in the Lavadome but he had a good eye for weaknesses and fault and his snout-picked thralls showed the quality of refined gold. Then there was LaDibar, of course, so that Anklene opinion might be consulted. NoFhyriticus stood apart, close to the wall, his gray skin darkening so that he seemed hardly present at all. The Copper asked him to attend because of his practical mind. He would have liked Nilrasha to be present as well, but she had business with the victorious Firemaids just returned from the Star Tunnel.

Just outside the entrance a few dragons of the principal hills waited so they might have their share in the discussion.

CoTathanagar was among the outer audience, of course. He'd found his way into the map room despite the lack of an invitation, probably to cadge for an Upholder apprenticeship for one of his relations. At a *griff*-twitch to NoSohoth he'd been ejected.

Thralls worked hard at the entrance, circulating air with fans. Despite its size, the map room tended to grow stuffy very quickly if more than two dragons stood in it. SiDrakkon had always been an aloof, solitary dragon, and couldn't imagine bringing other dragons into the map room, so he'd never improved the airflow in the chamber. He liked to brood in peace.

"Ever since the Ghioz claimed all those islands to the east in the Sunstruck Sea I've feared for Komod and Tuvalea. Men and blighters of the most primitive sort live there, unchanged in their worship of dragonkind since Silverhigh, and they cry and wail of Ghioz slaveships raiding their coasts. On the Windbreak Isles the Ghioz established relations with the headhunters there—they paddle their canoes into Tuvalea and whole villages disappear. They kill the old and take the young."

"One might ask the difference between a Ghioz slave-raid and our own thrall trade," LaDibar said with a sniff.

"The tribes willingly offer up strong sons and daughters as sacrifice to the Upholders for their favor," NoSohoth said. To the Copper's mind NoSohoth had his own ways of wasting time and breath, but even patient, courtly NoSohoth tired of LaDibar making the same observations over and over again.

"Ah, yes, that old swindle," LaDibar said. "After a poor harvest the Upholder explains that he was unhappy with the quality of the last offering and sent a warning. To think of dragons resorting to such tricks in this advanced age."

"We fight for them," HeBellereth said. "Remember the great migration out of the Black Tip. The Komod and Tuvalea would have been driven from their huts and fetish-places by those . . . one hardly wants to call them blighters. Primitives, more like."

"Thralls. I'm sick of hearing of them," the Copper said. "What are a few thralls a year compared to the cattle and goats we need?"

"Not to mention the oliban," NoSohoth said.

"Especially not to mention your profitable skimming from the oliban trade," LaDibar said in the airy manner that allowed the Anklene to claim he was joking if challenged.

"Worse news," HeBellereth said. "We saw many of those Ghioz roc-riders over the Sloai Horsedowns. If the Ghioz swallow Hypatia, as seems likely, the Ku-Zuhu could be lost to us. Without Hypatia's protection they'll become just another province of the Ghioz."

HeBellereth's chief of thralls put models of condor-like birds over a depiction of gently rolling hills.

"Ku-Zuhu is not ours to begin with," LaDibar said. "It's not even an Uphold."

"But they are friendly to us, as well as the Anaeans," the Copper said. "We and the Anaeans both benefit from their cattle and grains."

"And the cloths. There are no weavers like the Ku-Zuhu. They remember patterns even the elves have forgotten."

"Textiles!" LaDibar said. "We cannot eat textiles."

"But we trade the textiles to the other Upholds, you Anklene cloudhead," one of the assembly outside the door called.

"Who said that?" LaDibar called. "I'll have your—"

"Let's not spoil the sculpture with blood," the Copper said.

"Za! I'm not about to start a duel, Tyr," LaDibar said.

"We all know that," HeBellereth grunted.

"LaDibar, I would appreciate a suggestion," the Copper said. "Where should we counter the Ghioz?"

"It is difficult to make a decision. There's not enough information."

"There's never enough information with you," HeBellereth growled. His *griff* twitched in anger.

"None of that," NoSohoth said. "More oliban on the fire, there at the entrance."

The thralls perfumed the air.

"HeBellereth, you believe the Ghioz will move against Hypatia?"

"They've massed much of their marching army at the passes on the east slopes of the Red Mountains. We couldn't risk much overflight of Ghioz itself because of the roc-riders, but there is much river traffic heading up to the Iwensi Gap, heavily laden barges full of grain. That and even more rocs in the south over the Sloai Horsedowns may mean thrust into Hypatia."

"LaDibar, these rocs, are they fast fliers, or are they more for endurance?" the Copper asked.

"They're said to be the farthest-flying creatures of the sky over a distance. *Griffaran* are said to be quicker in a fast flutter, but like dragons they tire after the first sprint."

"Perhaps Ghioz used them to spread sickness to the Anaean crops," the Copper said.

"The elves once won a victory in the Age of Wheels by sowing locusts in Old Uldam's fields," LaDibar said.

"Anaea is remote and little known," HeBellereth said, tapping the sculpture of the plateau with his tail-tip. "That plateau cuts them off from all but the strongest climbers."

"Or fliers."

"Those hag-riders certainly knew it was important to us," NoFhyriticus put in. "They attacked Anaea first."

"Perhaps some of those roc-riders are former dragon-riders," LaDibar said. "The principles of flight are the same. Same knowledge of winds and safe altitudes, same survival skills . . ."

"The Ghioz seem to be waging a subtle sort of war against us," the Copper said.

"War! That's quite an ascent from a few slave-raids," LaDibar said. Growls of agreement came from the entrance. "Just because we can imagine them poisioning our kern doesn't make it so."

"We've just had a war, a hard one, against the demen," NoSohoth said.

The room went silent. The Copper's decade-long pursuit of a final victory over the demen had wearied the Lavadome. Every hill had suffered losses.

He knew there were whispers. That he was only settling an old score against the race who had wounded him.

"It served its purpose," the Copper said, breaking the uncomfortable silence. "There'll be no more *griffaran* eggs stolen now, and we have vast new areas of the Lower World open to traffic. We can use the rivers again without fear, and the Star Tunnel could one day support many dragons."

"We are short of wholesome kern now, my Tyr," NoFhyriticus said. "You can't eat cold, dark, and damp."

"Still, we have losses to make up," NoSohoth said. "It doesn't help that we've lost promising hatchlings to the kern-sickness."

"If it was the Ghioz, the Red Queen picked the perfect time to strike," HeBellereth said. "Let the Aerial Host go to the islands, Tyr. I'll burn their slaveships and smash their pens. The winds will be blowing hard in the Sunstruck Sea, they'll affect those featherweights more than dragons."

"Perhaps they wish us to do just that," LaDibar said. "I agree, the Red Queen might know we're weak now. If we attack her she could rally all Ghioz to the fight."

"We attack her?" HeBellereth said, stomping his feet so Yellowsand Desert seemed in danger of gaining a few new canyons.

"The Ghioz mass in the Horsedowns, stir up trouble in Bant, take slaves from our Upholds, and you speak of *us* attacking *them*?"

"Don't forget the kern poisoning," the Copper said. "As though we're rats in some grotty waste-shaft."

LaDibar stiffened. "That conclusion is utterly unfounded."

"I have reports of winged birds above Anaea this summer," the Copper said.

"My Tyr's information is always very carefully chosen," LaDibar said. "It always seems to support what my Tyr wants to do. We caught one deman raiding *griffaran* eggs and suddenly every lost egg is the fault of demen. If the Drakwatch had had trials in logical leaps during your famously long stay in the training caves, your scores would have astounded the Lavadome."

"I have a scar from an egg-raid and still feel the pain in my fire-bladder when I grow angry," the Copper said. "It's started throbbing again just now, LaDibar."

"My apologies, Tyr. But nature may have put the blight on the kern. Perhaps some new parasite has found its way to Anaea. Diseased crops are nothing new. Send an Anklene mission to investigate, and we'll have an answer after observing healthy crops against sick ones for a cycle or two."

"Years, you mean. We can't do without kern for years."

"Who else grows kern?" NoFhyriticus asked. "Perhaps we can trade, somehow, through intermediaries."

"It is a staple in both Ghioz and Hypatia," LaDibar said. "Ghioz is closer."

"Brilliant," HeBellereth said, banging his forecrest against the star-painted ceiling with a *thunk*. "We'll trade dragonscale for kern with the Queen who probably poisoned it in the first place. A few score more dead hatchlings, and then shields and arrowheads made out of dragonscale in the hands of our enemies. Well done, LaDibar!"

"I gave facts. I offered no opinions as to how those facts should be acted on, you Skotl egg-sack."

"Cry settled!" the Copper snapped. "NoSohoth, remember to

ask the plasterers to repair the damages. Let's have another ladle of oliban on the fire, there! All of you, just be quiet a moment, breathe, and let me think."

The Copper circled the Upholds. For some reason, he though more clearly when he walked. After two circuits he had an answer, an unusually elegant one, if HeBellereth's assessment of the Ghioz was correct.

After all, there would be no need of kern if the dragons could return to the surface. Kern, in and of itself, wasn't necessary, except for dragons who lived long without sunlight.

But he would be laughed out of Imperial Rock if he put such an idea forward. While still in egg, every dragon of the Lavadome was taught that they had to hide from hominid assassins, concealing their strength and egg-caves deep underground.

"What would you all say to an alliance with Hypatia?" the Copper asked.

"An alliance? With a hominid power?" HeBellereth said.

"They'd never keep their word," NoFhyriticus said. "We're talking about hominid kings, not dragons. If a hominid ruler keeps a promise from one solstice to another they etch the title *faithful* on their obelisks."

"My Tyr," CoTathanagar said, poking his head in through a hedge of crest and horn. He'd polished his scale to a blue as bright as the sky for the meeting. "I have just the dragon for you for this commission. My cousin CuNiss. His Parl, perfect! And such a diplomat! He knows just when to use sweet words and just when to bite a head off."

"I hardly think biting the head off some Hypatian noble would help negotiations along," LaDibar said.

"Oh, not a king or anything, just some ventwipe or whatever wretches important hominids employ to keep their orifices clean. It has a most salubrious effect on the waste-elves of Yellowsand."

"I shall give it my deepest consideration," the Copper said, tempted to add, *The next time I'm in difficulty at the Tyr's personal waste-chute and need something ridiculous to ponder.*

But it wouldn't be to advantage to insult CoTathanagar. He had relatives in most of the Upholds and Firemaid posts in the Empire.

"Perhaps we should continue this discourse another time," the Copper said. The idea of an alliance with a great hominid power like Hypatia needed time to sink in. If he left them talking, they'd resolve on it being impractical, even dangerous.

At a wink from his Tyr, NoSohoth called the meeting closed. Little factions formed between those inside the room and outside as dragons of like mind discussed the matter.

He thought about it all through his meal, eaten alone since Nilra-sha still hadn't returned from her meeting with those Firemaids. His former mate-sister was probably telling war stories.

He went to his gallery, alerted the *griffaran,* and took wing for a few circuits of the Imperial Rock.

The flight was an easy one. He never dared be too vigorous, since he still didn't quite trust Rayg's artificial joint, though it had not failed him since it had been properly installed. Rayg had just put some new rigging in it—some animal's tendon that blighters used in their bowstrings—and it would be a shame if he—

Later he wondered if it was his bad wing that saved him. He had it slightly closed as he flew, making his other side work harder to give himself the momentum to stay aloft. His instinctive protection of the injured wing caused him, at the first sense of a presence falling from the Imperial Rock, to close the wing, forcing a quick turn-dive.

He heard the sound of teeth snapping shut just behind his head and felt a blow across the back.

A flash of red scale passed. He felt the air of the scaly missile's passage more than the wing-strike. By the time he turned his head to see what was happening, the two *griffaran* converged on a smallish dragon.

The dragon made one more attempt to fly at him, lashing hard with *sii* and flapping through the *griffaran,* but his eagerness to come to grips with the Copper left him open to the *griffaran* talons. They tore at his wings and the red tumbled broken-winged to the earth below.

He landed hard, righted himself, and searched the sky.

Long necks projected from the Imperial Rock.

The *griffaran* dove, claws out, like hawks after a running rabbit. But this prey didn't run.

"Death to the Tyr, killer of hatchlings!" he shouted.

Then he turned his snout to his shoulder and bit himself just under the *sii*.

The *griffaran* struck but he made no effort to resist; he didn't even cry out as their talons tore flesh from neck and spine.

The Copper drifted over the body. Two more *griffaran,* attracted by the war-screams of his escort, swooped down from atop Imperial Rock.

The body arched away from the ground, the tail and one *saa* stuck in the air. He'd seen stiff dead dragons before—too many—but never a dragon who'd just died like this. The dragon was very young; his skin was striped with clear extrude where his wings had emerged. Not more than a few months since he'd begun flying.

And he'd expended his life in trying to kill the Tyr.

The Copper was so shocked he could hardly stay aloft. It was one thing to have a defeated deman charge you, quite another to have a young member of your own society, without apparent quarrel, try to kill you. He found that his *sii* and his tail were shaking.

"Return to your nest, sir," Aiy-Yip, the chief of his personal guard, called. "You two, keep close! Yes! Close! No tailfeather-slacking!"

Some young drakes, probably on a Drakwatch hike, were already trotting toward the scene. He was Tyr—he shouldn't just scuttle off to his hole.

"There's been an attempt on my life," he said, passing over the drakes. "The *griffaran* guard killed the dragon responsible. I don't know who he is, but two of you watch the body and two more send for help to the neighboring hills."

*   *   *

Later he learned that the dragon's name was RuPaleth. He made a brief appearance to concerned members of the Imperial Line out in the gardens—yes, he was fine, just shocked, no, nothing was known of the motive or grievance of the villain.

NoSohoth told him what he'd learned under the eyes of six *griffaran* in the throne room.

"NoSohoth, what was all that *killer of hatchlings* insult the fool shouted?"

His chief counselor shifted his stance and looked around, as he always did when choosing words. "Why should my Tyr pay attention to the ravings of a mad dragon?"

"What hatchlings have I ever killed?"

"None, my Tyr," NoSohoth said. "Forget his words."

But the Copper couldn't forget them. He had a double helping of Tighlia's brand of wine to calm the distress. Nilrasha returned, exhausted, clearly having had a dash of a flight.

"An assassination attempt. My love! My love! Oh, what wickedness," she said, wide-eyed. She ran her head this way and that, neck against his, as though checking for a hidden, festering bite.

"Never mind. It's over."

She sniffed his breath. "Who was it?"

"A young drake from milkdrinker's hill. RuPaleth."

"RuPaleth! I knew him almost out of the egg. He was half strangled in his fight for the eggs, but he was bit and the venom took hold. Grew up stupid because of it. That old tradition of squashing venomers was a good one, I think. They should never have abandoned it."

"So he wouldn't have thought of this himself?" the Copper asked.

"As I told you, my Tyr, his brain's deformed. Don't credit his words. Shall I have the thralls bring more wine? It may help you sleep."

"Did he rave?" the Copper asked, waving away the thralls.

"He'd never raved, or his parents would have squashed him for sure," Nilrasha said.

"I ask because he said 'Death to the Tyr, killer of hatchlings,' " the Copper said.

"Idiots," Nilrasha said. "Those Anklenes—their brains are too big. All they can do is dream up trouble."

"What's that?"

"Well, Essea told me she'd been to Anklene Hill to see about a sculpture and she overheard a couple of young Anklenes gossiping, or maybe *theorizing* is the word. They were going on about how you probably poisoned the grain yourself to get the dragons stirred up and start another war now that the one with the demen is finished."

The Copper could only blink for a moment.

"Sometimes, my love, I wish I'd never been named Tyr."

"Oh, don't say that, my love. Just today I was with the Firemaids and they all—all—praised you to me. Since the victory in the Star Tunnel there's been only one attack by the demen, and that was a rout. I had it direct from a messenger who was there. Ayafeeia rescued a dragonelle captive with some sad loss, but apart from that it's been two full seasons now without so much as a drakka taken in the Lower World."

"I hope my mate-sister is well?"

The Copper knew he was setting *saa* upon drift-ice in mentioning his former mate, a delicate dragonelle who had choked to death despite Nilrasha's attempts to save her.

At least that was the story he chose to believe.

"She sent her respects."

"Wait—you said the demen had one of our Firemaids held captive? I don't remember being told about that."

"That's because she wasn't a Firemaid. She's some dragon out of the wild. She'd been injured in a fall and the demen took her captive."

"A strange dragon? The Anklenes will probably want to talk to her. They always ask questions of anyone who travels in the Upper World. I'll send them a message."

"What shall we do with her?"

"Do with her?" the Copper asked. "Is she some criminal or exile?"

"No, or you would have heard of it from someone other than your mate chatting about her business."

"Offer her hospitality and show her the best exit to return to her mate or wherever."

"Unmated. She has friends in Hypatia, it seems. Ayafeeia has some idea of convincing her to become a Firemaid."

The Copper forgot the unfortunate business of the attack. This dragon had friends in Hypatia?

His adoptive grandfather had always said that he'd been born lucky.

"Hypatia?" the Copper asked.

"Yes, you know, the old—"

"I know where Hypatia is. Strange, we were just speaking of it this morning. My love, I've changed my mind. Please ask Ayafeeia to do whatever she can to get this stranger to take up residence here, even if she might not become a Firemaid."

"She may just wish to return to her home."

"Maybe we can mate her off to one of the dragons here," the Copper said. "In any case, visit her when she arrives. If she seems a dragonelle of wit and initiative, and her knowledge of the Upper World profound, hint that the Lavadome may have a high position for her."

"Certainly, my love."

"I may just adopt her into the Imperial Line, since we've had no luck with hatchlings."

Nilrasha dipped her nose.

The Copper shifted and put his tail around hers. "One disappointment just makes the rest of my fortune all the sweeter. No life is perfect."

"Can we trust a stranger, my Tyr?" NoSohoth asked. "If you're thinking that she might serve as an advisor on the surface, I would like to know her better before coming to trust her."

"I hope she proves trustworthy. She may lead us back to the surface."

Chapter 13

AuRon cursed the map he'd been given. The farther he traveled from Ghioz the worse it became. It was clearly the work of a cartographer with poor sense of direction and worse sense of scale. He found landmarks that were supposed to be on the east side of a mountain on the west side, rivers flowing the wrong way, and meadows flourishing where snowcaps were supposed to reside.

He would have blamed it on a careless hominid with a taste for wine with his work, save that some of the landmarks made sense only when viewed from the air, like a lake shaped like a dragon's *sii* or a mountain crevice with stunted brush growing in the sheltered crack. Had a dragon advised them, or some roc-rider with altitude-frost fogging his brain?

The map had a mark in the corner, a little design that resembled a cloverleaf with some scrawls within. AuRon decided that when he claimed his reward, he would ask which titleor was responsible for her surveys and pay him a visit. The dwarves of the Chartered Company would never have allowed such sloppy mapwork.

On one of his backtracks over the mountain forests to the south—rugged, tree-filled canyons pierced by needles of stone—a waterfall in three steps was simply not to be found. While searching for it he marked a line of those roc-riders, flying in a V-formation like migrating geese. AuRon counted nine.

Perhaps the fliers knew where the waterfall could be found.

He turned and flew hard to catch up to them. Low clouds dotted the sky and the riders wove in and out of them.

AuRon flew closer and saw that the birds held bodies in their claws—they looked like cow carcasses, but something was wrong with the shapes, both stunted and bloated.

They flew with purpose. The map, erroneous as it was, indicated that he was flying somewhere over the slopes of the Hypatian side of the Red Mountains.

He slowed, wondering if he should interfere. They might even attack him.

They altered course, dipping and rising, changing directions but keeping northward along what was some of the most difficult-looking ground AuRon had ever seen—steep slopes, tight canyons, woods thick as wolf's fur.

The lead flier dipped. They turned a slow circle. They must see him now! But they gave no sign of it. One more circle and they dove.

They folded their wings, falling, in succession, releasing the carcasses exactly where the leader had. The burdens spun as they fell. Again AuRon could think only of small cattle or sheepskins, tied off and filled to bulging with water.

He saw them burst when they hit, splattering flame in all directions. Flame that burned momentarily with a fierce greenish light before fading to a more usual orange and yellow as it caught or died, depending on the character of the surface it landed upon.

AuRon could not tell that this pocket of forest was much different than any other patch. The trees were perhaps a little thinner.

The fliers rose back into the clouds, and smoke pulsed from the forest.

Auron landed on one of the pillar-like needles, among bracken clawing for a hold in the wind, wanting a look at what might be worth such an effort of wing and oil.

He slipped across a sheer cliff-face, creeping, creeping, skin a perfect match for the pinkish granite, careful not to dislodge too many pebbles. He looked down into the canyon.

There were men down there, running with lines of horses, taking them away from the fire. He saw some women dragging or carrying children, and men rolling barrels or dragging sacks four at a time.

He looked carefully and saw shelters made of pulled-down fir limbs, with more branches laced within, forming crude shelters. Firepits, log bridges making paths through the woods, rope strung here and there with clothing and fabric drying on it—there were men settled in these woods.

Even at this distance, something looked familiar about one of the men, walking to and fro, gesturing.

"Naf," AuRon bellowed, but the wind took his words.

"NAF!"

They heard some of the noise he made.

Bowmen raised their weapons—no arrow could travel to his perch, but Naf had them lower their bows. Naf began to wave his arm, gesturing for AuRon to come down.

He had to do some intricate flying in the narrows between the sheer sides of the needle-rocks in two careful dives back and forth.

He landed in what he guessed to be an armed camp.

There was an awful sulfur-and-oil smell in the air, the residue of the fire-skins dropped by the roc-riders.

The fires, with dirt being heaped on them right and left, were being put out. AuRon smelled burned flesh and traced the odor to heaps of branches covering what must be bodies.

There he was, old Naf, smiling in that gap-toothed way of his, everything in his scarred face vaguely askew, as though it had been dropped and put back together again. His hair and close-trimmed beard were well flecked with gray, a gray that sometimes verged on white. Quite a change in the brief span of years since they'd last met.

His men looked half-animal, as men tended to look when long outdoors—shaggy, dirty and wolf-lean. Their tattered clothes were bound up with bits of leather cord, layers of rags thick about their legs and torsos. But all had well-kept weapons, sharp and bright with oil.

Naf embraced him, managing to put both arms around his neck. A few of the men pointed at his skin or claws and muttered.

"AuRon! I do believe you've grown. But what on earth happened to your tail? It's quite a runt."

"A long story, Naf."

"My men are suspicious. They've had nothing good from dragons of late." He turned and picked one out. "Ho! Dominof, remember AuRon, who visited the Silver Guard in the pass? He has returned."

"Aye. Right on the heels of those blasted birds. Strange timing."

"I would never have seen you if it wasn't for those birds," AuRon said.

"Tell me—I know nothing of those giant carrion hunters. Are they as intelligent as dragons? How do they keep finding us? Each time we shift camp, they find us again within six-day."

"I do not know those birds, but they strike me as no smarter than ordinary birds. I've never talked with one."

"What are you doing in these hills?"

"I was on my way south and became confused. I saw those riders and thought they could put me on the proper course."

"Those riders are from our old friends in Ghioz."

"The Queen. Yes, I've seen them over her capital."

Naf lowered his eyes. "I don't envy you the sights."

"They call you Naf the Dome-burner."

"I didn't start out as one. Far from it. I was as loyal to the Queen as any Ghioz-born subject. No, all the disloyalty came from her, old friend."

"How do you mean?"

Naf sat down and rubbed his thighs. "Oh, a battle started up with one of the Hypatian thanes. A fellow named Capoedia. There were so many refugees from the dragonraids piling up on his lands—Ghioz wasn't letting any more through the passes, you see—that he sent his men against the pass guardians and won, at least long enough to get those wretches off his lands. That kind of thing had to be answered, of course, and answered hard, so I led my men in a raid on Thane Capoedia. I'd learned a good bit about moving through woods and such quietly when I rode with the Red Guard on the eastern borders of Ghioz in those timberlands. So we took him by surprise and won soundly.

"The Queen rewarded me with the title 'governor of the Dairuss.' Well, if there ever was a worse governor than me, I'd like to meet and strike hands. I cut a fine figure."

AuRon wondered why more humans didn't use masks in the manner of the Queen. They made it so much clearer. Hominids didn't always speak their minds fully and expected others to follow them in expression and gesture, which could be as misleading as a dog's tail, which often wagged even as the other end snarled.

"The Queen said Hieba and my daughter must come and grow up at her court and attend the schools in Ghioz, the best in the world, so that she could follow in my place with better mind than I ever could hope to have, and like the saddle-tramp who's had some luck with his bow and spear I am, I thankfully accepted."

"You're no fool, Naf."

"Needless to say, I did not squeeze and bleed my people as thoroughly as she would have liked. I've seen too many hangings in my life, for in Ghioz crimes of property and crimes of blood are held equal, and I commuted the sentences of small thieves of property to terms building roads or digging drainage ditches. I freed families who'd lost their fathers in Ghioz's battles from taxation, thinking blood more precious than gold, and held court under those famous domes as I thought it was supposed to be held, with all free to speak and seek justice from their ruler without fear that their words would be turned against them."

"I think many would like such a poor ruler as Naf," AuRon said, wondering how Naf would deal with dragons who stuffed themselves with entire herds of sheep.

"I suppose I was warned. The Queen visited me, her mask turning from smiles to frowns, more frequently to frowns as the questioning progressed, and told me Dairuss was no longer the jewel of her provinces but a rather shoddy bit of brass. In desperation I hired some dwarves to open old mines in the mountains, but only succeeded in emptying my treasury still further, for the mines failed.

"Of course the Queen replaced me. She sent me a message saying she'd grown very fond of my daughter and the company of Hieba and would, with great liberality on her part, see to it that both were comfortable and Nissa was educated in the manner she'd promised, perhaps to one day rule and do a better job than her father. Oh, AuRon . . . the Queen's counselor who brought that message said that I must do all I could to help the new governor, the awful Hischhein, succeed. Hischhein sneered, a little, as he surveyed the governor's house and took inventory of the cookpots and lamps."

Naf looked off to the northwest, as though he could see through mountains. "Were that all he wanted was a fine house with a commanding view! Hischhein immediately grabbed my people by throat and hair and shook them so hard that he might profit by dropped boots, coats, and shirts. And to think I'd once counted him as a friend!

"My people didn't stand for it, and started murdering Hischhein's tax collectors and townheelers. It was they who started burning the domes of Ghioz, and did it in my name. They rampaged through the streets of even the capital, pouring out of their quarters like a mudslide, and burned the dome there, and then I knew the life of my wife and child would be forfeit. Was my governorship just a year ago? No, a little more. The messenger came in the spring, just as soon as the roads cleared.

"I did know how to fight. That's one lesson life has taught me, and taught me well. I organized such elements of my old Red and Silver Guard as loved Dairuss more than their quarterly pay and we fought, for one glorious summer. But what could Dairuss do against the might of Ghioz? Those torch-wielding mobs, chanting my name as they burned the dome, what did they know of the resources of a whole Empire, which would shortly be flung over them as you might snuff out a fire under a wet blanket?

"I was not ignorant of the situation. I tried to call for help from the Hypatians. The Hypatians must know of the Queen's designs against them. Has she not built a web of allies all around their lands, from the Ironriders in the north to the Usuthu in the south? Dairuss had many advantages: a people already opposed to the Ghioz, a choice of passes they could use to throw forces against the flanks of any Ghioz moving up from the south, control of the mightiest of rivers, friendly terms with the dwarves and their Iron Road, giving them a clear path into the heart of the Ghioz Empire for their legendary Indomitables. But my pleas met with words rather than swords, diplomats instead of arrows. They sent a general of theirs, a learned elvish fellow named Sandwash and a dwarf engineer named Ermet, but they seemed more interested in observing Ghioz destroy my poor people than offering assistance.

"I'll never forget the sight of the Ghioz armies, advancing in three columns, glittering golden serpents. That's the Ghioz for you, an army of gold, the only god they worship, the only truth they recognize. While I tried to slow them, for I couldn't hope to win a victory, the Ironriders struck in the rear. I'm told, and this is the one grim joy I take from the debacle to my people, that the Ironriders accidentally quartered Hischhein when he came out of hiding and presented himself to them as the Queen's governor. I suspect the Ironriders saw their chance for a bit of sport and took it.

"Now my people are worse off than before I governed them. The old Ghioz governor who stood in place before me is returned, and his punishments seem light, I suppose, after the destruction the Ironriders loosed.

"But for all the catastrophes, all my mistakes, I still have, each week, two or three sons of Dairuss appear in this camp, even if their shoes have fallen to ribbons while crossing the mountains and their horses are gaunt as scarecrows. They call me King Naf in the Mountains and speak of this bandit-camp as a freeman's hold. Ha! Oh, the world is a joke, AuRon! Life is a joke."

Naf laughed, no longer the hearty and controlled racket of the booming, friendly sound AuRon had known as a drake but a sound that made him think of a goose noisily dying.

"So, what brings you south? Seeking an old friend, or did you try to claim your title, promised long ago?"

"I'm on a mission of diplomacy for the Red Queen."

"You've found your sense of humor at last, I see."

AuRon blinked. "No, friend, I am serious."

"If she seeks my surrender—"

"Your name hardly came up in our converse. She sends me as ambassador to some dragons living in a great cave south of here. If her information is as faulty as her map, I expect I'll find a score of dragons huddling cold in a mushroom-cave, eating their own eggs."

"Interesting. That necklace, then, is hers? The chain looks like Ghioz artistry, though it's not the Queen's braiding on the chain, as you'd expect of a royal emissary."

"She did give it to me. I wonder about this crystal, though. It reminds me of something."

"Odd cut to it. You might find it convenient for scraping out your earhole."

"So you've never seen anything like it, though you were once high among the Ghioz?"

"No. I suppose fashions come and go. Perhaps white crystal is the new ruby. There was a time when rubies were all the rage among the Ghioz."

"Did the rubies—did the Ghioz jewelers know how to put light into their gems? This glows even in utter darkness. Faintly, but it does glow. I've known only one other stone that held such clear white light, a massive crystal NooMoahk kept in his library."

"That must have brought some titleor a hefty bounty. There's many a rich Ghioz dowager who'd see her brow glamoured by a stone that shines with its own light. Happy was the captain who found that!"

AuRon wondered how much of the burden DharSii carried was paid for with the crystal. Of course it couldn't be all gold, not even a dragon could fly with such a burden. Had he taken a piece of it for himself?

Or perhaps only a few tiny fragments had been shaved off, such as he wore. Was there some power in the crystal he didn't know? Why hadn't NooMoahk warned him? Even his failing mind had its lucid spells, and so important a subject would have come up.

"I wonder, Naf, if the stone wasn't the whole purpose of the raid, the war with the blighters there trumped up."

"Perhaps. You know, AuRon, I think you should carry out this commission for the Queen. A suspicious mind like yours might go far."

"As far from the Red Queen as my wings will carry me, once I have my gold. I shall have the dwarves of the Chartered Company account it for me so I may portion it out yearly."

Naf went all still. AuRon seemed to recall that he would always quiet his body when he became serious and thoughtful. "Will you return to the capital to collect?"

"Yes. To that mountain-face they work upon."

"I have another reason—no, *reason* is the wrong word. Hope. I have another hope, AuRon. It is that Hieba and Nissa still live. I must think and act as though they are dead, but Hieba and you were close. Let my hope live in your heart. Return to the Queen, your message delivered, and see if you can have news of her. It would be the most natural thing for you to ask. She knows that you and I spoke, about the threat of those dragon-riders, and Hieba was present when we did so."

"I will see what I can find out," AuRon said.

"Do not be afraid to return with bad news. It is better to know, I think. If I knew, I could cease thinking about it, or know exactly how to think about it. We shall look for you, and signal. A dragon with a stunted tail is easy to mark as he passes overhead. Look for us at dawn and dusk, so that we might signal you with fire if we are concealed. Two equal lines of flame meeting, vertical and horizontal, a dwarf-cross."

He looked so miserable that AuRon would have promised him anything to bring the usual gap-toothed grin back. "Very well. Perhaps you can help me with this Ghioz map. There's a waterfall I don't seem to be able to find . . ."

With Naf's advice AuRon set a better course and found the waterfall. From there he flew out of the mountains and into some high, dry plains inhabited by hominids—men, by the look of them, sun-dark and bronze-adorned. Though the cattle looked tempting, he avoided them and instead devoted himself to hunting the tiny jumping deer that lived in thornbrush between high outcroppings of rock that held fat, and tasty, rats.

He found a divided rockpile with a great sloping slab hung suspended between the two, thick with marks of men or blighters. While the iconography struck him as unique and interesting, he was nearing his destination and had no time for a lingering appraisal.

He hurried south into land that looked like it had once been sea-bottom. The ground was foul and salty and held only patches of desperate-looking green vegetation like stringy cactus that existed only to make white desert butterflies happy in its hanging blossoms.

Soon he found the great canyon at the bottom of his map. There could be no mistaking what must have once been a great watercourse but now was just a series of dry mudholes flaked like burned skin. He found some toads buried deep in the mud, but they were sour and dry and not worth the digging.

The canyon plunged into the earth, first in a series of breaks and then at last into darkness. He flew more cautiously here, wondering how such a land could ever support dragons, with the nearest edibles a long day's dry flight away, and not much even at that.

His eyes adjusted to the dark and he flew at a pace he could almost match on the ground, wary, wondering what kind of reception he might meet.

And so he came to the bridge.

Of course he wondered what dragons would need with a bridge. The sides of the canyon were striped with holds that even a young hatchling might use as a hominid used a ladder.

It was a superior piece of craft as he understood such things, looking almost as fine as a dwarf-built in his estimation. It passed from rock-column to rock-column, joining two bits of tunnel, fixed here to cavern roof, there to a column, and in another place held up by arcs of metal and twisted cable.

"Land, stranger," a dragonelle's voice called from the center of the span. AuRon marked sort of a mini-cave in the cavern ceiling. She would have an easy time pouring her flame on him if she chose.

A drakka emerged from the east end of the bridge and opened her *sii* in an odd gesture. AuRon guessed it meant they wanted him to land there.

So he did. Two drakka and a dragonelle stared at him from a wide, well-dug tunnel.

"Do not even you know him, Angalia?" one of the drakka asked the dragonelle.

She blinked. "There is grit in my eyes, I cannot be sure. Oh, I am ill. This bridge and these dry holes will be the death of me."

"For a moment, by the skin, I thought he was one of those awful monster-bats, but he's dragon-sized," the one in the cavern roof-hole called. "Who is he? Is there a gray in the Aerial Host?"

"I've not seen one, but I've been long away from the Lavadome," the one AuRon thought to be Angalia said. "It seems I'm always indispensable in some unhealthy clime."

The drakka eyed each other. The look they exchanged reminded him of Jizara and Wistala sharing a private joke at his expense. His hearts ached at the memory.

AuRon spoke his long-rehearsed speech, not really knowing the manners of the dragons here, so he fell back on old phraseology that he'd at times heard from NooMoahk. "My name is AuRon son of AuRel. I come from Ghioz, bearing a message in friendship from the Queen. If you could arrange for me to reach your Lavadome so that I may deliver her words, I will hereafter call you friend."

The dragonelles blinked at him, frozen, reminding him of nothing so much as startled monkeys he'd seen when he'd been a wingless hunter stalking the jungle south of Uldam.

"Some friend," one of the drakka muttered. "A travel-thinned gray with a stumpy tail who talks like a drunk Wyrr. The Red Queen can keep him."

Chapter 14

Wistala's introduction to the Lavadome left her thrilled yet mazed, speechless despite words of admiration at its beauties fighting to get out.

After the tall cavern of the river ring, *griffaran* were wheeling in and out of shafts of light from cracks in the surface as cold waters carried their secrets beneath. They swam across, hearts pounding in the cold, the pain half exquisite. She climbed out of the water feeling more alive than she ever had before in her life.

Ayafeeia, three dragonelles, and three drakka accompanied her from the other end of the Star Tunnel and through a maze of twists, turns, and ancient chambers.

She thought she'd seen beauty enough to remember in the bright colors of the far-off *griffaran*.

Then they passed through another tunnel on the other side of the ring and entered the Lavadome.

After, she sensed that the others had been watching her to see her reaction.

The space seemed an impossibility, like a sea rolling above clouds rather than below, or a mountain hanging from the sky instead of growing from the earth. It was a separate world deep underground, vast beyond imagining and lit by the earth's hot blood. At first she thought it an optical illusion, a strange effect like some of the murals she'd seen in the Hypatian libraries, or a garden-pool she'd seen near a seaside palace that visually met the ocean with many dragonlengths of sand and coral between the palace and the Inland Ocean.

Brighter than all the lava, a glowing orb topped the Lavadome, bathing a tall, squared-off rock Ayafeeia identified as the Imperial Rock, the residence of the Tyr and his family.

They ate a meal, food fetched by the youngest of the Firemaidens, immature females who, according to Ayafeeia, sometimes passed into the Firemaids.

Then they walked, walked until the light faded from the top of the dome, and they still hadn't crossed to the other side of the Lavadome. Ayafeeia brought her to a depression in the ground with several caves in its walls and floor.

"Odd that a sink should be called a 'hill,' but this place is called Halfhollow Hill."

The soil here was looser than elsewhere in the Lavadome. Wistala slid as she descended and had to brace herself with her tail.

"This is sacred ground to the Firemaids, Wistala. Here the First Score set tails-a-ring and promised to act for the defense of others' hatchlings."

"Why, could the mothers not defend their own?"

"Oh, it was a terrible time, during the war. Wyrr against Anklene against Skotl. Groups of dragons were seeking out egg-caves and smashing eggs, killing hatchlings, trying to break the will of the opposing clan or swap murder for murder.

"The First Score were all unmated females, from all three clans. The civil war was at its height. They swore to forsake their clans, guard any eggs or hatchlings brought into their protection, to remain neutral in the war.

"Mated pairs of dragons came from all corners of the Lavadome bearing an egg or two in their mouths. Many eggs were abandoned to the egg-smashers. Some were lost on the way.

"When Skotl came looking for Wyrr eggs they fought them as one, together. When Wyrr came looking for Skotl hatchlings they fought them as one, together. Only three of the First Score knew the key to their arrangement, and of them each knew only a part, so that pain could not reveal all."

In her imagination, Wistala could see the dragons running for the caves with eggs in their mouths. Dragons fighting dragons above— that she hardly needed imagination to picture. Her own memories supplied the details.

"Ever since, the Firemaids have lived to protect eggs not their own. We guard far-off holes and the hills of our siblings. We prowl unlit tunnels and stand guard in the burning sun at the Uphold entrances."

From her earliest dreams in the egg Wistala had thought herself a protector of her kind. Here stood a sister in spirit if not in body.

"How many dragons are in the Lavadome?" Wistala asked.

"A score of scores counted six, and another score of scores in the Upholds," Ayafeeia said.

Wistala had never imagined that so many dragons could live in one place. But she'd seen the pens and cattle that supported the dragons, the scruffy hominids toiling in the dark, spreading manure in mushroom fields and then grinding the grown mushrooms into chunks of feed for themselves and the cattle.

"The first great Tyr, FeHazathant," Ayafeeia continued, "he and his mate established traditions for the Firemaids, and set up the Drak-watch in imitation of the Firemaids. The idea was that Wyrr, Skotl, and Anklene would serve together and never come to blows again. The Firemaids and Drakwatch conduct skirmishes against each other. Many a mating has had its start in a good tussle against the drakes.

"But this space is important in one other respect. Firemaidens take their first oath here. As they pass into adulthood some take the second oath and are trusted to hold a position. Then there are those who take the third oath, to remain unmated, or rather to mate with all dragonkind and defend it as our own."

Wistala realized that she'd already made the decision when she heard the story of the First Score. Perhaps she'd found the meaning of her first memory, a hatchling dream in egg of flying above others, protecting.

Now she just had to find the courage to give voice to feeling and put it into words.

"May I . . . may I take the first oath? I would very much like to repay the debt I owe to the Lavadome. You did save my life—more than once."

"I'd be delighted to exchange the words with you, Wistala," Ay-afeeia said.

"How—" Takea squealed.

"She's a female dragon," Ayafeeia said. "That's enough, that's always been enough."

"But how can she ever be trained, if she didn't pass through the rigors?"

"She looks like she's seen rigors enough," Ayafeeia said. "You have no idea, drakka, of the dangers of the Upper World."

Wistala smiled. The other dragons looked at her as though she'd just vented herself, and she stopped. She'd been too long among hominids. "Oh, the Upper World has its hazards, but there are many fine things to see. It is rich in variety."

"Rich in everything but dragons," Ayafeeia said. "Dragons are hunted even into their egg-caves, like one long war."

Wistala didn't know what to say that wouldn't be a lie. It was possible to coexist with the hominids. She'd proved that. She'd even met a dwarf or two she'd liked in the halls of the Wheel of Fire, though they'd have her head if she ever returned.

"Takea, you will prompt her with the words. You've won the honor."

Takea's *griff* dropped and rattled. "Maidmother! It's an honor I'd as soon—"

Ayafeeia raised high her head. "Still that racket. You've won more honors than any other drakka present. It's your place."

The youngster shrank against the stares of the older dragonelles. "Yes, Maidmother."

Ayafeeia pointed with her tail-tip to the gritty bottommost part of the hollow. "Wistala, you stand where your mothers and sisters stood before you."

Wistala took her place and looked up at Ayafeeia and the other Firemaids.

"Wistala, if any part of this oath gives you doubt or pause, you may stop at any time. There is no shame or danger in not speaking the oath, only in not keeping it once spoken. Do you understand?"

"Yes."

Takea fell into place next to her.

"How do you come to this place?"

A long pause. Ayafeeia glared at Takea.

"A maiden female, leaving family, clan, and line, of my own free will and with clear mind," Takea prompted.

Wistala repeated the words.

"Why do you come to this place?" Ayafeeia asked. "Takea!"

"To join with my sisters in protecting our future," Takea said, tail twitching petulantly.

"To join with my sisters—" Wistala repeated the rest.

"Will you give up duty to family, clan, and cave for the greater duty of protecting all dragonkind?"

"Yes, I will," Takea said.

Wistala had a moment's doubt. Should she stop the oath? She was a librarian of Hypatia, after all. But librarians held other posts, some were priestesses, some attended thanes as advisors—the librarians would probably appreciate an account of the Lavadome.

"Yes, I will," Wistala repeated.

"Will you obey the orders of superior, maidmother, and Tyr?"

"Yes, I will," Takea whispered.

"Yes, I will."

"Will you brave want, pain, injury, and death in obedience to those orders and defense of this oath?"

"Same, again," Takea said.

"Yes, I will," Wistala said, after a moment's confusion of almost letting *same, again* pass her snout.

"Takea, one more trick and I'll put you on the southernmost rock as a watchkeeper," Ayafeeia said.

Takea hung her head, but Wistala heard *griff* rattle.

"Then come and meet your sisters and call me maidmother."

"Yes, maidmother," Takea prompted.

"Yes, maidmother."

"Welcome back to the Lavadome, our long-lost sister," Ayafeeia said.

Wistala's life had seen its share of happy moments, but this felt truer than most. Perhaps she'd been born for this and all her life had been training for this moment. Her hearts pounded with excitement.

"She's blushing like you're a dragon who's sung his song to her," one of the dragonelles said, twisting her head to and fro in amusement like a dog drying its ears.

The sisters embraced.

"I'm so happy," Ayafeeia said. "I don't know why, but I'm truly happy."

"What are my first orders, maidmother?" Wistala asked.

"We're going to have a first-oath feast. Your orders are to stuff yourself cross-eyed, Wistala."

"My family mostly called me Tala."

"Then Tala you shall be to us," Ayafeeia said.

Ayafeeia gave orders to some thralls in—almost—spotless white smocks regarding food.

She put Takea in charge of correcting Wistala's behavior, a duty that somewhat mollified Takea's dislike and cutting remarks. Able to devote herself to criticizing Wistala's bows, or wording, or tone, or knowledge evidently removed the incentive to treat her as a curse dropped into the Lower World to vex dragonkind, or at least Takea.

"Silly! Keep your eyes open as you bow. What if a blow were to come during an exchange of formalities? Even enemies will bow to each other," was a sample of the chatter, which tended to bend round back to where it began, like a dragon with a solid bite into her own tail.

The Firemaids and Firemaidens—the taxonomy was a little confusing to Wistala; it seemed that all wingless drakka were Firemaidens while some winged dragonelles who had no intention of taking further oaths were called Firemaidens and others were called Firemaids—she suspected it depended on whether a dragon seemed likely to sing his song in the near future—and all dragonelles who had taken their three oaths were titled Firemaids, with the ones no longer expected to do duty far from the Lavadome given ranks such as "advisor" or "superior" or "of distinguished merit," depending on overall health and ability.

She met one cave-bound dragonelle "of distinguished merit," an aged thing with scales gone unhealthy and almost yellow, with a great chunk of her head caved in and scarred over. She babbled about flowers and stars for the few uncomfortable moments Wistala spent in her presence.

"Dwarvish ax," Takea whispered. "Saka will be your first duty, cleaning her tailvent and reminding her to eat and making sure she raises her head to swallow."

"A lesson to always smell and listen first before putting your head into a hole," the Firemaid who attended several of the "distinguished merits" explained.

"Wouldn't it be kinder to just let her starve, if she won't eat?" Wistala said.

"Oh, she has a few good days every year. You hear some fine stories. Besides, bones from older dragons are worth more in trade. The alchemists claim they can age a dragon by the color of a cross section."

"You sell her body after she's died?"

"Just bits," Takea said. "It's an honor. You serve the Empire even after death. Your bones can purchase gold coin or whole herds of veal for hatchlings."

Takea watched her for a moment. "Don't be afraid to accept the harsher realities of life. Embrace them. We never die, in a manner. As long as there are new drakka taking the same oaths we did, we've helped that part of us live on."

They feasted, well and long. Wistala had never had such a banquet. Organmeats in rich sauce and quarter-sheep and great flanks of beef and glazed chickens lined up on a skewer ready for swallowing. She'd eaten well before, but it was always hominid food, overloaded with tasteless, juiceless vegetables that bloated one with gas and glazed fruits that made her throat close up and her eyes wince.

They talked of battles against the demen and hunting aboveground, and she heard the story of how the Tyr destroyed a Ghioz fortress by having rocks dropped on it by the Aerial Host. Ayafeeia corrected the stories on only one point, saying that the Tyr, though present, had only inspired the rock-dropping. The actual management of it belonged to an exiled dragon, a white named NiVom.

"He would have been Tyr, I think, but he was driven out," Ayafeeia said.

The bloodcurdling stories reminded Wistala of Rainfall's tales of when Hypatia was ruled by "barbarian kings."

Was this Tyr, whom all seemed to respect and admire, nothing more than a "barbarian king," climbing to his throne-shelf over bloodied heads of rivals?

"Ha!" Ayafeeia told her, when she asked the question, phrasing it more politely. "Our Tyr is many things, but he's no duelist, for all that he killed the Dragonblade. No, he was a compromise. As he came from no clan, he had fewer enemies who'd swear to die before they saw him in the throne room."

"His mate, however," Takea said.

"Hush. I believe Nilrasha herself comes."

Wistala was taught not to crane her neck to watch the Queen approach, but to turn into a respectful recline, facing the Queen, ready to do her bidding.

"What do I say to her?" Wistala asked.

"As little as possible," Takea said. "It's deeds that count, not words."

The Queen approached.

From a distance she seemed a fine-looking dragonelle. Wistala was improving in her judgment of the various clans. It seemed she had a bit of Anklene about the eyes—how like Mother!—and strong, thick *saa* bulging with muscle. Wistala guessed she must be a great leaper. She envied her long, graceful tail and elegantly formed forelimbs. Wistala thought hers oxlike in comparison.

She'd heard a story that the blighters called her "Ora"—her entire band of Firemaidens had died in an attack on a Ghioz city. She was the only survivor, the Ora—the one spared from slaughter at a great feast, by blighter custom.

Closer, her looks were marred somewhat by scars.

"She's seen her share of battles," Wistala observed.

"The Tyr has a scarred face as well," Takea whispered. "The scars look less strange when you see them together."

Nilrasha accepted her bows and crossed necks with Ayafeeia. Nilrasha asked a few polite niceties about the quality of the pig, sheep, and cow from the Imperial Herd that she'd sent to the banquet and received thanks and compliments in return.

"Maidmother, I understand you have news for me," Nilrasha said.

"I have an account of the completion of the war against the demen in the area of the Star Tunnel," Ayafeeia said, her voice flat, as though she were suddenly a stranger to Drakine. "Further, we have one new recruit, a stranger to the Lavadome named Wistala."

"Which is she, the one next to, errr—Takea?"

"Yes, my Queen." Ayafeeia touched Wistala with an extended wingtip. Wistala thought it a protective, motherly gesture and warmed.

Nilrasha's eyes widened for a moment and she swiveled her head on her neck to view Wistala from different angles.

"The shape of her snout. Good teeth and healthy gums, no mash of kern and onions for her. I would almost think—I see she has an injured wing."

"It is healing and will be sound again, I expect. We almost lost her a second time during Paskinix's escape. Young Takea here had captured Paskinix as he was about to kill Wistala, but he slipped away during our concern for Wistala as we climbed into the Star Tunnel."

"Bad luck, Takea," Nilrasha said. "The Tyr would have liked to see that egg-stealer brought to him in chains. But all know how slippery the old deman is. I shall be sure to mention it to my mate."

"Thank you, my Queen," Takea said, bowing—though she kept her eyes open.

Nilrasha stiffened a little. Wistala decided some slight had been offered.

Ayafeeia intervened, bowing with eyes closed. "My Queen, Wistala has just taken her first oath, so we all meet at feast. Will you join us?"

"Thank you for your kindness, sister, but a hard-flying courier bat has just come in." She pointed to a nick of blood at her shoulder. "He tells me there is an emissary on the way and we are to gather to hear what he has to say. Such talk! It has been years since the Imperial Rock has seen such a rustling. And the visitor! The arrogance, the presumption . . ."

Wistala thought the Queen was struggling with her firebladder. "But social gossip doesn't concern our brave Firemaids. I came to deliver my mate's word. Consider it a summoning. The Tyr would like to see this new Firemaiden and hear her account of matters in the Upper World."

Wistala felt the tingle of the gazes upon her such that it made her scales ripple. "I—I thank you for the opportunity to obey, my Queen," Wistala said.

"Don't let me stop you from enjoying your feast. You look as though you could use it. Ayafeeia, see that a body-thrall with sharp snippers and fresh file attends to her. Her scales are running quite wild."

"Yes, my Queen."

The Queen drew Ayafeeia away and said a few more words, quietly. They crossed necks again.

"Such an insult," an old Firemaid said, interrupting Wistala's concentration. "Send a renegade with a demand. We'll give her war, if she wants it."

"I expect she does want it," Ayafeeia said, leaving Nilrasha.

Behind her, the Queen touched nose-tip with a very young drakka standing sore-footed at the end of the line as she departed. A dragonelle at the opposite end said something quiet about *on the climb since she lost her hatchling teeth in milkdrinker's hill.*

Eyes narrowed in thought, Ayafeeia watched the Queen take off. "The losses from the dragon-riders are still within this generation. We've just completed a hard war with the demen. She knows we are weak."

Wistala had heard much talk of battles with the Ghioz. "How does she know? Spies?"

"Quite possibly," Ayafeeia said. "There are dragons who weigh gold above blood."

"A curse on such dragons," Takea said, looking directly at Wistala. "If I learned of one, I'd not rest until I saw her head left dry atop some mountain."

Wistala began to believe she'd dropped into a whirlwind: suspicions, jealousies, politics, worries of civil war, war in the Lower World, worries of war with the surface. Still, dragons did thrive on challenge, Father always said. *Dragon eat challenge and vent victory. It was surfeit that beat you.*

"May I ask a question?" Wistala asked.

"Of course," Ayafeeia said. "That's the beginning of wisdom."

"Why did she call you 'maidmother' at some times and 'sister' at others?"

"We are sisters after a fashion, though one presses the issue in this case. Her mate was married to my sister."

"I still say she did it," someone said quietly.

"None of that, now," Ayafeeia said. "I won't have the Queen disparaged, either in my hearing or out of it."

"When all is said and done, she broke her oath," one of the Firemaids said. "She took the third oath. Do our traditions count for nothing?"

"Yes. How convenient that your sister died when she did,

Ayafeeia," Takea said. "It couldn't have worked out better for Nilrasha."

"Takea, watch that tongue of yours. You have a little too much Anklene blood in you for decent manners. It could have worked out better for Nilrasha, if Halaflora had died with more witnesses to her choking. There wouldn't be all these foul rumors and adder-backing. I can believe the story they told. Halaflora always had more strength of heart to her than body. I'm not sure Nilrasha isn't the better Queen. A Queen needs energy."

"There's an old saying—defend loudest your deepest enemies, until it is time to strike," Takea whispered to Wistala.

"Could it be said that becoming Queen is a higher calling?" the young drakka Nilrasha had spoken to said, raising her voice. "The Queen is the spiritual leader of the Firemaids. Nilrasha just rose above any maidmother."

"Have some respect for her rank, and understanding of her character," Ayafeeia said, straightening. "I abhore all this nasty gossip. My adopted brother, our Tyr, has the best interest of dragons at heart. Nilrasha has the best interest of the Tyr at heart. He makes enemies; she deals with them. Not even dragons can be governed without a little fear, I believe."

She grated her teeth in thought. "Wistala, you must be made ready for presentation in court. I suppose I should attend. As usual I'll leave Malitha in charge of our hill. Takea, you've not been atop Imperial Rock since you were presented as a hatchling. You must go, especially as Wistala is in your charge. Whatever you do, don't let her pull up her lips like that in front of the Tyr."

Wistala enjoyed the experience of the body-thralls working her scale.

First, several of them gave her a good scrubbing with bristly, long-handled brushes that cleaned her scale above and beneath. She was the ruin of at least three brushes.

Then they trimmed her scale in such a way that misshapen pieces covering old wounds looked a bit more comely and in line with the others. Some were considered a lost cause and—rather painfully!—yanked out and carefully gathered.

Even worse, a pair of bats, muttering to each other and with many apologies in broken Drakine, nibbled and licked at her wounds.

"The bats are, well, creepy, but they do help one heal," Takea said. "To think, we used to eat or burn them out."

"I still gulp one if I get a chance," another drakka confessed. "The Tyr doesn't miss 'em. Rodents never run out. I think the thrall capture them too, to toast on sticks and wrap their food up in the wings."

Ayafeeia came by to check the progress. "Tuve, a little highlighting around the eyes," she said to an older thrall with a gloriously long mane like a lion. "And Wistala, at court keep those big wings of yours tucked high. More room for everyone else."

"And the males will notice you," Takea said, snorting.

"It'll be a fast suitor who can catch up to her, once she's flying again," the Firemaid in charge of the body-thralls said.

Wistala wondered about the thralls. They didn't chatter the way hominids on the surface did, but just exchanged a few quiet words as they worked. They looked healthy enough, though perhaps a bit undersized. There were no marks of lash or shackle on them, as she'd seen on slaves in some of the surface lands she'd passed through, but then it sounded as though troublesome thralls were simply eaten.

"How do you do?" Wistala said to the thrall working with her brushes, painting scale about her eye.

"My apologies, mistress, did I get paint in your eye?" she asked.

"No, I was just introducing myself. My name is Wistala. How do you do?"

"Your thrall is named Tuve, mistress," Tuve said.

"You must not mind dragon-breath, Tuve," Wistala said.

"Oh, Susiron help us," the Firemaid in charge of the thralls said. "Not another of these Anklene radicals."

Tuve smiled. "A little oliban ash and witch hazel in the nostrils, mistress," she said quietly. She took out a thinner brush and blackened it and went to work again.

"They're hypocrites," Takea said, tapping a scale that needed to be removed. "The Anklenes have three thralls to every one the Firemaids have. If they're so concerned about how they're treated, they can start with their own. The thralls die like flies over there. Bad air from all those illumination lamps."

"Some say they only report them dead, then sneak them to the surface."

"I'll wager they eat them. Always counting and measuring things. No one will cheat you like the one doing the accounting, my father used to say."

"Not enough honest dwarves to go around," the Firemaid in charge of the thralls said. "You can trust dwarves. They'll cut their own throats before they lie. If only they wouldn't starve themselves. Not like elves, who play games with definitions of truth and falsehood. Now a good stupid man, that's almost as good as a dwarf. If you ever mate and set up in a cave of your own, Tala, look for the ones who count on their fingers instead of in their heads. That'll be a thrall you can trust."

Wistala's painting thrall gestured to a younger version of herself with similar thick hair. The girl brought forth a polished sheet of tin. Wistala saw herself, as in a silvery pool at sunset. Her eyes looked bigger and brighter.

"Have her show her teeth, Tuve," Takea said. "She's a Firemaid now, and she does have a royal set of renders. She should be showing a lot of tooth."

Tuve smeared a foul-tasting grease on her teeth. Wistala's lips retreated in disgust, practically of their own accord.

"That'll impress the Tyr!" Ayafeeia said, having completed her own preparations in a very few moments with the aid of a single thrall. "Though the rest of him's a bit of a wreck, he bears very fine teeth."

"The Tyr's sure to remember you!" Takea said.

Chapter 15

The Copper sent the body-thralls away to hear the report from Gnash. He'd given her just a taste of his blood and promised her the use of a steer once her report was done.

"I saw them myself, great one," Gnash said. "Mighty birds, with men lumpy under fur riding them. They flew low over the kern, only at night and in cloud or rain, and dropped a bitter powder, like dried dung."

The Copper could picture it. He knew those midnight mists that settled over the plateau, where trees grew short and thick, filling the hillsides with their tangled black roots and boughs, giving way to the rich volcanic soil of the plains that produced running rows of strawberries and grapes separating the rows of kern stalks. The fierce, brilliant sunshine that seemed to come from all directions rather than one, the stars bright at night until the clouds collected and distributed the dew. The whole Aerial Host could glide in unseen by the Anaeans, quiet in their rich clay houses parsing out their horoscopes from the day's observations.

Those had been happy years, with Halaflora in the sunshine. He was more than half convinced it was the sun that set her on the mend and gave her the strength to believe herself to be carrying a belly full of eggs.

Didn't dragons deserve their share of the sun?

He brought himself back to Gnash, who was snuffling about where he'd eaten his mid-meal.

"Could you follow them when they were done?"

Gnash licked up some bit of skin and gristle that hadn't been cleaned yet by the household thralls. "No. They flew too high, too fast. I am but a poor bat in my master's service. The air is so thin, indeed, in Anaea I could hardly breathe. Everything, everything left me panting, even a short glide."

"Thank you for your fatigues," the Copper said. "Can you at least say in what direction they came from, and where they flew to?"

"To the north."

The Copper considered. He knew Anaea well, having served as first assistant to the Upholder there and then as Upholder himself. North? Hypatia was to the north, but there were no reports of Hypatia employing giant birds. Only the Ghioz used such mounts, since some years after their brief war in Bant, according to the Anklenes. The Ghioz would be more to the east of Anaea, perhaps northeast. And he knew little of the prevailing winds off the plateau in that direction.

"Well done. Rest some days, then fly back and get Wail and the both of you may return. I'm sorry flying was so difficult for you there."

"The Tyr is just, the Tyr is kind, thinking of his poor servants. Oh, and he is so generous, so generous."

"Yes, I haven't forgotten about the animal." He took a silver disc, a coin with the Red Queen's image upon it, and carefully bit through it with his most distinctively shaped fang. "Here, give this to the chief steward of the Imperial Herd."

The bat-creature, which the Anklenes had started calling a "gargoyle," took it and tucked it tight in an ear. He hardly noticed the flap as it left.

Ghioz.

He could put a stop to their flights easily enough. He could send part of the Aerial Host there. Under a skillful captain, they might trace the return flights and discover the base of the feathered giants. One swift, massive strike . . .

But all this was shadow theater, such as the thralls used to entertain young drakes and drakka of the Imperial Line. Perhaps the fliers were like those shadow images, their movements a provocation to draw him into just that sort of action. If he committed the Aerial Host to far-off Anaea, suppose she struck elsewhere. They could scrape out an existence for a time without kern—the Anklenes were even now experimenting with ways to cleanse it of the blight, starting with boiling and roasting—or, in a pinch, he could send a few hills to the surface to take the sun for a season, if the hills would trust each other not to pillage each other's properties.

That was the ridiculous part of being Tyr. All the little drakes and drakka thought if he gave an order, it would be obeyed. Some orders were obeyed, some weren't, it all depended on how carefully he watched and how advantageous his people considered his decisions. They found a hundred ways to interpret his words.

Dragons were altogether too selfish, when they weren't out and out dishonest, to put the Lavadome's needs above their own.

If dragons wouldn't change, they'd have to figure out a way to change the world to better suit their needs.

"My Tyr," NoSohoth said, breaking in on his thoughts. "The *griffaran* have met a most astonishing visitor to the Lavadome. He would speak to you."

The Copper limped up the short passage to the throne room. It was always a slow trip; it bent around to the right and he couldn't trust his left *saa*.

He looked out on the assembled dragons. He'd had Nilrasha invite a few key leaders of the various hills, the principal members of the Imperial Line, and the leaders of the Firemaids, the Aerial Host, and the Drakwatch. His *griffaran* guard straightened and fluffed their feathers as he stepped out onto the throne-shelf.

The old banners won in battle and glory could really use some stitching and cleaning. He recognized one taken in Bant, when SiDrakkon's swift-dashing drakes attacked the half-completed tower of the Ghioz.

Dragon-necks, waving this way and that as the gossipers took part in two or three conversations at once, stilled and heads turned to the throne end of the room.

Nilrasha stood talking to Essea and two other females, aged widows of some of the hills but still important in influence with their families.

Everyone had a polite mouthful of coin? he thought to her.

Yes, and they're still restless.

At a nod to NoSohoth, more oliban went on the braziers, filling the air with its thick, spicy odor. He sensed his dragons relaxing, *griffs* stilled, tails ceased thrashing, waiting for him to speak.

"Thank you for attending me," he told the assembly. "We have several matters to discuss. Questions to answer, options to consider.

"But first, the war with the demen is over. We are victorious."

That set them roaring to shake the dust from those rotting old banners. You'd have thought they'd spent the last score of years digging demen out of their holes personally.

Wistala, far at the back of the long, narrow chamber, could hardly see the Tyr for the waving dragon-necks and tight wings.

"Then where is Paskinix?" a well-proportioned young female with almost-healed wingcase wounds asked. "Do we get to see his head?"

"That's Regalia," Takea said, from her perch upon Wistala's back. Ayafeeia, being a high leader of both the Firemaids and the Imperial Line, was at the other side of the press of shoulder-to-hip dragons. "She and her brother, SiHazathant, don't much like the Tyr. They were just young drake and drakka when he became Tyr—otherwise, some say, SiHazathant might have taken the throne instead of RuGaard. They were of SiDrakkon's line, but related to Tyr FeHazathant as well."

Wistala swallowed the last silver coin she'd pocketed in her gumline. She'd taken a very modest mouthful from the offered platter and had swallowed each one slowly, to savor the taste. But her mouth was still thick with the slime that always came when one had metals, and her eyes were on the cascade of silver and gold descending from the Tyr's throne-perch.

"His forces are dead, captive, or scattered," the Copper Tyr said. "The hunt goes on."

"I hope so," a red said. His scales were so dark they verged on the brownish color of dried blood. "Wretched egg-thief."

"HeBellereth," Takea said. "He's the best—"

She didn't find out what HeBellereth was best at.

"It is not the past or present that I asked you here to discuss, but the future. You all know about the shortages of kern because of the blight."

That caused them to stir. Wistala liked the sound of the Tyr. He reminded her a little of Father with his deep voice, even if she could only glimpse a little scale here and there between the necks and wings and heads. He was probably broadly built, like Father, from what she could see, though he rested against his throne in such a way as to hide his right, and turned his back to hide his left.

A rather serpentine pose for such a noble dragon. Mother always taught her to face friend or enemy with all claws forward, weight distributed evenly—to better move, forward or back, right or left, as circumstances warranted.

"We have an important visitor from the north," the Tyr said. "He brings news that concerns us all. Make room at the back, there!"

The dragons parted, and the rather officious silver-and-black dragon—NoSohoth, that was it—who'd been going up and down the center aisle of the throne room with some muscular blighters burning pleasant-smelling chips of what looked like resin of some kind used his neck and tail to help clear a path.

A dragon or two gasped. Wistala felt as though her head detached from the end of her neck and dropped to the floor as though severed.

DharSii of the Sadda-Vale, looking haggard and bright-eyed, fixed his eyes on the throne and walked forward.

"I don't know who that is," Takea said.

"DharSii, a renegade," said an old dragon with thin scales so blue they were almost silver. "He once commanded the Aerial Host, but he tried to overthrow Tyr FeHazathant."

"That was a lie spread by Tighlia and you know it, cousin," an aged green said. "He saved the Tyr's life, is what he did. What did he get as a reward? His good name taken."

Wistala looked at Takea, but she was craning her young neck to see up the aisle to the throne.

Wistala had eyes only for DharSii.

"Have a mouthful of gold, visitor," Queen Nilrasha said. A few gasped, and the old silver-blue rattled his *griff*.

"More oliban, there," NoSohoth said quietly, but Wistala was near enough to overhear. Hearts pounding, she wished he'd shift his great black bulk so she could see better.

DharSii's horned head dipped and he pecked at the pile of gold at the base of the throne like a bird taking an insect.

"Thank you, Queen."

Another big, multi-horned blue dragon, *griff* down and scales bristling, planted his *saa* in an effort to still a thrashing tail. "How dare such as you—"

"Quiet," NoSohoth barked.

"Like that scalepainter ever tasted blood and sand in the dueling pit," the old blue grumbled.

"Uncle, you're no duelist yourself," the one called HeBellereth baited.

Why could these fool dragons not still tongues? She had to listen!

"I ask no hospitality, no justice, and seek no duel and will refuse any challenge," DharSii said.

"We've done away with that brutality," the Tyr said.

"Have you?" DharSii said, looking at the Tyr. "That's a jump in the right direction."

"No, dragons have always—" someone protested, and was lost in a general exchange of opinions. Voices rose to an excited crescendo.

Wistala shoved forward as everyone offered an opinion of the visitor. "Tear him to bits!" "No, let's hear him." She'd already heard a few whispers from her fellow Firemaids about her broad frame and the length of her tail, but muscle-mass had its uses. "He's done no wrong!" "Cowards, this is insult!" She forced herself halfway through the press so she could see and hear.

There was something about the way the Tyr held his head. Was it that bad leg he propped himself upon? No, it was the droopy eye, it made him look rather stupid, half-asleep or—

Blood and blaze. The Tyr. *It couldn't be.*

"Quiet, you fool dragons," Nilrasha roared. "Quiet!"

"Thank you," the Tyr said, not looking at her. His eye locked on Wistala.

Wistala found her reason again. She remembered the last time she'd seen her brother; she'd tried to kill him. She'd given him that injury to his eyelid and face—she almost smiled at the thought. How had he come so far, risen so high? Of course, anyone who would conspire with dwarves to kill his own family would be bound to rise. The ethics of the barbarian kings.

DharSii spoke, as from afar.

"I'm here to deliver a report. I recently passed over the eastern slopes of the Red Mountains near the pass of the Wheel of Fire. I have seen such a mass of men and horseflesh as has not struck earth since the time of Tindairuss. The Ghioz have gathered riders from across the plains and concentrate them in the Red Mountains to the north. I saw boat traffic, barges, all along the great river, though whether this is to aid the supply of the hordes to the north or shift this mass of men and horse to the south I cannot say. I come here with no expectations, and if my old crimes still hang about my name I am ready to answer the charges. I know, I know from being in her counsels, that the Red Queen means to claim the Empire's upholds as their own."

"What do you care, renegade?" the old blue called.

"I've heard you hire yourself out to the Ghioz Queen," a battle-scarred red said.

"That's HeBellereth, captain of the Aerial Host," Takea said, happy with the better view she had now atop Wistala's back, clinging to her fringe like a lizard on a leaf.

"The Upper World can tear itself to bits for all I care," DharSii said. "Perhaps they just mean to ravage Hypatia, but if so they've chosen a strange place to gather, for the Wheel of Fire could hold that pass against any number."

Hypatia! Those old temples, the libraries, the towns full of flower, vine, and tree. Rainfall's trees, each an old friend. Had DharSii said they were assembling at the old pass guarded by the Wheel of Fire? The Wheel of Fire were no more, thanks to her.

DharSii spoke on: "But Ghioz is assembling such a force as could tear through every Uphold of the Empire. There is one more fact you should be aware of. The Queen has taken dragons other than myself into her service, with more recent knowledge of events in the Lavadome."

"Who?" Nilrasha asked.

"NiVom the White and ImFamnia," DharSii said. "I am not in their confidence, but between themselves they speak much of the Lavadome."

More arguments broke out, debate on whether NiVom had planned to seize the throne or whether the "Jade Queen" and NiVom had been lovers before his flight from accusations of treachery. Takea started to explain, but the Copper quieted his dragons.

"NoSohoth, better send for more oliban," the Copper said. "Matters grow heated. The *griffaran* guard will have the first dragon to draw blood, I promise. Double the guard."

Wistala glanced up at the fearsome-looking birds, perched just above the trophy banners. They wore sharpened metal guards on their claws and beaks.

One of them, missing feathers from tears across his chest and with gaps in the trailing feathers of his wing, screeched. Other *griffaran* appeared from the shadows behind the Tyr and joined their fellows on the perches, an uncomfortable squeeze by the look at it, facing front and back so each looked at the assembly down the other's long tailfeathers.

"They tore an assassin to bits the other day," Takea whispered.

"Have them start on DharSii," someone called.

"He's my guest," Queen Nilrasha said. "Stop that talk. Any dragon who doesn't recognize the favor he's done us, or the courage it took, flying far into uncertain welcome, leave and don't return."

DharSii gave her a brief bow. Wistala couldn't see whether he shut his eyes or not.

Wistala thought the praise a little overdone. Perhaps the Queen had sent him to lie to the Lavadome? She eyed Nilrasha, who stared at DharSii hungrily, as though he were a bullock turning on a spit.

DharSii bowed to the Tyr. "What you choose to do with my observation is up to this fine assembly. I've done my duty to the cave of my birth and will leave you now. Unless the Tyr would hinder me?"

"Only long enough to thank you. Have another mouthful of gold. You ate but one before. Or have some roast pork. There will be a banquet after this meeting."

"I didn't come here for gold. But others may," DharSii said.

With that he bowed and turned. He glared at the dragons close around, and they parted for him, giving him a path to the door.

He stalked toward the entrance, eyes traveling over the assembly. Most dragons looked away as his gaze fell on them. But one did not.

DharSii froze in front of Wistala.

"You! You live," he said.

"I was rescued by the Firemaids," Wistala said. "They brought me here."

"I . . . I am relieved."

Takea slid off her back with a thud, righted herself, shaking her head.

"I have oathed myself to the Firemaids," Wistala said. "To repay my debt."

"Add impressed to relieved, then," DharSii said. "I tried to tell you, once, years ago. Not that it would have aided your purpose. The dragons here aren't much interested in the surface, except as a source of food and slaves."

"Who does he speak to, there?" Nilrasha asked.

Ayafeeia, who had a longer neck than most, raised her head. "That's Wistala, here for her presentation."

"What was that name?" the Tyr asked.

DharSii gave a brief bow and stalked toward the door, as stiff as though someone had plunged a spear into him, Wistala thought. His tail just brushed her across the base of her neck as he passed.

She watched every step, every swing of the neck as he left, but he did not look back.

"What did you say was—" the Tyr asked, but the growl of conversation smothered the rest of his words.

"My name is Wistala," Wistala said. "Daugter of AuRel and Irelia, granddaughter of AuRye the Red and EmLar the Gray."

Another babble broke out. "EmLar? Didn't explore . . ."

She pushed forward in earnest, felt a slight thump as Takea landed on her back again.

"AuRye," someone murmured. "Weren't he and his mate in that back-to-nature cult?"

"No. They fled the civil war when Sofol hill was burned out . . ."

"Anklene, wasn't his mate?"

She stared at her brother. "My Tyr," she said.

"Welcome to the Lavadome, Firemaid," her brother replied.

Nilrasha glanced from one to the other, as did Ayafeeia. Wistala couldn't say whether she enjoyed the moment or loathed it. Her emotions were buffeted as though by a fierce spring thunderstorm.

"Why, look at their snouts and teeth. They might be—" Nilrasha said aloud, but the words ceased as though snapped off like a brittle twig. Wistala felt the mind-speech more than she heard it.

"Wistala, you live!" a voice shouted from a dark alcove.

A dragon, smallish only by comparison to the great Skotl hulks flanking him, moved forward. Gray-skinned, he had a distinctive nub on his snout, his egg-tooth.

AuRon! Had she gone mad? AuRon? Here! She extended *sii* and *saa*, dug them as hard as she could into the stony floor.

This must be a dream. Surely she would wake, and vomit up some piece of wormy pork.

But would she dream an AuRon with an oddly foreshortened tail, or a glowing jewel on a chain about his neck?

"Our emissary from Ghioz has arrived at last, I see," NoSohoth said. "Wise of you to bring him through the *griffaran* gate. My Tyr, may I present—"

"AuRon, son of AuRel," the Tyr finished, stepping forward. "*Griffaran!* Be ready to kill. Who knows what sort of viper the Red Queen has found to thrust into our bosom."

Chapter 16

AuRon felt ... *disinterested* was the only word for it. There should be anger, hatred, but he felt none of that, nothing to make his *griff* rattle or make him imagine plunging his *sii* into the Copper's throat or eyes.

Perhaps it was the fatigue of the long underground trek. The mass of rock and earth above him—could the pressure of it be bothering him? The wonder of the Lavadome with its lava-streaked "sky" and unnatural outside-inside air, the smell of unknown dragons, these *"griffaran"* and tremendous bats and dragonelles who acted like a pack of wolves he'd once run with, only as disciplined as any of the Wyrmmaster's riders. Quick meals of dry, tasteless meat, water with strange metallic or chemical tastes, in the endless mosslit tunnels, when there was any moss to be found with dragonelles feeling their way along by markers in the stonework.

Exhaustion and lack of sunlight had numbed him.

He wondered how much the Red Queen had known about him, and his brother, when she selected him for this assignment. What would be the effect of an emissary from Ghioz making an assassination attempt on the ruler of the Lavadome—this mass of restive dragons, hidden beneath a volcano, forgotten or half legend to the world above? How would they react to such an attack? Would they unite and fly as one to Ghioz?

What would meet them there?

Wistala. Had the Red Queen arranged this too? What trick of fate had brought her to this place, at this time, mixing anger with joy, regret with regard? Where and what had she been all these years? Had she somehow found the Copper and come with him deep into the earth? If Wistala hadn't been there, would he have leaped, *sii* and *saa* ready to rend and tear?

The moment overwhelmed him.

Perhaps that's how it was for the other two. Each waiting for a third to make a move.

Say something.

His thoughts felt strange to him, as though from a voice in his head not his own. Mind-speech from Wistala? But it wasn't her voice either.

"I hope your subjects know what kind of king they've put upon their throne," he finally said. "A patricide."

"AuRon, don't," Wistala said. She stepped up, putting herself between AuRon and the shelf where the Copper rested. The Copper's mate took a protective step forward as well.

"Give us this message from Ghioz," the Copper said, glancing about.

Was the Copper gauging the reaction of the other dragons in the room or looking for somewhere to run?

"Fine one to speak of vipers," AuRon said. "Do they know your history?"

"If you've come here to plant some lie about my mate—" Nilrasha said.

"He can't hurt us, my love," the Copper said. He set himself as straight as a dragon with only three sound legs could. AuRon pitied him for a moment. The overdevelopment of muscles on the good side had left him almost twisted. "Say your piece. Then I will say mine."

AuRon hardly heard even breathing from the assembled dragons. Perhaps they were hoping for a fight.

Well, say it. Challenge him!

"Your Tyr bargained with dwarves for the murder of his parents and family," AuRon began. "He saw the murder of his parents, hatchlings sold into slavery or death. One treachery resulting in three deaths.

"For the truth of this, ask Wistala. She's of your own band, it seems."

"Ah, truth," the Copper said. "Truth is a messy business, shaded and colored by experience. Now, sister, let's have your truth."

Wistala's tongue went dry. It clung to the roof of her mouth like a dead bat, too frozen to drop.

She felt the attention of the dragons on her scale. "I can only speak to a mouthful of knowledge. The dragon who stands before you is my brother, of that I'm sure. I'm not so sure I was ever sister to him. I know I didn't try. In fact I begrudged every mouthful of food or bone he stole. Ours was a bare cave during a harsh winter.

"He did conspire with dwarves. It resulted in the death of his mother and sister. I don't know that he expected them to kill Jizara—his sister—and myself, however. I believe the dwarves came to capture hatchlings and take an older vengeance on our parents.

"My father died in honorable battle against a man who aided the dwarves, called the Dragonblade. Later I destroyed the dwarves and forgave the Dragonblade."

She heard a stir and gasps at that.

Wistala raised her voice. "I have no business holding a grudge against a crippled, hungry hatchling. As Tyr, you know the whole of him better than I."

"Strange fate," the Copper said. "That I would end up avenging my father in turn. I killed the Dragonblade, though it very nearly came to him killing me."

Wistala looked around, but no one argued with that seemingly impossible statement. The Dragonblade came to the Lavadome? What madness!

"You still had a tooth in the murder of our mother," AuRon said.

"You accuse me of murdering my family," the Copper said. He raised his voice so all could hear. "I reply they were no family to me.

"Our parents believed, I think, a strict code of isolation and barbaric survival by wit and wing and claw rather than through civiliza-tion. We know of a few dragons here who argue for the belief, even if they lack the courage to leave the Lavadome, with its thralls and its herds and its aid, to go off and fight for a cave of their own.

"Understand, I was not born into the Lavadome, where a hatch-ling who happened to survive the hatching duel could end up ad-opted into another cave. For me, the only dragons I knew cast me out. Why, they did not even offer me the dignity of a name."

"You deserved a name," Wistala said. "I had nothing to do with that. I know our parents told you to leave the cave."

"Did they shelter me, as Tyr FeHazathant did?" the Copper asked.

He looked at them, but spoke to the assembly. "Did they reward duty with honor? Did they lay down rules and traditions? Offer ad-vice as to how to survive in the world? Give me even a mouthful of silver so that my scales might come in thick enough to turn a dagger? No, I starved in silence, never hearing the voices of my kind."

Nilrasha rushed to her mate's side and buried her snout in his flank under the wing.

"My love, my love, you should have shared this with me!"

"No," the Copper said, though whether he was answering his own questions or his mate Wistala couldn't say. "Our parents abandoned these things, or never learned them. Perhaps they or their grandsires abandoned other ideals when they left the Lavadome.

"Tyr FeHazathant and the Imperial Line gave me a name and a station and taught me what it means to be a dragon. Have the two of you forgotten? Wistala, what bargains did you strike in the Upper World to allow your survival? Were you fed like some overgrown guard dog perhaps, or fitted for a saddle?"

Wistala felt the blaze in his eyes. She knew she had little cause for guilt, yet guilt she felt nonetheless. Perhaps for not making more of an effort on her brother's behalf. Jizara had once spoken to her about their Copper brother, that perhaps they should make an effort to meet with him and feed him, in secret as they hunted for slugs on the cave floor, but she'd seen him then as another mouth and there was already little enough food to go around.

"AuRon, you come here like a messenger-thrall, and you don't even do that task properly," the Copper said. "You've given us no words from Ghioz. Or was the Queen's message that the dragons of the Lavadome should doubt and despise their Tyr? I wonder why she might wish for that?"

Wistala could no longer read her brother. The stripes on his gray skin darkened—in layout they were not that different from Dhar-Sii's, perhaps a little thicker. He shifted his weight from one side to the other.

The Copper raised his head high and asked the assembly: "Does any dragon here have a complaint about how I carried out my duties in the Drakwatch?"

"No," a few dragons murmured.

"I've never had luck in duels. I did not fight for this throne, but for all the dragons of the Lavadome. They trusted me with this title, and if they want it back, knowing all this, I will quit it."

At this Queen Nilrasha raised her snout, glancing around alarmed as though afraid of a fight or a challenge.

No dragon stirred. "I am not a hatchling," the Copper continued, "maimed by my hatching, starved in sight of my own egg shelf, taken and broken by iron rods in the hard hands of dwarves. I am fortunate, today, in having the luxury of choices."

"Father's gold drove you to your choice more than the rods of the dwarves," AuRon said.

Ayafeeia spoke up. "It does not matter. In the Lavadome, whatever you were as a hatchling, or as a drake, is never mentioned again if you enter the Drakwatch or Firemaidens and grow into an honorable set of wings. The outcast is equal to the scion of the Imperial Line. My mate-brother RuGaard went into the Drakwatch and served, shed blood in battle, and rose to the position of Upholder. With that record I couldn't care less for the details of what came before. Wistala, settle down. You've no need to bristle so. There'll be no fighting. Or if there is"—she glanced up at the alert *griffaran,* leaning down and ready to drop—"it won't last long."

Wistala hardly heard her. She couldn't take her eyes off the jewel AuRon wore about his neck. It emitted a soft glow of a peculiar white shade, something between the pale luminescence of reflected moon off the snows of the north and the glitter of starlight.

"So did you come all this way just to accuse me of murder, AuRon?" the Copper asked. "Or is there a message from the Red Queen?"

AuRon felt his hearts hammering. His mind clouded.

"Yes, there is a message from the Red Queen," a voice that was only partially his answered.

Like speech in a dream.

He froze, seized by the same irresistible instinct that made him spin legs downward as he fell or that made him squat when he voided his bowels.

He found himself speaking in a voice not his own, high-pitched, with the words coming out at all the wrong intervals: "This pathetic, scaleless . . . excuse for dragonkind doesn't have . . . the backbone of a river fluke. We speak to you dragons . . . now as the Queen of Ghioz."

"What insult is this?" his brother's mate said, raising her head.

His voice continued: "We propose a division of influence. The Upper World shall be mine, and the Lower World . . . shall belong to the dragons, and we will have . . . peace and such commerce as benefits . . . us both. Accept this and enjoy prosperity, or reject Our terms and starve in the dark. Fight Us, and you'll . . . find your second offer to be much worse terms, with the alternative the extinction your kind . . . toward earning."

AuRon wanted to smash his head against the floor—anything that would remove the awful alienation his own body had taken on itself.

As though spellbound, he continued: "We will accept . . . a delegation of no more than two dragons to attend Us and discuss the arrangements further. In return, We propose to send . . . two dragons as Our representatives into your realm."

Horrified, AuRon wondered what would happen if his body just stood here speaking words not his own forever. Would he stand here, a living, speaking statue, soiling floor and self, until he starved or died of thirst?

The voice that wasn't quite his continued: "As for this wretch, We suggest you . . . kill it. It has a nasty habit of worming its way into the confidence of its prey and then striking from behind. That is what it did with the Wyrmmaster on the Isle of Ice, and it had some thoughts along the same lines with Our royal person."

Good-bye, AuRon. You were most useful to us, whatever your intentions. Even now our daggers are poised to strike that traitor Naf. Little Hieba will be heartbroken. Ah, well, there are plenty of balconies for her to hurl herself from.

With that, he jumped at the Tyr, his brother.

Two flashes of green.

One struck him, hard, the other interposed itself between his *saa* and the recoiling Copper. He felt his claws rake scale.

A tail struck him across the snout.

White and yellow stars obscured his vision. It may have been Wistala's, it may have been Nilrasha's. It hit too fast for him to tell. Then on his side, a *saa* clawing at his throat—

—But instead of opening him up, two claws hooked under his necklace and broke it away. He heard the clatter as it bounced off a wall.

Feathers batted from above to the sound of alarmed cries.

Limp as a water buffalo with a broken back, he realized Wistala was atop his neck. She'd scratched his neck where she'd ripped away the chain, and he bled. Hers was worse. He had cut both Wistala and Nilrasha along their sides and haunches.

"Wait, wait!" Wistala called. "This is not his doing! The Queen of the Ghioz—she spoke and acted through him."

The Copper pushed away a mass of feathers and claws. "*Griffaran* guard, back! It's over."

AuRon raised a *sii*, a pathetic gesture. But it was his own. He controlled his body again.

The Copper stared down at AuRon. "By our laws you should die.

"But being Tyr has its privileges. One is the ability to dispense mercy. Should you, AuRon, ever be able to hold death in one *sii* and life in another you'll come to know the temptation in both. Once, long ago, you might have killed me, quite easily, but you didn't," the Copper said. "All things are now equal, as far as I'm concerned. I will forget the present; I hope you will forget the past."

"The court has never seen such a tumult since the arrival of the Dragonblade," Ayafeeia said. "You came very near to dying, visitor, on the very stones where my grandmother's blood was spilled."

"The crystal," Wistala said. "It serves as a link with the Queen. I wonder if this is some doing of the great one that NooMoahk once possessed?"

That blighter fetish? AuRon wondered. How could an oversized hunk of luminous rock control a dragon's words and movements?

NoSohoth and the Firemaids were calming the crowd. The Tyr climbed back upon his perch.

"Crystal?" AuRon asked, righting himself.

"You weren't speaking those words, were you?" Wistala asked.

"No," AuRon said. "It was—I couldn't control my tongue."

"I think she can see and hear through it somehow," Wistala said. "How else could she know she was addressing the Tyr? How did she know there were many dragons present?"

"She learned that Naf still lives, and where he is," AuRon said.

"Naf?" Nilrasha said.

AuRon's mind was once again ahead of his voice. "Naf, the leader of—I must warn him."

Anxious, he looked to his sister. "Is there a faster way out of this place?"

"I confess—" Wistala said.

"To fly in which direction?" the Copper asked.

"North."

"You can climb out one of the *griffaran* holes," the Copper said. "Above the river ring. Not the easiest path, but the shortest."

"Or there's the wind tunnel," Nilrasha said. "You could fly out of that. This time of year the wind blows outward."

"But I wouldn't advise it," the Copper said. "Better to follow the *griffaran*."

AuRon looked at the feathered menaces looming all around. "Perhaps not."

"Ayafeeia, show him to the wind tunnel. It's his neck. Take some food before you quit us, AuRon. You'll need it as ballast in the tunnel."

With that, he turned and began speaking to a human servant wearing soft leather and furs.

Wistala embraced AuRon. "Come back, brother. I've a great deal to tell you."

"Perhaps. I have a mate and hatchlings of my own, far off in the north. Her name is Natasatch. She was a captive dragon as we might have been. I've been too far away from the home cave. It's in a place called the Isle of Ice."

"I know it from maps. Strange, I once passed close to it but was warned off by men mounted on dragons."

"They're gone now," AuRon said.

"In any case, Father would be overjoyed at that news. That's all he wanted for us. To have some hatchlings in peace and safety."

"Peace and safety," AuRon said. "If only the dwarves sold those, the world would be a better place."

"I see you still like to tease."

"I thought it philosophy. Well, I wish you would join us."

"Perhaps," Wistala replied. "But if there's hope for dragons in the world, I believe it lies here, in the Lavadome. Yet I fear for my friends in Hypatia, with the news we've had today."

"I've met some of them. At an inn with a strange sign."

Wistala's eyes widened. "You've been there?"

"You're right. They do fear the coming war. We were born into a hard generation, Wistala."

"We still have much to do, it seems. Well, I will not delay you," she said. "Our reunion is one worthy of a song or two, I expect. Good-bye again, AuRon."

He looked at Ayafeeia. "I am ready to fly, if you are ready to guide."

"You're quick to depart us," Ayafeeia said. "Would you not prefer to resolve matters here first, with your brother and sister?"

AuRon could not delay, not for a dwarf-hour. "I have a friend in danger."

"I'll show you the way out from the gardens. We shall simply fly from there."

He brushed Wistala's snout—how like Mother she looked, though not as thunderous in size. Or was she? He tried to imagine her from a hatchling's perspective, as she stood there sniffing at the wounds he'd inflicted, but it made his hearts hurt.

With that, he left.

The Copper sent one of the Drakwatch messengers to fetch Rayg. He had that young Firemaiden, Takea, tend to Nilrasha's wounds while Ayafeeia looked at his sister. No one had serious injuries, and scale would grow back.

He felt, if anything, exalted. He'd triumphed, at last, over his brother, the Gray Rat. AuRon seemed in a hurry to leave, and he would like nothing better than to see the tail of him.

The assembly had been a parade of horrors. First, DharSii's speech had put the fat pot on the boil. A low murmur started in the back and didn't cease until DharSii left. Dragons, even soothed by burning oliban, could be mercurial. He'd felt his rule creep more than once to the edge of a precipice as the three visitors spoke.

Names had come up that hadn't been heard on Imperial Rock in years: DharSii, NiVom, ImFamnia . . . there were still factions who thought NiVom, his old comrade in the Drakwatch, a superior dragon, and there was nothing like absence to let a memory grow up into a legend.

About legends—he'd once been told that there'd been talk of DharSii becoming Tyr. He'd won a terrible battle that saved some Upholds and brought them the cattle from the east and south and opened up the oliban trade. NiVom himself had apparently been selected to succeed Tyr FeHazathant, before being driven away by false—or were they?—charges.

The Imperial Line and the leaders of the principal hills had given him the title Tyr. If they chose to quit obeying him and support another, could he count on the Aerial Host, or the Drakwatch, or the Firemaids?

His rule had been mixed in accomplishments of late. They'd won the war against the demen, but at a cost in blood from drakes and drakka, dragons and dragonelles. The benefits would not be felt for some time, as more and more trade moved through the Lower World without being raided. Then there was the matter of the blighted kern.

Without kern, illness was on its way. How many dragons, seeing their hatchlings sicken or grow twisted and stunted and weak of tooth and claw, would blame him?

Suppose they decided his reign brought more trouble than promise? Every dragon made Tyr had died with the title.

Rayg, moving with the discretion of a human in a chamber full of restive dragons, spoke briefly with the Copper and then picked up the crystal and its chain and wrapped it in a piece of soft leather.

"I'm no wizard, my Tyr."

"I'm not expecting wizardry. For now, keep it somewhere deep and dark and just observe. The Queen of the Ghioz is using it—she sees and hears through it, I believe."

"Sees," Rayg said. "Hears. You are sure of this?"

"Speaks as well. She took control of a dragon. She responded to our conversation. I don't think she's hiding among the *griffaran*. It must have been through the crystal."

"It still must be a trick of some kind, or some form of special suggestion or training. Perhaps she manipulated that dragon's mind. I've heard of such things."

"Don't let the Anklenes have it unless I approve. I don't want another spy or assassin wandering the Lavadome. And above all, don't put it on yourself. The last thing I want is your mind overthrown."

"I shouldn't care for the experience either. Don't worry. I'll treat it like hot metal."

Rayg departed with his wrapped, deadly treasure. The Copper made a private note to keep a bat on him and watch for strange behavior.

With that, he turned back to the assembly, who were all speaking again. He heard DharSii and NiVom mentioned more than once in the chatter.

"So, Ghioz has sent us an offer," he said.

"They do seem to want peace," LaDibar said, speaking for the first time.

"Pieces, more like," HeBellereth, leader of the Aerial Host, said. "Pieces of our Empire."

LaDibar ignored the interruption. "But they offer a peace in which they would hold every advantage. They can survive without the Lower World. We will starve without the Upper."

That met with a growl of assent from the assembly.

The Copper was relieved to hear LaDibar talking sense for a change.

"If the peace is questionable, what of the alternative?" the Copper asked. "Is the threat credible?"

"Ghioz has raided our coasts," HeBellereth said. "Stolen our property. They've fortified their piece of Bant. And then there are those cursed birds. They're like *griffaran,* faster-flying and quicker-turning than dragon, and our fire is almost useless. They simply rise out of the way, they can climb faster than a dragon."

"They carried off thralls from my cousin's estate in Komod," one of the Wyrr leaders said.

At this the Copper wished Sreeksrack present. He'd enjoy his reaction to the idea that another headhunter might carry off thralls to which he was entitled.

"I have more recent reports from Anaea," the Copper said. "Great birds, which must have come from Ghioz, have been seen over the kern fields in the mists and dark. They do not fly all the way there to take the scenery, I think."

At this there was more grumbling.

"I was not aware of this," LaDibar said. "Did the Upholder send a new report?"

"I have sources of my own there."

"Can you trust the observation of one of those bats?" LaDibar asked, making the logical leap.

"I'm convinced that Ghioz put a blight on our precious kern," the Copper said, feeling his firebladder pulse at LaDibar's tone. "I think we can all guess who advised them as to the importance of the kern trade. Those of you whose hills lost hatchlings to the blight have my promise to avenge those deaths."

He let that sink in a moment, then continued.

"Ghioz has invited its own destruction. If we cannot have kern, we cannot long exist in the Lower World. Perhaps we can get a trickle from the southern provinces, but will that be enough to keep the Lavadome healthy?

"I offer an alternative. We only need kern because we do not see sunlight from year to year, unless our duties call us to the surface. I propose a return to the sunlight."

At that all gasped.

"The hominids will unite to destroy us," LaDibar said.

"Yes, they fight among themselves now, but let them know of our existence . . ." an elderly Firemaid agreed.

"I did not say this would be easy, or without danger. Wistala, you're familiar with hominids. I've been told you spent years in Hypatia. Tell us your judgment."

His sister stared up at him, wondering for a moment. "One

dragon is a curiosity. How they would react to a score of scores, I cannot say. But Hypatia, with a thousand or more years of culture dating back to Anklamere's time or before, has need of friends if she is to resist the Red Queen. We may find more welcome and gratitude if we but speak to them."

An excited murmur broke out.

"As equals," Wistala said.

And the excitement turned to growling. *Equals? Hominids? Stupid, short-lived, shortsighted . . .*

"Hear her," the Copper called. "Hear her, now."

He read new feelings in her expression, he thought. The pity and perhaps contempt had been replaced by something else. He thought it might be respect, but wondered if he flattered himself.

"Certainly, an individual hominid can't compare to a dragon," LaDibar said. "But together, they accomplish great things. They're like ants—they have a form of collective intelligence."

Wistala raised her head. "Tyr, if we must fight the Ghioz, we would do better to have allies."

"We would."

"Hypatia has warriors, men and elves and dwarves and the ships and roads to move them. If they were aided by your—our—dragons, it could mean a new beginning for hominids and dragons."

"I'm more concerned about an ending," the Copper said. "An ending to dragons hiding underground. Will you speak for us to Hypatia?" the Copper asked.

"What may I promise them in assistance?"

"At the very least a few of your Firemaids. Much will depend on the Red Queen's moves."

"If we return to the surface, who will have the Lavadome?" Co-Tathanagar asked. "Will there be more than one Tyr? Who shall rule the individual hills?"

"I am not saying abandon the Lower World. We will keep the Lavadome a cradle for dragonkind. Perhaps newly mated dragons will return here always, to lay in peace and safety." The Copper's emotions had given him a tongue for words. Might as well use it to talk of a happy future instead of one of battle and sacrifice. "Years from now we will bring our hatchlings and they will hear the story of how we rose anew out of terror, out of murder, out of persecution.

"But without gaining security in the Upper World, there will be no existence in the Lower. Does anyone doubt this?"

If they did, they didn't say so.

"So will we have peace or war with the Ghioz?" He looked down at the young Firemaiden at the front.

"You, you—"

"Takea," Nilrasha supplied.

"Takea. What do you think the choice should be? Will you speak for the Firemaids?"

The drakka paled, and her tail twitched nervously as she found her voice. "I say they've not given us a choice."

This one bears watching, the Copper thought.

"My thoughts exactly," the Copper said. "What is our choice? Life at the pleasure of the Red Queen?"

"Settle it quickly, then. One strong blow," HeBellereth said. "Unite the Aerial Host, the Drakwatch, the Firemaids and fly to Ghioz and lay waste to their capital."

"No," the Copper said. "The Queen tried to provoke us into exactly that move, I believe. They've made war against us at the edges of our empire, sapping our strength. I suggest we return their favor. We will attack them on the horsedowns and the savannahs. We will close mountain passes and rivers."

The Copper sensed their growing excitement. NoSohoth moved to put more oliban on the braziers, but the Copper stilled him with a glance. Now was the time to channel their anger.

"Dragons of the Lavadome. When I became your Tyr I swore an oath to all of you. That we would live to see an awakening of dragonkind. There's only one direction for dragons to go, and that is up. For years there's been talk that one day, when we were strong enough, we'd return to the surface united and resolved to overcome any difficulty. I believe that time is now. Let us inaugurate a new age for dragons."

He raised himself as high as he could, and spread his wings slightly so that all could see him.

"Will you follow me back to the surface?"

The Lavadome roared their assent.

"In the memory of our martyred hatchlings, let us strike."

They liked the sound of that.

"In the memory of our fallen fighters, let us strike."

They liked that even better. HeBellereth roared. Even little Takea hopped up and down, dodging waving necks and tails, growling.

"In the memory of our ancestors' glory and in the hope of our hatchlings' future—let us return! United we resolve. United we overcome. United we strike!"

They roared so as to shake the Lavadome. Even NoSohoth and the thralls joined the chorus.

BOOK THREE

Overcome

Oh, battle's the easiest thing in the world. Smash 'em up. Then smash 'em some more, then stomp what's left. It's the befores and afters what cause all the trouble.
—*AuRye, grandsire to AuRon*

Chapter 17

"In some months it blows out. In other months it blows in," Ayafeeia said. "The Anklenes told me why once, but I've forgotten. All that matters is that you'll have an easier time of it with the wind passing out."

AuRon noticed that she looked at a high rock as she spoke. He searched, saw nothing, then glanced over at her.

"My sister was mated here," she said. "To your brother."

"I'd rather think him your Tyr than my brother. Nilrasha is lovely, though this seems an odd place. Is it because of the privacy?"

"Oh, no, it's not a tradition. Mated dragons usually fly to the surface in the south, to the tips at World's End."

"Then why here?"

She told him, briefly. A crippled dragon and a sickly mate, jokes the whole way there and back.

"I was closer to Halaflora than—we don't speak of my other sister. She saw a quality in RuGaard. Have you ever heard the expression 'deephearted'?"

"No."

"It's one of the virtues we try to instill in the Firemaids. It means a dragon who thinks about others more than himself. I see it in our Tyr. I see the same in you."

"I'd be curious to know how you came to that conclusion."

"For whom?"

"Me. I'm curious."

"I saw how you looked to your sister at the assembly."

He should be saying good-bye, but he should probably rest a few more moments before attempting an ascent. "Is concern for a sibling so strange here?"

"One sometimes wonders. But not just her—that young drago-nelle next to her, and the others. No fear, no anger, just interest. I never thought you were deciding which part of the hide was the most vulnerable."

"It may have been that smoke in the air. It leaves one relaxed and fog-headed."

"That's oliban. Very valuable. Don't be surprised that NoSohoth uses so much of it. It's a rare commodity. His family controls the trade."

"Fascinating. But I must be off."

"Are you with us, then?"

"I delivered the Red Queen's message. She owes me a reward. I'm off to collect it."

"Don't eat any gold of hers. She'd poison it."

AuRon took a breath. "I'm after blood now, not coin."

With that he launched himself into howling confusion.

He felt like a leaf caught in an updraft. The wind slid him this way and that, threatening to send him crashing into the side of the tunnel.

Perhaps if he'd been a scaled dragon it would have been an easier flight, since the wind roaring up the shaft would not have pushed him so easily. But then again, his weight allowed him to ride the current, follow it as it swirled through gours and sword-edged scars.

He took painful bashes to each wingtip as the current sent him careening toward the blue patch of night sky above.

Out of desperation, he misaligned his wings, sending him into a spin. Though dizzying, it kept him to the center of the shaft.

And if he crashed into a rock, he'd be spared the moment of horror before the impact.

As the patch of lonely sky breaking the dark grew, the shaft widened, and he found himself having to flap his wings hard to keep rising.

An ascent at this angle is almost impossible for a scaled dragon for longer than a brief moment or two of furious wingwork, even with such a tailwind. AuRon found his body swelling with each deep breath, his throat one long wound forcing the rush of air in and out.

Out, with night sky all around, with the loom of a shorn-topped volcano above, dusted with snow and pocked with ice. AuRon, curious, circled up and over the crater.

Despite the smokes rising from tears in the side of the mountain, he had a good view down into the mouth of the crater. A lake lay there, with a thin bulge at the center that seemed to be a mound of ice, but he suspected it was in fact the crest of the strange crystal dome.

Off to the west a second volcano steamed, connected to the mountain by way of a rocky saddle.

It took him a moment to obtain his bearings and evaluate the air currents, for the stars were strange this far south. Once he knew north from south, he turned his neck for Ghioz.

An hour of flight passed and he idled in an updraft as the dry ground north of the Lavadome's mountain bled heat into the night sky. He spotted a watering hole shining below and started a slow circle down to see if it was safe to drink.

Motion caught his eye to the north. Two roc-riders, flying hard and a goodly distance apart, straight for the mountain of the Lavadome.

Something about the distance between the two bothered him. All the roc-riders he'd seen flying until now had kept close. These flew to observe as much sky and desert as possible, and still stay in visual communication with each other.

He alighted, trusting to shadow and coloration to conceal him from the fliers' eyes—hominid and avian.

A pebble-backed desert lizard with two rows of horns running along his back hissed a warning that he was poison to eat. AuRon glared at him—he'd not come hunting lizards.

Then he had a thought.

"See those birds above?" he asked.

"Too big for prey," the lizard said. "I hunt jumpmice."

"Do you see such birds often?"

"Wrong color for *griffaran*," the lizard said, rolling one eye skyward while the other kept watch on the dragon. "No, not see such birds before. Hawk and carrion-wing dayhunters."

AuRon wondered what two such hunters of the Red Queen, flying hard for the Lavadome, could be seeking in the night.

Had the Red Queen somehow learned of the hour and place of his departure?

Hardly moving, even to breathe, he let them pass overhead.

When they were thin black lines against the sky again he caught the lizard's attention.

"Thank you for the information. Is the water nearby wholesome?"

"Best drink in the world," the lizard said.

"I thank you again. Good luck with the jumpmice." AuRon raised a *saa* high and stomped, hard. Tiny rodents bounded away in panic. The lizard scrambled after them with an excited hiss.

AuRon resolved to fly low and slow for the rest of the night, and hide out of the sun.

He had an easier time finding his way back to Naf's encampment.

He overflew the woods, searching, searching, while wolves howled beneath. The wolves were complaining of men to the northwest devouring all the deer.

Naf's men must have moved—or perhaps they'd learned not to light campfires where the roc-riders could see.

Or he was too late, and his friends had been destroyed.

As he passed over thickly wooded hills on a blustery afternoon he heard a hunting horn—or so it seemed. He turned, following the sound. A flaming spark streaked up from the trees.

He altered course, saw another streak of flame rise.

He searched the sky, looking for the Queen's riders.

It was all very well for them to indicate where they were hiding in the forests. He was considerably larger than a flaming signal arrow. For a dragon to land there risked breaking a wing.

He had to settle for a messy, painful landing on top of the green canopy, quickly folding his wings as the limbs gave way . . .

Six *kraaaks,* a cascade of *snick-snaps,* and a very loud *swoosh-thunk* later, he stood on the forest floor, smelling the spring growth and the hearty rotting smell of last year's leaves breaking into detritus.

He righted himself and shook the twigs out of his *griff,* hoping he hadn't landed on anyone.

Coming up the slope, he heard running water and followed the sound to a camp at a creek curled up next to a tumble of water that was neither rapids nor waterfalls but something in between. But there were rocks aplenty and tree trunks placed upon them so men might cross without wetting their boots.

"Pfew!" a sentry on a high, twiggy platform whistled. "His lordship's dragon's back."

Men and their adaptive abilities. They could sound like birds when they chose. Run like horses by riding, fly like dragons by taming savage beasts, even dragons. They even had a desire to be turtles, judging from some of the armor he'd seen.

AuRon saw Naf's tall form standing in the center of a warren of crude huts, part tent, part shack, part burrow. The smell of cooking meat and boiling laundry rose from the camp.

He glided across the river and landed in a central strip of green that smelled of horses.

"It's fortunate for us that tail of your body is as distinctive as the tale of your travels," Naf said, smiling in his usual cheery manner. Naf could fall into a dungheap and have his house collapse and still find something to laugh about. "At first we were afraid you were one of the Queen's dragons. I've asked my cook to heap a shield with sausages and deer-vitals as a welcome. I'm afraid I lack the more civilized seasonings, but there's salt and some rosegift and butterbloom—"

"I see you've shifted camp again," AuRon said, trying to keep his mouth dry at the thought of sausages after so much flying.

"We were found again by the roc-riders, the fabled gods know how."

"I have an idea about that," AuRon said, wondering if he could manage a takeoff through a break in the foliage above the stream. "Naf, cling to my back. You must fly!"

"What have you seen?"

"Nothing. It's what I have done."

Naf raised an eyebrow to match the corner of his mouth. "I wouldn't leave my men! You must know that."

"Then run away with them. Just leave this place. The Queen is coming!"

Naf whistled, and gave a few orders. The men began to wake up and go to work gathering their possessions and harnessing their pack animals.

"How do you know?"

AuRon thought it the best compliment of all that Naf had issued his orders first and asked questions later. If there were more such men, he wouldn't be keeping them at a cold, stormy sea's distance on the Isle of Ice. "The last time we met, I had a necklace. The Queen saw whatever I saw, heard whatever I heard, through it. Some magic of hers."

"It didn't do her much good. My scouts report riders to the south and north, but they're back searching the column rocks and sweeping through the mountains, where we'd last been camping."

"Their columns would not be closing on these hills as they search the mountains?"

Naf's eyebrows narrowed. AuRon had been too long away to determine if that meant he was interested or suspicious or vexed. "Yes, they're passing close. But the search is proceeding in the other direction."

"Last time I was here you told me you had volunteers joining you, a steady stream."

"Yes. Some stay, others I send on to seek refuge in Hypatia. What's left of the elves at Krakenoor are happy to have men to help rebuild their city."

"Search your recruits who have joined since I visited you, or just before. I would not be surprised if one has a crystal similar to the one I wore."

Naf frowned. "Most of my men are Dairuss. A few Ghioz with reason to hate the Queen, some from the horsedowns who've lost their grazing lands . . ."

"A Dairuss or one of those others couldn't play you false, using a stone such as I wore about my neck?"

"I'll have some of my men search the most recent arrivals for such a stone. If one has it, they'll find him hanging when they close in on the camp."

"Naf, I unwittingly gave the Queen a view of your camp. If there is a spy in your camp, he may be just as unwitting. You're better off just burying the crystal, or better yet, smashing it."

AuRon had a thought. "Or better yet . . ."

He offered a suggestion for a way to turn the Red Queen's insight against her. Naf's smile widened as he thought the matter over.

Naf put a few of the men who'd been with him longest to searching the recent arrivals as the others broke up the camp.

A detail of six men rigged AuRon with a drag of beams, hoof on sticks, and a sort of rolling log rigged with worn-out footwear. AuRon could do his part in making a false trail, whatever the outcome of the search.

They turned up a Dairussian youth, in his first beard, in possession of a triangular chip of crystal set in a wrist-bracer for his sword arm. They showed it to AuRon, and he guessed it was of the same vintage as the stone he'd worn about his neck. Naf ordered the ornament removed and stuffed deep into a bag filled with clattering herb-bottles—no telling if the Queen could hear as well as see through the thing.

The boy said the bracer had been given to him by his uncle, a veteran of a term with the old Red Guard who'd retired with an allotment on the Queen's land-grant yet seemed strangely encouraging of his nephew's desire to join the rebels. The boy thought the leather looked rather new for such an old war trophy, but his uncle told him he'd replaced the sweat-stained old leather, keeping only the buckles and the attractive talisman.

"I wonder what the uncle receives for this service," Naf said, after assuring the boy that he was not in danger. "A perfect spy," Naf said. "He's intelligent and energetic. And he can both read and write. I was considering making him the messenger of my best scouting team, once he gained a little more woodcraftiness scraping his toes and rounding down his bootheels."

To be sure, they searched the rest of the new arrivals. It would be just like the thorough Red Queen, who always had another plan in place if the first failed, to infiltrate Naf's camp with multiple spies in case the first was discovered.

As they did this, a breathless scout arrived, panting that the Ghioz columns had turned and were moving hard against the camp from two directions.

Under Naf's direction and the guidance of a scout with the legs of saplings and the body of a scarecrow, AuRon dragged the contraption downstream, along with a pair of mules distinctly unhappy at being forced to walk in the odiferous wake of a dragon. When they weren't complaining of the stench, they were hazarding guesses as to which of the pair the dragon would eat first.

"You the plumper, Nok. Dragon eat you raw and juicy. I'm stringy. He smoke me good for later."

"I'm not eating either of you, as long as you step lively," AuRon said over his wing.

"Quicker we get there, quicker we're eaten," Nok said. "Hope I'm a bird in the next life. I'll find this gray stinkbomb by the smell and dump on him."

"I don't think birds can smell," AuRon said.

A *sii*-score of Naf's men walked ahead of him in a tight bunch, one wearing the bracer under a long piece of waxed canvas meant to keep it out of the rain. Through it, he gave the crystal a view of the backs of the men in front of him and an occasional look at the cliffs the river cut through above.

Another flaming marker arrow sputtered down, hissing as it struck the rushing water. AuRon looked up at the cliff above, a deep notch with trees growing on it cleaving the rock face into a shape like a pig's hoof.

The man with the bracer wrapped his canvas cover around it and stuffed it back into the bag with the clanking medicine bottles. They hurried along, with AuRon dragging his trail-creating contraption and the mules bellowing in protest. And so they came to a trio of fallen trees, cut from a wooded notch in the cliffside and blocking the path.

AuRon chewed his way out of the harness, half tempted to eat the noisier of the two mules to teach the other a lesson about complaining so much—*gripers get eaten first*. But he heard hoofbeats echoing down the canyon, and besides, it seemed unfair huntsdragonship to eat someone with whom you've bandied words.

As he looked at the barricade, with cloaks and old broken helms decorating the branches like warriors lined up behind the fallen timber, it occurred to him that the mules might be smarter than they let on and had engaged him in conversation with his sensibilities in mind.

No time to lose in filling his belly.

He examined the river. Next to the barricade and downstream the river widened and grew calmer, and probably shallower, judging by the shape of the waves. He couldn't hide there.

But upstream looked more promising.

AuRon plunged into the stream and waded—or swam, in the deeper pools—upstream to a mass of rocks breaking the river into confused froth. The water would carry away his scent as long as he kept under it. He found a pair of boulders that diverted much of the flow, and, muscles twitching and wishing to be active in the cold flow, he settled down between them, eyes and nostrils above water and a bit of driftwood camouflage stuck in the horns of his crest, awaiting events.

At least the river was a little wider here. If matters went ill he could rise from the water and escape the ensnaring branches in a few flaps.

The vanguard of the Ghioz column appeared, riders moving widely spaced with bows notched.

The men behind the barricade launched arrows at them. They fired madly, trying to send up a volume of arrows rather than well-aimed strikes. The Ghioz scouts turned their horses and rode back.

AuRon watched the main body approach, a black block of archers to the front, tightly packed like some enormous multi-legged insect. Behind them, AuRon counted riders interspersed with dismounted men with swords and axes or hefting javelins.

The dismounted warriors must mean their mounts were somewhere farther back. It should be easy to smell that many horses.

Under swarms of arrows, the Ghioz column approached the barricade. Many heads turned to watch the cliffs nervously, but perhaps the trackers and whoever might be in communication with the Red Queen assured them that the retreating rebels had followed the riverbank in hurried retreat.

Ghioz skirmishers ran forward, javelins and light axes at the ready, giving high war-yips like slim hunting dogs after rabbits. They flung the javelins and buried the axes in trunk or helm, vaulting up to the peak of the short, irregular wall. Others shouldered one of the trunks, opening a gap big enough for a horse. Seeing but a few men falling back before them, they yelled to their fellows, and horsemen came forward to complete the destruction of what they must have thought was a rearguard designed to delay their advance.

As the first rider passed through the gap in the trail-block, Naf acted.

A horn blew and a rain of arrows fell from the cliff. The Ghioz column reacted like a flock of sheep to approaching wolves; they whirled and tightened ranks.

An avalanche of rock and beam fell from the cliff. Some bounced off the cliff to land harmlessly in the river, but enough rolled into the Ghioz, carrying more with it, that the column dissolved into chaos.

Some desperate souls escaped into the river by jumping in and swimming.

Naf's men descended through the steep notch with the aid of ropes, under the cover of concealed archers. Still more continued to throw stones down on their enemies, leaving bloody men and horses scattered on the riverbank path.

A pair of roc-riders came shrieking down into the river canyon, perhaps seeing battle joined from far away but losing track of the action in their dive. One suddenly folded and fell, dashing its rider to pieces as it bounced off the cliffside, shafts from the cliff-top bowmen projecting from its head and neck like a lopsided mating display.

The remaining rider wheeled, and AuRon's hearts pounded when he saw the rider guide his mount up the river, flying low and gathering speed for a climb to the cliff-top level.

He'd never make it.

AuRon exploded out of the rushing stream, brought down rider and bird in a crash of avian forehead against dragon chest and *sii*. Feathers flew, the rider went head over heels into the river, and AuRon and his prey rolled into the flow. He stomped and tore and left the ruin of the bird tainting the white water red.

AuRon turned on the Ghioz, most of whom had their backs to the river, thinking that quarter safe.

Poor conventional-minded fools. But then, they would fight a lord with an old dragon friend.

Still more of Naf's men were now running for the barricade, having either come down another notch as the Ghioz approached or sent there earlier. They joined the men descending the ropes to harry the Ghioz, now recoiling up the riverbank like a snake backing away from a burning brand.

AuRon, with one eye cocked to the sky in case more roc-riders arrived, chose a likely spot and set fire to a mix of riverside brush, dry driftwood, and timber.

Retreat through that, he thought with satisfaction.

Then he launched himself up the river to seek out those horses.

He found them hardly a score of wing-flaps back, gathered in another notch with the baggage train and carts and wagons filled with feed and bundles.

He scattered the horse-guard with a lightning descent, gout of flame, and swipe of his tail. They didn't even have time to notch arrow to string. Then he circled back and landed hard in the water. Much of his splash fell on the backs of men fleeing or riding off at a gallop, leaving their baggage train.

It burned gloriously. The bags of grain caught fire with loud *whoofs,* and alarmed mules gladly tore themselves loose from picket-lines and trotted off, yelling their heads off in the beast-tongue: *Dragon draagon* draaagon!

The horses scattered in terror, fleeing flame and the alarming odor of a dragon—which AuRon was doing his best to enhance by voiding whatever he could onto the highest branches he could reach by cocking his leg like a flop-eared dog. He did his best to herd them into the river, where the current would put an end to many of them or carry them down to Naf and his men in the calmer waters.

He swam back downstream to find the Ghioz in full retreat, harried by archers popping in and out of the trees. They did not stop to aid their wounded, but AuRon saw many an ugly scene of those pierced by arrows thrown off their horses and dumped into the stream as a new warrior took saddle and rein.

Ghioz and its Red Queen, it seemed, could be beaten after all.

AuRon didn't understand even a fraction of what the Dairussians said. It seemed they were calling Naf "Lord Dragonheart."

"Dragons have more than one heart," AuRon corrected.

Naf and his men were enjoying a dinner of stick-toasted horseflesh. For AuRon, the grateful Dairuss bagged livers and hearts and kidneys into horse intestines, wrapped them in skins, and blackened them all over the fire.

AuRon thought it one of the most delicious meals he'd ever eaten, despite the smell of burning horsehair (which probably somewhat covered the odor of a well-fed dragon's sulfurous burps and emissions as his firebladder refilled).

He thought it best if he at least saw Naf safely to his new camp. This one was in some ancient ruin, nothing more than rings of stones set on a hillside in the forest and a few cairns running the ridgeline above like the bones on a blighter's back, but there were clay-lined grain pits that could be cleaned out and wells that would produce water once cleared of the deadfalls and wildlife.

Naf said he suspected it was an old elf settlement. There were yew trees aplenty, which elves always planted for the construction of their bows. A few limbs would be cut to replace worn wood or supply new weapons for recruits coming over the mountains.

Only these would stripped, bathed, and checked for crystals . . .

Already Naf was hearing back from his scouts and spies on the Ghioz borders.

"We've angered our good foes, AuRon. As the Ghioz see things, scattering horses and burning pack-trains is a violation of an honorable warrior's code."

"What does their code say about throwing wounded into a mountain river?"

"Oh, it's that whole victors and failures 'ethics of the strong' that their priests spout. To the victors the spoils, to the failures a new station serving the victors, so they might learn and do better next time."

AuRon was about to comment on men being born mad—was not the first sound every human made a wailing scream?—and dying even more madly, but was that terribly different from the fights hatchlings engaged in, with bits of wet egg still clinging about their snouts?

"My spies report that our obstinacy at the riverbank has incensed the Red Queen. She's claiming that the Hypatians have assisted us in battle—for how else could a scarecrow band like mine triumph over Ghioz arms?—and a state of war now exists between Hypatia and Ghioz."

"No wonder old NooMoahk was always glum when I spoke of the wider world," AuRon said. "I wonder how many wars he saw in his long years."

"It's not a man's thought but a man's deeds that count, AuRon. Same rule for dragons, I expect."

AuRon belched and felt his firebladder settle.

"A terrible reckoning is at hand," Naf said. "I wonder if I shall be blamed by both sides. Could be, no matter which empire wins, myself and the Dairussians will end up vassals. Again."

Hominids. If there were but six left in all the Red Mountains, they'd soon shave it down to three by fighting, and two would make the third their slave.

"Come with me," AuRon said. "Come to my island. You could live out your life in peace."

"The peace of an exile? I can't. It's hard to explain, but if my people believe me still alive, still fighting, it's as though some part of them hasn't been beaten. More so, I have to keep near, be a threat, or I fear it will be the end of Hieba, or my daughter."

AuRon felt a pang at Hieba's name. The little girl he'd hunted for and watched grow up, snared in all this, thanks to no crime but her love of this man. "How can you be so sure they still live? Have you had word?"

Naf picked a sizable hunk of meat from the gap in his teeth, worked it thoughtfully with his toadlike tongue. AuRon could never make up his mind which hominid line had the ugliest arrangement of features. "No. It's just—a feeling. And the Queen—she's too keen a calculator of chances. If matters were to go ill with her, she'd like to have them as goods to be negotiated in a final bargain."

AuRon tailvented enough air-volume to make the stars shimmer in their courses, interrupting his friend. "Horsemeat always does that in me," he said, by way of apology for the interruption.

"Can I suggest that you stay with me? I could use a pair of eyes in the clouds. Better still, bring your family here, and aid me in my cause. I could promise you and yours food and safe landings as long as the Dairussians call themselves men of honor. With the help of some dragons, I might be able to get my lands back. Then Ghioz would have a true enemy hard on her border. I might bring down the Queen herself."

"I'm not sure she can be killed," AuRon said. "She brags of immortality."

"It's the same hickory-dickory her priests spout. I think she uses doubles. If one is killed, another takes her place, and the Queen shows herself only to her most trusted courtiers in the safest of circumstances. She must keep four or five copies of herself, women of her height and shape who imitate her voice. You met her, saw the masks?"

"Yes."

"Once I thought only that she was hideous. Men are too easily swayed by appearances of women—one way or the other. I don't know how it is with dragons."

"We appreciate beauty in our mates, but the wise dragon chooses for other reasons."

"Well, now I think it aids her use of doubles."

"How do you know?" AuRon asked.

Naf looked thoughtful. "Because I killed her. In her own bedroom. I stole in, said I'd been summoned. The Queen has odd appetites. I fashioned a weapon from a bone hairbrush. I felt her heart flutter its last under my palm, but when I took off the mask. . . . Oh, if men only knew."

AuRon waited for more, but thought it best not to press him for further details.

"Just as well I didn't collect my ransom from her, I think."

Naf returned from his memories. "How's that?"

"I'd hoped to return to my island bearing coin."

"Then you won't stay?"

"I will always call you my friend. But I can't hurl myself into the flames of war. I have a mate and hatchlings to think of."

"I think of mine even as I draw my sword," Naf said.

AuRon could not find a reply.

"Well, I'd be a poor friend if I sent you back empty—errr, handed. I have a few coins. A very few. You're welcome to them."

He made a birdlike whistle.

An adolescent girl approached, tall and a little awkward in her movements. She had rich red hair braided out of the way of her duties.

"This is my camp helper and tentmate. She's the daughter of a man who rode with me, a son of Dairuss now dead. Get the dragon-box."

The girl scuttled off. She had slight swelling at her hips. AuRon's limited understanding of hominids allowed that the configuration meant she was ready to mate. "Hieba might wonder, keeping someone like that in your camp."

"Oh, it's not that kind of arrangement. I'm getting a little old for such antics, my friend."

Naf sighed, as if regretting either his age or hers. "We spoke of beauty earlier. Beauty for a Dairuss is a reason for lament. The Ghioz take what they like."

The girl returned with a wooden box. She carried it easily enough, as it wasn't much bigger than a loaf of risen bread. Dragon forms, rather more snakelike than the real thing, at least to AuRon's taste, decorated the lid, inlaid in dark wood.

"It's an artistic style. Dragons are mostly wing, and if artists were to draw them as they lived, there'd be less room for teeth and fire."

"Perhaps I will take up cave-painting and draw a few humans with tiny, flattened heads."

Naf laughed, that easygoing boom AuRon found to be his most appealing feature. "Let's forget the box and remember the contents. Behold! The mighty treasury of a onetime governor. Do not stare in wonder too long, AuRon, for I believe dragons can become be-witched by the sight of such riches."

He opened the lid on the box. It was almost empty. Perhaps three-score coins lay within, a mixture of gold and sliver.

Naf scooped out half of them.

"Here, my friend. I have a bag. Offer these to your hatchlings. A present from an old family friend."

"Naf, you must need this coin," AuRon said.

"It has its uses, but my men serve for vengeance, not for gold."

"Still—"

"There's more where it came from. I robbed for these, I can rob for more. AuRon, if you delay much longer I'll ram the whole thing down your throat, and your noisy digestion can make of it whatever fireworks it will."

"Thank you, my friend."

"Well?" Naf said, selecting a leather pouch.

"I will take four coins, one for each of my hatchlings, tokens of many wasted horizons, and four more for my mate. No more, or you will have another fight in these woods."

It turned out he left the camp more weighted down than he could hope for. Word passed through the rebels that their dragon needed coin, and even the youngest wood-carrier and water-scoop searched their boot-pocket for a Queen's silver. They filled four saddlebags heavy with coin and arranged them front and back of his wings with hitches of running knot.

Naf encircled his neck with his strong arms, and many in the camp passed their hands over his flanks, though their greasy touch made his tail twitch and he kept an eye rolling across them looking for drawn blade.

They sang a song in his honor as he left, the camp dividing it into three parts: the women and immature boys singing high, Naf and some of the deeper voices low, and the rest rather out of tune in the middle.

If he were to be honest, his digestion made far sweeter music.

But he kept circling back to get his bearings and watch the woods as he gained altitude, thinking of Hieba as a little girl, crying out her loneliness against his flank.

He wondered if he hadn't left something behind. Like a piece of his conscience.

Chapter 18

The day after the assembly, Takea was teaching Wistala a singsong about the different hills in the Lavadome.

Gryathus hill of Wyrr and wall
By river ring and deman hall
The next around, as river winds
The grazing fields of NuGrakat's lines

A member of the Drakwatch, a young drake, ignored the calls and jokes from the drakka as he delivered a message.

"I am here to escort the new dragonelle to Imperial Rock. The Queen requests her presence."

Wistala was happy to abandon her lesson in topography. It seemed there wasn't a dragonlength of space in the Lavadome that wasn't claimed by one line or another.

She followed the drake to the Imperial Rock. Takea trailed along, using the excuse that she could point out landmarks, but she spent much of it trying to provoke a fight with the Drakwatch messenger. Wistala had learned enough about the Firemaids to know that a victory in a wrestling match with a member of the Drakwatch was a sure way to get praised by the maidmother.

The drake ignored her taunts and tail-tags, chattering the whole way of a new muster of the older members of the Drakwatch to guard tunnel exits. "Firemaid work," he complained.

He led her to the "Imperial Gardens." They lost Takea near the exit for the Aerial Host's dining halls. Wistala marveled at the growth here, high under the diffused light from the dome-tip above. Strange purple and blue-green blossoms and artfully shaped ferns grew in the muted light of the sun circle above.

They found Queen Nilrasha at a series of splashes, half waterfall, half fountain. A statue of a hatchling spat a thin stream of water, artfully arranged so it bounced off a pair of carved mushroom-caps. Statues of lithe human and elvish girls, posed elegantly, filled jugs that Wistala's sense told her fed back into the fountain.

"Wistala, I would speak to you," Nilrasha said.

She looked down at the floor of the Lavadome. Wistala followed her gaze. Hills and pens and goats—was it milkdrinker's hill? Hominid servants—or rather thralls, as they styled slaves in the Lavadome.

"The Tyr and I ask you for the benefit of your experience. The Lavadome shall send a group of Firemaids to offer assistance to the Hypatians and build an alliance. Do you believe they will accept?"

"Hypatia is . . ." Wistala searched for the right words. "Hypatia is not like the Lavadome. It is not a matter of someone making a decision. There's no all-powerful Tyr to win over and settle matters."

Nilrasha gave a humorous *prrum* and resettled her wings. "When you understand the Lavadome better, you will not say such a thing."

Wistala, having figured out the flow of the water, watched the lava run down the other side of the crystal. Beautiful colors.

"Dragonkind is depending on you, Wistala," Nilrasha continued. "We can no longer stay underground, at least as dragons rather than some kind of slaves. I fear we'd turn into little more than a lava-lit stockyard for raising young dragons to be brought to the surface. To survive, we have to return to the surface. We've been so long underground, in hiding, we know very little of the Upper World. We need friends up there who can guide us to safety. Friends we can trust."

"I must ask you the same question. Can the Upper World trust dragonkind? If I am to go to Hypatia, do I know that you're offering an alliance of equals? Hypatia demands that even kings obey laws. I want to be able to promise aid, not obedience."

Nilrasha extended and settled her *griff*. Perhaps the Queen was not used to being questioned so closely.

"What kind of forces may I promise?" Wistala asked.

"So you will do it?"

"I am a Firemaid and will obey. Not that it matters, but I think it's a wise path the Tyr chooses. Dragons will thrive only if they learn flexibility in their relations with the hominids. It can't all be wars, thrall-taking, and 'Upholds.' "

"The Firemaids will be with you. Perhaps a score of dragonelles and threescore drakka."

"But the drakka cannot fly, and it is a long way to Hypatia."

"You haven't been long a Firemaid. Thanks to our experience with the new Aerial Host, we've learned the best way to fix some light straps punched through your fringe. The drakka grip the straps. It's not altogether different from hatchlings riding atop their mother's back. As long as they stay flat, flight is still possible. It's actually easier to carry two rather than one, for better balance."

Wistala thought of her desperate trip carrying dwarven wounded and messages from the doomed column, lost in the barbarian north so long ago.

"I'm no warrior."

"We will send Ayafeeia with you. She's our best. Do not worry. She is sensible. I spoke to her over my first meal. She will act as your maidmother when she sees fit, but will leave the Hypatians to you."

"Suppose I fail?"

"We will come to the surface in any case. Otherwise we will sicken and die."

Wistala had heard about the kern. But something else crossed her mind. She found herself liking the Queen.

"You love my brother."

"Yes. He's different."

Wistala watched her breathe. "True." She wondered if she should talk about the murder of her parents, expand upon a few details left out of the conversation at the assembly. No, no reason. Her brother had changed, it seemed.

She had too. She no longer wanted to claw his eyes out.

"May I ask one more question, my Queen?"

"Oh, you may ask. But there are questions I choose not to answer, sometimes."

"Why did you bring this to me? Does my brother fear my reaction?"

"Fear? No. But I frequently sound dragons as to his ideas. That way you can later be asked and assigned in court with proper pomp and ceremony."

"Perhaps matters of state in the Lavadome are more complex than they appear," Wistala said.

"You'll do well to support the Tyr, Wistala, and do your best for us. Like it or not, ever since that scene in the assembly, you're thought of as being in the Imperial Line, and a relative of RuGaard's. If the Tyr falls, you will too. Speaking of which, rank has its privileges. Take a roasting hog back to your sisters when you leave."

Wistala uttered a few more pleasantries and found Takea, who was wearing a fluffy rabbit's foot hooked in her *griff*. Together they managed to drag a whole hog back to their hill.

Wistala asked Takea what she'd occupied herself with during the audience, and the drakka described a visit to the Aerial Host to hear stories.

"And the rabbit's foot?"

"From a thrall boy, Zathan, the son of one of the Free Thralls in the Aerial Host. You know they raise many rare rabbits in the host caves? Not just for meat. They grow long hair that the riders stitch into their jerkins to keep them warm aloft. I promised to let him ride me one day, and he took a loose scale and I took his rabbit's foot. We'll keep the tokens until my wings come."

Wistala left the Lavadome with more than a score of dragonelles and twice that in Firemaids. The Tyr, at a ceremony full of all the pomp and pageantry Nilrasha had promised, insisted that they take a few bats along as he wished them good fortune on the surface.

The Firemaids chuckled. The Tyr and his bats.

Blighters banging giant drums shook Imperial Rock as they offered to endure hardships and death in the Upper World.

He wished them farewell, calling them the first explorers of a new history for dragonkind, representing the rehatching of their species—as dragons emerged from protective egg, so to would they leave the dark.

"Rise, and rise with you the hopes of dragonkind," the Tyr said.

The flying straps were well designed. They didn't interfere with wing movement, and allowed the drakka to hang on to either side of the fringe—the nerveless tissue was pierced by wooden handles to help them hang on—and they rode easily enough out of the wind.

Their flight northwest to Hypatia began in confusion. A few members of the Aerial Host guided them for three horizons, then returned with a warning to keep well west of the horsedowns.

Luckily Ayafeeia knew what the horsedowns were.

Wistala did not know these lands, and the Lavadome's maps were old and inaccurate. She had to trust to hope that they would reach the southern provinces, where she'd traveled with Ragwrist's circus a score or more years ago.

At least the hunting was good. The savannah, broken by empty seasonal watercourses in what looked to be the dying part of the year, had herds of antelope and half-horse following the rains north. A few primitive bands of blighters and humans followed the herds, skirmishing with each other as they went.

Of course the Firemaids wanted to gossip about old wounds between her and their Tyr. She admitted only that both she and her brother had been greatly altered by their experiences.

Luckily, the herds were moving in the right direction.

Sooner or later, the stars must turn familiar, if she just flew north long enough so that the flying dragon of the southern skies disappeared and the bowing dragon rose.

They passed into rich grasslands and she recognized the distant spine of the southern tips of the Red Mountains. And with that she was back in familiar lands, the southern provinces of Hypatia. She'd once searched this far south looking for dragons, but had decided that the empty plains beyond didn't look promising. Perhaps, had she just gone south as long as land held, she would have come to the range holding the Lavadome—though only *griffaran* showed themselves above the dragon mountains.

She took her Firemaids to the coast of the Inland Ocean, and they dined on fresh fish, crabs, and sea turtles. They passed over the ruins of the old elven sea-city—she'd seen Krakenoor in its glory, sadly, before the race war of the dragon-riders that she'd missed while hunting AuRon in the east.

When they reached the coastal marshes she knew they were less than three horizons from Hypat. The marshes had been settled and then abandoned long ago, but roads and paths still crisscrossed the wet mass.

There was food and game to be found, if you didn't mind crayfish, smelly water-rats, and raccoons.

She'd once been told that the gods smiled on the foundations of Hypat.

She knew the air on this part of the coast well. Ragwrist's circus rested here, so that old talent could be paid off in changing-house funds and new talent hired and trained from those drawn to the marble city from across half a world.

From above, the city reminded her of a jawbone of some big herbivore. The long, toothy side hugged the river creeping into the Green Tidetwist of the Inland Ocean, with the great thick bulge of the city on somewhat higher ground overlooking some marshes that provided nutritious mud for the city's gardens—even the most impoverished resident could scratch a living hauling wet mud—

By some trick of river, ocean, wind, and sun the city saw sunshine almost every day of the year—bright, cool sun that burned off the fogs that rolled in off the Inland Ocean and into the famous vineyards. A half-day flight to the north and you cursed the fogs and the cold wet that bypassed your skin entirely and settled in around your bones; a half-day flight to the south and the air was humid and the black-bark forests smelled like rot filled with rain-slicked squirrels and torpid turtles. Only the ants hurried anywhere.

But the pocket of dry air and sun surrounding Hypat seemed ordered by nature herself; she'd decided that whoever dwelt along these brief horizons should enjoy cool nights and afternoon sunshine just warm enough for napping. Wistala had been told they paid for it with wild storms roaring in off the Inland Ocean at the equinoxes, but even those were brief.

Her first duty would be to pay a call on the librarians at the keeper's school. Though Hypat was not as great a center as the giant archive at Thallia, the librarians there would be better acquainted with whatever trials faced Hypatia, for they educated the sons and daughters of the prominent families and advised the directors.

She wished she'd paid more attention to her old mentor Rainfall when he spoke of the Hypatian Directory.

The keeper's school lay to the south of the city, on grounds ringed by homes piled atop each other on the remains of a rock-slide. Connected gardens and courtyards formed green squiggles between the homes. Colorful awnings shaded rooftops or the street fronts.

Her descent and landing caused a stir. Everyone from fire wardens to fruit vendors fought their way through the streets to get a view over the library walls.

After identifying herself, she waited in the garden behind the school. She listened to the clatter of shutters being opened and passed time by counting young faces in the windows.

The head librarian himself came to speak to her. He knew her by sight. She'd met him years ago but couldn't remember his face. According to him, half the city was anxious about war with Ghioz. They'd taken two thanedoms in the southern reaches of the Red Mountains and demanded gold from four others so that a new set of trading posts might be built for the benefit of both empires.

There was much talk of war ruining the spring rites and the traditional revelries of blessing the new plantings.

He summoned two officials of the Directory—optimates, in the Hypatian tongue, but where they ranked in the complex hierarchy of the Directory Wistala couldn't remember. There were twenty-seven different titles. They had long names that would do a dragon credit and wore a variety of robes and decorative sashes. The stouter one, Ansab, walked so that his belly rode high—just under his chin, it seemed to Wistala—and the other, called Paffle, was aged and always rubbing his hands in anxiety.

When they learned she was ranked as a librarian they gave her brief tips of the head, so she guessed they stood somewhere above librarians.

"A half-council is already in session and the agenda is full," stamped Ansab.

"But she is an ambassador."

"Ah, but not from an acknowledged state! Remember what happened when that churl arrived claiming to represent the Moon King of Gaiyai!"

"Pleasant fellow," Paffle said. "Well spoken. Always made me laugh."

"Ate in half the Directory's houses and borrowed money from the other half, then *fsssst*!" Ansab's meaty arm shot out and up.

"I've no intention of committing a *fsssst*," Wistala said.

"Oh, no no no!" Paffle said, shrinking like a worm caught in the sun. "We never meant to suggest—well. I do apologize, librarian. Oh, dear."

"Perhaps in twomonth," Ansab said. "There's a meeting of the Directory. You can get on the agenda for that, though I warn you, a quarter-Directory's decision can only be ratified by a meeting of the full Directory, and you can't imagine how busy those are."

"Are you at war or aren't you? I come to offer help," said Wistala.

"Oh, dear! Another warmonger," Paffle groaned, scabbing at the sides of his head as though to protect his ears from an unpleasant noise. "The Directory is divided already."

"It's all a matter of commerce. Once the question of use of the Falnges is settled, matters will calm down," Ansab said.

"But suppose they aren't settled?"

"Doom, doom, doom," the librarian put in. "It's been foretold every generation. Those dragon-riders, for example. Supposed to burn the city to the foundation. Every refugee coming in had a worse story. But they never came. I always said there was never anything to those stories, but people would rather alarm themselves. It settled itself down and the doomsayers found a new object of anxiety."

"May I speak to the Directory or not?" Wistala asked, eyeing the cording stitched about Ansab's robe. He had silver and gold rope-work decorating his cloak.

"Oh, of course you may speak," Ansab said. "As a Hypatian citizen and a librarian you have every right to speak to the Directory. I'll have you on the agenda in no more than sixmonth."

"I thought you said two?"

"That's for an uncredentialed ambassador. Sixmonth is as a Hypatian librarian. If she still is a librarian," he added, eyeing the head librarian. "I don't know what librarian policies are for dividing allegiance. We optimates ensure that affairs of Directory are run smoothly and fairly, and such matters fall outside our province."

"Good. I need an expert to explain all this to my Tyr," Wistala said. She reached out and picked Ansab up by his robes. "I'm taking you because you show some fat on you," she said out of the side of her mouth. "I'm afraid that thin one will perish in the cold at the higher altitudes."

"Wha— Put me down!" Ansab squawked. "Help! Paffle!"

Wistala thought he smelled like a wet chicken.

"Oh, dear," Paffle said. "If you're going to carry someone off, couldn't you just grab an arbiter? They're more accustomed to travel."

"Paffle!"

Wistala gave her wings an experimental beat and Ansab screamed. "Don't worry. It's just four or five hard days to the Lavadome. You won't lose too many toes."

"L-Lavadome?" Ansab asked.

"Yes."

"I thought that was a myth," the head librarian said.

"No, it's where the Tyr lives," Wistala said. "He always has room on his agenda. I just hope he's in a good mood when I have to explain why threescore dragons wasted their time coming to save your miserable hide."

"Are there really demen with whips?" Paffle asked, looking livelier than he had the whole conversation. "Hold your temper, Ansab, old fellow. A full court bow would be best. You'll be the laughingstock of the baths if you're all striped from the lash."

"Shut up, you old fool," Ansab shouted. "We'll put you on this afternoon's agenda. Just put me down!"

"Thank you," Wistala said. "I doubt that fine robe would have held you the whole way."

Ansab plucked at a bit of torn cording. "It's ruined as is."

"Oh, that was wonderful," Paffle said. "I'll buy you a new robe, and count the price cheap in return for the entertainment."

"Your librarians should have better manners," Ansab said, glowering at the head librarian.

"She is a dragon, optimate. She's something of a librarian-at-large. It's Thallia's doing, anyway. They just use naming a dragon among their staff as a way to raise funds. Never fails to impress the patrons when they read out her account of the Wheel of Fire–Varvar war. I hope I do not give offense, Wistala."

"I labored hard over that account," Wistala said. "I'm glad it's of some use."

They brought Wistala up the high road, which ran through the city between the old gates and the Ziggurat. A sort of mobile crowd followed, being dribbled away from and added to as they passed up the elevated road.

It was a pleasant walk. The high road ran two or three humans high most of the way and was flanked by columns with statues of the great figures of Hypatia. Wistala saw bearded dwarves with modest

visors partly shielding their faces, elves with victory garlands growing in their hair, and men. There was even a blighter carrying a hammer and chisel.

"Doklahk, a celebrated stonemason," the head librarian said as
he walked next to her, following the optimates. Evidently his duties
at the library school weighed lightly enough so he could come to the
Directory and watch events.

She wondered if Rainfall's grandsire was among the statues.

Flanking the high road were two streams of flowing water.
Smaller channels and even pipes diverted the flow off among the
rooftops to other quarters of the city.

"Hypat is a city of baths and gardens," Paffle said, puffing even
on such a slight incline. "You need a good deal of water for either."

"Water!" Ansab said. "Any beaver can claim the same level of
civilization. Lamps are the glory of Hypatia. Two thousand public
lamps, twice that about private domiciles, and a whaling fleet to keep
them lit."

"They're both wrong," the head librarian whispered. "Courts
where citizens can get a fair hearing and criminals a fair punishment—
that's our glory. The Ghioz, whom all seem to praise for their vigor
in war and commerce, know only the rich man's law, where wealth
and justice are one."

Laborers lounged outside the water-house that somehow fed the
streams lining the high road and others descending from the Temple
Hill. They circled north around the hill and came to a round building
of vaguely bluish marble, columned outside and in, with dozens of
stairways. Vendors and idlers and messengers lounged, sold, or hurried as their duties required.

They passed up the stairs. The only armed men she'd seen,
guards in purple, white, and gold, stood on pedestals overlooking the
stairs and shifted doubtfully as she approached. The guards looked to
Ansab and Paffle for guidance and relaxed when they smiled and announced her as a citizen and dignitary. She didn't blame them. Their
spears appeared more ceremonial than functional, and their great

square shields had so much artwork on them she doubted they could be easily braced in battle.

Then she entered the Directory.

It reminded her a little of the grand court in the Sadda-Vale, in that there was a hole in the ceiling admitting light and air, though it was smaller. Columns of various colors and types of stone stood all around, ones of limestone much decorated, with a pair of old black obelisks set off in an alcove in dignified isolation. Benches, stools, chairs, and statues of mighty beasts littered the open space—there was even a dragon, though the artist had become carried away and it bore entirely too many horns and tusks and the wrong number of toes.

Perhaps ten-score men met here, talking or drinking or eating from long, tiny platters built to easily extend a tidbit. They wore robes of black and white. White trimmed with black seemed to be the most popular, but some had black trimmed with white. Scribes and servants sat on little cushions, writing messages or keeping track of a debate.

Clever stairways and rests were built into many of the statues. Some men had climbed to the top of the larger ones to be better heard.

All eyes turned to her as her shadow fell across the floor.

Ansab rang a gong as they entered. Paffle leaned over to say something to one of the scribes. The scribe picked up sort of a wooden case and, holding it steady as though afraid to disturb the contents inside, carried it in their wake.

Ansab climbed onto a black statue of a pair of teamed horses rearing and leaping. A platform stood between them, carved to look like traces.

He spoke in a tongue only slightly familiar to Wistala. As best she could make out, he said, "Let the ears of those of the Directory hear, and through their tongues those of the city speak, and through their loins those of future generations remember, our words."

An elf stepped forward, long grapevines hanging to his waist growing from his hair. He wore a draping sort of garment tied this way and that about his torso.

"I am Cornucus, Voice of the Directory," he said, climbing the dragon statue until he stood just behind its horned crest. "Are you the same Wistala granted citizenship in Hypatia under the request of the librarians of Thallia?"

Wistala was grateful that he spoke so clearly. She had an easier time understanding him.

"I am."

Assorted shouts broke out from the men in black and white robes.

"Dragon. Librarian. Emissary," the Voice said. "*Ahem.* Which do you come as?"

"A daughter of Hypatia. A sister of dragons. I will be true to both."

Some of the directors shouted advice to the Voice, but he gave no sign of recognition.

"Say what you have been asked to say," the Voice said.

"The Tyr of the dragons asks me to say: We share a common enemy, the Red Queen of the Ghioz. In the end she will want the whole world. Should Ghioz claim either of our two kingdoms, the other would fall quickly. Only together can we see victory."

"Then you also come as a mother of troubles," a man in a white robe called.

Shouts and whistles broke out as she spoke. They were losing their awe of her quickly. Men were ever thus, plunging from fear to contempt. She tried to remember the respect for Hypatian institutions that Rainfall had taught her—after all, they'd known peace for years not easily counted.

"There will be no war," the Voice said. "Not if the Directory acts wisely."

Behind her she heard the head librarian mutter something to Paffle.

"You are wrong," a voice called in a more familiar accent of the Hypatian tongue.

Wistala followed the echo to a dark young man in riding apparel. He wore a heavy necklace of rectangular pieces of gold.

"We've already heard you speak—ahem—Thane of Hesturr."

Hesturr. Wistala remembered that name. The ruins of Hesturr tumbledown, the evil thane who'd stabbed gentle Rainfall. She looked at the man afresh. There was something of Vog in his wariness.

"But she has not heard me, sir."

He stepped up beside her and raised his palm in salutation. "I know the name Wistala of Mossbell."

At that there were more murmurs.

He ignored them, raising his voice. "While we speak through the day, dine and dance at night, and sleep long into the morning, Ironrider scouts move through Thul's Pass and raid our flocks in the north, steal horses, and assemble piles of firewood. I do not believe they do all this for the sake of amusement, though it may be hard for some of those here to imagine any other pursuit."

An older man stood up and hopped up on the pedestal supporting the dragon statue. "Roff, trade has always passed though Thul's Pass and the Ba-drink. The dwarves keep the pass."

"Yes. They always have as long as we remember. But that does not mean they always will."

"The Ironriders mass in the Iwensi Gap as well."

"The thanes of the north always cry war and ask for help to avert disaster," another director said, joining the others with the Voice at the dragon. "Salted cod and cries of disaster is all we receive from the north. The Empire would be better off without both."

"If I may return discussion to the dragon and her offer," the Voice said. "Do you have anything to add?"

"I did not come with just words. A force of dragons waits among the bugs in the marshes to the south," Wistala said.

"Hypatia would have more friends in the world. If your— ahem—Tyr would like to establish communication and commerce, Hypat would be pleased to see again the old routes reestablished in the south. We will not take sides in a war with Ghioz."

* * *

Wistala left the Directory, alone and dejected. Even the head librarian stayed behind to talk matters over with the Voice.

Roff, the thane from the north, hurried to catch up with her.

"Dragon, wait."

"Dragonelle," Wistala corrected. He was stocky but powerful-looking, like a tall dwarf. His eyes were as pleading as a dog's, but more intelligent.

"If you will accept the friendship of a piece of Hypatia, rather than the Directory, I would hear your answer."

"Does not the rule of the Directory apply to her thanes?"

"Oh, they weary me. But I had to make the trip. I found them as deaf as usual to difficulties in the north. We're poor provinces, compared to those south of the Falnges."

"I know. I spent years in the north."

"Yes. You once met my father, the night he died."

"Your father."

The man waved his hand, as though casting something away. "Yes. I know it's against tradition, for a thanedom to fall to a son, but more and more the thanes are going their own way on such matters, with so little contact or help from the Directory."

"No. I just—I expected a different reaction."

"You shouldn't. I grew up in my father's house. He was a jealous, ill-tempered man. I promised myself I'd be different, both as man and as thane. Ragwrist is a friend of mine, and our two poor lands are friendlier now."

"I am glad to hear it."

"The Hypatian order is failing. The Empire is no empire at all but a historical anachronism."

"Rainfall of Mossbell did not believe that to be true."

"He is dead. I fear in my lifetime I may need to make other arrangements for the security of the lands under my protection. With the Ironriders scouting my borders I'd make a pact with demen to save my thanedom. I will take the alliance you offer."

"I am not sure elves know death as you and I, but I do agree he is no longer the master of Mossbell."

"How many dragons do you offer?"

"A sc—fourteen have accompanied me, and twice that number of drakka—wingless females."

The thane lost some of his composure for the first time since they'd met.

"Fifteen! With you. That is a force to be counted as great. I know what that number of dragons can do, I saw it in the late war. We may be able to turn back the Ironriders after all."

"I'll settle for chasing them out of Hypatia."

"I should think you would be glad of its passing. The Hypatians killed dragons who stole from their flocks."

"There are more recent wrongs I am attempting to forget."

"You know the ruins of Hesturr—Tumbledown, some call it, I take it."

"I do."

"Bring your dragons there, but take care to fill their bellies with turtles or whatever you may find in the marshes before they arrive. My entire thanedom will have difficulty feeding so many dragons. Even on the easy path of the old north road, I fear you may arrive before us. A descent of dragons upon my lands would be met violently."

"We will make do somehow. We came to fight, not to eat. Your lands and flocks will remain undisturbed. If there is fighting, we will find sustenance."

Roff laughed. "A dragon-army at war. To think I lived to see such things."

"I will ride as quickly as I can to see to the muster. We meet again at Hesturr!"

She brought her dragons north into familiar lands in easy stages, flying at dawn and dusk. Under Ayafeeia's direction they flew north in four groups, with the lead turning south every few horizons and flying south until they were the back group. By such crossing patterns, watchers on the ground might be confused.

They landed in the ancient Hypatian ruins of Hesturr, piles of overgrown rubble that some would call picturesque. To Wistala they brought back mostly bad memories—the trip that ended in the loss of her father and Rainfall's wounding that night of the brush with the old thane, Vog.

Now the ruins of a great city held only sheep. The shepherds ran as the dragons landed and began to explore.

"Thick forests around here," Ayafeeia said. "Bad ground for fighting, especially against horsemen. They can use the trees as cover. We can't go after them without breaking wings."

Wistala suspected that the shepherds of Hesturr would be missing a few sheep when next they counted. Drakka kept flitting off to hunt and returning with bits of wool stuck in their snouts.

The lack of discipline rankled. "We came here to make friends, not impoverish the locals. The thane will give us sheep enough once he catches up to us."

Ayafeeia sent out dawn and dusk patrols to make sure the Ironriders weren't already on their way. They reported nothing of interest except game and livestock. Wistala warned them away from the livestock again.

Her maidmother granted her permission to visit the inn near Mossbell.

Either the village had shrunk, despite the new buildings, or she'd grown.

She could only pay a brief visit to the Green Dragon Inn, sticking her head in through the half-door in the back as in the old days, after receiving many embraces upon her landing.

The cats seemed most disturbed by her presence. Old Yari-Tab had long since died, but one of her kittens was now an aged, scrawny black cat named Aroo.

"Does the rainy season end soon, you think?" he asked Wistala.

"Wistala! Your brother has been here," Hazeleye said.

In response to that, she had to tell the story. And then tell it again, with fewer digressions into what the Lavadome was, who the Firemaids were, and why demen would bind and starve a dragon.

Widow Lessup still lived, though she had difficulty getting about.

They were still talking when Ragwrist and his mate, or rather, wife, Dsossa, rode in on lathered mounts.

"Can we expect a visit at Mossbell as well?"

"I must return to my comrades at Tumbledown."

They talked of war and trade on the bridge. Ragwrist had a plan for taking apart the repaired center span of the great bridge that his estate was responsible for keeping in order and hiding the pieces in Wistala's old troll-cave.

"AuRon left some kind of message for you there, if you wish to read it."

She did, that night. It was detailed instructions on how to fly to the Isle of Ice and which dragon to ask for and some talk of wolves.

She came to regret the trip. It reminded her of how happy she'd been at Mossbell. Perhaps, once she'd helped the Firemaids of the Lavadome and paid off, in part, the debt she could never pay in full, she would be able to return. This troll-cave was a splendid spot, though it needed a good cleaning thanks to the rooks and pelicans.

When she flew back to the ruins, she found Thane Hesturr there with a few of his retainers.

"It seems your company started on the sheep without me," he said. "I smoothed it over and told them I said you might feed yourselves from the flocks and I would reimburse them. But I'm not a rich man."

"Our help has a price," Ayafeeia said, when Wistala passed on the thane's complaint. She bit off a response. If this would be her role as a diplomat, "smoothing" over matters of poached sheep, her term as ambassador would be short-lived—she'd rather be telling fortunes with the circus again.

"I'm sorry we're taking up your shepherds' grazing space."

"It matters not. They like to bring the sheep here so they can poke around in the ruins. There's always some new rumor about where gold is buried."

"If there is gold buried here we'll soon have it up. Dragons have noses for refined metals. We were hunting those here when we had the unfortunate dispute with your father."

"I was a boy when he died," Thane Hesturr said, sounding very much out of humor. Before, he'd spoken of it lightly. Perhaps he was just tired from his journey, or perhaps he'd heard multiple complaints about missing animals. "I will take your help. While you are of aid to Hypatia, I offer you my courage and strength and support. Should you fail in your alliance, I will take my grandfather's revenge upon you."

Wistala translated that for Ayafeeia. She asked what he meant by support.

"Meat, fowl, and fish. Also, such irons as you might like. We'll be collecting old nails and broken tools for you."

"By the Stormbringer and the Nightdeath, we can use that," Ayafeeia responded to the translated offer.

Wistala flew out on a night reconnaissance to see how many of the rumors were true.

One she could verify at once: The Ironriders had moved before the Hypatians could gather, it seemed.

The carrion birds led her to the work of the Ironriders.

She passed over burned villages, with heaps of the dead staked out lining the roads. Heads, black with flies and poked and torn by birds, lay in the road like oversized onions.

Other villages and homesteads lay empty. She hoped the owners had fled and the pieces of torn clothing and footwear were just bits and pieces dropped by the riders as they carried off their loot.

From the heights, she saw groups of riders. They'd set up tall, narrow tents from which the fragrant aroma of smoking meat rose into the skies.

So these were the mighty Ironriders. Both the men and their horses appeared bony and undersized, but Wistala knew better than to rely overly on appearances.

The Ironriders, meeting no resistance, had already divided. One column of riders went north, a second stabbed east, and a third headed off to the south, perhaps to seize the river gap where the mighty Falnges fell past the dwarves of the Chartered Company.

The northbound column she would not worry about. If they intended to pass into Varvar lands seeking plunder they'd be in for the fight of their lives, in thick, wolf-haunted woods crossed by many rivers. She knew how quickly the barbarians there would drop their eternal feuds to unite against invaders.

As for the southbound column, they would have a long and difficult trip across hills that would meet them like a series of walls. They would not be able to use their horses to advantage, and the few settlements in the wild mountain foothills would have plenty of warning of their arrival and drive their flocks even higher into the mountains. They would lose many horses on the thin soil of the foothills.

The center column, however, was the most numerous. It aimed straight for the old road that passed through all the thanedoms of the Hypatian north. Once on that, the horsemen could travel like poison in a bloodstream from town to town and finally into the sun-blessed city of Hypat itself. The Ironriders would burn art a thousand years old to toast their horseflesh on sticks and strip the temples of their silver statues.

But perhaps, just perhaps, Hypatia would summon its legions in time, put competent generals at their head, and destroy the northern invaders, then turn to meet the southern.

Hypatia would like to know what sort of numbers had come across the pass, thanks to the treacherous Wheel of Fire.

She passed to the other side of the Red Mountains and trembled. Winking lights of charcoal fires dusted the open plain everywhere there weren't corrals of horses and goats and sheep. Laden carts sat full of hay and grain, and packs of dogs ran here and there.

The greatest summer priestly festivals in Hypatia didn't draw a third as many people. Yet these were warriors, with feathers and furs trimming shield and scabbard, under the painted bones tingling wind chimes of a hundred nomadic princedoms.

No wonder DharSii had brought a warning. Had he told of another army such as this to the south? She'd heard talk of it.

She wondered what the Red Queen had promised the princes of the Ironriders to gain their cooperation. Loot? Would each warrior be allowed to carry off one woman and one child as slaves, bound across the leather and sheepskin of their saddles?

What did Mother say about fighting? *Hit them where they're thin.* A deer is vulnerable at the leg or neck. A man at the knee, elbow, and throat. Of course, dwarves present a problem—they're thick everywhere to look at. Thin only in flexibility, dwarves, and she'd improvised her way into breaking a king who would not bend.

The Ironriders ran thin in this pass.

"Excellent ground, Wistala," Ayafeeia said, when she took her up after dusk that night to view the pass. "I have never seen a finer place for dragons to do battle."

"Between us we should be able to burn the boats they use to cross the Ba-drink."

"Yes, but there's another road around the water, it seems. We can only make things more difficult for them at the lake. No, we must fight in the pass."

Wistala's knowledge of warfare was limited to observing men and dwarves in battle, and the dragon attack on the blighters in Old Uldam.

"Horsemen," Ayafeeia said. "They may be masters of warfare on four legs, but we will fight so that their charges and lances avail them not."

Wistala saw what she meant. Or thought she did.

"Where the pass narrows there, by the rock-slides."

"If only the dwarves would fight alongside us, yes, that would be the place," Ayafeeia said. "With such a wall there, we could hold many."

Wistala saw only a steep cliff on one side and a mountain broken and sharp in three places like one of her rear teeth. The road traveled around the three turns like a snake's body.

"What kind of wall?" Wistala asked, befuddled. Would the drakka drag rocks, or push snow?

"The same sort that keeps rocks from rolling uphill, my dear. Yes. Yes. This will do very well. Perfect ground for the drakka."

Wistala flew back to Mossbell. Ragwrist had left his estate to see to the muster of his huntsmen and militia levies.

"There were four new babies born over the winter, still alive after the winter's sickness," Lada said. "I cut and washed each one myself. What will happen to them, I wonder."

"They'll be eating mash mixed with their milk by the fall, if I have a part in the matter," Wistala said. "But I would hide them somewhere in the hills. Perhaps a shepherd's shelter."

"I'd rather they died of cold than crushed under the hooves of the Ironriders. I've heard terrible stories."

"What does Ragwrist intend?" Wistala asked.

"He's mounted a small company. But they're hunters of deer and foxes, not warriors. For the rest, he says he will hide as much as he can in the old mines on the twin hills. The entrances are blocked up, but the old airshaft has a new ladder. Though it's been a dirty business cleaning out the bats."

"Don't speak to me about bats. We've a few of these great toothy ones with us, to lick clean our wounds and trim ragged flesh. Rodents who ride in bags. Our Tyr's idea."

Dragons, flying all this way with vermin snug and warm against hot wing-muscle in their bags. She shuddered at the memory.

"There's wisdom in your Tyr's notion, if they're the sort of bats I'm thinking of, cattle-feeders. Their saliva numbs and it cleans."

* * *

Back at the dragon encampment at Tumbledown, Ayafeeia put the Firemaids to work sharpening their claws.

The thane had installed some of his retainers in a corner of the ruin, and the men pounded together a new roof for three empty walls. Wistala sent for him through the warriors.

"Remember your oaths," Ayafeeia said, walking up and down the line to inspect the leather straps and wooden pins the drakka used to hang on to the dragonelles. "Remember the years of comradeship. In this next battle they will be tested. It will take true hearts to face the coming danger and death and pass the highest test asked of our sisterhood."

Hesturr rode in.

"What news, green allies? I have none good. There's rumor of burned villages east of here. I believe they make for the road here."

"They do," Wistala said. "I've seen them. This is but a vangard for what is coming across the pass."

Thane Hesturr gripped his sword in its scabbard tightly. "It will take time for us to join battle, then. We cannot fly, and there are already many riders on this side of the mountains. We must meet them first."

"More importantly, defeat them," Wistala said, after translating for Ayafeeia.

"Let us put the past behind us, from this day on," Thane Roff said.

"I have no particular grievances to burn," Wistala said. "But I am happy to call you an ally."

"It is a long walk back to my horses and dogs. They won't easily come near your dragons, I'm afraid. We'll meet again on the slopes of the Red Mountains."

"They'll be red with more than sunlight, if we're still there when you come."

"Every rider that can be kept from crossing is a victory," Roff said. "We'll meet again, Wistala."

"I hope so."

The thane pointed to his retainers and standard-bearer, and they departed.

The drakka were mounting for the ride to the pass.

"I must send a messenger back to the Lavadome," Ayafeeia said. She'd been taking more and more charge of matters as the time of battle grew closer. "Angalia, you've been ill since those swamps. I will send you back to the Lavadome to let our Tyr know where we will make our stand."

Angalia, a pale green Firemaid with the wrinkles about the snout and flanks that showed her to be one who suffered from much sickness, nodded.

"May I send a messenger as well?" Wistala asked.

"Angalia may carry more than one message."

"Not there. To my brother, on the Isle of Ice. A fast flier, and intelligent."

"Yefkoa would be a good choice. She is young and fast."

The dragonelle came forward, eager for her chance at distinction.

"Yefkoa, you must find a place strange to all of us. My brother is there. Go to the great river just north of where we camped. You can't miss it—there's a long bridge with a repaired patch in the center. Downstream from the bridge on the north side there's a hole shaped like a dragon-eye. In it you'll find instructions in Dwarvish notation for finding an island to the north.

"Find my brother AuRon there. Tell him that we have gone into battle. I know he lives with other dragons. Ask their aid, for their good and ours. If we fall, beg him, in my memory, to save those at Mossbell who I love best. Fly them to safety."

"But—the battle."

"Oh, from what I've seen we've a long fight ahead of us," Ayafeeia said. "There'll be blood enough for all of us, sisters."

Chapter 19

The conduct of the battle of the pass surprised Wistala.

Luckily, it surprised the Ironriders even more.

It was a battle of angles and slopes and gravity, fought in mountain fogs and bright sun. The science-minded Anklenes might have called it a war between vertical and horizontal.

They arrived at the pass in the dead of night with the moon down so that they wouldn't be spotted, circling in well north of the star-charting tower at the Wheel of Fire fortifications, which Wistala knew well from her brief time as an ally of the dwarves.

Wistala, clinging in a deep crevice so long to the mountainside as she waited for the order, finally decided the horses passing up the road were the ones in strange perspective, walking sideways before her.

Ayafeeia kept her forces hidden in the clouds of the mountaintops.

There were deep seams in the vertical mountain-face. The dragons settled themselves into them, latching on with *sii, saa,* and wing-spurs. One could even rest, hanging in that manner.

The drakka opened the fight in the dusk, creeping down into the pass to slay horses and pack animals following a long, triple file of riders passing through. There were no warriors tending the burdened animals.

Wistala watched it from high on the sheer mountain half of the pass. The drakka dashed and jumped on the animals, which screamed as they died. Their tenders fled, east and west, screaming in their unknown chopping tongue for help.

"We will have meat tonight. I'm sick of cold fish and burned raccoons," Ayafeeia said.

The drakka jumped back onto the cliff-face and climbed to shelter.

"I think you fight just to fill your stomach, maidmother," a dragonelle said.

Wistala, her throat tight with fear of battle, hid her anxiety by
picking at a crevice.

The Ironriders sent horsemen to investigate. They walked their
mounts forward, archers just behind the scouts with spears, men on
foot behind them walking their mounts with swords out. Wistala's
eyes picked out the frightened pack-train leaders talking and pointing to dead animals.

Ayafeeia carefully crept across the rock face to her reserve.

"I want them in doubt as to what they face as long as possible,
Verkeera," Ayafeeia said to the greatest of the Firemaids, a massive,
mature dragonelle with a bluish tinge to her deep green. "Let some
of those rocks on the mountainside do your talking."

"Yes, maidmother," Verkeera said. She launched herself and
glided over to the other side of the pass.

A mist passed through the mountains, obscuring what came next.
Perhaps Verkeera, lower down, could see. In any case, Wistala heard
a *krrack!* followed by a series of descending booms matched with
screams of alarm and pain from horse and rider.

"Now that they know we're here, we might as well get some work
done. Crack rock, Firemaids. Let's claw ourselves a shelf or two."

The dragons cleared fallen rock, carved falls of ice, or even
wedged boulders into chimneys and chutes in the cliffside to make
themselves perches so they might rest more easily.

What any ears down in the valley made of the strikes, rattles, and
steady fall of small rocks and ice chips Wistala could only imagine.
Perhaps they thought trolls were at work.

Wistala heard crashes and screams and the sound of galloping
hooves headed back toward the Ba-drink or riding for the eastern gap.

The dragonelles flew down and collected dead horses, mules, and
donkeys, then took them high into the mountains and laid them out
"on ice" so they might be eaten fresh later. Then they dined, heartily,
on corpses. The drakka ran down an injured horse.

"Dragonelles are suited for this kind of fighting," Ayafeeia told Wistala. "With the Aerial Host, they get blood in their nostrils and they refuse to relent until there's blood and flame everywhere. This isn't the kind of fight that can be settled in one stroke."

Nor was it.

The next day the Ironriders came through the pass in force.

The dragonelles and drakka taunted the Ironriders to come up in the hills and get them.

Of course they tried, riding as steep a rocky slope as they could, with many horses slipping down to injury thanks to the snow and ice that still lurked in crevices and shadows.

When the Ironriders dismounted, chasing after the dragons in groups with spears, archers behind, the drakka hid until the men had passed and then leaped onto the backs of the archers, gutting them and then running under showers of arrows, leaving the Ironriders the depressing task of bringing down the dead or wounded. Otherwise their much-chewed bones would be neatly arranged in the road by dawn the next day. When they charged through the pass as fast as they could trying to simply run by the dragons, one or more would drop from cover in the cliff and loose fire onto the screaming men and horses, or they would drop *sii* and *saa* full of rocks from great heights so that gravity did the killing work.

They couldn't pass at night, either. After a successful test run of a small troop, they tried to walk a larger contingent through. The dragons first panicked the horsemen and then batted the crowd back and forth along the mountain road, attacking first the east end and then the west.

An overzealous drakka died during that, speared after she knocked a wounded rider out of his saddle.

Another dragonelle was wounded when an arrow hit a soft spot and shot straight through her lung, at such an angle and doing so much damage that she could no longer fly. She had to be content standing watch at night and trumpeting warnings when the Ironriders tried to force the pass.

Wistala could feel the despair and frustration of the tormented riders below. While the others counted bodies or, worse, brought back heads, she could only fight the cold queasy feeling in her stomach.

Was she to blame for the bloodshed in this pass? She'd humbled the Wheel of Fire, and the dwarves were taking revenge on those west of the mountains by leaving their pass open.

But the knowledge of the depredations of the riders who had already passed through to the west steeled her. Warriors and their mounts must die so that Hypatian villages would go unburned.

Of course they burned the boats the Ironriders used to cross the Ba-drink, and they downed the bridge where Wistala had once made peace with the Dragonblade, bashing at the keystone with their tails and once that gave way, widening the breach by jumping up and down on the edges.

Their greatest difficulty was coping with the cold. Though spring had come to the lower altitudes, the mountains were thick with snow. Dragons like the cool of a deep underground cave, but being caught out in the open with icy mountain winds and snow gathering in their scales leaves them ill-spirited. They slept tightly, side by side, alternating front to back, with the drakka tucked under the protection of motherly wings.

The cold made them torpid and slow until the activity of battle heated their blood.

It was glorious fun. "Better than tunnel fighting, and horsemeat twice a day," Takea said.

As the days of sporadic fighting wore on, the dragonelles noticed a slight change. Traffic began to flow the other way over the pass. Ironriders, in ones and twos, with horses laden with loot or bringing sore-footed captives behind with necks bound in rope-line.

The Firemaids were only too happy to spread havoc among exhausted men and worn-out horses. They were easier to chase down and devour. Ayafeeia gave them the contents of various captured saddlebags and their pick of whatever they wanted from the corpses now littering the pass.

The Firemaids had never enjoyed such a variety of rich, refined metals. While their enemies grew weaker, they became thick-scaled and stouthearted on devoured steppe ponies and their riders.

Then there was the freeing of the Ironriders' captives. Wistala had the most gentle-winged dragonelle fly them to a sheep-trail down the western slope of the mountains, heavily laden with smoked meat, skins, and traveling clothing thickened by stolen furs.

Hopefully, the liberated captives would return to their villages and hearths with a tale of outrage—and the kindness of dragons.

Chapter 20

The Copper received news of the opening of Ghioz's war in the map room.

None of it was good. All his Upholders to the east and south reported fighting, all begging for the immediate aid of the Aerial Host or the land was sure to be lost.

"Four cries of disaster," the Copper said. "One Aerial Host. What should we do?"

"Start at the south," HeBellereth said. "The Yellowsand reports only a roc-rider or two, and bandit attacks on our caravans. The Ghioz will be weakest there, and easiest to locate. Then sweep north. Move slowly and surely so the rumor of our coming travels faster than the dragons themselves. Terror will do half our work for us."

"Should we let our enemies choose the ground of the fight?" NoSohoth asked. "They are plundering our Upholds. We could send the Aerial Host to burn out a few of their lands."

"I would think Chushmereamae is the base of their attacks on us," LaDibar said, tapping his tail on the depiction of the islands on the map in thought. "Destroy that base. Then we may restore order in the Upholds."

"Fine idea," Nilrasha said. "We must commit the Aerial Host, my Tyr. With their boats burned, the threat in the south will be ended."

That gave him pause. Nilrasha didn't much like LaDibar. To see her supporting him in a debate made him wonder if she was really speaking her mind or playing some political game to win support of the Anklenes.

"I fear all of these are feints," the Copper said. "The Red Queen doesn't care where we react, as long as we do. As soon as the Aerial

Host is committed, she will launch her counterstrike. Their roc-riders worry me. They can beat our dragons to any fight."

"You are too cautious!" HeBellereth said. "Let them come. We have been practicing flying in a new, tighter formation so that our riders may better cover each other with bows."

The Copper stared at the map. The little statues representing the type and kind of Ghioz forces scattered up and down the eastern Upholds seemed to be mocking, willing the arrangement to reveal the Red Queen's mind. "I fear I'm not being cautious enough. I'll choose when to commit the host, and where. I won't have the Red Queen make that decision for me. We've lost too many skirmishing over Bant already. Curse the eggs that hatched those featherbrains."

He was just in a foul mood because Wistala had made a mess of things in Hypatia. According to Ayafeeia's courier, the Hypatian "Voice," or whatever they called the king, had rejected his offer of an alliance. They were fighting in the Red Mountains to help some Hypatian provinces north of the Falnges River.

Practically the other side of the world.

Well, Ayafeeia knew her business. Perhaps she would occupy the Ironriders so they wouldn't come rampaging through Bant. But he ordered Ayafeeia to return with as many of her Firemaids as she could.

His mood didn't improve until he received a bat with his evening meal. Paskinix had been found, hiding close to the river ring where he could keep in contact with the demen settled there to keep in contact with the "Tyr's demen," as they were beginning to be called.

"Tell the Drakwatch," the Copper ordered. "I want him captured. Alive. Don't bring me a charred corpse and say he committed suicide, or I'll yank every scale out of the capture-party leader myself."

Angalia returned from the Tyr with a complaint about shooting pains in her joints caused by the altitude and a message that war had broken out all through Bant and the southern provinces. As Hypatia had rejected his appeal for an alliance, he had other uses for the Fire-maids. He ordered Ayafeeia's return with her forces.

That night it snowed—probably a heavy spring rain on the woods west of the mountains but at their altitude it made fighting impossible and even movement dangerous. They talked it out over a meal of dragonflame-warmed horse.

"I won't withdraw from this pass, with battle begun. We're teaching them to fear the smell of dragons."

"You can plague them here at your leisure, Wistala. I leave you in charge. You've learned enough about this sort of fighting to handle the rest."

Ayafeeia departed with those who'd suffered small injuries that limited their ability to climb or run but could still fly, or hang on. She left Wistala with the most experienced and battle-tested of the Fire-maids and a handful of drakka, including Takea.

On the third day after Ayafeeia left, the roc-riders attacked.

They came screaming out of the sky as the dragons were occupied dropping fire on stone-throwing machines that they later decided had been built solely to provide them with targets for their fire. The rocs raked two dragonelles across the back, tearing wing and ligament and sending them tumbling through the air into the Ironriders.

If the fall didn't kill them, they were soon speared by the Ironriders.

Now it was the Ironriders' turn to jeer.

The roc-riders stole the food they'd kept on ice on a high glacier. One lucky rider plucked a drakka and lifted off with her, carried screaming higher and higher as two dragonelles tried to pursue in vain. The roc dropped her, just to hear her scream as she fell, and Wistala cursed the eggs that had sheltered them.

They managed to avenge themselves on two roc-riders when Wistala suggested a tactic that had very nearly worked on her when a troll plunged out of the sky upon her. They buried two dragonelles in snow so they wouldn't be seen, and then they fell on the riders as they rode through the pass. The dragons did better than trolls, though—they could use their wings to control their dives. When they struck the riders, rider and mount disappeared in a burst of blood, flesh, and feathers.

Takea returned that night with the top half of a beak, wearing it as a human would a helmet.

Now the sky and the heights belonged to the Ironriders. Wistala and what was left of the Firemaids had to keep clear of swooping roc-riders and their arrows.

"We could sneak away. Why do we hold this pass alone? Where are the men who would fight at our side?"

"They have troubles enough with the riders who are making it across the pass."

"How long do we stay here?"

Wistala bristled. "Until they stop coming or we breathe our last."

The Firemaids needed more than that, she decided. Each would lay down her life gladly if they guarded the mouth of a tunnel that had hatchlings at the other end. But the reasons for fighting here—how could she put them into words?

"I believe humans will never trust us unless we prove our loyalty to our word and their law by dying for it."

"What's human law to us?" a Firemaid asked, both nostrils and lips caked with blood and the marks of the desperate dagger-strokes of some Ironrider she'd finished off. "I say withdraw!"

A Firemaid muttered that they would be climbing out if they withdrew. There were no longer enough healthy dragonelles to carry the drakka.

"What's dragon tradition to humans?" Wistala replied. "If we keep our word, do our duty, they'll know they can rely on us in the future."

"We should keep our word for ourselves, no matter what the humans think," Takea said.

"A future we won't live to see," another replied.

"Maybe," Wistala said. "No one knows. But every day we create a future. Our fight here creates a better one."

"I still say they deserve these steppe-demons. Letting us die up here in the cold, alone. It's their lands. I would not expect a bunch of dwarves to die protecting my tunnel."

"The rest of you may go, if you wish," Wistala said. "I'm staying here. I will prove it." She tore off the brace on her wing, threw it down, and smashed it on an angled rock, breaking it anew.

"There," she said through the pain. "I can't fly off."

Little Takea could take no more. She ran and stood before Wistala. "How do we live, Firemaids?"

"Together!" they responded.

"How do we fight?"

"Together!"

"Then how should we die?"

"Together!"

She organized all her Firemaids into pairs or trios. One would always keep watch for the roc-riders while the other dug sleeping holes in the snowdrifts or stole down into the pass looking for a loose horse or a lost dog to eat.

It was while watching the drakka melt snow for everyone to drink that Wistala had her idea.

A dam of ice and snow had built up on the southern slope. Snow exposed to the sunlight and warming spring winds was melting and running down into the pass, but as it passed into the shadows of ridges and other mountains, it froze again.

The mass created hung heavy in the mountains, an avalanche waiting to happen.

They tried making noise, for noise sometimes triggers an avalanche, they knew, but the loudest dragon roars had no effect on the ice-dam and the glacier of snow behind. Their cries brought satisfying sounds of alarm from the end of the pass.

Wistala studied it, remembering what Rainfall had taught her about bridges, loads, keystones, and so on. It seemed to her that the ice-dam resembled an upside-down bridge, with a line of rocks and boulders blocking it.

She waited for a storm to try her theory. As the blowing snow reduced the horizon to a few dragonlengths and turned the sky a smoky gray, they went to the base of the dam.

"If we can't block the pass ourselves, maybe ice and snow will do our work for us. Ready?"

"Be sure to take off as it gives way."

"If it gives way," a Firemaid said. "But what about you?"

Wistala pointed with her tail-tip to the cliffside just to the left of the dam. "I'll dash there."

"Hope you're a good dasher."

"Together," Wistala said.

They vented their flame across the base of the ice dam.

The ice and snow, or possibly rock, groaned. Wistala heard cracks.

Wistala remembered being caught in the tunnel as a hatchling with Auron. They'd battered their way out with their tails, Auron hurling himself against the ice with his body until it broke.

She turned, beat the rock with her tail, beat it until she smelled blood.

"More flame!" she gasped.

They vomited fire again. Running water turned to steam in the heat—

Krrrrrack!

A stone gave way.

The ice shifted, the whole mass moved perhaps a clawsbreadth.

Wistala held her breath, every nerve alert.

"Run, Wistala, it's giving."

She felt wingtips lash across her back as she hurried for the rocks. The ground slid beneath her feet.

Thunder in her ears, a roaring so loud that one felt it rather than heard it, engulfed her. She lunged, leaped, managed to cling to a fall of rocks at the base of the wall of rock.

Ice and snow roared down behind her, dragging her feet with them. She felt the ground pull at her—a strange sensation, not being able to trust the ground. Instinctively she opened her wings and tried to take off, but her broken wing just pulled against the lines and braces that held it to her body.

The flow dragged at her, its icy dust trying to choke her, but still she clung. Then she realized she was lost as well—tumbling, tumbling—and she curled her wings about her.

Then her breath was gone. Somehow she sensed which way was up and, heaving with every muscle, fought her way toward the surface. But the snow was so very heavy and she was cold and tired and broken, and oh so very sleepy . . .

She woke to a bright orange eye, found a great feathered roc staring down at her, its reins piercing its beak like a leathery mustache.

It had its claw on her throat, ready to rip out her neck hearts.

She was lying in the pass, but something was all wrong. She was at the wrong height, halfway up the sheer cliff on the south side. Then she realized that she rested on a mound of snow the size of one of the twin hills on Rainfall's old estate.

Spirits and snowdrifts, they'd done it! She knew the weather at these heights—it would be full summer before the pass would be warm enough to melt all this down into the Ba-drink.

"It's alive," the rider called, in Parl, to a group of Ironriders behind. They wore baskets upon their shoes to allow themselves to walk on the snow.

"You. Hold still," he ordered in Parl.

She wouldn't be a prisoner again. She'd rather breathe her last in the clean mountain air than be flung into some new dungeon.

Wistala realized that only a thin layer of snow covered her body. She flexed her body, struck out with all the power in her cold-stiff tail, and a wave of snow flew out toward the bird.

As birds always do when startled, it flapped its wings and jumped back.

That was all Wistala needed. Her body stiffened and she spat flame—a thin stream, more a series of *torfs* than an actual stream of fire given that she'd been on short rations lately—striking bird and rider.

Both screamed and they flew off, the rider beating at the liquid fire across his saddle.

The Ironriders waddled comically, dropping the lines and chains they'd brought to drag her out of the snow.

Wistala felt too tired and cold to give chase. But shadows crossed the sun, shadows of dragons—

"Wistala, we are coming!" cried the Firemaids.

Drakka came shooting down the snowy slope, heads up, *sii* and *saa* tight against their sides, steering with their tails.

Roc-riders, drawn by the motion, dived and whirled, their riders firing arrows.

The drakka shot past her, flying like scaly arrows across the snow.

The Ironriders didn't have a chance. They couldn't run with the baskets on their feet, and they couldn't move through the snow with the baskets off. One after another fell, knocked down by the drakka.

Takea lay behind, an arrow through her throat.

Wistala went to her side.

"Bats! Some bats here!" Wistala called.

"It doesn't hurt, Wistala," Takea whispered. Wistala put her head close to the drakka to better hear her words. "I can feel the wound. It is bad, isn't it? But it doesn't hurt. Strange." She still wore the brown beak on her head. Wistala thought the horn-lines in it made it look like an agate.

"We'll get that shaft out and close you up. You'll sit the rest of this fight out."

Takea tapped her tail. Wistala heard her hearts fluttering. "Sister, do not lie to me. I can feel my hearts slowing. We loosed HaVok himself on them, didn't we?"

"For a while," Wistala said. She'd failed. She'd failed her sisters in the Firemaids, all for a stupid hatchling's fancy-dream.

"I would have opened my wings next year. I wonder if some male would have wanted me, with the glory of a fight like this to my name."

"I expect so," Wistala said.

She removed something from deep in the pocket of flesh behind her ear. It was the rabbit's foot. "Tell Zathan—I must break my promise to him. Return . . ." She began to pant.

Wistala, half choking and blinking tears, looped the little ring on her wing-spur.

Takea's voice grew quiet and clear. "Pity the humans never showed up. It's a good idea you have, though, Wistala. I mean, why couldn't we share white cities in the sun. Dragons would even make fine thanes, I expect. We could see brigand camps from miles off and keep the roads safe. Dragons could even—"

Her head lolled and her body seemed to shrink, save for the swelling wing-cases.

The Drakwatch pried Paskinix, with some difficulty, out of his hole. He, of course, had a hidden exit, but the bats had discovered it and an expert blighter thrall-netter waited where the bolt-hole joined river-tunnel.

Paskinix showed admirable dignity as they brought him before the Copper in the empty assembly hall. He was so gaunt the Copper wondered if a soft tail-tap would pass right through him. The horny plates of his self-grown armor looked oversized, some old trophy of a ancestral deman worn in tribute, perhaps.

The Copper ordered food to be brought. Paskinix, sensibly, did not even make a pretense of refusing. Instead, he opened that strange swinging deman jaw and began to stuff himself.

"Not too much, or you'll make yourself sick," the Copper said, by way of starting.

"My last meal, I suppose, now that you've holed me at last," Paskinix said. "May as well enjoy it."

"I am ready to make peace if you are," the Copper said.

"Peace? With what? My people are destroyed."

"This old war is not my fault. It was going on when I came here."

Paskinix swished out his mandibles and spat on the floor. "We have claim to the Lavadome too, dragon-king. It was here the sun-shard fell to earth, and it was here the first demen recovered it at the dawning of thought. Only the Eternals are older than ourselves."

"All the more reason to share its control. I propose to give you a voice in the Lavadome, my old friend."

"Our people have shown a curious brand of friendship."

"We've forged a history. We've learned to respect each other. Out of that respect, cooperation can bloom. I have some lovely gardens here atop the rock, and the blueblooms are bigger than ever since I put them on that mix of bat-dropping and dried cow dung. I could show you the old pools one of my predecessors put in, a very fine set of caves, and I know you like things warm and moist and comfortable. Perhaps you could move your household there temporarily while we work out an understanding?"

"I am . . . suspicious."

"Of course."

"You hold every advantage. Were I to have conquered the Lavadome the way you had the Star Tunnel, I would not be inviting you to the most comfortable cavern off the Wisterfall."

"You've played so many tricks yourself you expect them in others. I have spoken honestly to you. If I have been generous, it is because I wish your help as an ally."

"Ally? All my warriors together would hardly be a match for a pair of your dragons."

"Ah, but you count your experience in the Lower World cheap. I am engaged in a war on the surface."

"Then I wish you fortune. The Red Queen burned out our sun-mines on the surface years ago."

The Copper wondered what a sun-mine was but decided not to ask.

"Would you care to play one last trick? Strike one more blow against your surface enemy?"

"Perhaps."

"If I wished to reach the lands of Ghioz in secret, could I do it with dragons? I have examined the maps of the Norflow. It seems to me it runs right under Ghioz lands."

Paskinix shut his eyes in thought.

"It does. It does at that. But why not fly?"

"My dragons cannot get near her capital because of those roc patrols," the Copper said. Paskinix clucked in confusion. "Great birds, bigger than our *griffaran*. They can outfly and outfight dragons in the air. She would have two days' warning, at least. If I could cut that down to two hours—"

"Getting there is not the problem. Reaching the surface is. But if I had a dragon or two instead of just my warriors—"

"You might get your sun-mines back."

"I could refuse."

"Gigrix could just as easily lead your people. I've consulted him on the matter already, and he is drawing us a map."

"Then why not just kill me?"

"You fought the Firemaids and the Aerial Host to a standstill for years, with numbers less than a quarter of what we believed you to have, if the talks with your general have led the Anklenes to the correct conclusion. I would be mad to kill such a resourceful warrior."

"Tyr RuGaard—your dragons said you were unlike any Tyr since FeHazathant. I am beginning to understand their opinion."

"Thank you. But I warn you, praise in the Lavadome often comes before the bite."

"My Tyr, I saw many deman skulls about the entrance to your fine towering rock. I've no wish to see mine displayed in a place of prominence, especially with such a meal as you've fed me dissolving so pleasantly within." He belched. "My compliments to your cook. It's been long since I ate flesh flavored with anything but the tears of the meal's friends and family."

Chapter 21

The courier dragonelle's arrival on the Isle of Ice set all the dragons to talking and arguing. Yefkoa spoke of a time of decision for the dragons.

And of their Tyr, a prophet who would lead them all into the bright sun of a new age.

For such a young dragonelle, she spoke well, fearless in the face of strangers.

War in the south—a lost kingdom of dragons—Ironriders on stout horses with big, hearty livers—dragonelles and drakka dying in battle.

The population of the Isle of Ice was mostly female, and their sympathies naturally ran to the dragonelles fighting for their lives. She painted pictures with her words and the dragons began to stamp and roar in agreement.

Save for AuRon. Wistala had joined with the Copper and had flown herself into this scrape. She would have to fly herself out.

"Is the isle flying to the aid of the dragons, Father?" Varatheela asked, her hindquarters dancing.

"Did I ever tell you how I came to be in that cargo hold?" Natasatch asked AuRon.

"Not willingly. I asked you once about it, I recall. You said you were captured while hunting."

"That was true—after a fashion."

"Tell me," AuRon said.

"I was a few weeks from my first trip aboveground," she said, toying with a dry shard of one of their hatchlings' eggs she'd kept as a piece of memory.

"We did not have a large cave, but there was a long tunnel leading to the surface. I liked to explore the tunnel, at least the dragon-length or two near the mouth of the egg-cave. To me, that was like going aboveground. I was exploring, when suddenly I saw a pair of legs walking past me.

"Before I knew it I had a sword-point before my eye. The elf offered me a choice, speaking Drakine. *Silence or death.* I was at the high end of the egg-cave. My voice would have carried had I screamed. The family might have been saved. I tried to scream. I decided on it. But the sound never came. I was frozen. I bought my own life with their death."

"That elf—was it the one from the boat? Hazeleye?"

"No. A friend of hers."

"They made you a captive."

"Yes. Less than I deserved. I've carried this with me, told myself I was young and frightened. Deep down, I know I chose myself over my parents."

They regarded each other in silence.

"AuRon, I don't think dragons can survive by isolation and hiding. It just gives our enemies more time to increase and organize."

"We will organize too."

"We can't even keep our flocks intact," Natasatch said.

"That's not important. If we were threatened— We'd make this place a name of dread and terror. Boats burn easily. I've seen it."

"Yes, we may last long on this cold, foggy island. But eventually we'll be a crowded, sick isle full of thin-scaled dragons eating seal-blubber and fish."

"Difficulties that can be overcome. Why could we not fashion tools and mine as the dwarves do? Are our limbs weaker, our brains smaller?"

"Our bodies are bigger. We would have to engineer tunnels tall and wide."

"If we fight for one set of humans, we'll just make enemies of the other set."

"Better than both allying against us."

"You're too clever," he said.

"You're too cautious. Even a few dragons may make a difference. You told me an old friend was in trouble. Can we not help him?"

"A few dragons wouldn't help him. I've seen the fliers who hunt him. They're a match for a dragon."

"All the more reason to fight now. Will not these fliers be just as much a match for us tomorrow?

"I think," Natasatch said, "this has gone beyond reason. You're worried that your brother may be on to something. Is it his success that troubles you?"

AuRon felt his firebladder pulse. He'd never felt like biting his mate in his whole life until now. The impulse shamed him. "Whatever he has planned, it's not for our benefit, or that of dragons. There is no interest but his own in these doings."

They watched the dragonelles stomp and roar as they talked to the courier.

The young dragonelle took off. Three others joined her, one of the isle's altered males.

"Coming, AuRon?" Ouistrela called. "We're off to inaugurate this 'age of fire.' A new age of dragons! Battle screams and horseflesh as far as the eye can see!"

"Will you go?" Natasatch said.

"I haven't decided."

"Every moment could be important."

"If you don't go, I will."

"What about the hatchlings?"

"You and your sister were fending for yourselves by this point. Not all of our kind are leaving. There are dragons on this island hoping some men would land for a change of diet. I expect they'll survive. Just as well. The sheep will be lambing soon and they could use a break."

AuRon read the resolution in her eyes. "Well, if we're going to get involved in this war, we might as well do so with some force. I will join you."

"Let us go, too, Father!" the hatchlings clamored in various iterations.

Perhaps there would be wounded we could let them finish, Natasatch thought to him.

"Let them take care of themselves while we are away. That is experience enough. Remember, hatchlings," AuRon said, looking at their disappointed faces, "talk to the wolves as often as possible. They will teach you much about moving in cover and in the open, hunting, and above all, cooperation. *The strength of the wolf is the pack,* as they say."

"I've often heard that quoted," Natasatch agreed.

AuRon, with his mind made up—or made up for him—felt at ease. All doubt and regret had vanished. There was just need for action. "I've an idea where our first stop should be. We fly to Juutfod."

AuRon had not been to the dragontower since his time as a courier for the Wizard of the Isle of Ice, though he had visited the wharves where Varl tied up his boat and some of the oceanside sights.

The men of Juutfod accepted dragons as part of their daily lives. Without the Wyrmmaster, they'd happily given up their raids on the south and used their dragons to protect fishing fleets and remote settlements.

The tower was much the same. More outbuildings had sprouted around it, like warts. And the town beneath had taken inspiration from the tower—there were round houses of stone, long buildings with thick walls and heavy-timbered roofs, and wooden homes and pens and workshops all around with smoke rising from the chimneys.

A dragon-rider rose to meet him.

He'd been told a few of the riders and their mounts had survived. The female dragons of the Isle of Ice had come to this place looking for males. Some dragons were content to be saddled and reined, it seemed, as long as they were well fed and rested in comfortable housing.

His old friend Varl had settled in this village. He smoked fish and made crab paste that the dragons had always found tasty on the Isle of Ice.

"Perhaps you'd better talk to them," AuRon said to Natasatch. "I'll keep watch above."

Once he was sure of Natasatch's reception—they let her land and she began to speak with the dragons and dragon-riders there— AuRon went seeking Varl among the mead-dens and group-houses near the docks. His boat wasn't in, but Varl sometimes took months off between the seasonal fish runs.

He did, however, see a pair of familiar hominids outside of the dens. The warrior Ghastmath, looking thinner without his armor, and the elf with the raven walked down the street, tossing colorful rings back and forth between them using a small stick.

"I see you made it off my island again," AuRon said.

One of the rings clattered to the paving stones.

"You," said the warrior Ghastmath.

"Here I was looking for the mariner Varl to help me find you," AuRon said.

"Can we talk somewhere out of the wind?" the elf asked.

"What is your name? I don't believe I ever caught it."

"I don't believe I ever gave it," she said. "Halfmoon, if you must know."

"Halfmoon, what is an elf doing in this town? Ten years ago, these men would have weighted you with rocks and dumped you in the bay to attract crabs."

Ghastmath planted his oversized feet. "They'd have to go through me."

"They like the gold I bring into town," she said.

"There are worse places to live," Ghastmath added. "No king pushing you around. No edicts rewriting last year's edict which rewrote the one that was beaten into you as a child."

AuRon scratched himself behind his *griff*. "You're thieves. Would you like a tip about the location of a flow of gold?"

"A dragon's going to tell us where to find gold! Laughable," Ghastmath said.

"I don't bother with gold."

"That's right. He is a gray," the elf put in.

"You'll have to fight for it, or be very clever thieves. You might even get the help of those dragon-riders in the tower. The Ironriders are on the rampage south of here. I've some experiences with the princes of the Steppelands, and I can tell you they're carrying off every item of value they can get their hands on and strap across their saddles. I suspect they'll raid into your lands as well, and if the Varvar bands have anything to say about it they'll ride back a good deal faster than they came in. The way they're getting back is across the Ba-drink and through the pass of the Wheel of Fire. If you hunt around the paths and trails leading to that, I expect you'll find more gold and valuables than you can carry being ridden out of the northern half of Hypatia."

"Sounds as though you need some gallant fools to do your fighting for you," Halfmoon said.

"Gallant remains to be seen. Fools who can sneak on and off an island with dozens of dragons hunting the hills and shores are fools I would rather have think favorably of me and mine."

Later, Wistala decided it would have been much more dramatic if they'd arrived in the middle of a battle.

But the war in the pass, which once burned as bright as dragonflame, had sputtered out.

Three dragonelles and ten drakka remained.

The Ironriders had opened a precarious path around the avalanche blocking their pass, a piece of needlework threading through boulders and across ridges like braiding. In good weather with plenty of daylight they could be across it in half a day.

The Firemaids were moving only under cover of weather, watching for Ironriders taking the new path.

What she was, in fact, doing when the riders appeared in the sky to the east was speaking to a Firemaid about having the Firemaids fly off carrying the drakka. She and the four drakka who couldn't be carried would leave.

The dwarves had finally come out of their holes and were hunting them. The only way they could escape the dwarves was to climb, for the dwarves could not follow without much effort with ropes and anchors.

There seemed no point to staying. The Ironriders could bring only a trickle over the pass, and what little traffic there was traveled back to the steppes. The dragonelles who'd flown over the eastern slopes of the mountains reported that the great camp had vanished, with many trails leading south.

It was time to return to Mossbell and Hypatia.

The dragonelles—and a few dragons—of the Isle of Ice arrived, not in such a way that would make a fine song, or an exciting story, but only to offer the news that a few dragons, men, and dragon-riders were scouring the northern thanedoms, chasing down the Ironriders still on the west side of the mountains.

Her brother was not among them. They said he'd flown south with his mate and a strange assortment of elves, men, and dwarves.

Back at Mossbell, the dragons ate their fill of smoked horseflesh. The Ironriders had lost or wounded many mounts as they first advanced, then retreated, across the northern thanedoms.

"A call for an all-muster has gone out," Ragwrist said. "Every thanedom in Hypatia is to gather what forces it has and march them to either the Founding Arch on the north bank of the river or the King's Marker on the southern coast of the Inland Ocean."

"The Firemaids were in that very spot," Wistala said, "a month and a score of days ago."

"Perhaps it's a portent of victory," Ragwrist said.

"It is a well-chosen site," Roff said. "The bay is calm, and there's a long, easy beach where boats may be landed and drawn up. The marshes make it difficult for the soldiers to reach the city. Sometimes a civilization must be preserved from its defenders. That is where you'll find the last muster of Hypatia, if anywhere. That is where I'm bound, as thane."

"That is where I'm much overdue," Ragwrist said. "I sent Dsossa ahead with our light riders. Mossbell and the twin hills will be represented at the muster."

"I fear we'll be one of few," Roff said. "The thanes in the north are dealing with the Ironrider raiders. Thanks to Wistala's stand in the pass, they are not tens of thousands riding hard for Thallia or Hypat, but raiding villages to steal chickens."

Chapter 22

The Copper spent a score of days having his bats scout the Nor'flow, working matters out with the *griffaran,* and planning.

The Lavadome was in an uproar. The eastern Upholds, source of food and thralls, were falling to the Ghioz like so many dominoes. There were daily delegations and deputations by dragons ranking from the rich and distinguished SoRolotan to the thrall-trader Sreek-srack demanding that he do *something*.

His only relief was in talking to Rayg. Rayg didn't bring complaints; instead, they talked solutions.

Rayg had investigated the Queen's crystal, which had been torn from his brother. Though it had been cracked and scuffed by the scene in the throne room, Rayg had set it in a brass frame with a chain lanyard so that he might work with it without touching it, and he'd made a remarkable discovery.

When one gazed through the crystal, images sharpened. One found oneself reading more quickly, with better comprehension. Details previously unnoticed leaped out.

Daring the Red Queen to try to overthrow his mind, the Copper tried it himself.

He found he could fix the lens in his damaged eye in such a way that it held the lid open. Whenever he wore it in this fashion, he felt alert, as though perceiving the world through a mind sharpened in the manner he might sharpen his claws. He made a jest that had even SiHazathant and Regalia turning their heads entirely upside-down in laughter; he noticed a new design beneath Nilrasha's eye; and he tore through the latest tally of livestock left in the Lavadome. Sadly, the columns were all too brief.

He set the Drakwatch to rationing what was left of the food and livestock.

"Where is the Tyr who threw himself against the Dragonblade?" SoRolatan asked.

"Waiting for Paskinix and some bats to complete a reconnaissance of the Nor'flow," the Copper said.

"Paskinix! You've placed our fate in the hands of a long-standing enemy?"

Ayafeeia returned with some of her dragonelles, which was some comfort. She reported that her fast-flying courier, Yefkoa, had seen fighting in Hypatia. A few Ironriders had come across the Red Mountains before the dragons seized the pass, and many times more had roared through the river gap and were riding up both sides of the great river, burning and stealing as they approached the city of Hypat.

"They may be more amenable to an offer of help now," Nilrasha said.

At last Paskinix returned with the bats, and a favorable report. They'd found an old dwarf-mine that led to the surface.

At last he could unleash the Aerial Host. Someplace where it might make a difference.

"The day we have planned for has come. Now we can move," the Copper said, talking over his thoughts with Nilrasha. "Engage the Queen's attention by sending Ayafeeia and the Firemaids to Hypat. I'm a firm believer in second chances. You'll stay and oversee matters in the Lavadome, of course. It'll be easier for you. I'm taking the Aerial Host and every dragon who'll come. And many of the *griffaran* and my personal guard, of course. There'll be more food. If you have to, use the food stored in case of earthquake."

"Of course. My Tyr, the Queen leads the Firemaids. If they're to be hazarded in such a battle, I should be with them."

"But the Lavadome still must be guarded. We have hatchlings, eggs, newly mated drago-dames heavy with eggs. With only a handful of Firemaids and young *griffaran* left behind to guard them, who shall be responsible for them?"

"NoSohoth is happy to remain behind. Was there ever a dragon who cared less for glory?"

"You're not calling him a coward."

"No, I admire him. He's survived longer than any Tyr, quietly attending to thrall sick lists and banquet menus and allocation of caves. He shows better judgment than any of us."

The Copper felt his muscles go liquid at the thought of what might happen to Nilrasha in battle.

"I'd be lost without you," he said at last.

"Allow me the same feeling for you, my love. What should happen to me if you fall from the sky? A small, quiet cave with a good supply of wine, as Tighlia had?"

"Suppose we both should fall?"

"I suspect the world will manage without us. It did well before we breathed. Life will go on after our hearts stop."

He pressed his nose to the pulse-point behind her *griff*. "Still, we are responsible to, and for, dragonkind. The Tyr is called the 'Father of the People' in hatchling rhymes. I would not have the Lavadome orphaned."

"Then you stay. If one of us should die, better that it should be me. A Queen may be replaced. All you'd have to do is mate again. The third try is often all the more glorious after two failures."

She withdrew, watching. He suspected she wondered if she'd gone too far. Anytime Halaflora came up, even obliquely, he became moody.

The old dueling pit had dragons on the shelves, on the old sand in the pit, and two even stood in the entrance.

The Copper stood on the old spur, a long flange of rock where the duel-judges used to rest after giving instructions and announcing the start. From here he was above most of the dragons, except those at the very top.

"Thank you for coming to hear the news," the Copper said. "What has come to my ears is all bad.

"One chance remains," the Copper continued. "The Red Queen has launched war on our Upholds and Hypatia at the same time. We do not have the strength to fight her everywhere at once. There is only one course left to us, a battle of desperation."

"You began this war, RuGaard," LaDibar said. "Now that matters have turned against us, you would have us destroy ourselves."

"Tyr RuGaard—at least for the present."

"The Red Queen offered us peace and you rejected it."

"She didn't offer us peace—she offered us terms of surrender. What price would we have had to pay to keep cattle and kern flowing, I wonder? Hostages to good behavior? Strong young wings to fly her messengers around?

"I propose a strike at the heart of Ghioz." He launched himself into the arena. "When I was a hatchling, I learned that the strongest snake could be felled if you but crushed its head."

The Copper limped through the sand ring, walking around so that he could look each dragon in the face.

"I need every fit dragon who can fly and fight. I've no idea what we may face in the coming battle. If we are to reclaim our place in the sun, every dragon must take his part.

"How many will fly with us?"

They looked at him, at each other. Scale grated against scale and weight shifted.

"My Tyr, there are hatchlings in the cave."

"The thralls in my hill are restive. Suppose they should murder my mate while I am away?"

"I'll return to find not a scrap of silver. Who will guard my hoard if not I?"

The Copper thought of his grandmother's rant, on the last day she drew breath, when she alone hurled herself against the Dragonblade in a court of cowards. She'd called them a lot of backscratchers, and she'd been right.

"Ghioz is three days of hard flight," an aged dragon said, the swirls of the old Aerial Host from the early days of Tyr FeHazathant faint on his sagging wings. "If we come at speed we will arrive exhausted, hardly able to stay in the air. If we take our time she will have warning and assemble those roc-riders."

"I don't propose a flight, until the end."

"Then how shall we get there?" the old dragon asked.

"When the peak first glows tomorrow, meet me at the north river ring beneath the nests of the *griffaran*. It shall be a trip that will go into many a lifesong, I promise."

There were grumblings and complaints, with not a few saying some variation of "you have to live through it to sing about it."

Had such an assortment ever left the Lavadome by the river ring?

The Copper doubted it. It would have been in the battle stories he'd learned in the Drakwatch.

They'd wrecked flatbed dwarf carts and filled nets with the surprisingly buoyant mushrooms that were normally ground into cattle-feed. There were driftwood logs dried, bound together, and formed into rafts.

They'd made traces out of leather, chain, and rope. The dragons of the Aerial Host would drag the rafts and boats behind in the manner of horses pulling carts. But this time the horses would ride. Cattle and goats rode in the improvised armada, ready provision for eating along the journey. The riders of the Aerial Host sat along with the livestock in the boats, their armor and weapons tied down rather than worn in case the boat upset in rough water. From everything he heard of the Nor'flow, the ride would be treacherous.

Even unhappier than the most miserable, lowing cow was the *griffaran* guard. All but a bare minimum of *griffaran* stood perched on logs and gripping canoes in talons so tight-set that the sawdust dribbled from beneath their talons.

Aiy-Yip and his feathered warriors, usually as placid as statues until they exploded into fury, were white-eyed and losing feathers as they bobbed toward the river tunnel.

"Hate-hate-hate water!" Aiy-Yip said as his boat bounced in the current. "Bathing one thing, but this is *yaaak!* like drowning!"

Nilrasha watched them depart.

Her mate would have his own way. A Tyr shouldn't leave the Lavadome to go into battle—it just wasn't done. A tour of the Upholds, yes, but to lead dragons into battle . . .

If he died, how long would she last as Queen?

She climbed back up from the riverbank and into the tunnel to the Lavadome. She passed an alcove where a Firemaid should be standing watch—the Lavadome was emptying of dragons faster than they could breed.

Taking wing, she was back at the top of Imperial Rock before the smell of her mate had left her nostrils. She called for Ayafeeia and NoSohoth.

While she waited for them to arrive, her body-thralls attended her. She envied the thralls and their simple lives. Follow orders, do your job well, please the dragon you belong to. No doubt, no anxiety, transitory passions and heartbreaks forgotten in an hour.

If she lost RuGaard she would live with the pain for a thousand years.

"The Tyr told me to act according to my best judgment, Ayafeeia. My judgment rarely counsels caution."

"How have circumstances changed, my Queen?"

"Simplicity itself. As Queen, I am now making decisions for the Lavadome, and the Queen wishes to lead her Firemaids into battle. Maidmother, prepare your daughters for a flight to Hypat!"

Paskinix showed them where to leave the river.

It wasn't so much a landing as a gap in the ceiling, ringed with the shells of long-dead water-creatures. The demen had some difficulty with ropes and so on until LaDibar suggested that they just ride up one by one, clinging to the crests of the bigger dragons.

The *griffaran* still had a terrible time of it. They didn't like walking and the tunnels were far too small for flight. The water-carved tunnels improved by the demen gave way to the old dwarf-mines.

In the end, the Copper convinced his dragons to drag the *griffaran,* each riding on a dragon-tail with beak hooked on the trailing edge of folded dragonwing.

So they went, the bats foremost, echo-sounding off the walls as they flew back and forth between the demen, who came next, and the darkness ahead. Then the dragons, with the Copper in front keeping in touch with the demen. And finally, what was left of the livestock, being driven by the men of the Aerial Host.

There was hard work at blockages. The dwarves, in their ancient fights with the demen, had walled up parts of the mines. While the demen had long since broken through these, they'd opened them only wide enough for demen to crawl through, not dragons. The demen, men, and the smaller drakes sweated and cursed in three different tongues doing the hard labor to break down the iron-reinforced masonry and open the passages further.

"I came to fight, not to dig. This is thrall-work," HeBellereth complained.

"Would you rather dig or fight roc-riders?" LaDibar asked.

Chapter 23

Natasatch had a grueling flight south. She'd not had AuRon's recent exercise in distance flying, and though she struggled with a dragon's heart and AuRon did their journey with frequent stops for food and rest, she arrived at Naf's warrior camp utterly exhausted, her skin loose and sagging and her eyes glazed with fatigue.

"I've . . . never . . . flown . . . such distances," she said.

"A few days on a good diet is what you need," AuRon said.

Naf misunderstood the reason for her exhaustion and thought she was dying for want of metal. He sent word through the camp that every piece of scrap and old coin or trade token be gathered at once.

The soldiers made them presents of food and the gathered metal. Old belt buckles and scabbard caps, broken tools and worn-down knives, as well as a smattering of coin lay in a heap the size of Natasatch's head.

"I thank you," she said in her rough Parl.

She ate two roast pigs, seasoned and softened with the simmering spices popular in these foothills. When AuRon saw his mate sleeping comfortably at last, breathing easy and with a full belly, he joined Naf and two of his most trusted captains over mugs of spruce ale.

Naf told them how all Ghioz seemed to be coursing through Hypatia with only the briefest show of resistance.

What forces Hypatia had not engaged in the border thanedoms hurried toward their rallying points along the coast or the Falnges River.

"All the more reason to try my plan," AuRon said.

Naf shook his head. "Impossible."

"Impossible why?" AuRon asked.

"No body of armed men could get into the city. The gates are too well guarded. The only large groups of men who move together are Ghioz soldiers, and we could never imitate them. The others are slaves, who wear the barest kinds of clothing. There would be nowhere to hide our arms."

"Suppose you weren't armed."

"A hundred loinclothed men against the Citadel Guard? It couldn't be done."

"Suppose I could provide you with arms and armor."

"Our own? My men's own bows and blades?"

"Yes."

"We would have a chance. Just a chance. Could I count on your help at the citadel gate?"

"Of course."

"It could be for nothing. Hieba is probably dead."

"Then we will avenge ourselves upon the Queen."

"And kill one of her doubles as you die."

"I've thought much about that," AuRon said. "I cannot help but think there is some deep mystery to the Queen. The being I've spoken to is no double, no matter how well trained. I spoke to the Queen herself. I'm sure of it. So she is either speaking through her doubles, as she did with me in the Lavadome, or . . ."

"Or what?" one of Naf's captains asked.

"Or there is a deeper enigma still to the Red Queen."

Paskinix sent a messenger-bat back, with a report that there'd been "a fight and a capture" in one of the upper chambers while the dragons dined and waited for the drakes and demen to clear a blockage.

The Copper went to see the results himself.

Three dead demen lay together, facedown with their arms linked according to the custom of the hominids.

The chamber the bat led him to must have been near the surface. Old bones, flat bits of dried hide, thin as leaf and held together by a coat of hair and mud, droppings, and mushrooms and lichens feeding on the rest dirtied the floor of what looked like a dwarven sleep-hall, judging from the many notches in the wall. He'd seen old dwarven cells. When away from their homes they liked to sleep in little chambers reminiscent of the partitions in honeycombs.

The Copper found himself face-to-face with his old friend NiVom.

The demen had multiple lines around his neck, his limbs, climbing hooks through his wings and buried painfully into his spine and tail.

"Tell me one thing. How does she know of our movements?"

"She didn't know dragons were coming, just demen, otherwise I suspect you'd have met more than just myself and my mate."

"Your—mate?"

"Imfamnia. Your mate-sister."

"You would mate with such a traitor to her kind?" the Copper asked.

"Says a dragon who had a tooth in the destruction of his family."

The Copper did not want to have that conversation again. "Where's your mate now?"

"She ran as soon as the demen attacked. Valor in combat is not one of her charms."

"May we bleed him, my lord?" one of the demen asked, sharpening his knife against the cavern floor.

The Copper sniffed at his old Drakwatch leader's wounds. "And you were always so bright, NiVom."

He heard rumblings of the Jade Queen from the Aerial Host. Imfamnia would pass into history through some very creatively-worded songs centered around her alleged deeds with various temporary mates.

"I'd forgotten how quietly demen could move rock," NiVom said. "If you're going to kill me, do it. I have no heart for talking."

"Kill you? NiVom, I'll be happy to rescue you. Join us and help us bring down the Red Queen."

"It's impossible. She'll see you coming. She's always one step ahead. I wonder if she didn't tell Imfamnia to come with me to this dirty hole and then flee at the first spine-scrape of the attack. I'm beginning to think she wanted me dead."

"All the more reason to join us."

"What are your conditions?"

"Only this. Once we are out of this hole and in the air, travel through Ghioz and warn the people that the vengeance of dragons is about to be visited upon them. Any who wish to surrender should mark their homes and barns and watercraft in some manner. Is there a common fabric color? Something bright we can see from the air, by daylight or good moonlight?"

NiVom considered the matter. "Better than that. The Ghioz are great consumers of white paint. They use it on all the inner walls of their buildings."

"Paint? Oh, yes, of course, that color-splash. Yes, white paint will do. Have them mark the rooftop or at least the roofline to indicate their surrender."

"Brave of you. I see why they made you Tyr. I might just fly away."

"The NiVom who fought with me in Bant kept his word. If that dragon is gone, I'll see to it that the renegade hiding in his body is killed as well."

The Copper looked at him, hard, and NiVom gave a brief bow.

"I—I will see to it, my Tyr."

He gave orders to the demen to let him go.

The demen led the Aerial Host to the surface. The Copper offered them their freedom when they saw naked daylight.

"You are welcome to any caves north of the Star Tunnel," he said to Paskinix and the rest. "Or you may continue to live close to the river ring, but you must accept the Tyr's word in the Tyr's tunnel."

"If the Tyr keeps word to us, he'll find Paskinix a firm ally," Paskinix said.

With that they departed back for the deeps.

The dragons waited until dusk.

NiVom left first. The Copper and HeBellereth and Aiy-Yip watched him fly off

"Oh, to spread my wings!" Aiy-Yip squawked.

"Tonight," the Copper said.

"Why did you let him go?" HeBellereth said. "He may go to the Queen."

"I don't think so," the Copper replied. "Watch behind him."

A pair of roc-riders dropped out of the clouds and followed NiVom, all three fliers oddly dark against the night sky.

The Copper nodded. "As soon as we met him, I guessed the Red Queen would be having him watched. Had we killed him, at least one of that patrol would have lingered aboveground. They had Imfamnia to follow and now NiVom. I hope that is as many as they had waiting above these lands."

"My Tyr is clever," HeBellereth said.

"We shall see just how clever. If the Red Queen felt or saw a few-score demen coming, imagine what the approach of this multitude of dragons is to her. We may be in for a fight worthy of many a lifesong."

"All the more reason to finish what's left of the livestock, then," HeBellereth said, and Aiy-Yip ruffled his feathers in agreement.

The dragons were in the sunlight. They'd need it to navigate their way to the Queen's City—the mountains where it lay were a purple smear on the horizon.

He'd released Paskinix and his warriors, granting him this exit on the surface for as long as dragons breathed in the Lavadome for their use as a sun-mine (which had finally been explained to him—it simply meant an area used to grow crops, preferably fruit).

The dragons filed up and out of the old dwarfworks. They rested on a grassy hill somewhere at the north end of the rolling hills that started in the horsedowns.

"Now is the moment, dragons," he said to the assembly.

"We were driven from Silverhigh and scattered. Then we were

tempted to the Lavadome and enslaved. For generations we have hidden in fear of armies and assassins, egg-thieves and scale-gatherers. Our bones have been sold for medicines and our hearts have been burned for sacrifice to the totems of idiotic hominid gods.

"This is the last morning of dragonkind as we know it. Perhaps it will be a terrible last morning, a deathsong, a judgment where we match courage and brain and sinew against numberless adversaries who would reckon our destruction a boon.

"Or perhaps this is a new beginning for dragons, where we cease to let the world shape our destiny. If we see victory this day, we will become the shapers of the world and take our place in the sun, with generosity to our friends such as the *griffaran* and ferocity to our enemies."

The Copper saw some of the dragons glancing about them, unsettled by the light and space of the Upper World, or perhaps fearful of roc-riders screaming from the clouds.

"I am sorry to have to ask this of my dragons, but I need a few dragons to remain here and guard this entrance to the Lower World. If matters go ill for us over Ghioz, what is left will probably be pursued on the way back. A few fresh dragons, firebladders full and ready to fight, may save many lives. No one will think the worse of any who answer my request to guard this tunnel-mouth."

At that the doubtful eyes brightened. Four gave their names as willing to be the rearguard.

"Whichever way this next day goes, I am proud to have my share of it. Proud of our brothers, the *griffaran*. Proud to name myself as one who flew with HeBellereth, with CoTathanagar and NoFhyriticus and SiHazathant and Regalia."

With that, they rose into the sky and formed two great arrowheads heading north, each dragon taking advantage of the wake of the dragon in front and in turn passing on the savings in effort to the one behind. The *griffaran* flew above and between, their long tailfeathers making them look like darts in a hail of arrows.

Arrows aimed at the heart of the Ghioz Empire.

The Copper noticed that they seemed to be following storm-clouds sweeping northeast.

"A storm on its way to Ghihar. It is good we're behind that," He-Bellereth bellowed. "The air'll ride easier."

How fitting. A storm on wings would follow.

Chapter 24

They'd painted Natasatch using a sticky compound of dry clay, honey, dyes, and AuRon didn't want to know what else. Whatever it was, it clung to scale like hide-ticks.

He circled his mate, surveying the result. Darker stripes ran down her sides. Once it dried they had her fly, circling higher and higher. Of course, she still had her glorious fringe running down her spine, but nothing could be done about that.

When he mentioned it, however, Natasatch began to worry at it with her teeth, trimming it down to the shorter, serrated length of a male. It broke AuRon's heart to see his mate so disfigured, but it would grow back eventually.

"From afar, it doesn't look too bad," Naf said. "Her tail's a little too long and too thick, but apart from that . . ."

The men cheered. According to Naf, the Dairuss loved a good trick played on enemies. They'd been a subject people for much of their history, under Anklamere, under the cruel Ironriders, and lately under Ghioz, and they had learned the value of the sly wit and clever trick that fools the harvest collector or the labor bondsman.

Naf's whole camp crackled with excitement. For every man he accepted for the dangerous trip to Ghioz, he had to turn away three. Then he culled that group through contests and exhibitions of sport and strength, with Natasatch acting as judge. A rumor spread through camp that she could smell a hero born by the sweat of his skin.

"Show yourself every day," AuRon told Natasatch. Eyes watching the rebel camp would be sure that Naf remained with his ally dragon. "Fly off to the west in the morning and return in the afternoon. They will think you are communicating with a Hypatian column."

"Yes, yes, my lord," she said, with the tone of exaggerated obedience she used to mock him. "Just show myself, and above all don't start any fights with the big beaknoses. No matter how hungry I get for some fireroasted squab."

They nuzzled each other, scratching behind the jawline with *griff* points.

"I suppose it's no good asking you to be careful," she said.

"You were the one who wanted to join in this war."

"To form a bond of friendship that will last until our hatchlings have their wings," she said.

He glanced around. "Men have short memories. But I would like to see this Queen struck down and Hieba safe with Naf, if she still lives."

"And let us not forget a hoard this time. Glory and gallantry are all well and good, but our hatchlings need coin. Carry off all you can."

"Yes, yes, of course. Naf will be generous, if this works."

When Naf had his band selected and properly oathed to whatever gods men imagined in charge of such affairs, they removed to another camp a little east. From there, scouts set out to explore the trails and passes.

While in camp, they placed all their arms and shields in bags of netting running along AuRon's sides and he tried a test flight. He could not even get off the ground and managed only a short glide until they relieved him of the burden of everyone's chain shirts.

"A decent meal of metal for your mate, at least," Naf laughed.

"Save them," AuRon said. "The workmanship's too fine for a dragon belly."

"The dwarves of the Chartered Company are old friends of ours. They feel the weight of the Queen's grasping hand and have sent armorers to aid our cause."

"Then I'm doubly sorry I can't carry them."

AuRon tried one more flight and found he could bear the weight creditably. If this was anything like flying with a coat of scale, his mate was ten times the dragon he was, to fly so far so fast under such a burden.

Without any complaints except an occasional groan. He didn't deserve such a dragon-dame.

Naf's picked band gathered their shields and spears.

"I'm sorry," AuRon gasped, his wings aching. "The rest are too heavy to carry."

"Shields and helms will have to do for a start. We can scavenge from the dead if we must."

"They'll laugh themselves to death, seeing loinclothed men attacking with nothing but spears, helms, and shields," one of the warriors joked.

"Are you ready for your chance in a thousand?"

Naf laughed. "The spirits my men are in, I say it's a chance in a hundred now. But if I'm to die, it's best for my people if I do it under the walls of Ghioz. Better for me, too. If I'm to take up residence in the other world, I'd just as soon be near my beloved."

They made their way into Ghioz in easy stages, taking old smuggling trails between Hypatia and Ghioz. AuRon walked most of the way with the men, though it galled him to crawl along at a foot pace after years of flying.

The borderlands were empty. Even the usual watch stations at the main mountain passes had only a handful of soldiers in them and a single messenger horse.

The scouts found a group of young men hiding in the woods, avoiding the Queen's service. According to them, every pair of legs who could walk were either raiding in the southlands or aiding the Ironriders in their invasion of Hypatia.

"They're risking being sold on the auction block by avoiding the Queen's bondsmen," Naf told AuRon. "When I rode with the Red Guard, we rounded up a score or two like those every year. They all said the same thing—better service in the fields under a taskmaster than facing arrows and cutthroats in the Queen's garrison houses."

*   *   *

They crossed over into Ghioz, and gradually the lands gave onto mountain pastures and terraced fields. The rivers and streams began to run off to the southeast—they'd made it across the flow divide and into Ghioz.

When they could see the lights of the city—amazing that you could see a city at night from a horizon away—they said their goodbyes.

Naf had his men divest themselves of their weapons and arms and rig AuRon's netting in a tree so he could easily slip into it.

"We will travel faster if we go by road, as a labor levy."

"We might even beg a meal or two at the Queen's breadhouses," one of the scouts, now dressed as a taskmaster, said.

They made arrangements to meet in the Queen's woods outside the citadel, at moonrise three days hence.

"I feel naked without so much as a dagger on me," Naf said, shivering in a bare loincloth, sandals, and a blanket wrapped about his shoulders and closed with a bit of twine.

"Let's hope that the Citadel Guard has been stripped as completely as the border posts," a captain said.

"See you at moonrise, three nights hence," AuRon said.

"I hope so," Naf replied, his usual smile absent. "I don't care to spend the rest of my years knee-deep in the irrigation ditches or breaking road-gravel."

After they moved on down the mountain trail through the high fields, AuRon stayed under tree-cover and waited, watching the skies and sniffing the wind and hoping for good weather three nights ahead. He was tempted to raid livestock, but satisfied himself with wild goats that had evidently escaped captivity and learned to live in the mountain forest. They were alert, and it was all he could to catch the old and the sick without using flame to aid his hunting.

Finally, the time came. The weather was cooperating in their endeavor at the moment—bluster but likely to rain. Depending on when the rain arrived it might be a good thing or a bad. He got into his harness of netted weapons and shields, climbed to a steep hill where he'd have a nice drop, and launched into the night air.

He stayed so low on the trip that he sometimes touched treetop on his downstrokes.

A light drizzle set in. He was glad he'd overflown the city in perfect weather and so had some idea of the land Naf selected for their meeting.

The river was in full flood, it being spring, and Naf and his men were waiting on a dry island surrounded by river. They were in a cold camp.

"In happier days Hieba and I walked these woods," said Naf. "The view of the city and the sculpture on the mountain is incomparable."

On the other side of the river were many wharves and built-up sections, and a few lights burned through the mist. The citadel itself.

AuRon remembered what Naf had told him of it as the men buckled on their helmets and shields.

Ghihar. The old city of the Ghi men, walled in the days when they had enemies on every border or fought civil wars with the population downriver.

It was a simple enough plan. They'd size the old city's small garrison, free Hieba from her house—and whatever other hostages the Queen kept who wished to leave the prison that masqueraded as fine homes—and leave before the sun rose, Hieba and her daughter upon AuRon's back, Naf and his men riding on the fresh horses under the standard of the Citadel Guard, who would have been taken prisoner in their beds and then locked up tight in one of the old towers. AuRon could fly quickly enough that they'd be back in the borderlands by the time the sun rose.

Dirty weather would only slow the roc-riders and make their search difficult. It seemed likely that they'd see some, judging from the wall of clouds coming up from the south.

Of course there was the problem of the dragons the Queen was known to employ.

AuRon would take care of diverting them. And even if he did see them, he could outfly anything scaled.

The first job was to get the men across the river and onto one of the lesser roads leading to the citadel.

He did the swimming. All they had to do was hang on to his fringe, half in and half out of the water. They showed admirable fortitude in the crossing, sucking air as the cold water struck their loins and puffing like nervous baboons he'd hunted in the jungles.

Four trips later, he and Naf and the men were hurrying up the road toward the citadel, while residents barred their doors and shutters.

A pair of men ran off up the hill toward the citadel, ringing handbells.

Naf made a hissing noise and arrows brought the unfortunate pair down, three in one and two in another, tightly grouped around the upper spine.

"I'm glad your bowmen aren't shooting at me," AuRon said.

"Firewatch, I think," Naf said, lifting their belts and examining the buckles.

The walls of the citadel appeared out of the rain. Water streaked down their sides, running down crevices worn into the masonry over hundreds of years. They were impressive walls for man's handiwork. AuRon guessed they were wide enough at the top to allow horses to ride upon them or animals to pull siege engines. Dripping fabric sunscreens at the top flapped in the wind.

What had once been a ditch around the walls was now filled with muck and refuse.

"To the gate! Hurry!" Naf called, pointing to a small arch between two towers, like twin legs of some great troll, torn by arrow-slits.

The gate, under a low arch, was a trifling affair of iron bars. He saw lights beyond, an open courtyard of some kind. A horn sounded from the wall at the sight of the soldiers. A glass shattered on the paving stones in front of the gate.

AuRon flung himself against the gate and tore it from its hinges in one solid piece. It landed flat and Naf and his men dashed across it.

"Siegecraft isn't necessary when you've the aid of a dragon," Naf said.

A man in a twilight-red tunic appeared in the gap to a stairway. AuRon lashed out with a *saa,* and knocked him back where he had come from, and dragon-dashed out into the courtyard.

Naf's men paused as they took their bearings, then divided into three disciplined columns, save for a few who stayed behind to care for men blinded by the contents of that smashed glass that had fallen behind him. One file made for a staircase climbing the back of the walls, a second moved toward an angled-in tower, almost a pyramid, at the center of the citadel, and a third, led by Naf, went up a road lined by fine wooden and stone homes with sharp-angled roofs like a row of teeth.

He watched the center column enter the angled-in tower and the other column divide to move around each side of the walls. There was hardly any guard at all atop the walls, and what there was dropped their weapons and ran for the tower doors.

AuRon flew up to the wall and helped the wall-storming party by bashing in a barred tower door with his tail. In another tower a trio of men cranked around a boxlike war-machine. He was tempted to use his flame, but a sudden burst of fire would draw whatever might be riding above in the clouds.

Above all, he must keep the roc-riders busy elsewhere.

He flapped hard in the direction of the face on the mountainside as angry lightning began to flash.

AuRon noticed a strange glow from the top of the face, at the crown of the head. At first he thought it was some reflection of a fire in a chimney, but no fire he'd ever seen burned white.

He suspected he knew the source of the star-like light.

AuRon decided that the easiest way to enter would be through the mouth. The scaffolding blocked the way like wooden bars.

He picked up speed, folded his wings so they angled back as if he were diving into water after tuna. He went through the wood as though it were riverbank reeds.

The scaffolding made a satisfying crashing sound as it fell.

He marked fleeing forms of humans in various states of nightdress.

A pair of guards charged in, spears at the ready. AuRon roared at them, and they charged out with the same enthusiasm as they had entered with.

"What is this insult?" a commanding voice called.

AuRon saw the Red Queen standing in a stairway. She wore a mask that looked as though it was made of carefully pressed paper.

"You owe me a ransom of gold," AuRon said. "I am here to collect."

"You did a poor job of delivering my message. We keep our bargains. We will give you a quantity of silver, and we may part in peace."

"Give me what I have earned, or die."

"That is an easy choice. Kill me. It will save us a chest full of coin, that we may then find a better use for."

"I do not desire your gold," AuRon said. "You may satisfy my demand by paying me in flesh."

"Naf and his men have failed, you know. All your clever planning simply put him and those men of his in our hands with less trouble than it would have taken to hunt him out of those mountains."

AuRon bristled.

"What did you want in the citadel, I wonder?" the Red Queen said, walking out into the center of the nexus of stairs.

"If you give up Hieba and her child, I will forget your betrayal," AuRon said, listening to cries and arguments of the servants.

"Is this some exotic appetite of dragons? We have heard rumors of such compulsions."

"Let us go in peace."

"So you can return them to that—traitor? Young Desthenae is being raised to lead her people under the title of governor. She promises to be beautiful enough to keep poets and songwriters inspired for generations to come. We would not like to let such grooming go to waste."

"Then pay me the ransom promised or die."

AuRon loosed his flame and the Red Queen vanished in a brief scream. Was she insane?

A burst of bluish light darted from the conflagration. It danced before his eyes like a lost firefly. Then it whirled up the stairs.

AuRon followed it, up and around turns, through the palace. Servants stared, not at the jumping light but at AuRon pounding up behind. Even as he panted from the chase, AuRon suspected that, like some hues of cave moss glow, the light could not be seen by human eyes.

They burst through the double doors at the back of the mountain's head. The light raced up the ridge of the mountain to the tiny temple high on the mountainside.

He took off, circled the giant sculpture and looked down into the city. Perhaps he imagined it, or it was some trick of rain and wind, but it seemed that wings glided over the citadel.

He raced to the temple, burning its image into his eyes as the light faded.

Upon alighting, he listened, but only the mountain wind entered his ears.

He descended through graceful elvish sculpture built on stout dwarvish foundations, went down a wide, curving stair, and then squeezed through a crude blighter passage.

And so he came to the chamber.

The roots of the world itself held up its ceiling, or so it seemed.

AuRon had the strange feeling the mountain had grown up around this place. The rocks felt old, as if even they were tired and worn down by the ages.

A tree stood at the center, though it was an odd sort of tree, like two sets of roots joined at the trunk. One set of roots gripped the ceiling, the other the ground.

In places the roots bulged like diseased skin. Some of the perturbations were small, red, apple-like, others were as swollen as a bloated pig.

One of the swollen nodes moved, pulsing as though it were taking breaths. AuRon bent his head close. Its skin was stretched tight, reminding him of his own back before his wings broke through.

A face looked back at him.

The face of the Red Queen.

He recoiled in shock.

He had his flame. Would it be enough? He scored the trunk of the tree, and the pulpy wood gave way in sheets more in the manner of flesh than bark.

A hand punched out of the egg-node. Red webbing hung about it like a long veil.

The flame came out of fright. He spread it, concentrating on the tree. The bark hissed rather than burned as the flame lashed across it, like dragonflame vomited upon seawater.

He paid special attention to the nodes. They steamed, swelled, and exploded.

The air boiled with smoke, but he had to complete the destruction. He lashed out right and left, breaking and smashing the nodes. Not fast enough. He rolled, burning himself, smearing freshly grown blood all over himself.

Out out out! Out of air, out of hide, out of time.

He fled up the stairs, dragging flame behind, and out into the clean mountain air.

Horror awaited him in the citadel. Naf's men hung from the walls, already being pecked by crows, with bloated vultures waiting beneath, evidently experienced enough in the ways of the Ghioz citadel to know that the bodies would fall eventually.

There was fighting outside the sloping tower at the center of the citadel. Those within the tower exchanged arrows with rocks fired by war-machines outside.

A green dragon, long and light-framed, circled above the tower, and above the green dragon two roc-riders circled higher.

Had he been thinking rationally, given time to plan, he would have glided high above the roc-riders, then dove on them from straight up. He could strike at one and drop flame on the other without much loss of speed, and fall on the dragon jarring the tower with strikes of her tail.

But like a fool, all he could think of was Naf, and possibly his men, on the inside of that tower as its walls were battered and opened by the war-machines.

He dropped fire on them. The rocs dove, talons out, rending and tearing out chunks of wing. He crashed to the ground, rolling and scattering soldiers and their horses and oxen.

He dragon-dashed for the ruins of the door. Arrows struck him along the sides but did not slow him. He snapped off feathers as he squeezed through the door.

It was a vast, square room with four fat columns running from floor to ceiling, stairs running up each side and what seemed to be old horse stalls filled with crates and chests and bundles.

Naf's men, dressed in a mixture of their own armory and Ghioz breastplates and chain, were lighting flaming arrows to fire at the war-machines as other bowmen covered them.

At the center of the four columns was an old throne. A simple thing, wooden with brass feet and arm caps, almost unadorned.

Naf lay sprawled upon it, an arrow in his shoulder and stomach. Hieba held him in her arms. She'd aged greatly since he'd last seen her. Two long ropes of gray contrasted with the black in her hair.

"Well, AuRon," Hieba said, "you've made it in time for the last act of our heroic tragedy."

"Your daughter?" AuRon asked.

"The Queen sent her off to the southern provinces," Hieba said.

Naf chuckled, a stream of saliva and blood trickling out of his mouth. "I am glad, though I wish Desthenae could see my final repose. Would you believe, today I sit on the ancient throne of Dairuss? The first kings of Ghioz dragged it all the way here and forgot about it in this old tower. Do me a courtesy. Once I've breathed my last, burn me in it."

Chapter 25

W istala, heading south with the muster of the north to the aid of Thallia and Hypat, was met on the road by Dsossa and a twin column of riders escorting what looked like a group of thanes and their families.

The thanes went far off the road to avoid Wistala, but Dsossa trotted ahead.

"Hypatia's surrendered," Dsossa said.

"When?" Wistala asked.

Dsossa shook her head. "Does it matter? What can be done? The Ironriders swept through the Iwensi like a storm, over a dozen passes and down the Iron Road. The Ghioz had barges laden with grain for their horses—trade that was supposed to be coming to Hypatia."

"Fount Brass has mustered a herd of mounted thugs and war-carts. There are even four dozen Knights of the Directory with trained warhorses and remounts—not that they would stand a chance against the thousands of bowmen of the Ironriders. Shryesta sent spearmen and horsemen. Had they only made it to the city in time!"

"With such a force, perhaps something could be attempted."

"The Directory have surrendered."

"We haven't."

"We're Hypatian."

"So we obey the Directory. If they have surrendered, we have as well."

These Hypatians and their legal niceties!

"I'm also a dragon of the Lavadome. The Lavadome hasn't surrendered to Ghioz."

"If the dragons of the Lavadome attack, can we count on your support?"

"What will be left? The docks and the iron-quarter are burning."

"I wonder if the Ironriders have ever had Hypatian wines and brandies?"

"If they haven't, they will wish they'd lost their heads in battle."

"The Ironriders wouldn't be so foolish as to let all their riders pillage. There must be some force still keeping order."

"I'm told there are chieftains and their personal guard squatting in on the Ziggurat and the Directory hall."

"We'd best come in two waves, light/heavy," Ayafeeia said. "Heavy wave will wait for the light to go to ground fighting, then fly in and support. We'll grind them between ground and sky."

"Opportunities for glory in the light wave, I think," a dragonelle said.

"I shall lead it, my Queen—"

"No, Ayafeeia. You shall lead the heavy wave, to more judiciously direct their strength. You have the more experienced eye for that sort of thing."

"No! The Tyr would never."

"It's a poor Queen who shouts 'go' and remains behind."

"Yes, but a live one."

"Oh, I've heard the whispers. 'She does it for the bows.' 'She lives to humble those who once stood as her betters.' 'She murdered the Tyr's first mate.'

"If the only proof they'll accept is a corpse, so be it. My mate has said this is the beginning of an age of fire. I will put my flame where his words are.

"Are you coming, Essea, to represent the Imperial Line in this red dawn? Or were you only my friend these years to better pass around gossip about the private habits of the Tyr and his mate?"

Wistala had never seen such beautifully shaped claws on a dragon before. Her servants must have labored hard perfecting their shape. But they'd also perfected the points.

Essea looked doubtful. "I am your friend and loyalist, my Queen." She stepped forward. "Admit me into the first wave."

"Who else will fly with their Queen?"

Other Firemaids stepped forward, by tradition the oldest and toughest or the young seeking the glory of being named as the leader of the attack.

"That's enough!" Ayafeeia cried, seeing old Verkeera step forward, her battered scales stitched together with Ironrider-rein and bound up in blood. "Verkeera, you have the biggest firebladder of any of us. Let me have it in my line to pour down on the enemy."

"I would rather shield my Queen's other flank with my body," Verkeera said.

"I intend to move too fast to have much care for my flanks, Verkeera," Nilrasha said. "The last time I led a line into battle against the Ghioz, we were trapped under walls and destroyed by Ghioz fighting from their fortifications. But this time our opponents are strangers to the city too! A house collapsed on me. I've been waiting years to return the experience to a few Ghioz."

"Carry full bladders into battle," Ayafeeia said. "We are matched against horsemen. But horses don't care for the smell of dragons. Spray your water as carefully as you spray your fire, for once."

The dragonelles chuckled at this and some made jokes about fighting with both ends. A few coarse jokes passed among the green ranks.

"What about you, Wistala?"

"I'm afraid to trust my wing to the air again. I will go in with the Hypatian horsemen."

"We'll count on you to come to the rescue of the first wave," Ayafeeia said. "The sounds of fighting shouldn't be hard to find."

"Maidmother, would it not be better to let the Hypatians lead the attack? It's their city. Let them keep their honor by winning it back."

"It is an accepted rule of the battle art that air should pass ahead of ground, the way the rain strikes before the flood."

The quote stirred Wistala's hearts. She'd read an old battle-treatise of Rainfall's grandsire. Strange that one of his maxims passed over to dragon-strategy in such a manner. Perhaps dragons had fought with the Hypatians in those ancient battles.

She brought herself back to the present.

"The Hypatians' approach may draw the Ironriders out into battle."

"Or it may send them to the walls and war-engines."

"I've been in the city. The walls are old and ill-kept, and if they have any war-engines, they weren't on display when I passed through. The Hypatian numbers are few. Would not their princes send their horses out to fight in the fields such as would be most familiar to them and their manner of fighting?"

"You argue like an Anklene, Wistala. Very well. We shall stay concealed in the marshes until you launch your attack."

"I'll leave it to you to best judge when to launch your fliers. Just do not leave us out there too long on our own."

"For our gardens and our vineyards," Sandwash shouted, leg hooked in perfect balance atop his strange sidesaddle, his enormous bow held with long, slipper-covered toes of one extended leg. The pose reminded Wistala of the dancers who'd traveled with the circus, who could hook ankle around behind ear like a ruin-cat.

"For our roofs and our hearths," Ermet called, perched atop his thug on the horny ridge just above the eyes. A long-handled ax hung easily in one stout arm, a forked mancatcher in the other.

"For our fathers and our daughters," Roff called.

"For our libraries and our courts," Wistala said, finding her Hypatian again.

"For all this and all we hold dear," an aged, bent elf in the shining armor of a Knight of the Directory called, just barely keeping his great, steel-shod warhorse under control.

"Let's get to some stompin' already," the horse muttered.

"For all this, forward, Hypatia. Forward, the Last Host!"

"Forward, the Last Host!"

They came into the open fields beside the riverbank and passed through the vineyards, tearing away stakes and stalks as they went.

The advance wasn't quite so splendid as a charge. The horses moved at a fast walk, having to keep behind the vanguard of thugs. But it allowed Wistala to keep up at an easy pace.

Yet there was something to be said for a slow advance. Wistala wondered how it would look to the bleary-eyed Ironriders as they woke to the drums of battle.

The thugs had been trained to go into battle in step, and their heavy footfalls shook the ground. Behind them one felt it rather than heard it, a boom ... boom ... boom ... as the creatures swayed forward in their odd, sailorlike gait. What would such a noise sound like to the Ironriders, far from home in a strange city?

But for all that their pace was slow. The Ironriders had plenty of time to prepare and draw their plans.

The Ironriders, or some part of their number, rode out to meet them.

They rode out in three long columns, a trident of black emerging from three different points in the city. Wistala, peeking between the thugs and kicking up as much dust as she could as she walked to hide her presence, guessed the Hypatians were outnumbered ten to one or more.

She marked three tall banners drawn by horse-carts, as high as ship-masts. Bodies hung from them, arranged in frightful and gory poses. She recognized among them women and the black-and-white robes of the Directory.

So much for a peaceful surrender.

Ah, well, the center would make a fine aiming point for her leap.

"Do not take alarm at what I'm about to do," Wistala said.

The thugs halted and lowered their heads. The men riding them dropped shutter-like shields down to cover their faces and forelimbs. A mobile wall had sprouted on the battlefield.

Arrows of the Ironriders struck the shields, sounding like hail on a metal-plate roof.

Wistala marked the approaching center banner. One of the Hypatians shot a flaming arrow into it, trying to burn it. But the bodies had been well coated with pitch to preserve them.

"I do so hate this sort of thing," she muttered.

She gathered herself behind the line of thugs.

"Mossbell and Thallia!" she roared.

Even the thugs jumped.

Wistala tore forward, leaped, using the heavy hindquarters of the thugs as a vaulting-point. As she sailed into the air she extended body and wings, getting every dragonlength she could into her arc.

Arrows rose to meet her, but most passed behind or stuck into her tail, for she gathered speed as she fell, or so it seemed, for in battle all motion was slowed to a dreadful crawl.

She fell against the banner and its cart, knocking the totem down. Using wreckage to shield her breast, she lashed out with tail and spat fire across the ranks that faced the Hypatian right.

Horses screamed and scattered.

Wistala thought it best to keep moving. She trotted, tail lashing to keep them off, head held low where a sword-stroke couldn't get behind her extended *griff,* and simply used her body as a sort of mobile linebreaker against the ranks of Ironriders.

If there were any old hands at dragonfighting among their number they showed no sign of it. They didn't try to trip her with lines or get a rope-drag on her tail. A few halfhearted charges and thrown lances against her side left her with feathered shafts dangling from her sides and backbone. She broke up more organized charges by beating her wings, hard, into the horses' faces. The brutes didn't care to be peppered with wingblown pebbles.

"Hy-yah! Hy-yah!" came the war cries from behind as the Hypatians charged forward to support her, the great Knights of the Directory leading the way on their tall horses, half again as high as those of their opponents.

Still, the battle would have gone ill for the Hypatians. Despite the chaos in the center, the two Ironrider wings stayed in order and reached out to envelop the Hypatians. There were not nearly enough thugs to form an armored ring capable of covering all the horsemen, archers, and footmen. Elvish arrows flew far to tear gaps in their line, but the dark riders closed each gap as remorselessly and unfailingly as ants.

They harried the Hypatian flanks. As the edges of the Hypatian battle line went ragged and uneven, the Ironriders charged, snipping off sections of spearmen and sending archers tumbling back with the precision of a skilled-body thrall shaping up a ragged scale.

Then the Firemaids struck.

The dragons came in low, with the rising sun to cover their approach.

The drakka were already in the city, hiding in garbage piles and pigsties, anywhere that would hide their scent.

None knew from where a drakka might strike next. They slithered out of sewer holes and plunged from rooftops, attacking Ironrider messengers and officers rousting the riders out of the beer-halls and tobacco-dens.

Following their example, the population forgot their fear, and their surrender, and rose. They flung crockery from balconies and dumped boiling water from high windows. Angry Ironriders set fire to houses, bringing mobs with ax and rope ready to fight either flame or invader.

Many a booted, long-haired rider ended up hanging from a laundry line strung between two buildings.

The Ironrider princes upon the Temple Hill had forgotten more about warfare than the thug-riders entering the city in street-filling columns had ever known. They organized their reserve into rows of archers guarded by spearmen, with riders ready to ride from point to point and dismount wherever an attack might develop.

It was against their ranks that Nilrasha's first wave flung themselves.

Some landed behind the lines, some in front, some atop roofs and some in the confusing tangle of decorative gardens. Orange blossoms of dragonflame colored the hillside.

The second wave of Firemaids, kept under control by their maid-mother and the veteran warriors, circled Temple Hill, dropping to strike and then retreat when the arrows grew too thick.

The Ironriders, with courage of desperation, hurled themselves against the dragons. They climbed onto haunches to hack and stab, wormed their way between slashing *sii* and stomping *saa* to sink their daggers into vulnerable undersides.

For generations after, the phrase "died like an Ironrider" passed into Drakine, used for a dragon who succumbed to wounds with teeth and claws and spurs gripping enemies.

It was easy for Wistala to find the Queen. All she had to do was listen for the high dragon cries of "Blood bats! Blood bats!"

Wistala hurried up the corpse-littered streets, between buildings roaring as flames consumed them, to find Queen Nilrasha stretched out in the ruins of an old Hypatian temple.

"I did think the roof could hold my weight," she said. "The columns looked so thick. But here I am. The columns are still standing and I'm not. I've just no luck with buildings, that's all."

Ayafeeia stood by her, sadly surveying a torn wing. Nothing but a bloody stump remained of her left. The rest of it was a flat, gory mess under a fallen pillar.

"Perhaps his next mate will lay down a string of eggs worthy of a Tyr." She smiled.

"Yefkoa," Ayafeeia said, "you're our fastest dragonelle. If ever you flew for love of your Tyr, fly now and tell him his Queen needs him."

Chapter 26

"Aerial Host," the Copper bellowed, trying to summon the words from his hard-pumping heart and heaving lungs. "Dive!

"*Griffaran* guard, with me!" he called. "Keep the roc-riders off them."

"Teach those coop-hatched fools the terror of a free wing and a loyal heart," Aiy-Yip shrieked.

No dragon could keep up with fast-flying *griffaran*. The Copper found himself tailfeather-slacking, as Aiy-Yip might have styled it.

Roc-riders rose to meet them. For one instant, the formations, rising and falling angles, turned to meet, like the spearheads of opposing armies. Then it dissolved into a whirlwind of combat.

When roc-riders attacked the dragons, *griffaran* swooped and dove, knocking riders loose for a long fall or tearing at wings so the roc-riders spun earthward, their mounts keening and the men screaming.

But if the roc-riders tried to turn on the *griffaran,* the *griffaran* applied the same principles that served the roc-riders so well in their fights with dragonkind—they outturned and outclimbed the big, laden birds.

Scale against feather, flame against arrow, ball-and-chain against beak-and-talon, the two forces left feather, blood, and glittering scale falling to earth as they swooped and parried, a mad aerial dance of ever-changing partners.

The Copper watched one roc fall in a blaze of flame, leaving a dark smear of feathers.

"Behind you!" one of his two remaining guard said.

Two roc-riders swooped down. They must have been high up

and far off when the encounter started and both the Copper and his guard over-attentive to the spectacle below.

The Copper turned to protect his bad wing. The fliers bored in on him, diving around the *griffaran*. Their men loosed arrows from curved bows and the Copper felt the missiles punch him.

One passed behind, one in front. If he'd had use of his flame he might have started a feathery blaze. As it was he had to settle for turning and a futile snap of teeth in the fast-flying birds' wake.

A *griffaran* got the frontmost rider, as it turned out. Or part of it, anyway. The Copper doubted the legs left in the saddle would be of much use piloting the bird.

The Copper turned to meet the other. Perhaps he could distract it long enough for one of his *griffaran* guard to strike.

The other roc-riding warrior, watching the *griffaran* tearing toward him from behind, only turned to look at the Copper when his mount shrieked and shied. The Copper flapped hard and narrowed his wings, lowered his crest at the end of a ram-stiff neck.

They struck, the roc open-winged and evading, the Copper driving.

Messy pieces of roc fell away, spraying the sky. Or worse, clung to the Copper's scale and horns and *griff*.

One of his guard dropped down to glide close beside. The Copper flinched from the sudden flutter of wing, hating his nerves. That was no way for a Tyr to act, startling at your own guard.

"All right?" a *griffaran* asked while the other circled above, searching for more enemies.

"I'm well. Follow," the Copper said. He dared a glance back at where the arrows had struck. Two feathered souvenirs stuck into him, one high in his mass of wing-driving muscle, the other at the base of his tail.

Then there was the blood dripping and drying from his snout and crest. He must look a fright.

Dusk had settled into the arms of the valley. Dragonflame flashed bright as the Aerial Host spread terror across the tenting. The bats hadn't mentioned that great sculpture looking out south toward the Lavadome.

The dragons who had no flame left picked up wagons and thatched roofs, coops and trees, anything that could be set aflame and carried a little way, there to have the process repeated.

So the flame spread from roof to warehouse to dock to boat. Flapping, diving *griffaran* attacked knots of men who gathered to fight either dragon or flame, or patrolled the outskirts of the city to look for reinforcements. Now and then a *griffaran* rose to report to HeBellereth, who circled above all with his dragons, looking at the wounded, sending members of the Aerial Host to protect downed dragons as they retreated toward the outskirts of town.

The destruction had not been achieved without loss. He marked a fallen *griffaran,* bloody atop one of the city's famous domes. A collapsed building had an unmoving dragon-tail projecting from the rubble.

"The whole city united will not stop that fire now," the Copper said, smelling the awful sweet stench of burning flesh. "Recall the host. Let's go to the palace and see what's left."

He felt a pang for the Ghioz. Any people who could shape mountains into art, apparently just for the satisfaction of it, had his grudging respect. Perhaps he would let some part of their society blossom after this too-long-delayed trimming.

He wondered what kind of effort it would take to shape that great flat face into a dragon-head. It would be a project mostly of cutting away, after all. Or perhaps a frieze of a profile. That might be even easier.

Such a monument would let the world know what had happened here this day, for all time.

A small portion of the Queen's guard held her palace until death.

Dragons breathed fire onto the balconies and dropped their riders. They met AuRon and his raggedy Dairuss under their war-chief fighting inside the temple with what was left of the Red Guard.

The Copper decided he much preferred having AuRon as an ally. He seemed to have the knack of making friends who didn't demand blood or gold or rank in exchange for their service.

Some of the Queen's servants took their own lives rather than surrender. The Copper found a heap of corpses, male, female, even children, lying peacefully beneath a statue of the Queen.

The sight depressed him.

Dragons, at least, had more sense. They accepted a new Tyr and got on with their lives.

Time, indeed, for dragons to get back to the purpose of living.

They found the crystal in a blue-domed chamber, high in the mountain. Careful star-charts were etched above. He picked out patterns both familiar and unfamiliar. AuRon wondered if the stars bore some purpose related to the crystal or if they'd preceded its installation. There was an even smaller passage, too cramped for any but a human, that led up to a tiny platform with a good view of the sky.

AuRon guessed the crystal chamber lay just behind the forehead where the eyebrows met, or perhaps just above.

He sent for his brother. The Copper might be interested in this if he could squeeze up the stairs.

HeBellereth made it, well dusted with scrapes and scraps from the stair-passage walls, along with a slender young Firemaid named Yefkoa who had distinguished herself with fast flying.

"I was afraid I would have to go for oil to work him through," she said.

"I wanted to see the source of so much misery."

So they stared, the four dragons, at the Red Queen's seat of power.

She'd set an impressive throne against it, built a comfortable seat and arm and footrest. Instead of facing outward, the throne-chair faced toward the crystal, so that one might peer deep into it. The throne itself was built on some sort of mount that allowed it to rotate around the crystal.

"So careful, with each and every step," Naf said. "Until she found this. Then she thought she could see everything."

"She saw how weak her enemies were," the Copper said. "More, she knew how to exploit faults, primarily greed. The greatest stone gives way if you tap it in the right crack. It is a strange thing. It almost seems to be—to be looking at me." Did the stone dislike him? What did a piece of crystal care who its owner was? "I can't help but feel it doesn't like me."

"Perhaps you're just seeing your conscience in the reflection," AuRon said.

"Don't speak to the Tyr that way!" HeBellereth snapped. "He saved your thin little hide, you know."

"And helped himself to a new Uphold. One worth all the rest put together, I expect," AuRon said. "My profound admiration, Tyr RuGaard. You've won a gamble for the ages."

"What shall we do with this trophy?" HeBellereth asked.

"Perhaps we should smash it," AuRon said.

The Copper tapped it with a *sii*. "Go ahead. Try."

"Perhaps some dwarves could do it," HeBellereth said.

"I know a man who would enjoy spending some time with it. Or perhaps the Anklenes."

"It could be dangerous," AuRon said.

"I thought NooMoahk lived with it for years," the Copper said. "And you, and our sister, spent some time in its presence. It is only fair that I take my turn to see what mysteries it holds."

"It seems to me there's danger in it," AuRon said. "Anklamere used it, the Red Queen. Were they who used it corrupt, or did the power within it corrupt them?"

"In the end, it seems it did them more harm than good. They were defeated despite its power," HeBellereth said.

AuRon looked at the crystal. He'd lived with it for years. Yet it seemed different. Not in general shape. It still had a heavier end and a curve to it, an upright kidney, but he could have sworn it had grown.

Perhaps it was just a trick of the light in this chamber. "I am not convinced she is dead," AuRon said. "The Red Queen may turn up again."

The Copper gave orders for a guard to be placed at the entrance to the stairs.

Then he slept, more or less comfortably, on some hay in the stables at the side of the palace. And still dragons disturbed him, flying in to report a barge sunk or some cattle pinned in a box canyon. If only so many of his dragons weren't illiterates, he would hang up a sign outside that said "Decide for Yourself." Parl would do. It was a good vigorous language that allowed you to make your point with a minimum of words.

He woke to a glorious dawn. Maybe this was why the Ghioz made their capital here, for the views of the sun coming up as clouds raced around the end of the mountains from southwest to northeast in furrows like the fresh-plowed fields he'd seen while flying.

So much to do. Crippled *griffaran* who had survived their plunge, wounded dragons and men—he gave orders that the dragon-rider wounded were to have as much dragonblood as they could stand. If nothing else it would ease their passage into death. The citadel fortress might make a good place to house them, for now.

Already men were arriving from Ghioz, answering warnings that they should mark the roof of house and barn, warehouse and temple, with white linen or paint if they wished to avoid destruction.

Most of the Ghioz Empire would fall to pieces, he expected. Just as well. AuRon had already planned to set that human friend of his up as king in Dar—no, Dairuss, it was called. It would be well to have an armed body of men, as long as they remembered to whom they owed their liberty.

He didn't have anything like the dragons to manage all this. He'd have to see about taking the best and the brightest of the thralls from the Lavadome and setting them up here to act as go-betweens for the dragons and their new domain. The Anklenes had thralls who could read and write in several tongues. He would have positions for even CoTathanagar's endless stream of relatives now. But there must be dragons to serve and protect them, Drakwatch and Firemaids to keep order.

NiVom had done an admirable job of spreading the word. He would probably make a good governor of the Ghioz Uphold, come to think of it.

He expected that he and Nilrasha would spend much time traveling between Hypatia, Ghioz, and the Lavadome. He'd have to find a nice cave somewhere—there looked to be some fine ground where those spearlike rocks stuck up toward the sky, about the right distance from each—and set up a small refuge cave, where just he and Nilrasha and a few thralls could take their ease from the travels.

What a world of possibilities awaited them.

That lithe little Firemaid he'd met the previous year arrived and collapsed almost on top of him.

"My Tyr," she gasped, "your Queen needs you. Nilrasha was hurt in battle in Hypatia, and Ayafeeia asks that you attend her."

Hypatia?

"What is she doing in Hypatia?" he asked, angering. "How did she come there?"

"She led the Firemaids in battle, my Tyr."

The Copper swung his wing, and . . . It wasn't this little flash of green's fault.

Oh, Nilrasha. What have you done now? Once she had an idea in her head it was like digging out an obstinate dwarf.

"I'll come at once. You look worn-out, ummm—"

"Yefkoa, my Tyr."

"Of course. The one who begged an escape from a mating."

She glanced around at some of the Aerial Host, who cast admiring glances her way. "A mating to fat old SoRolatan, my Tyr, and he already mated."

He called HeBellereth over. "I must fly to Hypatia."

"Eat first, my Tyr. I believe it is a long way."

"Over a day's hard flight," Yefkoa panted. "For me."

"That means three days for me," the Copper said. "Consult with NiVom on matters here. You two were good friends when we were in the Drakwatch together. It should not be too difficult to remember old times and forget the recent past. Consult, I said. You're in charge, not he."

"Yes, my Tyr." HeBellereth studied his *sii*.

"HeBellereth, suppose NiVom asserted an old claim to the Tyrship."

"In that case, white dragons will be even rarer, Tyr," HeBellereth said. "I've little patience for renegades."

The Copper relaxed. A little. "He may turn out to be no more a villain than that DharSii."

"How long will you stay in Hypatia?" HeBellereth asked. "The Lavadome has no ruler while you and the Queen are away."

He looked at Yefkoa. The dragonelle looked away, stricken.

"Long enough to burn my dead mate, I expect."

It was a long, exhausting flight, lengthened by having to go to ground and wait out a thunderstorm. He was tempted to test his artificial wing-joint against the winds, but the *griffaran* guard practically dragged him to earth, where they knitted him a shelter out of pine branches laced by the effort of their beaks.

He arrived at Hypat thin and hungry, but would take no food until he learned the fate of his mate.

"She still breathes, my brother," Ayafeeia said, as she led him up the hill toward a ruined temple with a great piece of canvas stretched between the broken columns.

"The remaining Directors of Hypatia are more willing to hear your words now, Tyr."

"Tell them the worst of the danger is past. Ghioz has been humbled."

He found Nilrasha stretched out in a ring of rubble. A trio of blood-fat bats snored, hanging like bulging sausages in a broken crevice. Essea reclined near her, next to a pot bubbling with what smelled like liver soup. Essea's flanks were crisscrossed with sword wounds, and she had grease-covered burns about her *sii* and wings.

He observed the bound-up, blood-black stump of Nilrasha's wing with horror.

"Nilrasha, what has happened?" he said, shocked too stupid to say anything else.

"I appear to have got my share of Firemaids killed again," she croaked.

"Will you . . . will you live?" She was cut up all about the neck and face, and there were deep scars all along her flanks.

She rolled her head and lifted her snout. The drakka attending to his mate gasped. "Her head's up!" one whispered to her gaping sister.

"The sun is lovely, my lord. It reminds me of Anaea, except here the air smells of the sea."

Word passed back. "The Queen's head's up!"

Ayafeeia blinked in the sunshine. "That's all she needed. A glimpse of her mate. Perked her right up."

"The Ironriders tested their blades against my scale as I lay in the ruins, pinned," she said. "They would have cut my hearts out if I hadn't chewed through my wing."

"A proper punishment for disobeying your Tyr's orders," the Copper said, his voice choked and harsh. But he found himself rubbing his snout against hers the next moment.

They chatted with mind-pictures for a few moments, quietly catching up on each other's experiences, but he was still Tyr, among dragons who'd fought bravely and deserved recognition. A Tyr who thought only of his mate was no Tyr at all.

"I must learn more about the situation here," he told Nilrasha. "I will return as soon as I may."

"I will just be asleep anyway. But bring me some silver, if you see any plate about. I'm absolutely famished for silver."

The Copper joined his chief Firemaid, and heard her account of the battle.

"By the way, Ayafeeia, your sister slipped off again. NiVom begged mercy, and I granted it. I'd have that DharSii fellow back too, if we could just find him."

"Wistala knows more about him than she gives away, I think," Ayafeeia said.

He had no reason to be embarrassed at his sister's name.

"Speaking of relations, how is my sister?" the Copper asked.

"She managed to break her wing again in battle in the pass. Intentionally, as it turns out."

"You don't mean she did it to feign injury?"

"Quite the opposite, brother. She did it to tell the other Firemaids that they stood there until either victory or death. They bought a little of both with their valor."

"Would you have her action rewarded?" the Copper asked.

"Yes. She did good service with the Hypatians in battle before the city."

The Copper considered. Could he trust Wistala with the management of matters in Hypatia? Where would her loyalties ultimately lie?

"Your mate will be well, my Tyr. Her appetite is good, her heartbeat strong," Ayafeeia said.

"Hmmm?"

"You looked worried. You always bob your head when you're concerned about something," she said. "Do not be alarmed. The secret is safe with me."

Chapter 27

The summer wore on and left. That next fall was as brightly colored in the north as if all the blood spilled in the Iwensi Gap had run down off the mountains and been drawn up into the leaves of the trees.

Lada said it was the trees showing their approval of the dragon alliance—at a whisper from Rainfall.

In Hypatia, it made the day warm enough so that it was pleasant in the sunshine, but not so hot that the crowds filling the street to observe the ratification of the Grand Alliance sweltered.

The city reminded AuRon of bones all jumbled together. Unlike a rural village in the north, where the same set of carpenters built all the homes and barns in a similar fashion, varying details only to defeat prevailing winds or to take advantage of the lie of the land, the city, uniform in color but variegated in components, clustered with the haphazard density of whelks clinging to an old bit of pier.

The high road sloping up to the Eternal Light had never seen such a crowd—at least not in living memory, according to the old timekeeper on the fourth level AuRon spoke to.

Each of the columns flanking the road held a drake or drakka, leaning out and looking down, or a *griffaran*.

Wistala stood on the level just below the Eternal Light with her collection of elves and dwarves and men, a jewel glimmering above and between her eyes on a silver-chain headdress. He spotted Halfmoon, Ghastmath, and Fyerbin standing in the throng, ermine-edged robes held closed with jeweled brooches as big as a dwarf's helmcap.

As usual, Wistala had been a fountain of information about Hypatian history and custom and the meaning of this oversized stairstool.

His brain had become befuddled somewhere between the Contract of the Kings and the Restoration of Truth.

He watched his brother limp up the long road, those thick-beaked birds above, spine-painted demen in heavy, sun-shading helms all around, carrying not weapons but banners in thick limbs. The crowd stared at them in particular, a rarer sight than even long-haired elephants—which trailed at the back, bearing booty taken from the Ironriders.

The Copper looked well, thick scales polished to the highest sheen, trimmed neatly and, he suspected, subtly edged with black paint to make them weave fascinating patterns as he stepped. One hardly noticed that he limped.

He had enough sense to keep those horrible bat creatures out of view, if they were with him.

Strange, the difference that glass made. The Copper no longer looked vaguely stupid with sleep, but alert as a startled snake.

AuRon saw Natasatch and the hatchlings—he really must stop calling them hatchlings, for they were drakes and drakka now—and edged over toward them. They'd been in and out of the dragon-parade at the old circus pavilions all morning, meeting the Lavadome representatives of the Grand Alliance.

"This is how it should be," Aumoahk said, sighing in satisfaction at the display with a slight whistle through his slit nostril.

"Father. Tremendous news!" Ausurath said, his *sii* spread gravely as he bowed to his father, *saa* jumping all about and tail thumping as though they belonged to a different drake. "The Tyr had promised me a place in the Drakwatch. It's the surest path to the Aerial Host. NoSohoth himself told me so!"

"The Firemaidens do all the real work," Varatheela said. "Nilra-sha says that if you want a lot of noise and dirt, summon the Drak-watch. If you want a victory, call in the Firemaids."

AuRon read excitement in all their faces. Their father, dull and gray and full of little but correction and reproach, how could he compare against such shining glory? Had he lost his hatchlings to the Copper? Of all that stood or slithered or flew through the two worlds, him?

You have doubts, Natasatch thought to him. *Even on a day such as this.*

It's my temper. The pageantry's nice enough, I suppose. It's this Grand Alliance business. Everyone is fresh off fighting for their lives and sharing out spoils. It'll look different after the first famine when the hominids start grumbling about how much dragons eat.

The Copper and the Hypatian high officials bowed to each other, speaking words long arranged. He'd heard most of it from Wistala, grand-sounding bargaining that put a lengthy dwarf-contract to shame.

"I know there's more behind, husband."

"Yes. Well, there's a lot of talk about the glories of Silverhigh in the Lavadome. I don't think brother RuGaard, as he styles himself, has new poems composed and read at his dinners to offer lessons about its folly."

The Copper and various representatives of the Hypatian races added tinder to the eternal flame. The dwarves threw in some sort of chemical that sparkled bright blue, the elves added wood, and men bits of oily charcoal. As for the dragons, Wistala and the Copper spat.

They'd asked him to add his own fire, representing the Isle of Ice, but he'd declined and his siblings hadn't pressed him. Besides, there was hardly space at the top of the Ziggurat for two dragons, let alone three.

I wonder if the lessons of Silverhigh must be relearned, or can they be learned from? Natasatch thought to him.

The lives of many a hominid and dragon alike will be shaped by the answer.

You can't think your sister is part of it. She thinks all her elves and humans and so on are quite her equals. AuRon. So cautious. Except once—on the day you won me.

And almost lost you just as quickly. It rather reinforced the lesson.

So what shall we do? Go back to the island and scrape out a living? After the hatchlings have seen all this, can they be content with play-hunting sheep? I'd have them know more of the world.

AuRon sniffed the air. Scents from across half a world rose from the crowd. Not just smoked meats and fresh-baked breads, but the decorative scents, floral or woodsy, metals, sweats, dried herbs being smoked or stewed, the dust of the poured stone the Hypatians used in so much of their construction, dogs, cats, horses, and other beasts, and above all, dragon. The Isle of Ice smelled like sheep, peat, and melting glacier.

I'm being a blockhead. Let's enjoy this day, bask in the sunshine, and see my sister's dream come to life. For one day, at least. Maybe one day will be example enough.

The future's an unlit path, yet to be made, Natasatch thought.

"Where'd you get that?" AuRon said.

"My thoughts, as I watch the hatchlings crane their necks to see better. It seemed appropriate."

"My beloved has become a philosopher."

"It comes from being mated to an enigma," she returned.

"An enigma who loves you, and lives only to see our hatchlings thrive," AuRon said aloud, looking at her.

She took a deep breath and spread her wings a little.

"Hatchlings," Natasatch said. "Mind each other and enjoy the ceremonies. Your father and I are going to fly for a bit, so that we might see events better."

Together, they soared.

A Few Words of Drakine

Foua: A product of the firebladder. When mixed with the liquid fats stored within and then exposed to oxygen, it ignites into oily flame.

Griff: The armored fans descending from the forehead and jaw that cover the sensitive ear-holes and throat pulse-points in battle.

Laudi: Brave and glorious deeds in a dragon's life that are incorporated into the lifesong.

Prrum: The low thrumming sound a dragon makes when it is pleased or particularly content.

Saa: The rear claws of a dragon. The three rear true-toes are able to grip, but the fighting spur is little more than decoration.

Sii: The front claws of a dragon. The claws are shorter, and the fighting spur on the rear leg is closer to the other digits and opposable. The digits are more elegantly formed for manipulation.

Torf: A small gob from the firebladder, used to provide a few moments of illumination.

Photo by Ronald D. Frisch

About the Author

E. E. Knight graduated from Northern Illinois University with a double major in history and political science, then made his way through a number of jobs that had nothing to do with history or political science. He resides in Chicago. For more information on the author and his worlds, E. E. Knight invites you to visit his Web site, vampjac.com.